W9-DAA-427

THE LOST CITY

THE JAGUAR STONES
Book Four

THE LOST CITY

J&P VOELKEL

EGMONT
Publishing
New York

AUTHORS' NOTE

The Jaguar Stones are fictional, as are all the characters in this book except for the legendary Boston Red Sox players who saved many a game at Fenway Park, and Friar Diego de Landa, the true-life Spanish priest who made one big bonfire of ancient Maya books and artworks. San Xavier is a fictional country based on present-day Belize.

EGMONT
We bring stories to life

First published by Egmont Publishing, 2015
443 Park Avenue South, Suite 806
New York, NY 10016

Copyright © J&P Voelkel, 2005, 2015
All rights reserved

1 3 5 7 9 8 6 4 2

www.egmontusa.com
www.jaguarstones.com

LIBRARY OF CONGRESS CATALOGING-IN-PUBLICATION DATA
Voelkel, Jon, author.
The lost city / J&P Voelkel.
pages cm. – (The Jaguar Stones ; book four)
Summary: While awaiting his parents' release from jail, fourteen-year-old Max Murphy is sucked into yet another scheme of the Maya Death Lords' that sends him on a quest to the United States. Failure could mean the end of the world . . . again.
ISBN 978-1-60684-376-5 (hardcover)
1. Mayas—Juvenile fiction. 2. Extinct cities—Juvenile fiction. 3. Revenge—Juvenile fiction. 4. Paranormal fiction. 5. Adventure stories. [1. Mayas—Fiction. 2. Indians of Central America—Juvenile fiction. 3. Revenge—Fiction. 4. Supernatural—Fiction. 5. Adventure and adventurers—Fiction.] I. Voelkel, Pamela, author. II. Title. III. Series: Voelkel, Jon. Jaguar stones ; bk. 4.

PZ7.V861Lo 2014
[Fic]–dc23

2014034629

Book design by ARLENE SCHLEIFER GOLDBERG
Illustrations by Jon Voelkel

Printed in the United States of America

All rights reserved. No part of this publication may be reproduced, stored in a retrieval system, or transmitted, in any form or by any means, electronic, mechanical, photocopying, or otherwise, without the prior permission of the publisher and copyright owner.

R0456715445

To Harry, Charly, and Loulou

k yahkume'ex

In remembrance of Thunderclaw Branagan

ST. LOUIS

CAHOK[

NEW ORLEA[

GULF OF

[X]ICO

TO CENTRAL AMERICA

CONTENTS

CHARACTERS

In order of appearance

MAX (Massimo Francis Sylvanus) MURPHY: fourteen years old, only child, video gamer, drummer, pizza connoisseur. (Nickname: Hoop)

HERMANJILIO (*herman-kee-leo*) BOL: Maya archaeologist, university professor

LADY COCO (Ix Kan Kakaw—*eesh con caw cow*): Maya queen, Lord 6-Dog's mother

LORD 6-DOG (Ahaw Wak Ok—*uh how walk oak*): ancient Maya king

RAUL: Uncle Ted's butler at the Villa Isabella

TZELEK: evil sorcerer, Lord 6-Dog's adopted brother

LORD KUY (*coo-ee*): owl-headed messenger of Xibalba, the Maya underworld

AH PUKUH: Maya god of violent and unnatural death

LOLA (aka Lily Theodora Murphy; aka Ix Sak Lol—*eesh sock loll*): Max's half-Maya cousin, daughter of Ted and Zia Murphy. (Nickname: Monkey Girl)

TED MURPHY: Max's uncle, Lola's father, banana exporter, and reformed smuggler

ZIA: Ted's wife, Lola's mother, former housekeeper for Max's family in Boston

LUCKY, aka Jaime Ben: student teacher, Uncle Ted's former foreman and bodyguard

LOUIS: manager of Baron Saturday's Inn

BARON SATURDAY, aka BARON SAMEDI: New Orleans boss of the dead

THUNDERCLAW, aka the CHEE KEN OF DEATH, the FOWL OF FEAR: mangy black rooster (deceased)

BLUE SKY, RAINBOW, PHOENIX: friendly campers at Old Cahokia

ANTONIO DE LANDA, aka TOTO: Spanish aristocrat and descendant of Diego de Landa, the priest who burned Maya books

LADY KOO: Landa's wife, former beautician at the Grand Hotel Xibalba

FAY: wardrobe assistant at Old Cahokia, archaeology student

DR. DOLORES DELGADO: head of Maya Studies at Harvard

FRANK and CARLA MURPHY: Max's parents, famous archaeologists

CHAN KAN: Maya wise man, Lola's grandfather (deceased)

NASTY (Anastasia) SMITH-JONES: Max's friend, Boston music blogger

PLAGUE RATS: Max's favorite band

PUNAK HA: ancient Maya king, Lord 6-Dog's father

JADE FROG (Yax Tuun Ah Muuch—*yash toon awe mooch*): ancient Maya king, founder of the Jaguar Kings dynasty

IXCHEL (*eesh shell*): ancient Maya moon goddess

FACES AT FENWAY

EUSEBIO, chili farmer and boatman; OCH and little OCH, brothers from Lola's village; OSCAR POOT, head of the Maya Foundation in San Xavier City; VICTOR, head waiter at Hotel de las Americas in Puerto Muerto; SANTINO GARCIA, Spanish law student; DOÑA CARMELA: Santino's relative, owner of Casa Carmela guesthouse; FABIO: Venetian gondolier

MAYA MONSTERS, DEATH LORDS, PADDLER GODS, and BOSTON RED SOX: please see glossary pages 356–359

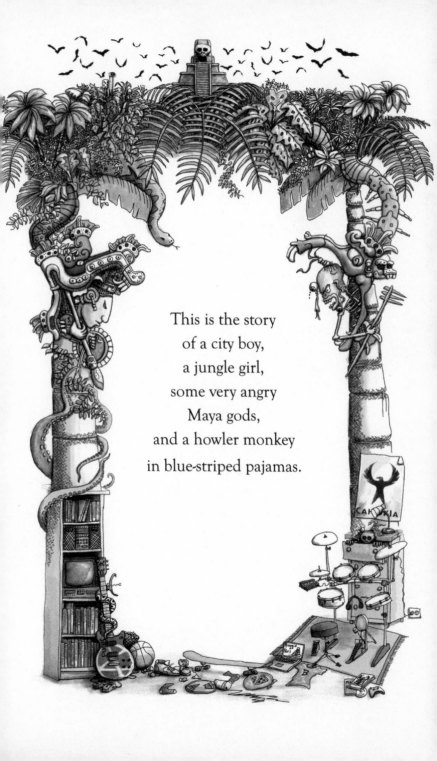

This is the story
of a city boy,
a jungle girl,
some very angry
Maya gods,
and a howler monkey
in blue-striped pajamas.

THE DREAM

Most mornings when Lord 6-Dog woke up, it took him a few moments to remember that he was a howler monkey. In his dreams he was still a Maya king, strong, handsome, and ten feet tall in his magnificent feathered headdress.

But that had been twelve hundred years ago—and a world away from the night he'd been summoned back by a red-haired boy named Max and a Maya girl named Lola, who'd persuaded him to take over the body of a howler monkey.

Lord 6-Dog stretched his furry arms. It wasn't so bad, this new life, he thought. If only he could understand the crazy dreams that played in his head every night.

Like all his people, he viewed dreams as messages from the gods and mulled them over carefully. For example, when he dreamed about his former life in the royal palace, he took it as a reminder to behave like a king even though he looked like a monkey.

But recently, his dreams had defied all interpretation.

Night after night, why did he see himself hurtling along with little wheels on his feet and a red cape streaming out behind him?

What could it mean?

What, he wondered nervously, did the gods have in store for him next?

CHAPTER ONE
REMEMBER TZELEK?

Deep in the jungle, something roared. It was loud enough to make Max Murphy, who was focused on battling a zombie horde, pause his game and look up uneasily.

The creature roared again.

Whatever it was, it was close.

Even though he was safe inside, Max suddenly felt very small and very edible.

He couldn't help remembering the scariest night of his life, when he'd first come to this place a few months ago and found himself lost and alone in the jungle, surrounded by things that wanted to prick him or bite him or eat him.

A third roar, even closer.

Calm down, he told himself. It was probably just a howler monkey proclaiming its territory or a wild pig squaring up for a fight.

A smell of mold and rotting vegetation wafted in through

the window screens, underlaid by something pungent and musky.

Definitely wild pig, then.

Max wrinkled his nose and thought about the skunk that frequented his backyard in Boston, and how they'd have to close the windows on summer nights to keep out its skunky odors. Once, a girl from school who'd come over to work on a project had thought the smell was Max's feet. He still cringed at the memory.

He supposed the windows were all closed in Boston now. The weather would be getting cooler, the leaves would be turning red, the kids would be planning their Halloween costumes, the stores would be stocking up on pumpkins and orange marshmallows.

He missed Boston.

But until his archaeologist parents were released from jail, where they currently languished on suspicion of looting, he was stuck here in the Villa Isabella, his uncle's house in the Central American country of San Xavier.

A huge hairy spider skittered out from under the couch. Max watched it contemptuously. In Boston, he reflected, spiders knew how to go about their business silently.

He returned to his zombie game and groaned in outrage— his foe had disappeared. Before he was distracted by the creature outside, the living dead had been lurking by some trash cans. Now, they were nowhere to be seen on the frozen screen. How was that even possible?

Indignantly, he pressed play and directed his avatar to crouch behind a wall to wait for the zombies to show themselves again.

A hand on his shoulder made him jump out of his skin.

"Hi, Max. Is Lola around?"

He turned to see Hermanjilio Bol, an archaeologist and local university professor, standing behind the couch, clutching a pile of books.

Max shook his head. "She's gone out with her parents. Again."

"No problem," said Hermanjilio. "I was just dropping these off for her. I'll leave them with you, if that's okay."

"Sure. But I never see her anymore."

"I thought you two were best friends?"

"So did I. But since she found out we're cousins, it's like she hates me, or something."

"What? I can't believe that! After all you've been through together? Going down to the Maya underworld, battling the Lords of Death . . . ?"

Max shrugged. "It's like it never happened."

Hermanjilio set the books down. "I guess she's got a lot on her mind. Think about it, Max. All her life, she thought she was an orphan. Now, suddenly, she discovers she has parents and a family. That's a lot for anyone to deal with."

"It's a lot for me, too. I have to get my head around the fact that her father is Uncle Ted, my dad's brother, and her mom is Zia, our housekeeper from Boston. I didn't even know they knew each other, and it turns out they're married."

"You should be happy for Lola. Besides, don't you have more important things to think about?"

"Like what?"

Hermanjilio pulled a crumpled card out of his back pocket. "Like this."

Max didn't need to look to know what it was.

Hermanjilio began to read out loud. " 'Memorial service

for Massimo Francis Sylvanus Murphy. To take place on 13-Water, the coming day of no hope, no escape, and no happy endings. All welcome.'" He waved the card at Max. "It's an invitation to your funeral. Doesn't that bother you?"

Max tried to look nonchalant. "It's from the Death Lords. You know what they're like. They have a twisted sense of humor. I'm pretty sure it's a joke."

"A joke?" With his beaky nose, long black hair, and imposing profile, Hermanjilio had always reminded Max of a Maya king in an old stone carving. But right now, the way he was screwing up his face in distaste, he looked like a Maya king who'd just stepped in monkey dung. "After everything you've been through, how can you talk about jokes? You know very well that the Death Lords are plotting the funerals of every man, woman, and child on this planet. There's nothing funny about that."

"You're a university professor. Surely you don't believe that some ancient Maya ghouls could bring about the end of the world?"

"They have all five Jaguar Stones. They can do anything they want."

Max shrugged. "Anyway, 13-Water's at the end of December. I'll be back in Boston by then."

"I'm impressed that you know your Maya calendar, at any rate."

"Uncle Ted's got an app for it on his phone."

"I might have known. So when do you fly back to Boston?"

"As soon as my parents get out of jail."

"Jail? I thought they were in police custody?"

"Same thing. They're locked up, no visitors allowed. All they did was try to report a looting."

Hermanjilio nodded sympathetically. "The authorities in San Xavier like their paperwork."

"Yeah, well. I just wish they'd hurry up and get it figured out, so we can go home and things can go back to normal."

Hermanjilio put a hand on Max's arm. "I know you don't want to hear this, but it might not be that easy. Like it or not, you have unfinished business with the ancient Maya Lords of Death. Wherever you are—here, Boston or Timbuktu—they'll find you. And when they're done with you, they'll start on the rest of us. The truth is that until somebody puts a stop to their evil plans, nothing will ever be normal again."

A howler monkey wearing oven gloves and an apron walked into the room, carrying a tray of food.

"Hello, Lord Hermanjilio," she said.

"How nice to see you, Lady Coco," he replied. "And what delicious concoction do you have there?"

Lady Coco loved compliments on her cooking and she rewarded him with a toothy monkey grin. "Something special. It's a delicacy from the old days."

Max didn't think twice about the fact that their hostess was an ancient Maya queen who was currently residing in the body of a small reddish-brown howler monkey. Nor did he bat an eye when her son, Lord 6-Dog—an ancient Maya king who was now a large black howler monkey—bounded in and sat next to him on the couch.

What he *did* find alarming was the pale brown porridgy paste in the dish set before him.

"What. Is. That?" he asked.

"It's called '*eek*,'" said Lady Coco, pronouncing it in Mayan as *eh-ek*. "It was 6-Dog's favorite when he was your age."

"Roasted wasp larvae." Lord 6-Dog licked his monkey lips

and nudged Max with his monkey elbow. "Thou art in for a treat, young lord."

Lady Coco smiled proudly. "I found the nest myself."

"They call it the caviar of the rainforest." Hermanjilio spread a little paste on a piece of tortilla and offered it to Max. "Try some."

"Thanks." Max chewed glumly. It wasn't what he was eating that depressed him—the wasp paste wasn't actually that bad—but Hermanjilio's grim predictions for the future. The funeral invitation still sat on the table taunting him. No matter how much he tried to downplay the gravity of the situation in his own mind, he knew that what Hermanjilio had said was true. The Death Lords were on the warpath. Long ago, at the start of creation, they'd been defeated by two human brothers who were known forever after as the Hero Twins. But now the balance of power had shifted. With a little (unwitting) help from Max and Lola, the Death Lords had acquired the Jaguar Stones, the five legendary stones of the Maya kings. Now, with the power of the stones behind them, the Death Lords could do anything they wanted. And what they wanted was to take revenge on the Hero Twins by destroying the entire human race.

Starting with Massimo Francis Sylvanus Murphy. Otherwise known as Max.

"A cacao bean for your thoughts," said Lady Coco.

"I . . . I . . ." Max cast around for another subject. "I wonder where Lola went?"

In Uncle Ted's office, a phone rang.

Max watched Raul, Uncle Ted's butler, scurry from the kitchen to answer it.

"I think they went out to eat. Lord Ted mentioned

something called won ton soup," said Lady Coco dreamily. "There are so many foods I have yet to try. It was all corn, beans, and squash in my day."

"And wasp larvae," added Lord 6-Dog happily.

Now Raul was walking toward them, the leather soles of his shoes rasping on the stone-tiled floor as he made his way slowly across Uncle Ted's sitting room, a huge vaulted chamber the size of a great hall in a medieval castle.

He stopped in front of Max and gave a little bow. "That was a lawyer from San Xavier City on the telephone, sir."

"What did he say? Have Mom and Dad been released? Can I talk to him?"

Raul shook his head. "I'm sorry. It was not a conversation. He said his piece and hung up. He merely wished to serve notice that you are a person of interest in your parents' case."

"What case? Why me? What have I done?"

"They are considering bringing charges against your parents. Your name has been entered as a potential witness. He said to warn you that you will be arrested if you try to leave San Xavier."

"So I can't go home until the police say so?" Max put down his tortilla and stared at his plate.

"It's just red tape," Hermanjilio consoled him.

"Have courage, young lord," urged Lord 6-Dog.

"We made your favorite pineapple cake for dessert," said Raul.

"With mango frosting," added Lady Coco.

As Raul and Lady Coco went back to the kitchen, Hermanjilio patted Max on the shoulder. "It's just until the case is heard. Your parents will be free soon. I'm sure of it."

"I'm not sure of anything," said Max.

Hermanjilio nodded understandingly. "This must all be so confusing for you. I'm sure they do things very differently in Boston."

"It's not that," said Max. "It's my parents. They find trouble like heat-seeking missiles. If they're not leaping into the Maya underworld, they're getting arrested and locked up. I can't trust them to behave like normal parents. I mean, it's their fault that the Death Lords are after me. They started all this."

Hermanjilio and Lord 6-Dog looked shocked at the outburst.

"What?" said Max.

"It was *you* who brought this on your parents," said Hermanjilio gently. "The Death Lords needed you and Lola to find the Jaguar Stones. They used your parents to get to you."

"If my parents weren't archaeologists, none of this would have happened." Max held up his palms. As far as he was concerned, the conversation was over.

Lord 6-Dog stared at him in disbelief. "Hast thou learned nothing from our adventures? Dost thou not understand that what *must* happen will happen? Thy fate is written in the stars; thou canst never escape it."

"I don't buy that," said Max.

Hermanjilio smiled, in spite of himself. "You've just dissed the whole of Maya civilization."

"I don't care," said Max. "I refuse to believe I can't control my own future."

Lord 6-Dog looked a bit like his head would explode. "What heresy is this?"

"I'm sorry," said Max. "But it's like when someone calls

you a loser and it makes you a million times more determined to beat them. If you tell me I have no free will, I'll automatically do the opposite of everything you say just to prove you wrong."

"In my day it was simple" said Lord 6-Dog. "Thou didst not have a choice. Thy future was determined by the day of thy birth and that was that. In many ways, that was the cause of the rift between myself and my adopted brother, Tzelek. I was born to be a great king. He was born to be an evil want-to-be."

"Wannabe," Max corrected him. "That's harsh."

Lord 6-Dog bounded off the couch and landed in between the two giant stone heads that dominated Uncle Ted's artifact-stuffed sitting room. "Dost thou know the story of these sculptures?"

"Of course. Mister Angry on the left is Tzelek; the other one is you."

"Indeed. And my destiny is to battle Tzelek until the end of time. It is the age-old story of good versus evil."

For a moment, Max felt a pang of pity for Tzelek and the role he'd been cast in. Destined always to be the bad guy, he'd died twelve hundred years ago in a battle with Lord 6-Dog. But, since there had been no winner—they'd killed each other—the brothers had vowed to fight again. As Lord 6-Dog was currently living in the human world and Tzelek was technically confined to the Maya underworld, the evil brother was always finding ways of escaping and taking up residence in unsuspecting mortals. (The only giveaways to his presence were an increasingly bad mood and a slight limp—easy enough signs to miss.)

As Max stared at Tzelek's stone head, he could swear that the statue was staring back at him with an intensity that made him shiver. He'd seen those eyes, that hatred, in real life—once when Tzelek had squatted in Hermanjilio's brain, and again in Spain, when he'd taken control of a creep called Count Antonio de Landa.

"Where is Tzelek now?" asked Hermanjilio uneasily.

"Last time I saw him was in Spain," said Max. "We were in a boat. He fell overboard."

"Let us hope he drowned," muttered Hermanjilio.

Lord 6-Dog shook his head. "There is only one way to put an end to Tzelek. It is written in the stars. He and I will duel to the death."

"But you've already done that once," said Max. "How can you duel to the death again?"

"Tzelek killed my father, Punak Ha, the man who raised him. With one plunge of a dagger Tzelek threw the cosmos out of balance. It is my duty to avenge my father's death. I will die, and die, and die again, until that one great wrong has been righted."

A chill ran around the room.

"It's cold tonight," said Hermanjilio. "Let's build a fire and get cozy."

Max looked around at the soaring ceiling, the expanse of cold floor, the antique furniture, and Uncle Ted's museum-like collection of Maya pottery. It would take more than a fire in the grate to make this room cozy.

Hermanjilio saw his dubious expression and misread it. "It's okay, Max, you're safe. Tzelek can't get you here."

"None of us are safe," said Lord 6-Dog.

And then the power went out.

CHAPTER TWO
RUNNING SCARED

Max groaned. "Not again. How can you live in a place that has so many blackouts?"

"You get used to it," Hermanjilio replied, "especially in hurricane season."

"It's always hurricane season," Max pointed out.

Hermanjilio laughed. "I know it seems that way. Blame climate change."

"Blame Tzelek," muttered Lord 6-Dog darkly.

"So sorry for the inconvenience," said Raul as he and Lady Coco bustled in with armfuls of candles.

"Candlelight is more flattering to the complexion," Lady Coco reassured him, apparently forgetting that her own face was temporarily covered in monkey hair.

"I thought you had an emergency generator," said Max.

"We do," replied Raul, "but it's not working. I sent someone out to fix it this morning, but I haven't heard anything. I just wish Jaime was still here."

"Jaime? Jaime Ben? You mean Lucky Jim?" Max's ears pricked up at this mention of the young Maya man who'd once saved him from Tzelek.

Raul nodded. "He took care of those things when he worked here. But now that he's training to be a teacher, we haven't seen him in a while."

"I have some experience with generators, Raul," volunteered Hermanjilio. "Want me to take a look?"

"If you wouldn't mind. It's in a clearing behind the warehouse. Can you find it?"

"Max can show me the way."

Max shook his head. After those roars he'd heard earlier, he had no desire to go outside.

"Not scared, are you?" asked Hermanjilio.

"No," lied Max.

"Good. I need you to hold the flashlight while I work on the generator."

Max thought quickly. "I have to stay here in case the lawyer calls again."

"No worries, young lord," Lady Coco informed him brightly, "the phone is down as well."

"Grab a machete and let's go," said Hermanjilio.

Uncle Ted's house was built on the jutting point of a ridge that encircled a sandy bay. The banana warehouse and loading dock sat on a pier at the water's edge. It was usually a sheltered little harbor, but today the boats bucked wildly and the tide roared as it pounded the shore.

At the top of the steps, Max hesitated. "The quickest way is straight along the beach, but . . ."

Hermanjilio surveyed the crashing waves. "Is there another route?"

"There's a trail through the jungle," said Max, already soaked in spray. "It's kind of overgrown, but I think I can find it."

"Lead on."

The watery setting sun barely tinted the gray clouds. As they walked along the trail, Hermanjilio pointed out a dark silhouette flitting through the sky.

"Look, a vampire bat!"

"Yech, I hate them," said Max. "One of them pooped on my pizza at the Grand Hotel Xibalba."

"That's odd."

"They were roosting in the roof of the restaurant," Max explained.

"No, I mean it's odd to see vampires around here. We usually get fruit bats. And you don't usually see bats awake so early. "

More and more vampires filled the sky.

"I wonder what's woken them?" mused Hermanjilio.

A bloodcurdling shriek pierced the air.

"What was that?" Max looked around warily.

"Probably a hawk. They come out to hunt the bats."

Hermanjilio stood for a moment scanning the trees. "Over there!" He pointed to a gap between the treetops where a large black bird, as ungainly as a turkey doing the backstroke, was thrashing and weaving through the sky.

Max stared at it. "It's flying upside down. Is that a thing? What bird does that?"

"I've
only heard of one . . .
my grandfather told me about
it . . . but it was just a story. That
bird was mythical."

"What was it called?"

"Mesa-hol, the bird that flies upside
down. Grandfather said that if it was ever to
land on your roof, your house would cave in. And if it ever
learned to fly right side up, it would foretell the end of the
world."

As they watched, the great black bird suddenly righted
itself and flew gracefully over their heads.

Max's eyes opened wide. "Did you see that?"

"It's just a big hawk," insisted Hermanjilio, "with an
unusual bat-catching technique."

"But it was flying upside down and then it flew right side
up. Just like the bird in your grandfather's story."

"Pure coincidence." Hermanjilio looked around,
narrowing his eyes. "But let's hurry. I think I see the warehouse
through the trees."

Max pointed to a fork in the trail. "This way to the
generator."

Hermanjilio shone the flashlight on a pattern in the dirt.
"Fresh tire tracks. Must be the repair truck. I'm guessing the
guy is still working on it."

"So he doesn't need us," said Max. "Let's go back."

"We should check he's okay. And then he can give us a lift. Come on. . . ."

Hermanjilio started running down the trail, and Max followed behind.

Suddenly, Hermanjilio stopped dead. Max barreled straight into him, almost knocking them both to the ground.

"Stay down," whispered Hermanjilio. "I don't like the look of this."

An overturned jeep lay abandoned in the clearing. The door of the shed was hanging off its hinges, and the roof had caved in, taking one of the walls with it. Smoke drifted up to the sky. There was no sign of the workman.

"Hello?" called Hermanjilio. "Is anybody there?"

As if answering his call, the big black bird landed on the rusty upturned underside of the jeep. As the bird turned its head to survey the clearing, it looked directly at Max. Its eyes were empty sockets.

"That hawk . . . ," he began, but Hermanjilio shushed him.

"I think I hear something. . . ."

Max listened. He could hear nothing but the buzzing of insects and the distant crashing of the ocean.

But then, from somewhere inside the broken shed, he heard a sob.

"Stay here," Hermanjilio instructed. "I'll go and look."

"Be careful," Max whispered. His insides felt swampy with fear.

With his machete at the ready, Hermanjilio ran across the clearing and picked his way through the doorway of the

31

shed. Then he disappeared from view behind a pile of rubble.

There was silence for a worryingly long time. Then: "Max, come and help me."

As Max got closer, the smell of burning oil and melted rubber stung his nostrils and he pulled his shirt up over his nose. He could hear Hermanjilio talking Mayan in a soothing tone. He followed the voice into the shed.

"Over here, Max!"

In a corner, trapped by debris, huddled a young Maya man. He wore dust-covered overalls and a yellow hard hat that had probably saved his life. He whimpered quietly as, one by one, Hermanjilio cleared away the sheets of tin, pieces of wood, and chunks of cement.

Max quickly moved to help.

"I've tried English, Spanish, and every Maya language I know," Hermanjilio explained, slightly out of breath from all the lifting. "He hasn't responded to any of them. I think he's in shock. We need to get him out of here before those fuel tanks blow."

They helped the workman to his feet. "Are you hurt? Can you walk?" Hermanjilio asked. In answer, the workman limped forward, holding on to his rescuer like a drowning man clutching a life preserver.

Once outside, they led the workman to the far edge of the clearing and tried to sit him down against a tree trunk. All the while, the man was trying to get away.

"It's okay," Hermanjilio assured him. "You're safe now."

BOOM! BOOM! BOOM!

"There go the fuel tanks! Get down!" Hermanjilio pushed Max and the workman to the ground, covering them with his own body, as an explosion blew through the clearing. There

32

was a flash of light, a wave of intense heat, a terrible screech of metal as pipes and machine parts were ripped apart. Max was unsure if the ground beneath them was shaking or if it was just his own body shaking in fear.

Leaves and branches rained down on them.

When all was quiet again, Hermanjilio sat up. "Everyone all right? That was a close call."

Max looked back at the shed.

It was gone. In its place was a smoldering heap of ashes.

On the jeep, the big black bird squawked triumphantly.

"Mesa-hol!" whispered the workman, staggering to his feet. He took Hermanjilio's hands, babbled a rapid stream of Mayan, then ran into the jungle as fast as his injured legs could carry him.

"What did he say?" asked Max.

"He said he crashed into the tree when he saw the bird. He hid in the shed, but the roof caved in. He said he has to find his family before it's too late."

"Too late for what?" asked Max.

"I don't know."

They watched as the bird flapped its great black wings and took off in the direction of the Villa Isabella.

"That bird is Mesa-hol, isn't it?" Max insisted.

"I don't know, Max. Let's just get back as fast as we can."

"What if Mesa-hol lands on Uncle Ted's roof?"

"Just keep running."

Max could see the Villa Isabella outlined on the ridge.

Not far now.

A voice floated out of the jungle. "Help me! Please help me!"

Max stopped and looked around. "That sounds like Lola."

"It's not Lola. Keep running."

"She needs help."

"Ignore her! Keep running!"

"Hoop! Hoop!" called the voice.

"It *is* Lola. Only Lola calls me Hoop. I have to go to her."

"No, Max!"

Too late. Max had disappeared into the undergrowth.

By the time Hermanjilio caught up, Max was staring as if hypnotized into a thornbush. The branches waved as if beckoning him closer.

"She's in there," said Max. "Can't you see her face? She's trapped in this bush. We have to help her."

"No." Hermanjilio locked his arms around Max to stop him going any nearer. His muscles bulged with the effort of holding the boy back. And, all the while, the branches reached out and tried to entangle them both in their thorny grasp.

Hermanjilio put his mouth next to Max's ear. "Look away, Max. Don't meet her eyes."

"But it's Lola—"

"It's not Lola. Her name is Ixt'abay."

"Eesh-ta-bye? You know her?"

"I know *of* her. She was another creature in Grandfather's stories. She calls to her victims like the sirens in Greek myth. If you go to her, she'll choke you to death in her thorns."

Even as Max struggled to go to her, he nodded to show he understood.

"Fight it," said Hermanjilio.

"Can't," gasped Max.

"Lean back on me, I'll drag you to the house."

"Can't do it."

"I'm losing you, Max. She's winning. Don't let her win."

34

"She calls to her victims like the sirens in Greek myth."

"S'okay. Lola won't hurt me."

"She will kill you. It's not Lola."

"Let me go."

Just as Hermanjilio was losing his grip and the branches of the thornbush were twining around Max's arms and pulling him in, heavy footsteps shook the ground behind them.

"Good evening, travelers," boomed a man's voice. "Is there a problem?"

Max felt Ixt'abay's power over him ebb away. Now, when he looked into the thornbush, he saw not Lola's face, but a haggard old witch fading into the darkness. He backed away as far as he could.

"Who are you?" Hermanjilio asked the voice. "Where are you?"

"My name is Che' Winik." (He pronounced it *Chay Weeneek*.) "And I am here."

"Where is here?"

While Hermanjilio was trying to locate the owner of the voice, Max was inspecting the cuts on his arms. Those thorns were as sharp as needles. He felt rather foolish for falling for the Lola trick. He made a mental note to ask Hermanjilio to leave that bit out of the story when they told it at the villa.

"Hey, Hermanjilio, could we—?"

He was whisked up into the air, high up into the air, as high as the forest canopy. He fought against whatever squeezed his waist and saw that it was giant hairy fingers. Hardly believing his eyes, he followed the fingers to a gnarly hand on a muscular arm attached to a chest the size of a house, above which was the biggest, ugliest head he'd ever seen. And the head was opening its giant mouth to eat him.

"Max! Max! Where are you?" called Hermanjilio.

"Up here! He's got me!"

Down on the forest floor, Hermanjilio looked tiny. "Don't let him eat you!"

Max could smell the giant's bad breath and see the stumps of his rotting teeth. Saliva dripped on Max's head. "How do I stop him?"

"Hey, Che' Winik!" called up Hermanjilio. "Watch me! I'm going to dance!"

Max watched in confusion as Hermanjilio started dancing, a sort of lurching, hip-hop slide. He thought the professor had lost his mind. But the giant looked down with interest, and his mouth twisted into a horrible smile.

Hermanjilio did a march like a drum majorette, using a small leafy branch as his baton, and the giant gurgled with pleasure.

Hermanjilio stuck out his elbows and bent his knees to do a chicken dance.

He kicked his legs like a solo Rockette.

Then he gripped the branch between his teeth and tangoed with himself.

A rumble like thunder emerged from the giant's throat. Terrified, Max braced to be crushed in the massive fist. But, if anything, the giant's grip loosened.

A tear as big as a birdbath ran down the giant's face.

He was laughing.

He was laughing so much that his monstrous tree-trunk legs were shaking, making the surrounding forest shake with them. Birds screeched, howler monkeys roared, and little kinkajous screamed in protest as they crashed out of the branches to find safer perches.

Down below, Hermanjilio kept dancing: a body wave, a robot, a one-man conga line.

With a snort that bordered on pain, the giant keeled over and Max plummeted to the ground in his hand, the giant's chubby fingers cushioning him like air pillows.

Hermanjilio ran to help Max out of his fleshy cage.

"Quick!" cried Max. "Before he gets up again."

"He can't get up," said Hermanjilio. "He has no bones in his legs. Plus, did you notice that his feet are on back to front?"

"No," said Max, "I didn't."

"But you saw my dance moves?"

"About that . . . what just happened?"

"That was Che' Winik."

"I got that."

"He attacks travelers. The legend says that the only way to defeat him is to do a dance with a branch and make him fall over laughing. Then he can't stand up again."

The fallen giant's tears of laughter were forming a pool on the jungle floor. Bullfrogs and small lizards came out to drink from it.

"Seriously?" Max watched with contempt. "As monsters go, he's not very effective."

"Not if you know his secret. But if you'd been on your own, he'd have had you for dinner."

"I thought you'd lost your mind," Max admitted.

"Was my dancing that bad?"

"Yes," said Max. "It was terrible." He took several deep breaths and tried to slow down his racing heart.

"Well, it did the job." Hermanjilio scratched his head. "But I have to tell you, until this moment, I had no idea that

Che' Winik was real. I thought he was just another one of my grandfather's stories."

"Like Mesa-hol and Ixt'abay?" asked Max.

Hermanjilio nodded. "Exactly. It's like there's something in the air tonight. Let's get home before we meet anyone else."

"Who else *is* there?" asked Max as they walked around Che' Winik and retraced their steps to the trail.

"If you're asking about all the creatures in Maya mythology, the answer is too many to count," said Hermanjilio. "But if I were you, I'd be more concerned about all the vampire bats that were hovering above my head."

Max looked up. "There are millions of them!"

"I believe the collective noun for bats is a *colony*," added Hermanjilio helpfully.

"What do they want?"

"What do vampire bats always want?"

"I'm guessing blood." Max took a few paces forward and the bats followed him. "But why *my* blood?"

"That's a good question. This behavior is quite out of character. Vampires usually wait until their prey is asleep, and they rarely bite humans. All those Dracula stories have given them a bad name."

"They deserve a bad name," said Max, stepping up his pace. "I hate them."

Wherever he looked he saw little mouse faces, greasy brown fur, leathery wings, and yellow blood-hungry fangs. The sulfurous-smelling air was thick with bats, and they perched on the trees at the edge of the trail like an honor guard.

Max felt like a sheep being herded to market.

"One touched me!" he yelped. "It's in my hair! It's going to bite me!"

"It's a leaf," said Hermanjilio, picking off the offending greenery. "Just stay calm, okay? We're nearly home. And remember, when we get to the villa, the most important thing is to keep the bats out of the house. Don't let them follow you inside."

Max was horrified. "You think they'd try it?"

"Who knows? Just keep your wits about you."

The Villa Isabella was close now. They could see Raul standing at the window.

"He's waiting for us," said Hermanjilio. "He must see the bats."

"He's pointing at the front door," said Max.

The bats chirruped excitedly.

"Ready to run for it?" asked Hermanjilio. "Go! Go! Go!"

As soon as Max approached the heavy oak front door, it swung open and sent out a blindingly bright beam of light. A hand grabbed him, and Hermanjilio pushed in behind him.

"Did we do it?" asked Max, leaning against the door to make sure it was shut. "Did we keep the bats out?"

Raul nodded. He was holding a dive light like a ray gun.

"Thanks to Raul's quick thinking," said Hermanjilio. "Bats hate bright lights."

Max and Hermanjilio high-fived.

They'd done it. They'd reached home. They thought they were safe.

But in their rush to enter the house, neither of them had noticed the huge, eyeless black bird crouched on the parapet above the front door.

CHAPTER THREE
THE CREATURES OF THE NIGHT

Raul seemed agitated. "Did you get to the generator?" he asked. Then he took in their scratches and smoke-stained clothes. "What happened to you?"

"Let's just say," said Hermanjilio, "it's a jungle out there tonight."

Max slid to the floor, relieved to be safe.

"I need to tell you—" began Raul.

THUD! THUD! THUD! The bats were throwing themselves at the doors and window screens.

Max jumped to his feet. "They can't get in, can they?"

"We must close all the shutters," said Raul.

"And barricade the doors," added Hermanjilio.

"Wait!" Lady Coco hobbled painfully toward them. "My 6-Dog is still out there. He went to get firewood."

Max stared at the little brown howler monkey. "Your leg— it's all bandaged. What happened?"

"I was about to tell you," said Raul. "We have a bigger problem than the bats."

Hermanjilio paused from dragging a heavy wooden trunk across the tiles. "What do you mean?"

"Lady Coco and I. We were set upon by centipedes."

"Centipedes?"

"In the cellar."

Hermanjilio relaxed. "Is that all? Damp, dark places often attract centipedes. Just call the exterminators. They'll soon get rid of them."

"These were not ordinary centipedes," Raul insisted. "One of them was six feet tall."

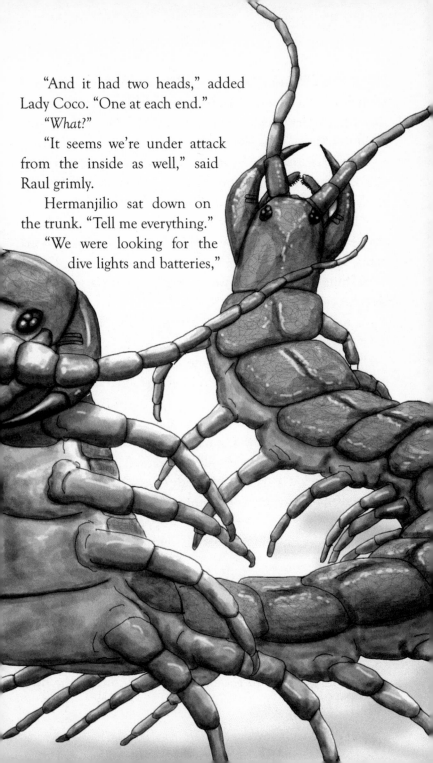

"And it had two heads," added Lady Coco. "One at each end."

"*What?*"

"It seems we're under attack from the inside as well," said Raul grimly.

Hermanjilio sat down on the trunk. "Tell me everything."

"We were looking for the dive lights and batteries,"

began Raul. "You know what it's like down there, a maze of tunnels and dead ends. And the first thing we saw was that the whole place was squirming with"—he shuddered at the memory—"*Scolopendra gigantea.*"

"Otherwise known as giant centipedes," translated Lady Coco. "I've seen them in caves before, hanging off the roof to catch bats, but I've never seen them as big as this."

"Luckily, the flashlight kept them at bay," continued Raul, "so we carried on to the dive room. Then, just as we found the lights, this huge *thing* appeared out of a side tunnel. . . ."

"Thing?" Hermanjilio was trying, and not succeeding, to keep his voice calm.

"I told you," said Lady Coco impatiently. "It was six feet tall with two heads."

"I can only describe it as a monster," agreed Raul. "When it reared up, it was as tall as the tunnel. It stood there . . . just . . . *undulating.*"

"Undulating?" repeated Hermanjilio.

Raul nodded. "It was waving its legs at us. It had legs everywhere. And big pincers like a lobster. "

"It was Eek' Chapaat," said Lady Coco flatly. "I'm sure of it. I've seen it many times in paintings."

"Eek' Chapaat?" Hermanjilio stopped trying to sound calm. "The mythical, man-eating centipede? Did it attack you?"

"We didn't give it a chance," said Lady Coco. "It has weak eyesight from living in caves, so we shone our flashlights into its eyes—"

"All four of them," added Raul.

"—and backed away as quickly as we could."

"But in my haste to get away, I dropped one of the dive

44

lights and it smashed and Lady Coco gashed her leg on some glass," explained Raul. He turned to Lady Coco. "I am so sorry."

"Not at all," said Lady Coco. "You rescued me. You're a hero."

Raul shook his head. "I am no hero. For one thing, I only managed to salvage one light and one battery. For another, I am no match for Eek' Chapaat. If that creature had wanted to kill us, it could easily have done so. I had the distinct feeling that it was looking for someone else."

"It's like we're trapped in a Maya horror story," said Max, bug-eyed with terror. "Whatever we do, we have to stay together. I've seen the movies. They pick you off, one by one."

Lady Coco bit her lip. "I wish my 6-Dog would come home."

"Is Eek' Chapaat still down there?" asked Hermanjilio.

"As far as I know," replied Raul. "I used the flood defense system to seal off the main tunnel. If it got through that, it would have to climb the spiral staircase up to Mr. Murphy's office, break through the trapdoor, smash through the secret bookcase, and knock down the office door."

They all stared anxiously at the door.

"Even if it could do all that," reasoned Raul, "it's a centipede. It likes the dark. Why would it come up here?"

"Still," said Max, "let's not take any chances."

They heaved a chest of drawers in front of the office door, then upturned an antique desk and piled that on top for good measure.

"Round up every candle you can find," Hermanjilio ordered. "It's getting dark early tonight."

"It's the bats," said Raul, looking through a shutter slat.

45

"They're all over the windows. They're coating the house like shingles."

Max took a peek. Layer after layer of bats clung to the window screens, crawling over one another and trying to chew through the wire. The bats squeaked in protest as the house was shaken by a loud banging on the front door.

"Open up!" came Lord 6-Dog's voice.

Hermanjilio ran to unbolt the door. "Enter quickly, your majesty," he called through the oak. "We are besieged."

"Wait—" called Lady Coco.

But she was too late. As Raul switched on the dive light and Hermanjilio inched open the door, a black monkey arm shot through the gap.

Quick as a flash, Lady Coco sank her teeth into it.

There was a cry of pain and the arm withdrew.

"Shut the door!" shouted Lady Coco. "I command you!"

Shocked by her newfound assertiveness, Hermanjilio obeyed but cast a worried glance at Max and Raul.

"Lady Coco," said Raul gently, "I think you may have a concussion. Do you remember that your son is a howler monkey?"

Lady Coco rolled her eyes. "Of course I do. Bring me the pineapple cake."

"But—"

"Bring it! Now!"

Shocked into action by her bossy tone, Raul did as she asked.

Outside, Lord 6-Dog banged again.

"Lady Coco, this is madness," Hermanjilio argued. "I have to let him in. I can't leave him out there with all the bats."

"Just a moment." Lady Coco took the cake from Raul. "Now you can open the door."

"Hey, that's my cake," joked Max. "Don't give it to *him*." His expression of welcome turned to horror as he realized that the black howler monkey on the doorstep had flaming red eyes. "That's not Lord 6-Dog," he cried.

"Take that, *alux*!" shouted Lady Coco, hurling the pineapple cake at the visitor.

Instantly distracted, the howler uttered a cry of delight. As soon as his hairy hands caught the cake, he transformed into an ugly little gnome, spattered with mango frosting. So engrossed was he in eating the cake and licking off the frosting that they easily pushed him away and closed the door.

"Sorry, Lady Coco," said Hermanjilio. "We should have listened to you."

"I knew he'd reveal his true self in the face of a cake," said Lady Coco. "The *alux* has a very sweet tooth."

"Can someone tell me what just happened?" asked Max.

"We had a visit from an *alux*," Lady Coco told him.

"What's an *aloosh*?"

"It's a shape-shifter, a mischievous sprite," explained Hermanjilio. "You're half Irish, aren't you, Max? Think of it as a Maya leprechaun."

"But why did it come here? What did it want?"

"I wish I knew," said Hermanjilio. "Why did Mesa-hol appear? Why did Ixt'abay pretend to be Lola? Why did Che' Winik block our way? Why did the bats follow us home?"

"And what's with the giant centipedes?" added Lady Coco.

"Indeed," mused Hermanjilio. "It's as if someone is playing a very elaborate and unfunny joke on us."

"The Death Lords like playing jokes," said Max in a small voice.

Lady Coco shook her head. "What happened in the cellar was not a joke. Eek' Chapaat was deadly serious. He was out for blood. I could sense it."

Raul shuddered. "Let us hope we will have no more uninvited guests."

WHOOSH!

In a cloud of soot and ash, a black howler monkey shot out of the chimney into the hearth.

They all froze, waiting to see Lady Coco's reaction.

"It's him!" she cried. "This time it's really him!" She brushed flakes of ash off her son's fur. "I'm so glad you're safe, 6-Dog. Did you see the *alux* out there?"

"Aye, Mother. The *waayoob* are massing around this house."

"What are *waayoob?*" asked Max, his voice wavering.

"Spooks and demons, the creatures of the night," explained Lady Coco. "But why have they come? Why here? Why tonight?"

"Thy guess is as good as mine, Mother. But let us not waste time talking. We must build a fire to keep the bats from following me down the chimney." Lord 6-Dog looked disparagingly at the decorative pyramid of logs arranged in the grate of Uncle Ted's massive fireplace. "We will need more wood. Much more wood."

Hermanjilio brought the machetes.

Uncle Ted's chairs were first to be chopped up, then his tables, his cabinets, his couches, his bookcases, and every piece of furniture that wasn't being used as a barricade.

Only when a bonfire was blazing in the hearth and every

flammable antique had been reduced to kindling did they sit down on the floor to discuss their situation. On the other side of the window shutters, the bats still dive-bombed the house.

"Whomever they seek is inside this house," said Lord 6-Dog.

Without a moment's hesitation they all looked at Max.

"Hey! It could be one of you," he protested.

"Ixt'abay called to you," Hermanjilio pointed out. "Che' Winik captured you. The vampire bats followed you—"

"Stop! I get it!" Max swallowed nervously.

"We'll protect you," Lady Coco assured him.

"Protect me from what?" asked Max miserably. "What's happening?" He followed Hermanjilio's eyes to a crumpled piece of card that lay on the floor where the coffee table had been. "Is this about my funeral? Is this how it starts?"

"Calm down, Max." Hermanjilio picked up the invitation and threw it into the fireplace. "The creatures of the underworld are scary, but they're stupid."

"I concur," said Lord 6-Dog. "Whatever is happening out there, we are more than a match for it."

Lady Coco stuck out her chin. "Bring it on," she said, trying to sound tough.

There was a distant booming like giant footsteps.

Max jumped. "What is that?"

"My guess is Che' Winik," said Hermanjilio. "And he's heading this way."

Lord 6-Dog listened carefully. "Thou art mistaken."

Max looked at him hopefully.

"Those are the steps of at least *two* ogres," concluded Lord 6-Dog.

"Please don't let them take me," whimpered Max.

"Fear not, young lord. We shall easily defeat them. For we know their weak spot."

"We do?" Max was shaking.

Lord 6-Dog nodded confidently. "Do you remember the old saying, Mother?"

Lady Coco thought for a moment, then she burst out: *"The creatures of the night fear courage and light!"* She clapped her hairy hands. "You are a genius, 6-Dog. Courage we have in abundance. Light we can make."

"No we can't," said Max. "The generator exploded."

"And the dive light won't last much longer," added Raul.

"Then we will fight by firelight," announced Hermanjilio. He sounded defeated already.

"What is the matter with you three?" Lady Coco demanded. "Pull yourselves together! I am injured and you don't hear me whining. Where is your fighting spirit?"

"It would be a tight fit, but we could hide under the stairs till they've gone," suggested Raul.

"A king does not hide," barked Lord 6-Dog.

Lady Coco stood to attention and saluted him. "What are your orders, your majesty?"

"I will take charge of courage, Mother; thou art in charge of light."

Lady Coco chuckled. "If there's one thing a Maya queen can do, it's bring light to the jungle night. Raul, I need your help."

"More candles?" said Raul, wearily.

"Candles? No! Think bigger! I need woven rags, coconut oil, and some sturdy bamboo canes. As many as you can find."

50

Raul looked at her blankly as the footsteps outside grew ever louder.

"Jump to it, Raul! Don't worry about what's out there, just listen to my voice. It will be like we're cooking in the kitchen—except, instead of cakes, we're making my famous flaming torches. Come on, now, follow the recipe. Rags! Oil! Canes!"

Raul jumped into action. "Yes, Lady Coco!" He considered her list. "How about dish towels, barbecue lighter fluid, and broom handles?"

"Perfect!" Lady Coco tried to smile brightly, but her smile dissolved into a wince.

"What am I thinking?" said Raul. "You are wounded. You must take the weight off your leg." He found some pillows that had not been burned and arranged them into a monkey-size mattress near the fireplace. "Rest while you can. Tell us what to do and we'll follow your instructions."

For once, Lady Coco didn't argue.

She lay back on the pillows and supervised as Raul, Max, and Hermanjilio assembled an impressive stash of homemade torches.

"I hope we have made them to your satisfaction," said Raul.

Lady Coco nodded weakly.

"Light alone will not repel them," said Lord 6-Dog. "We must arm ourselves for combat."

Max surveyed the collection of conquistador weaponry that lined his uncle's walls. He wondered if antique Spanish steel would be effective against the creatures of the Maya underworld.

Raul, still fragile after his encounter with the centipede,

chose a full suit of armor. He could hardly move and wouldn't be much use in a battle, but maybe, Max thought, the sight of an entirely metal man would be terrifying enough in its own right to a primitive ogre.

Lord 6-Dog took a dagger to use as a short sword. Max and Hermanjilio settled on swords, pikes, and breastplates. From her bed on the pillows, Lady Coco requested a slingshot.

All the while, the beating of bat wings outside the windows and the scratching of bat claws against the doors intensified into a rhythm like the drums of war.

Lord 6-Dog sniffed the air. "And so it begins," he said. He pointed up to the ceiling. "The Ookol Pixan have arrived."

"*Ock-ole pee-shan?*" Max directed his flashlight up to the rafters. There, in the shadows where the wall met the ceiling, sat a tiny, almost transparent man. He was bald with long, pointed ears and a sharp nose. Max ran the flashlight over the rest of the beams. More little men squatted like toads at the ends of every one.

"Who are they?" he demanded. "How did they get in?"

"They enter where they please," explained Lord 6-Dog. "They are the soul stealers. They appear when a human is about to die."

CHAPTER FOUR
THE MONSTER PARADE

"**S**hoo! Get out of here!" shouted Max at the ghostly beings in the rafters, aiming a pike like a javelin at the nearest one.

Lord-6 Dog stayed his arm. "Save thy strength, young lord. The soul stealers cannot hurt thee, not while thou art still alive. They are like vultures. They watch and wait."

And then it started.

BOOOM!

The house shook from top to bottom as if a colossal wrecking ball had been aimed at its walls.

BOOOM!

Deep cracks spread across the plaster.

BOOOM!

One wall of the great hall exploded, hurling stones across the room. Through the gaping hole Max could see what looked like two trees carrying a huge uprooted trunk between them. "The trees are attacking us?"

"Not trees. Ogres!" Lord 6-Dog shouted over the din.

Again and again, the tree-like ogres pounded on the wall with their makeshift battering ram. When the dust cleared, they left behind an opening big enough for a school bus.

Raul, in his suit of armor, clanked into position in front of Lady Coco, ready to defend her.

"Here we go," said Hermanjilio, lighting torches and passing them around.

Formations of vampire bats poured through the hole like dive bombers. The air was a blur. Within minutes, anything that remained of Uncle Ted's precious antiques collection was dripping with tarry black bat guano.

There was a horrible ripping sound as a large chunk of ceiling fell in.

Max looked up, expecting to see Mesa-hol.

But to his surprise, it was quite a different bird.

This one had little flint daggers all over its body in place of feathers. It landed on a Persian rug, its beating wings grinding like scissors on a sharpener. Within seconds the rug was shredded into strips. The bats (and Max) shrank back from the bird, squeaking in terror.

Max looked at Lord 6-Dog.

"The bird of blades? Its name is Waay-Pop."

"What does that mean?" asked Max distractedly.

"It means," said Lord 6-Dog, "that the stories of my ancestors have come back to haunt us. Like all witches and monsters and demons, that bird was invented long ago by a mortal telling tales by candlelight."

"Are you saying I'm imagining it?" asked Max.

"I am saying that it feeds on thy fear."

An enormous black-and-white-striped lizard with a bright

pink underbelly strutted into the room. It had a knot tied into its tail, and it whipped it from side to side.

Lord 6-Dog gripped his sword. "Ix Humpetz' K'in. The knot in its tail is to flay thee, but what it likes best is to bite thy shadow."

The lizard flicked its forked pink tongue menacingly at Max and took up a position at the end of the room like a game show contestant standing on a pre-arranged mark.

After that, it began to feel like some kind of grotesque beauty pageant, where every new contender was uglier than the last.

Next came a man made of stone with a vulture sitting on his forehead. Scorpions nested in his mossy green dreadlocks and small lizards crawled between his toes. His fingernails were as long and curved as scimitars. He took his place next to the lizard.

Max looked questioningly at Lord 6-Dog.

"They call him Unik-Tuun-Uh. He is the agent of death."

"That doesn't sound good," said Max

Lord 6-Dog shrugged. "He is just one more simpleton who fears courage and light. Ignore him."

"But his vulture is staring at me like it wants to eat me."

"It is a vulture. What dost thou expect?"

"Vultures are supposed to wait till you're dead," Max pointed out.

"Ah," said Lord 6-Dog, with one eye on a large ash-colored snake that was slithering into the room, "Eek' Unehil can help thee there." The snake paused in front of Max and raised its black forked tail menacingly. "Its delight would be to suffocate thee by forcing the twin tips of its tail up thy nostrils."

"Please tell me you're making this up," said Max.

"Unfortunately not, young lord. And here comes Wawa' Pach."

A giant with the hooded eyes of a snake marched in and stood with his legs wide apart, arms folded, head in the rafters. He smiled at Max, revealing three tongues like knives, and twirled a necklace of glistening brown blobs.

"I know I'll regret asking," said Max. "But what's that on his necklace?"

"Human kidneys. The kidneys of the crushed. He stands like an arch and waits for humans to walk between his legs. Then he crushes them and threads their kidneys on strings like beads."

"Make it stop," Max begged Lord 6-Dog. "Can't you just ask them what they want?"

"Cover thine eyes!" commanded Lord 6-Dog as a shaggy black animal with horns and a twisted corkscrew neck entered the room.

"Is that a sheep?" asked Max through his fingers.

"It is the goat-witch. If thou shouldst look into its eyes, thou wilt lose thy mind."

"I feel like I've lost it already," said Max. "What's happening now?"

"The goat-witch is moving to the back to make room for the new arrivals."

"Not more? Where are they all coming from?"

"From the depths of hell," replied Lord 6-Dog.

He pointed at the incoming monsters with his dagger, like a herald announcing new arrivals at a ball. "That's Ah Wayak', who will break thy bones . . . Waal Am Paca, who will capture thy soul, but can only hold one soul at once . . . and here comes K'aak'asbal."

The assembly fell silent as the ugliest creature Max had ever seen stepped through the hole in the wall. It was a hairy monster, rather like the chief wild thing in *Where the Wild Things Are*. But this one was covered in random arms and legs. Worse still, in between the limbs and hair hung assorted hearts and lungs and livers. His tail draped behind him like a snake. Nothing about him made sense. It was as if a blindfolded kindergarten class had drawn him into being.

"That's the grossest thing I've ever seen," said Max.

"They call him 'the sum of all malignancies.'" He is a walking war zone. Those organs that hang off his skin are from different animals that hate each other."

K'aak'asbal stood perfectly still, while his stolen organs throbbed and pulsed.

"What do they want?" Max was trying to sound brave, but his knees were weak. "Why are they all just standing around?"

"I can only assume that they are following orders."

"Whose orders?"

"That is the question."

While the major monsters resumed their acquaintance with each other, mingling like guests at a party, an entourage of hangers-on slimed in—giant brown toads with bulging yellow eyes, hairy spiders as big as cats, angry-looking moths, more lizards, more scorpions, more snakes—a slithering horde of snakes.

Yet none of the creatures took any notice of the residents of the Villa Isabella.

Max and Lord 6-Dog joined Hermanjilio and Raul to stand in a semicircle in front of Lady Coco. They each held a flaming torch. Max noticed that the monsters chose to congregate at the far end of the room, but he was disappointed that they didn't actually scream or collapse to see the fire.

For a several minutes, nothing happened. The five good guys and the hordes of bad guys eyed each other shiftily, but none of them made the first move.

The monsters seemed to be waiting for a signal.

Then a cold wind—the kind of wind that cuts right through your clothes and chills your bones—whistled through the hole in the wall.

It had the effect of an orchestra striking up at the theater to let you know that the action is about to start.

The monsters stood to attention.

The room fell quiet.

The candles and torches sputtered dramatically.

The tension became unbearable.

Just as Max was imagining what kind of mutant could command the lurching lowlife army currently assembled in Uncle Ted's great hall, a Maya warrior appeared. His skin was painted black, and he wore a headdress of white skulls and black feathers. He carried a flint spear, and an obsidian ax hung from his belt.

"Tzelek?" asked Lord 6-Dog.

"Well, well, well," said the warrior. "If it isn't my beloved brother, Lord Monkey Butt. I was hoping I'd find you here. Are you ready for our showdown?"

"This is it?" asked Lord 6-Dog, sounding surprised. "Our last epic battle is to be fought in a mortal's sitting room?"

"Beggars can't be choosers." Tzelek drew his spear. "Let's fight."

Lord 6-Dog wagged a finger. "If our showdown is to be recorded in Maya history, we must obey the rules."

Tzelek blew a raspberry at him.

"Who would I be fighting?" continued Lord 6-Dog. "Last I heard, thou wert a spirit in Xibalba. How didst thou get that body?"

"I've been working out."

Lord 6-Dog looked at him blankly.

"Joke," explained Tzelek. "I forgot you still live in the dark ages."

"I still live," harrumphed Lord 6-Dog, "in an age of chivalry and honor. How darest thou dress like a king? Thou hast no right to wear that garb."

"Oh, lighten up, bro. Why do you speak like that? Nobody speaks like that. You are a pompous idiot, 6-Dog. The scepter of the Jaguar Kings was wasted on you. I should have been king."

Lady Coco groaned in protest. She tried to get up, but she was too weak.

"Oh hello, Mommy. Is that you?" sneered Tzelek. "I might have known you'd be nearby. 6-Dog was always your favorite. It's all in the psychology books, you know. I'm a classic case of infantile alienation syndrome."

"You're a classic case of ignorance and ingratitude," countered Lady Coco.

Tzelek let loose another raspberry. "Much as I'd like to debate this further, I have an old score to settle."

"But whose body is that?" persisted Lord 6-Dog.

"This old thing? Who knows. It's just a loaner."

"A loner? It has no friends?"

Tzelek rolled his eyes. "It is on loan. It's temporary. I have to return it when I get back."

"Back where? Art thou living in Xibalba again?"

"I'd hardly call it living."

All this time, the assembled monsters had been patiently following the conversation, quietly cheering for Tzelek and hissing at Lord 6-Dog.

Now Lord 6-Dog pointed at them. "Is this thine army, Tzelek? Art thou too cowardly even to fight me single-handedly?"

Tzelek laughed. "I have never knowingly turned down an unfair advantage, but sadly these killing machines are not with me. I merely sneaked through with them when the door between worlds was opened."

"Then why are they here?"

"They're here for Max Murphy."

Max's legs nearly gave way under him. "Why me?"

Tzelek winked. "What can I tell you? You're a popular guy. Everyone wants a piece of you. Literally."

As if snapping out of a spell, Lord 6-Dog leapt into action.

"Be gone, foul demon!" he shouted, hurling his dagger at Tzelek.

His aim was perfect.

All eyes followed the dagger as it flew straight toward Tzelek's heart. (Or where his heart would have been if he actually had one.)

All eyes widened as the dagger abruptly stopped inches from Tzelek's chest and burst into flames.

Max had seen that trick before. Not so long ago, he'd fought for his life against Tzelek on top of the Black Pyramid. That time, the evil priest had dug his fingernails into Max's throat and would have pitched him into Xibalba if Lucky Jim hadn't saved him. Now, with the backup power of these grisly ghouls, Tzelek would have the upper hand for sure.

"Courage and light!" called Lady Coco. "Courage and light!"

Lord 6-Dog waved his torch at Tzelek. "Flee from the light, thou spawn of darkness. Shrink back into the shadows from whence thou came."

Tzelek giggled. "I wouldn't be playing with fire if I were you. That monkey suit looks pretty flammable."

"Unlike thee, I fear not firelight," announced Lord 6-Dog, thrusting his torch into Tzelek's face.

For a moment, Tzelek looked baffled. Then he clicked his tongue. "Oh, I get it now. It's that old saying about courage and light, isn't it? Well, I hate to break this to you, but we don't follow that rule anymore. We've been to training courses. These days, we don't fear anything."

He leaned forward and blew out Lord 6-Dog's torch.

Then, with a single breath as strong and as cold as the north wind, he blew out the remaining candles and torches. Even the bonfire in the grate flickered. "But that's better, don't you think? More atmospheric?"

The monsters roared their agreement.

"Let's get this party started!" yelled Tzelek.

Hermanjilio, who'd been standing dumbfounded, found his voice. "Stop right there! Given that we are mortal and most of you are mythical, I don't think it's possible for you to—"

"I know that voice," interrupted Tzelek. He peered at Hermanjilio. "I've been inside your head. Nothing but history, dates, and boring facts. I think I'll do everyone a favor and finish you off tonight, as well."

"Leave him be!" cried Lord 6-Dog. "Thou didst come to fight me!"

"Turns out I hate your friends almost as much as I hate

you. I may not be in command of this army, but I do have a few allies in the ranks." He put his bony fingers to his tongue and whistled. "*Keekaanoob!* Dinnertime!"

Raul was shaking so much that his visor clanked down over his eyes and blocked his view. He stood in front of Lady Coco in his heavy suit of armor, jabbing his sword at the air. "What's happening?" he asked.

"He's sending in the snakes," said Lady Coco indignantly. "*Keekaanoob* are boa constrictors."

Sure enough, a battalion of big, fat boas slithered forward.

Lord 6-Dog, Max, and Hermanjilio tried to put up a defense, but the snakes were surprisingly fast, sneaking up behind them and coiling around them almost before they knew what had happened.

In some ways, it was worst for Raul. Although not a big man, he was bigger than the average conquistador and his suit of armor had been made for someone shorter. It didn't take long for a few nimbler snakes to find the gaps between the pieces and pry them apart. Soon they had wiggled inside and, from the look of alarm on his face, begun to crush him.

Meanwhile, Lady Coco's little body was encircled by snakes from her neck to her toes.

"You should be ashamed of yourself, Tzelek," she gasped. "6-Dog's father and I did our best for you. We brought you up as if you were our own. You wanted for nothing."

"Be quiet, old lady. It's too late to start playing the mommy card now."

At another whistle from Tzelek, the snakes that held Lord 6-Dog knocked him off his feet and bound him like living ropes. The monkey king was stretched out on the hearth like a sacrifice victim on an ancient altar.

Tzelek snickered and fingered the blade of his ax. "Time for a little heart to heart."

"Wait!" shouted Max as his own serpentine jailers encircled him. "Why take a monkey heart when you could have a human one?"

It was the bravest and most stupid thing that Max Murphy had ever said in all his fourteen years on planet Earth.

His companions groaned in their scaly shackles.

"It's not an either/or situation," said Tzelek. He lifted his ax over Lord 6-Dog's helpless body.

"Excuse me, Lord Tzelek?" asked the mossy-dreadlocked stone man.

"What is it? Can't you see I'm busy?"

"It's just that most of us are man-eaters," explained the stone man. "And we're hungry."

"Fine." Tzelek rolled his eyes. "Share with the snakes. Whatever. Just make sure they suffer horribly."

The monsters advanced in a circle, drooling and licking their lips.

"Hold it right there!" shouted a woman's voice as a sickening smell filled the room. "I command this army!"

The monsters froze in their tracks.

Tzelek held his nose. "Can't a person sacrifice his own half brother in peace around here?"

A fork of lightning zigzagged to the floor, melting a hole in Uncle Ted's tiles, while a deafening crash of thunder made every creature in the room jump out of their skins—in many cases, literally.

When they looked again, a giant bat stood in front of Tzelek.

"Kamasootz', queen of the bats," he said. "To what do I owe this honor?"

She bared her fangs and flapped her leathery wings. "The boy's blood is mine. How dare you feed him to your snakes?"

"Well, you should have showed up on time, shouldn't you?"

"This is no business of yours. I agreed that my vampire armies would help storm this house in return for the boy's blood. He is mine, and mine alone."

"I feel like a short order cook," said Tzelek in irritation. "So 6-Dog is mine and Max Murphy belongs to Kamasootz'. If no one else has any special requests, the rest of you can share the other three." He motioned toward Hermanjilio, Raul, and Lady Coco. "Everybody happy?"

A crash came from the office, followed by a roar.

"What was that?" squeaked Raul, his voice high-pitched and echoing from inside his snake-filled suit of armor. "What's happening?"

"Eek' Chapaat," said Lady Coco. "He must have broken through."

"I hate to be the one to tell you this, Kamasootz'," said Tzelek with a snigger, "but the Murphy boy was also promised to Eek' Chapaat."

A murmur of protest went around the room. Apparently, there was honor among monsters.

"Eek' Chapaat doesn't share with anyone," the stone man pointed out.

"Then I must move quickly," said Kamasootz'.

As the thump of Eek' Chapaat's many footsteps drew nearer, a black cloud of bats engulfed Max's body, gripping him with their claws to immobilize him. He looked to his friends, but they were too busy fighting off the surge of hungry monsters moving in for the kill.

Max heard wood cracking and splintering as the office door was ripped off its hinges by two giant centipede pincers.

Kamasootz' placed her webbed fingers and strong thumbs around Max's neck to hold him still. She had pink eyes like a mouse and a little snout like a pig. As she bared her fangs, her army of bats squeaked in excitement.

Max closed his eyes. He'd read somewhere that the teeth of vampire bats were so sharp, their victims never felt the incision. He hoped it was true.

CHAPTER FIVE
FREEZE-FRAME

As nothing seemed to be happening, Max opened his eyes again.

The room was suspended in freeze-frame.

Kamasootz', queen of the bats, hovered over him, fangs bared, so close he could smell the blood on her breath.

The tidal wave of monsters was poised motionless mid-rampage.

Even the flames in the hearth did not move.

Only a flurry of owl wings disturbed the stillness.

"Greetings, Max Murphy," said Lord Kuy, the owl messenger of the underworld, as he landed between Max and Kamasootz'. His sinister yellow eyes blinked slowly and his sharp beak glinted in the moonlight. "I have come to rescue you."

Max looked at him in confusion. "Why would *you* rescue me? You work for Ah Pukuh—and he hates me."

"Ah Pukuh wants to talk to you."

"What about?"

"I am but the messenger."

"What if I don't want to talk to him?"

"Then I will fly away and this little scene"—Lord Kuy flapped a wing at the demonic diorama—"can play itself out. Kamasootz' will drain your blood while Eek' Chapaat chews on your bones and the rest of the guests feast on your friends. Is that what you want?"

"And if I talk to Ah Pukuh?"

"All will be butterflies and rainbows," sneered Lord Kuy.

Max sneered back at him: "Lord 6-Dog says that butterflies are the souls of the dead, and rainbows mean the moon goddess is angry."

"Lord 6-Dog is a buffoon. Make your decision."

"Where *is* Ah Pukuh?"

"He awaits you in Xibalba."

"Why can't he come here?"

"The Maya god of violent and unnatural death is not at your beck and call. Come or don't come, the choice is yours. But make up your mind. I haven't got all day. And Kamasootz' looks thirsty."

"How do I know Ah Pukuh won't kill me?"

"You don't. It's Ah Pukuh. He's volatile."

I need this to be a dream, thought Max, *and I need to wake up right now.* He pinched himself hard. It hurt. This was no dream.

Meanwhile, Lord Kuy looked bored and inspected his talons for mouse entrails. "Are you coming or not? Ah Pukuh does not like to be kept waiting."

Max considered his options.

His friends were about to be sacrificed or eaten.

Kamasootz', queen of the vampire bats, was about to sink her fangs into his neck.

Eek' Chapaat, the gigantic man-eating centipede, was about to burst into the room and tear him limb from limb.

When he looked at it that way, he didn't have much choice. So, for the second time in five minutes, Max Murphy found reserves of bravery he didn't know he had.

"I'll come," he said.

It was like one of those extreme roller coasters where your feet hang free, except a million times scarier because there was no safety bar, no carriage, no track, and no guarantee that Max's feet wouldn't hit all the obstacles that loomed at him out of the darkness.

Lord Kuy gripped him in his talons as he soared and swooped into the night, diving down, down through the raging ocean, into a tunnel of blackness, through caverns of mist and fog, along dripping passageways of slime, before dropping Max onto frozen flagstones in a room as cold as an icebox.

Max lay there for a moment as his eyes adjusted to the darkness. He looked around the chamber and shivered. Torches flickered in sconces, but their flames gave out no heat. The air was thick with the smell of mold and flatulence.

Lord Kuy poked Max with a claw. "Get up. Lord Ah Pukuh is here."

And there he was. Through the gloom, Max saw the

blubbery, plague-marked figure of the god of violent and unnatural death sitting cross-legged on a carved wooden throne at the far end of the room.

Lord Kuy pushed the boy forward.

"Greetings, Massimo Francis Sylvanus Murphy!" trumpeted Ah Pukuh, his many chins wobbling in welcome. "Or can I call you Maxie?"

He was wearing a spectacular headdress featuring shrunken human heads carved out of beeswax and impaled on bamboo spikes. The heads peered out of green feathers that waved like jungle plants, and each head was topped with a shock of orange hair like a troll doll's.

"Greetings, Massimo Francis Sylvanus Murphy!" echoed the heads in squeaky voices.

Under Ah Pukuh's chins was coiled an extraordinarily lifelike snake necklace. It was thick and brownish gray, with a pattern of yellow diamonds. As Max studied it, the snake raised its head and flicked its tongue at him.

He jumped back in alarm.

"Come back!" commanded Ah Pukuh. "Come and tell me all your news. We have a lot of catching up to do. I've missed you, Maxie."

"We've missed you," agreed the heads.

Max backed away even farther. "That snake," he said. "I recognize it. It's a fer-de-lance."

"Want to hold it?" Ah Pukuh unpeeled the snake from his neck and held it out to Max. "It won't bite."

"It won't bite," repeated the heads.

"Yes, it will," said Max. "It's one of the deadliest snakes in the world."

"You're not in your world, you're in the underworld.

69

Down here, we say *lively* not *deadly*. So it's one of the *liveliest* snakes in the world."

The heads tittered.

"It's still a fer-de-lance. I'm not touching it."

The heads tutted.

Ah Pukuh sighed and passed the snake to a loincloth-wearing attendant. The snake instantly bit the attendant, leapt out of his arms straight as an arrow, and slithered off into the shadows. The attendant took three steps and collapsed on the floor.

"You said it wouldn't bite," said Max accusingly.

"Oops," said Ah Pukuh.

"Oops," giggled the heads.

"Is he dead?" Max asked as the attendant's body was loaded onto a bamboo stretcher.

"Who cares?" said Lord Kuy. "We're all dead down here. Let's get on with business."

Max looked at him cautiously. "What business?"

Ah Pukuh smirked. "I have some good news for you, Maxie. But perhaps you want to thank me first."

"Thank you? What for?"

Ah Pukuh and the heads looked hurt. "For rescuing you, of course. From what I heard, Kamasootz' and Eek' Chapaat were about to have you for dinner. I couldn't let that happen. Not to my friend Maxie."

Max looked at him suspiciously.

Ah Pukuh smiled innocently. "Why are you looking at me like that?"

"I smell a rat," said Max.

Ah Pukuh shrugged. "What of it? There are thousands of rats in Xibalba. It's our house fragrance. *Eau de Rat.*"

"You know what I mean. How did you know exactly when to send Lord Kuy?"

"I sensed you were in trouble."

"Did you? Or did you order up those monsters in the first place?"

The heads looked at each other uncomfortably.

Ah Pukuh feigned shock. "Me? No! What makes you say that? Besides, they were under strict instructions not to harm one little hair on your head."

"I knew it!" said Max. "I knew it was you! You do realize that you've destroyed my uncle's house? Why would you do that?"

"Because I love you, Maxie!"

"What?" Max spluttered.

"It was a cry for attention. I sent the monsters so I could rescue you. So I could prove how much I love you."

"You don't love me," said Max coldly. "What's this really about?"

"You've got me all wrong, Maxie. I brought you down here to tell you how much I've changed. And I've got you and your cousin Lola to thank for it."

Max was scoping out the room for an escape exit. Now that his eyes were accustomed to the gloom, he saw that part of the room was separated by a thin cotton curtain, behind which shadowy figures could be seen reclining on low platforms.

"How's that?" he said vaguely.

"Thanks to you, I've boarded the peace train."

"I'm sorry?"

"I've renounced evil."

Max burst out laughing.

71

"Why is that funny?" Ah Pukuh and the heads looked offended.

"You *are* joking, right?"

"Is it so hard to believe?"

"To be honest, yes. Evil is what you do."

"I hear you, Maxie. But I've given it a lot of thought. I've realized that just because I've always been known as"—he made quote marks in the air with his sausagey fingers—"the god of violent and unnatural death, that doesn't mean I have to label myself for all eternity. I watched you and Lola at the Grand Hotel Xibalba, how you worked as a team, and I envied you. Yes, I've enjoyed being boss of the lowest and most evil level of the Maya underworld. But it's lonely at the bottom." Ah Pukuh's lower lip trembled like a vibrating slug. "I've never had a friend."

Tears formed in the wax eye sockets of the heads.

Max looked away, embarrassed. "What about the Death Lords?"

"Savages, the lot of them. They don't know the meaning of loyalty."

"Where are they, anyway?"

"I've sent them to charm school. It's time they learned some manners."

"There's Lord Kuy," suggested Max. "He could be your friend."

"That oily avian? He'd leave me in a heartbeat if he got a better offer. You've taught me that real friends stick around. It's you and me, Maxie. BFFs."

Max stared at him in horror. "What?"

Ah Pukuh gave a ghastly smile that looked like it hurt his mouth. "It means best friends forever."

The heads blew kisses at each other.

"What about your plans for world domination?" asked Max. "Last I heard you were going to use the Jaguar Stones to destroy planet Earth—starting with me."

Ah Pukuh smirked. "Oh, that funeral business. You didn't take it seriously, did you? It was just my little joke."

"It wasn't funny," said Max.

Ah Pukuh's face grew solemn. "I see that now. I'm a reformed character, Maxie. I'm on your side."

Max shifted uncomfortably. "What does that mean?"

"I don't want to end the world anymore. I want to use the Jaguar Stones as a force for good—healing sick children and that sort of thing." Ah Pukuh tried to look saintly.

"Why would you do that? Evil is your life. It's taken you an eternity to collect the Jaguar Stones. If you use them for good, you'll be throwing away everything you've worked for."

"You're a good influence on me, Maxie. I want to be just like you. I want us to hang out together all the time. What do you say?"

Max chose his words carefully. "I think it's great that you're turning your life around. But maybe you should choose someone else to be your friend, because I'm going home to Boston soon."

"Is that so? Have your parents been released?"

"No, but—" Max narrowed his eyes suspiciously. "What do you know about my parents?"

"Never mind *them*." Ah Pukuh's voice took on an edge. "Work with me, Maxie. Here I am, trying to make a fresh start, and all you can do is reject me." The heads in the headdress glared at Max angrily. "I have feelings, too, you know." Ah Pukuh pulled down a head and used its hair to dab at his eyes. "You can hardly blame me if I react by lashing out." He looked at the head and sighed. "It looks like the end of the world is back on track."

The heads cheered.

"Is that a threat?" asked Max.

"Absolutely."

Max rolled his eyes. "You're saying that if I won't be your friend, you'll go back to your evil ways? But if we hang out, you'll drop the whole end of the world thing?"

"Exactly! We'll eat pizza, play video games, make playlists, shoot hoops. I've got it all planned out. Let's do a blood oath right now, to swear our loyalty!" He produced an obsidian blade and offered it to Max. "You first."

Max pushed the blade away. "That's not what best friends do anymore."

"It's not?"

"No way."

"So what do they do?"

Max thought quickly. "They give each other space."

Ah Pukuh looked crestfallen. "That doesn't sound fun. Can we at least send each other pictures of cute fluffy kittens?"

"I guess," said Max without enthusiasm.

"I've never had a best friend before!" Ah Pukuh clapped his hands like an excited prom princess. "Promise you'll do anything for me? Promise you won't let me down? Promise on the little fluffy-wuffy head of a kitty-witty?"

"Yes."

"Promise on the snuffle-wuffle nose of a puppy-wuppy?

"Yes."

"Promise on the fuzzy-wuzzy tummy of a bunny-wunny?"

"Yes."

"Promise on the pinky-winky little heart of your cuzzy-wuzzy?"

"Stop! I get it, okay?"

"Do you promise?"

In less stressful circumstances, Max might have concentrated a little harder on what Ah Pukuh was saying. He might have realized that a cuzzy-wuzzy was a cousin and that he'd just put Lola's life on the line. But he wasn't really listening. All he heard was Ah Pukuh's girlish tones and his nauseating giggle. He was spooked by the whole situation, and he just wanted to get back to his life.

So, without giving a thought to the consequences, he said again, irritated by this childish game: "Yes. I promise."

"Slumber party! Slumber party!" chanted the heads.

Ah Pukuh looked hopefully at Max.

"Maybe another time," he said diplomatically.

"I get it." Ah Pukuh nodded wisely. "You want me to stay cool and give you space." He clicked his fingers. "Kuy, please escort Maxie back to Middleworld. And take good care of him. He's my new best friend."

CHAPTER SIX
BEST FRIENDS FOREVER

"What have you done?" said Lola. "We only went out for Chinese food, and you demolished our house."

"Haven't you been listening? *I* didn't destroy your house; Ah Pukuh did. He summoned all the monsters so he could save me from them."

"And that's another thing. You shouldn't be making friends with Ah Pukuh."

Max had a sudden pang of guilt, a flashback to a moment when he had possibly made a promise that involved Lola's pink little heart. He decided not to mention it. "Ah Pukuh said he's changed. He wants to use the Jaguar Stones for good. He said that if I rejected him, he might go back to his old ways. What was I supposed to do?"

"Ask yourself why he wants to be friends with you."

Max felt vaguely insulted. "What are you getting at?"

"You think he's interested in your sparkling personality?"

"Is that so impossible?"

"Dream on."

"Why are you being so mean to me? I've just survived the most terrifying night of my life. While you were slurping won ton soup, I was battling the entire Maya Book of Monsters."

"Is that what this is about, Max? Are you jealous because I've got a new life?"

He noticed she was wearing makeup. In her skinny jeans and flip-flops, she looked less like a Maya princess and more like a high school kid from Boston. He also noticed that she'd called him Max. The old Lola, the one who used to be his best friend, had called him Hoop. It was short for *chan hiri'ich hoop*, which was Mayan for "little matchstick"—a reference to his thin white body and reddish hair. In return, he'd called her Monkey Girl for her habit of talking to howler monkeys.

"Why don't you call me Hoop anymore?"

"People change."

"You'll always be Monkey Girl to me."

"Good to know," she said coldly.

"That came out wrong."

She shrugged. "Whatever. I have to go. I have stuff to do. You better get this room cleaned up before my parents get back."

"Where are they?"

"At the furniture store, replacing all the stuff you chopped up for firewood. If I was them, I'd never forgive you."

"I told you, it wasn't my fault—" Max protested, but she was gone.

In the old days, she would have stayed and listened

77

to his story. She would have pored over every detail with him, wondering what it all meant. She would have told him that possessions don't matter as long as all the people and monkeys and ancient Maya royals were okay. She would, he thought ruefully as he reached for the mop, have helped him clean up.

He surveyed Uncle Ted's sitting room. She was right. It was demolished.

The wild party had ended as quickly as it had begun.

When Max had returned from Xibalba, nearly all the monsters were gone. Only Tzelek and the snakes that bound Lord 6-Dog had remained. Tzelek still leaned over his brother, frozen in time, brandishing his knife.

"Good night, Lord Tzelek," Lord Kuy had said pointedly.

Tzelek's mouth had regained motion. "Don't be a spoilsport, Kuy. Just let me finish off my brother and I'll be out of your hair—I mean, feathers."

"No, Lord Tzelek. This is neither the time nor the place."

"But—"

"Your time is up. You are due back in Xibalba," Lord Kuy had insisted.

"You'll have to catch me first." Then Tzelek, still wearing his enormous headdress, had taken off through the hole in Uncle Ted's wall and out into the rainforest.

The snakes had slithered out after him.

"Why can no one around here stick to a plan?" Lord Kuy had muttered to himself.

"You're an owl. Can't you hunt him down?" Max had had several run-ins with Tzelek and really did not like the idea of his evil spirit running wild out there, even if it was easy to spot in its Maya king costume.

"That body is temporary. He must surrender it soon," Lord Kuy had said, almost to himself. Then he'd swiveled his owl head around to Max. "Do not forget your promise, Max Murphy." And with that, he'd flown away.

Max had still been dazed when Uncle Ted, Zia, and Lola had arrived home soon after, clutching boxes of leftover Chinese food. (Weirdly, they'd used the front door, even though there was a gaping hole in the side of the house.) He hadn't even had time to tell the others about his trip to Xibalba, let alone begin cleaning up.

Max knew that as long as he lived, he would never forget the expression on his uncle's face as he took in the sight of his devastated sitting room by the light of the moon shining through the hole in his roof.

"I . . . we . . . can explain," Max had said, looking around at his fellow survivors for moral support. But none of them spoke up. Hermanjilio sat with his head in his hands, speechless with shock. The injured Lady Coco slept on Uncle Ted's last pillow. Lord 6-Dog had headed into the night to look for Tzelek. Raul was nowhere to be seen.

So it had been left to Max to explain what had happened.

"The power went out," he began. It sounded like a lame explanation for a room so totally smashed up, empty, and plastered in bat guano.

"But the wall? That hole . . . ?" Uncle Ted sounded stunned.

"Ogres. They had a battering ram."

"And the roof?"

"I think that was the bird with knives for feathers."

"My furniture . . . ?"

"We burned it. For firewood."

"And the rug . . . ?"

"Shredded. That bird again . . ."

"I can't believe it. We should call the police."

"Good luck explaining what happened," said Zia.

"But we were only gone a couple of hours." Uncle Ted's voice was barely louder than a whimper.

"Forget about the house, Ted, we should call a doctor." Zia crouched by Lady Coco and gently stroked her fur. "And a good vet."

Lola had stood there, arms folded, looking at Max with contempt.

"It wasn't my fault—" he had begun again, but was interrupted by a clanking sound behind him. He turned to see a suit of armor making its way into the great hall, holding a can opener.

"Can someone help me?" came a muffled voice. "My visor is jammed shut."

"Raul?" Uncle Ted sounded like he might cry.

"I can't handle this," said Lola. "I'm going to bed."

And she'd stomped off, leaving Max to try to extricate Raul and somehow make peace with his shocked uncle.

Now it was morning.

And Lola still blamed Max for all of it.

Meanwhile, in the halls of Xibalba, Ah Pukuh's servants lifted off his headdress of shrunken heads and tied a white bandanna in its place.

He clicked his fingers, and the shadowy figures behind the screens came out and sat in rows at his feet. Mostly they were skeletons, although some were more recent corpses with a little flesh still hanging from their bones. They all jabbered into small conch shells clamped to their ears like cell phones.

An efficient-looking skeleton in a headset took center stage. "And now," he said, "those of you who have hands, please put them together to welcome our new Head of Marketing."

Polite applause rippled through the chamber as two smaller skeletons carried in a female head on a bamboo litter and set it down on a bench facing the audience. She was recently deceased from the looks of things. Her black hair was drawn back into a bun, and a pair of horn-rimmed spectacles balanced on her nose.

Ah Pukuh roared with laughter. "Good one! She is literally the *head* of marketing!"

The Head cleared her throat. "Good evening. Let us get straight down to business. As most of you know, I have been tasked with rebranding Xibalba for the thirteenth *bak'tun*—or the twenty-first century as this era is now called by the youth market."

A skeletal hand went up.

"Yes?"

"Why do we need rebranding? Xibalba has been the leading name in underworld intimidation since time began. Why fix what isn't broken?"

A murmur of assent went around the room.

"Even classic brands like Xibalba need refreshing from time to time," the Head explained to the dissenter. "For example, let me ask how you would define our core values?"

The skeleton thought for a moment. "Evil, obviously.

81

Death. Disease. Pain. Misery. Affliction. Our values are the same as they always were. We exist to cause maximum suffering to the citizens of Middleworld."

"Exactly." The Head of Marketing paused and looked around the room. "And those values are still alive and well in Middleworld. But if mortals no longer believe in our existence, how can we take credit for our work? And that, ladies and gentlemen, is why we need to rebrand Xibalba. We will launch a new age of suffering. We will make mortals quake in their boots again, before we destroy them, once and for all."

The audience cheered, and clapped, and whistled.

"So let me now move on to the nuts and bolts of our rebranding campaign, otherwise known"—her lips pursed in distaste—"as Operation Fluffy Kittens."

"O-*purr*-ation," Ah Pukuh corrected her. He smirked proudly. "I named it," he told the audience.

The Head of Marketing ignored him and continued. "Since the aim of the operation—"

"O-*purr*-ation. Say it properly," interjected Ah Pukuh.

"—since our aim is to mount a charm offensive, perhaps Ah Pukuh could debrief us on last night's opening event?"

"All in good time," replied Ah Pukuh. "First I demand to know which bright spark let Tzelek slip through the door between worlds? He could have wrecked everything! Here I am, working on a plan to destroy the world, and there's Tzelek using my snakes to tie down his monkey brother." Ah Pukuh tossed his head. "It's not okay."

There was much shaking of heads and pointing of fingers as row after row of executives denied responsibility for Tzelek. Eventually, a hapless-looking skeleton holding a jaguar-skin briefcase was pushed to the front. "I am s-s-sorry,

Lord Ah Pukuh," he stammered. "Tzelek told me he had your permission to accompany the monster party. He said he was your ambassador to Middleworld."

"You fool! Tzelek has his own agenda. All he cares about is settling scores with 6-Dog!" Ah Pukuh shouted so loudly that several major bones fell off the executive's skeleton. "You're fired!"

None of his coworkers moved to help as the executive gathered himself up, bundled bits of himself into his own briefcase, and left the room.

The Head of Marketing tried to regain control of the meeting. "Although Tzelek's appearance was regrettable, it did not impact our effectiveness, and I would like to commend everyone involved. All the monsters, especially Kamasootz' and Eek' Chapaat, played their parts masterfully."

Ah Pukuh coughed pointedly.

The Head got the hint. "Of course, our most fervent praise should be reserved for Lord Ah Pukuh. Last night, he did an excellent job of hoodwinking Max Murphy and exacting a promise from the boy that will serve us well in our campaign. So, without further ado, let us all show Lord Ah Pukuh how much we value and appreciate him."

Lacking any hands herself, she stared expectantly at the audience.

No one clapped.

The Head raised an eyebrow. "Anyone who is unhappy in Marketing will be transferred to Transportation. The rivers of pus and blood have immediate vacancies for ferryboat operatives. Say good-bye to your expense accounts, ladies and gentlemen, and hello to your ticket punches."

Faced with this alternative, the assembled executives

applauded so enthusiastically that several hands and arms clattered to the floor.

Ah Pukuh nodded sulkily in acknowledgment. "Let me tell you, it wasn't easy. Pretending that I wanted to be friends with that brat made me want to vomit."

"Your sacrifice is appreciated, Lord Ah Pukuh." The Head waited for the attendant to finish sweeping up the fallen bones.

"I don't understand why we couldn't just threaten him with violence like last time," grumbled Ah Pukuh.

The Head of Marketing nodded knowingly. "I hear you. Bullying always feels like the right way to go. But, shocking as it may seem to us, our latest research indicates that mortals respond better to positive encouragement."

The audience sat in baffled silence for a moment and then, deciding that the Head was joking, it began to laugh.

"I'm serious," boomed the Head. "We will not conquer Middleworld until we win hearts and minds."

"I'd settle just for hearts," cackled a skeleton. "And I'd rip them out with my finger bones."

The Head sighed. "You will all be retrained in courtesy and kindness."

The audience let out a collective groan.

"Or should I say," the Head corrected herself, "how to *fake* courtesy and kindness. Our most needy trainees, the Death Lords, have been shipped off to charm school already. You will all join them there."

A desiccated arm shot up. "But I thought," said its owner, "that once we had all five Jaguar Stones, Middleworld was ours for the taking."

"As did we all," agreed the Head. "But it turns out, it's not that simple. There are over seven billion mortals alive today, and we are horribly outnumbered. We cannot begin to destroy them all without winning at least a semblance of cooperation. Starting right now with our old adversaries Max and Lola."

"I hate those Murphy brats!" called a voice from the back of the room.

"Like it or not," said the Head, "our end-of-the-world strategy depends on gaining their trust. We cannot move to the next stage without them. And apparently, they are more likely to do our bidding if they believe that Ah Pukuh has joined the good guys. "

Ah Pukuh retched.

"It's a revolting thought, I know," sympathized the Head. "But I promise it will be worth it. And now, for a little more market background, let me pass you over to Brand Development."

A perky-sounding skeleton took the floor. "I'm not going to chocolate-coat this, guys. Competition within the end-of-the-world sector is tough. A breakaway group has appeared with its own set of Jaguar Stones. We highly doubt that they're the real thing, but the mortals are buying into them, hook, line, and sinker."

A gnarly old skeleton waved his femur. "What's the new group doing that we're not?"

"That's a good question. I think it comes down to visibility. They've put themselves on the map with a strong social media presence, and a bricks-and-mortar tourist attraction."

"You said the Grand Hotel Xibalba was going to put *us* on the map," said the gnarly skeleton accusingly.

All heads swiveled toward the perky skeleton.

He was losing his perk.

"It turned out that our Central American location was not ideal for optimum exposure," he conceded. "We're in a 'learning on the ground' situation."

"So have you learned why the new Jaguar Stones are attracting so much attention?" continued the gnarly one. "Why is no one interested in *our* Jaguar Stones? We have the real ones, all five of them. We were supposed to have taken over the world with them by now."

Murmurs of rebellion were floating around the room.

"Chichen Itza was not built in a day," snapped the now positively un-perky skeleton. "As soon as we reclaim brand share, we'll be back on track."

"Speaking of brand share," called a female voice, "focus groups suggest that name recognition for Xibalba is at an all-time low. What are we doing to reestablish our fear factor?"

There was a chorus of agreement.

The Head of Marketing bellowed for quiet. "Trust me, it is all under control. In a short time from now, we'll have shut down the new group, stolen their social media platform, attracted the attention of a global audience, sacrificed the Hero Twins, and established ourselves once again as the leading household name in apocalyptic scenarios."

"Where do the Hero Twins fit in?" called a voice. "Aren't they ancient history?"

"An excellent question. The Hero Twins, Hunahpu and Xbalanque, are at the center of the Maya creation story. A sentimentalist might even call them the most beloved characters in our mythology. Mortals glorify them for coming down to Xibalba and beating our Death Lords at the ball game. It was the Hero Twins who made Middleworld a safe place for mortals. For that, we will always hate them."

The audience began to hiss and jeer and shake their loosely connected fists.

The Head nodded in agreement. "My feelings exactly. So what better start to the new age of Xibalba than to sacrifice the Hero Twins and rewrite the old myth?"

A doddery old hand crept shakily up. "When you say 'sacrifice the Hero Twins,' do you mean Hunahpu and Xbalanque? Because they became the sun and the moon. It's going to be difficult to tie them down."

The Head sighed impatiently. "No, of course, I didn't mean the original Hero Twins. We will sacrifice the new, photogenic, media-savvy Hero Twins, otherwise known as Max and Lola. And now, ladies and gentlemen, if we could get back to—"

"One more question," called a voice from the back. "How will we trick the girl, Lola, into cooperating with us? She's not as gullible as the boy."

"I am sure Lord Ah Pukuh can work his charms on her," replied the Head of Marketing.

Ah Pukuh groaned. "Not another one. I won't do it."

"Just once more," begged the Head. "Win over Lola, like you won over Max."

Ah Pukuh's pasty face turned green. "Pass the sick bag," he growled. "Those brats turn my stomach."

The Head of Marketing nodded in sympathy. "I have an idea," she said. "We'll give the job to Lord Kuy instead. Lola is not as tough as she pretends. And I know her weak spot. If asking nicely doesn't work, we will demolish her."

Max lay on his bed. He was feeling tired, hungry, and sorry for himself. Last night he'd ridden down to Xibalba in the talons of an owl, but not one person had listened to his story and helped him understand what had happened. Instead, he'd been cleaning up monster mess all day with no help from anyone. (Lady Coco and Raul were confined to their beds on doctor's orders. Lord 6-Dog was apparently exempt from helping as Maya kings never did housework. Hermanjilio had a full day of teaching at the university. Uncle Ted and Zia had been meeting with builders.)

But Lola? What was her excuse?

She'd been holed up in her room all day.

Now it was nearly dinnertime.

How could she be so lazy?

Max checked his phone. Still no signal.

He jabbed at the keyboard of his laptop. Dead.

He switched on his bedside light. Nothing.

He closed his eyes and concentrated on detecting an aroma of dinner.

Still no good smells.

"It has not arrived yet," said Lord Kuy.

Max sat bolt upright. "What—?"

"Your dinner. It hasn't arrived yet. Your aunt and uncle ordered pizza from that new place over by the docks. I think you're in for a treat. It has wood-fired ovens just like the joint I visited with the Death Lords in Venice. We had the Four Seasons with extra cheese. *Molto bene!*"

The owl messenger of the Maya underworld was sitting in a chair by the window.

"What are *you* doing here?" said Max.

"Your best friend asked me to call on you."

"Lola?"

"Ah Pukuh."

"Why?"

"He asked me to give you this." Lord Kuy handed Max a loop of what looked like yellowy translucent nylon wire.

"What is it?"

"A friendship bracelet. Ah Pukuh wove it for you."

"Cool." Max held it up to the light. "What's it made of?"

"Bat intestines."

Max dropped the bracelet onto the bed.

"Don't you like it? He gutted the bats himself."

Max tried to look grateful.

Lord Kuy rolled his owl eyes. "I told him not to waste his time on you. I knew you'd let him down."

"How have I let him down?"

"You call yourself his friend but you're not."

Max squirmed. "You don't know that."

"If you were his friend," said Lord Kuy, "you would have warned him about the new king and the new Jaguar Stones."

"What?" Max stared at him blankly. "What are you talking about?"

"It's all over the news. Hashtag Jaguar Stones is trending everywhere."

"It is?'

"Don't pretend you don't know."

"Our power's out. And our Internet's down. And since when did ancient Maya messengers talk about hashtags?"

"Since our new Head of Marketing sent us all to social media training." Lord Kuy touched the keyboard of Max's laptop and the screen sprang into life. "Here, watch this."

"How did you do that? The battery's been dead all day."

"Just watch."

On the screen, news footage showed crowds bowing down at the foot of a grassy pyramid. A modern birdlike statue commanded the top platform of the pyramid, rising from the roof of a tented metal structure. Figures in Maya dress moved about up there, but the camera was too far away to show them clearly. Five points of different colored light glowed in the sunshine. Red, green, yellow, black, white.

"Are those the new Jaguar Stones?" asked Max.

"Yes."

"They look like the old ones. Where did they come from?"

"The new king says he dug them up. Which is patently ridiculous."

"Who is the new king?"

"We don't know. He claims to be Maya, but it's hard to tell under all the face paint."

"Can you get some volume?"

"No can do. We're having sound problems with our satellite link. Xibalba is very low-lying. It makes getting reception difficult."

As the camera pulled back farther, Max saw that all around the pyramid lay open fields and green mounds. A wide river glinted nearby.

"Where is that?" asked Max. "Is it in San Xavier?"

"It is in your homeland."

"In the States? It doesn't look familiar."

"It is a native American city called Cahokia. You must find it, and go there."

"*What?* No."

"I knew it. I told Al Pukuh you'd let him down."

"Why would Ah Pukuh even care about this place?"

90

"He went to a lot of trouble to get the real Jaguar Stones. This imposter at Cahokia is stealing his thunder."

"So what? Who cares?"

"Ah Pukuh cares. You want him to be happy, don't you?"

Max groaned. "Please don't drag me into this."

"You promised you'd do anything for him."

"Oh, come on. That's not fair."

"I'll tell you what won't be fair. When Ah Pukuh, spurned and betrayed by his one and only friend, declares war on Middleworld."

"Not that end-of-the-world stuff again? I thought Ah Pukuh had boarded the peace train?"

"The peace train will come off its rails if you don't grab those fake Jaguar Stones."

"Why can't *you* grab them?"

"You saw the footage. Mortals are flocking to Cahokia. It will be easy for you to mingle with the crowds. You need to leave as soon as possible."

"I can't do that," said Max.

"I don't think you understand the gravity of the situation. If you don't sort this out, Ah Pukuh will literally explode. And he will take your beloved Middleworld with him."

"Maybe I could talk to him? Persuade him to chillax?"

"Seriously? Have you met Ah Pukuh? He is not a chillaxing kind of guy."

"The thing is," said Max, "I couldn't help you even if I wanted to. I would be arrested if I tried to leave San Xavier."

"Do you want world peace or not?"

"Of course I do."

"Then do yourself a favor. Find this new guy and get

his Jaguar Stones. Do it for friendship." Lord Kuy looked pointedly at the bracelet of bat guts and twirled it on a claw. "Remember, you promised on your cousin's pink heart."

At that moment, Lola stuck her head around the door. "Pizza!"

Max stuffed the bracelet into his pocket.

Lola and Lord Kuy exchanged a glance. They didn't seem surprised to see each other.

"Ah," said Lord Kuy, "it is the Maya princess with more names than a goddess."

Max smiled in spite of himself. Lola did have a lot of names. When she was adopted by Chan Kan as a baby, she'd been given the name Ix Sak Lol or Lady White Flower, which her friends shortened to Lola. Recently, she'd discovered that her birth name was Lily Theodora Murphy—but everyone still called her Lola.

"Oh," she said to Lord Kuy, "you're still here."

"I am indeed. I decided to pay a visit to your cousin while I wait for your answer."

"I told you, my answer is *no*."

"What's the question?" asked Max. "What are you talking about? Why did you say he's *still* here?"

"If you must know, Lord Kuy has been bullying me all day to follow your example and make friends with Ah Pukuh. But I have respectfully declined that invitation."

"You said no?"

"Of course I said no. I'm not an idiot."

"Meaning I *am* an idiot?"

"Look, do what you like. Have fun with your new besties in Xibalba. I don't care. My mom just sent me to tell you that the pizza's here." Lola turned to go.

"Wait!" called Max. "Did Lord Kuy tell you the full story? About the new Jaguar Stones?"

"I'm not interested. I have other things on my mind right now. I just found my parents, remember? "

"As if I could forget," muttered Max.

Lola narrowed her eyes. "What's that supposed to mean?"

"I never see you anymore. And *my* parents are still in jail, in case you hadn't noticed." As soon as Max said it, he hated himself for sounding so needy.

Lola sighed. "Look, I'm sorry, I promise I'll spend more time with you, okay?"

"I think I can help," said Lord Kuy. "If you two would like to spend more time together, I have a great idea. You can go and get the new Jaguar Stones before Ah Pukuh blows a gasket. It's perfect! Max and Lola save the world—again!"

"Not going to happen," said Lola. "I meant we'd play video games or something."

"Why settle for video games," asked Lord Kuy, "when you could have a real-life adventure?"

"Because," said Lola, "I'm done with adventure, I'm done with running errands for Ah Pukuh, and I'm done with the Jaguar Stones. I just want to hang out with my family."

"I see," said Lord Kuy. "That's awkward. Did you know that your cousin has already staked your little pink heart on this mission?"

"What?" Lola turned angrily to Max. "What have you said now?"

"They tricked me."

Lord Kuy nodded. "It was artfully done."

For a moment, Lola looked furious. Then she relaxed. "You know what? It's fine. Whatever. I'm not playing this game anymore. As far as I'm concerned, none of this has happened. And you know why? Because the ancient Maya underworld does not exist. You trapped me once before when I thought I was an orphan, because the old stories were like my family and I needed them. But not anymore. Whatever you made Max say, it doesn't count. You can't get me this time. I'm a citizen of the twenty-first century. I have a family and a birth certificate and soon I'll have a vote. All I care about is the future and how to help my people move beyond superstition and lies. So fly back to whatever hole you came from and leave me alone. Good-bye."

It was a great speech. Max felt like applauding. "That goes for me, too," he said.

"Wow," said Lord Kuy. He looked impressed. "I had no idea you felt that way. This changes everything. I hereby officially release Max from his promise."

Max and Lola exchanged a hopeful glance.

"You do?" asked Max. He felt cautiously giddy with relief.

"I do." Lord Kuy assumed his wise owl face. "I see now where we went wrong."

"And where was that?" asked Lola sarcastically.

Lord Kuy fixed her with his yellow raptor eyes. "You seem to think you can hide behind your newfound family and pretend that none of this is happening. I therefore decree that you will not see your precious parents again until you have completed this mission."

"What? You can't do that!" Lola was outraged.

"Watch me," said Lord Kuy.

"That's not fair!" Max protested.

"Not fair, you say?" Lord Kuy's owl head swiveled to focus on Max. "In that case, you will not see your parents either."

Max and Lola stared at the owl-man, dumbfounded.

"*Your* parents"—he pointed a claw at Lola—"will take a vacation in Xibalba. And your parents"—he pointed at Max—"will stay in jail. If you fail to complete your mission, you will never see your parents again. Either of you. Ever. Good-bye."

And with that he disappeared.

CHAPTER SEVEN

INTO THE VOID

Lola raced downstairs, screaming "Dad! Mom!" the whole way, but no one answered.

Max ran down behind her.

In five seconds, they had searched the entire first floor. No one.

"They were here! They were right here!" Lola stared accusingly at the pizza boxes and plates on the kitchen table.

Max shifted uncomfortably. "You heard what Lord Kuy said."

"You know I don't believe that stuff!" Lola opened the front door and looked out. "Their car's still there. They can't be too far away."

Max shrugged. "Maybe they went for a walk," he suggested halfheartedly.

"Why would they go for a walk when dinner's on the table?" asked Lola. "This isn't 'Goldilocks and the Three Bears.'"

"Do the Maya tell that story, too?"

"Don't be stupid. We don't have bears in the jungle. Or girls with golden locks."

"I only asked. You don't have to bite my head off."

"If you must know, Dad just told me that story. We were reading some of my old baby books. He was trying to fill in some of the gaps in my education." Lola paced around the kitchen. "They wouldn't have kept my baby stuff all this time if they were going to leave me again, would they?" She started pulling out drawers and looking in cupboards like a crazy person. "Where are they? Why didn't they leave me a note?"

"You know where they are," said Max quietly.

"Nooooooooo!" Lola wheeled around. "I can't lose them again! I have to find them."

"Should we eat?" asked Max. "The pizza's getting cold."

"Did someone say pizza?" Hermanjilio had ducked in through a gap in the plastic sheet that covered the hole in the wall and was surveying the bare space that used to be Uncle Ted's sitting room. "I came to help with the cleanup, but it looks like I'm too late." He helped himself to a slice of pizza. "I half thought I'd come here this evening and find out it had all been a dream. I've been going over and over it all day. Why did this house suddenly fill up with mythical monsters? And why did they all vanish as quickly as they came? I've been wondering if there was something in that wasp larvae paste."

"They vanished because they'd done their job," said Max. "And that was to frighten me into going down to Xibalba with Lord Kuy."

Hermanjilio stopped chewing. "Wait, what? You think you went down to Xibalba? But that's impossible. I was in the room with you the whole time. You never left." He felt Max's forehead. "Have you been eating wasp larvae again?"

Max pushed him away. "You didn't see it because Kuy made the room freeze. But I can prove it. Ah Pukuh sent me a gift." He pulled the bracelet out of his pocket and showed it to them.

Lola grimaced. "What *is* that thing?"

"Bat intestines."

Hermanjilio put down his pizza. "I seem to have lost my appetite."

"But you believe me?" asked Max.

"Yes. I'm sorry for doubting you. It's just that the whole evening was so hard to believe." Hermanjilio sighed. "If only I could have filmed those monsters for my Maya Mythology class. That would increase attendance." He looked more closely at Max and Lola. "What's wrong with you two? Has something else happened?"

"Lord Kuy came back," said Max.

"He's kidnapped my parents," said Lola.

"He's keeping mine in jail," said Max.

"Not again," groaned Hermanjilio, remembering how Max's parents had been held captive in Xibalba when he and Max had first met. "Why this time?"

"Ever heard of a place called Cahokia?" asked Max.

"Yes, of course. It's famous in archaeological circles. It used to be the largest city in North America," said Hermanjilio. "Nothing left now but some mounds of earth. Why do you ask?"

"Because some guy has set himself up as a Maya king there. He has his own Jaguar Stones and everything."

Hermanjilio looked at him like he was crazy. "That can't

be right. A Maya king at Cahokia? But it's not a Maya city. It was built by the Mississippian culture."

"Whatever," said Max, trying to get Hermanjilio back on the subject. "But Kuy wants us to steal the guy's Jaguar Stones."

"Are they real?"

"Of course they're not real. How could they be real? The real Jaguar Stones are in Xibalba," said Lola impatiently. "Which is a place I don't believe in." She saw Max about to argue with her. "Even though I've been there," she added.

"Kuy said that we won't see our parents till we do it," Max finished up.

"I don't understand," said Hermanjilio. "I thought Kuy and his friends in Xibalba would be busy with their own Jaguar Stones, bringing about the end of the world and all that? Why do they care about a sideshow in Cahokia?"

"It's complicated," said Max. "Ah Pukuh said he's reformed and he wants to use his stones for good. He doesn't want this new guy getting in his way."

Hermanjilio looked confused. "If Ah Pukuh's reformed, how does he explain the monsterfest last night?"

"He said he was trying to get my attention."

"Well, he certainly succeeded. So are you going to Cahokia?"

Lola didn't hesitate. "NO!"

"I'm not allowed to leave San Xavier," Max pointed out.

Hermanjilio was thinking. "Something doesn't add up. Why, with the whole world in his grasp, would Ah Pukuh care about some crackpot in southern Illinois? And why does it have to be you two who go and investigate?"

Max and Lola looked at him blankly.

"Have you considered," he continued, "that these *are* the

real Jaguar Stones? That they somehow got transported from Xibalba to Cahokia? And now Ah Pukuh wants them back? That would explain why his world domination plans have stalled."

"But if they're real," said Max, following Hermanjilio's logic, "who is the new king?"

Hermanjilio rubbed his hands. "I vote we go to Cahokia and find out."

"Seriously?" Lola raised an eyebrow. "Why would we do that?"

"First of all, to get your parents back. And second of all, to find out what's going on up there. Whether the stones are real or not, we need to understand Ah Pukuh's little game. *Know thine enemy*, as Lord 6-Dog always says."

"We're not going to Cahokia," said Lola.

"I understand that after everything you've been through, you're reluctant to get involved. But the future of the world is at stake. You're not going to live a long and happy life with your parents if no one stands up to Ah Pukuh."

"Why does it have to be us?" asked Lola. "Why can't someone else stand up to him?"

"Because most people on this Earth have no clue about the danger they're in. And they wouldn't believe us if we told them. Sooner or later, Ah Pukuh is going to make good on his promise to end the planet. And before you say anything, Max, I do not believe for one second that he's reformed. So if we have a chance to foil his plans, we have to take it."

"*We?*" echoed Max. "You'd come with us?"

"Of course I would. After what I saw last night, this is my battle, too. Are you in?"

"We need to do this, Monkey Girl," said Max.

"Where is this Cahokia place anyway?" asked Lola.

"It's near St. Louis, on the Mississippi," replied Hermanjilio. "I'd show you if we had Internet. Does your dad have an atlas?"

"Maybe in his office."

"There's a map in my room," said Max. "I'll go and get it."

When he came back, Hermanjilio was telling Lola about Cahokia. "I've always wanted to see it," he was saying. "We could fly direct to Chicago and drive down from there."

Max felt a rush of excitement. Then, just as quickly, the feeling drained away. "I can't do it. They'll arrest me at the airport if I try to leave San Xavier."

"Then we'll smuggle you out," said Hermanjilio. He took the map from Max and spread it out on the floor. "Here's San Xavier. And here's the Gulf of Mexico. And here"—he tapped on the map—"is the mouth of the Mississippi River." With his nose almost touching the paper—"This map is old, it's hard to read"—he traced the blue line of the river up from the sea with his finger and jabbed at a point about two thirds of the way along. "Here it is! Cahokia Mounds!"

Lola knelt next to him to study the route of the river. "New Orleans, Memphis, St. Louis. I've read about those places. Mom and Dad were going to take me on a road trip. It was going to be my first-ever vacation."

"They'll still take you," said Hermanjilio. "Come to Cahokia with us and we'll get them back."

Lola said nothing.

Max was still staring at the map. "But how would we get there? Could we drive all the way?"

Hermanjilio shook his head. "Too risky. Armed guards at the border."

"A boat?" suggested Lola. "Across the Gulf of Mexico and up the Mississippi?"

Hermanjilio sounded dubious. "The coast guard is always on the lookout for smugglers. And the waters around here are dangerous. Too many reefs and strong currents."

"But look." Lola pointed at San Xavier on the map. "There's a dotted line just off the coast. Someone's drawn in a shipping lane around the reefs."

Hermanjilio looked closer. "That's no shipping lane. Where did you get this map, Max?"

"It was in Sylvanus Morley's car."

Hermanjilio did a double take. "Sylvanus Morley? As in Vay Morley, the great archaeologist who excavated Chichen Itza?"

"Yes. I met him at the White Pyramid when we were running from the zombies. He threw me the keys to his car—his jalopy, as he called it. Eusebio drove me and Lola home in it."

"Of course! That old car! How could I have forgotten?"

"You were too angry to remember anything that day."

"Why was I so angry?"

"That was the day you found out that Lola had stolen the White Jaguar and Chan Kan had jumped into Xibalba with it," said Max. "I've never seen you so mad."

"We were talking about shipping lanes," said Lola, quickly changing the subject.

Hermanjilio tapped the map excitedly. "I think we've found our escape route! Do you know anything else about Vay Morley, Max?"

"I know that it's his fault my middle name is Sylvanus."

"Well, I'm sorry about that. But did you also know he led

a double life? He used his cover as an archaeologist to spy for the US navy. He was looking for German submarine bases along the Yucatán Peninsula."

"Cool," said Max flatly, not understanding the relevance of this fact.

"Don't you see?" Hermanjilio was yelling. "That dotted line, it was drawn by Sylvanus Morley! It must be the submarine lane."

"This sounds like an interesting conversation," said a young Maya man coming in through the terrace doors.

"Hi, Lucky!" called Max.

"Hi, Jaime," called Lola.

Jaime Ben, known by almost everyone as Lucky or Lucky Jim, was Uncle Ted's former right-hand man and now a trainee schoolteacher. "Hey, you two," he said, high-fiving them. "Is this pizza up for grabs?"

"It's cold," Lola warned him.

"Even better," said Lucky, taking a huge slice. "So what's going on? I had a message from Mr. Murphy to come by after school. Sounds like he has a construction project he wants my advice on. Whoa!" Lucky dropped his pizza in surprise as he registered the damage in the sitting room. "What happened here?"

Max plunged into the story from the first time he saw the upside-down bird through to his encounter with the queen of the bats to his late-night flight down to Xibalba and Lord Kuy's return visit to the villa. Most people wouldn't have believed any of it, but Lucky wasn't most people. He knew all about the craziness that was the Maya underworld.

When he was caught up, Max showed him the map. "So this is Cahokia Mounds, where we need to get to."

"If we decide to go," added Lola.

"But Max is not officially allowed to leave San Xavier," explained Hermanjilio. "So we're thinking of ways to sneak him out."

"And that's why you were talking about submarines?" asked Lucky.

They nodded.

Lucky had a strange look on his face. He opened his mouth to speak, then seemed to think better of it and clammed up again.

"What were you going to say?" asked Lola.

Lucky shook his head guiltily. "I better not."

Max thought for a moment, then leapt to his feet. "Uncle Ted's got one, doesn't he?" he screamed excitedly. "Down there in the cellar?"

Lola turned to Lucky. "I know Dad used to be a smuggler, but that's crazy. Isn't it?"

Hermanjilio looked from face to face in disbelief. "Are you telling me that Ted Murphy has a submarine stashed away somewhere?"

"It's just a small one," said Lucky defensively. "A mini-sub."

"I knew it!" said Max. The first time he'd stayed at the Villa Isabella, he'd discovered the secret staircase leading from Uncle Ted's office down to the cellar and the underground HQ of his smuggling operation. Since many of the tunnels led out to sea, he'd imagined finding a James Bond–type submarine dock in among all the high-tech equipment. Now he was delighted to discover that his fantasy had been true all along.

Lola looked shocked. "But Dad promised me he'd given up smuggling."

"He has," Lucky assured her. "He bought it just before he made that decision. He's never used it, I promise. But it's not that easy to offload a sub without people asking questions."

"I can't believe it," Max said gleefully. "My. Uncle. Has. A. Submarine."

"Can you drive it, Jaime?" asked Lola.

He nodded. "But please call me Lucky. I tried to go back to Jaime, but even my family calls me Lucky. And we're going to need a lot of luck to pull this off."

"We? You're going to help us?" Max punched the air.

Lucky laughed. "So who's coming with me?"

Max and Hermanjilio put their hands up straightaway.

Slowly, Lola put hers up, too.

"I'm going to regret this," she said.

Hermanjilio put an arm around her. "You're doing the right thing. You can't run away from problems. You have to face them. And we'll face this one together, the four of us."

"Four's a full load," said Lucky. "I warn you, it's pretty cramped in the sub. It wasn't built for comfort."

"How far can it take us?" asked Hermanjilio.

Lucky knelt over the map and took some measurements with his thumb and forefinger. "You're headed for the Mississippi River, right? The sub can go fifteen hundred nautical miles without refueling. That should get it to New Orleans and back."

"Can't you take us all the way to Cahokia?" asked Lola.

"If people saw a sub refueling on the Mississippi, it might attract attention, don't you think? Besides, I'm a teacher now. I have a class full of children waiting for me."

"So how long to New Orleans?" asked Max.

Lucky thought for a moment. "At a cruising speed of twenty knots, I'd say two days at most."

Max looked worried. "Does the sub have a kitchen? What will we eat?"

Lola nudged him playfully. "Don't worry, Hoop. We won't let you starve."

Hoop! She'd called him *Hoop!* Things were back to normal between them! Max grinned at her. "So we're really going to do this, Monkey Girl?"

"I guess so." She looked like she couldn't believe what she'd just said. "I guess we're going to Cahokia." She shook her head in wonder. "Looks like Lord Kuy was right. Max and Lola save the world—again!"

CHAPTER EIGHT
SUBMERGED

Lady Coco didn't want them to go. "It's too dangerous under the water. The ocean is filled with vengeful ghosts."

Lola laughed. "These days, I think it's just fish and deep-sea divers."

"You're Maya, you should know this," Lady Coco rebuked her. "Before the Earth was born, the ocean was a sea of blood where gods and monsters battled. We call it the fiery pool."

"It's not like we'll actually get wet," Max reassured her. "The sub is like a little house."

Lady Coco was not convinced. "You have no business underwater. It's not natural."

When she couldn't talk them out of it, she insisted on rising from her sickbed and hobbling down to the kitchen to bake batch after batch of cookies, muffins, and scones. Raul, too, came down in his dressing gown to ransack the store cupboards and find every possible household item that could be of use to the brave submariners.

Lord 6-Dog, on the other hand, received the news impassively.

He was stretched out on a hammock, dressed—incongruously for a howler monkey *or* a Maya king—in a pair of child's blue-and-white-striped pajamas (castoffs from one of Lucky's younger siblings) with a hole cut out for his tail.

"May the Jaguar Kings watch over thee," he said.

"Don't you wish you were coming with us?" asked Max.

"Into the fiery pool, the primordial sea of blood? No, young lord, I do not."

"It's just across the Gulf of Mexico, not far at all."

"I care not for oceangoing vessels. My people lost many boats on trading expeditions."

"Technology's advanced a bit since then. They have radar and sonar now to avoid shipping hazards."

"They cannot avoid the rocks of destiny," said Lord 6-Dog darkly.

"Okaaaay." Max turned to go. "Any last-minute advice?"

Lord 6-Dog thought about it. "Heed my words," he said, sitting up in his hammock. "If the raging main should cause turmoil in thy stomach, be sure to void thy guts on the leeward side of the galleon lest thy puke should blow back in thy face."

"It's not a gal—oh, never mind," said Max. "You really don't like boats, do you?"

"Water is the realm of the underworld."

"You could at least wish us luck."

"I wish thee courage, and strength, and wisdom. I do not believe in luck." He lay back down. "And now, if thou wilt excuse me, it is time for my nap."

108

Loaded up by Lady Coco and Raul with more food than they could eat in a month at sea, Max and Lola said their good-byes. Then they climbed down the remains of the spiral staircase, now buckled and bent under Eek' Chapaat's weight, to the defunct HQ of Uncle Ted's smuggling empire. They could hear the distant sounds of Lucky and Hermanjilio shouting to each other as they readied the sub and, by flashlight, they followed the echoing voices down the dark and dripping tunnels.

"Watch out for centipedes," said Max.

"They're gone," replied Lola. "Lucky and Hermanjilio checked the tunnels. Ugh! Can you imagine how disgusting it must have been down here last night? Lady Coco and Raul were so brave."

"I have my own bad memories," replied Max. "Did you know that Lucky once arrested me down here?"

"Yes, you've told me that story a million times. He caught you trespassing."

"It's not trespassing when you're a guest in your own uncle's house."

"It was for your own good. You'd been warned not to snoop around."

With Max still seething at the injustice, they turned into a short tunnel that sloped steeply down into the water . . . and there was the mini-sub, bobbing on the tide. Suddenly, Max forgot everything but the vessel in front of him. It was smaller than he'd expected: about as wide and long as a school bus, tapering toward the stern. Halfway down the body, a fin-shaped bridge gave it the look of a sleek, blue shark.

"Ahoy there, me hearties!" called Hermanjilio.

"Okay, one thing, before we go anywhere, you have

to promise to drop the accent. That pirate thing could get majorly annoying," said Lola.

Hermanjilio saluted. "Aye aye, milady."

Lola rolled her eyes. "Something tells me this is going to be a long voyage."

Voyage. Max liked the sound of that. It sounded exciting and adventurous, but with a hint of luxury ocean liner. He didn't even mind Hermanjilio pretending to be a pirate. In fact, he kind of liked it. He viewed the sub approvingly.

"What are those for?" he asked, pointing to two pipes sticking up at the back of the fin-shaped bridge.

"Periscope cameras and air intake," explained Lucky.

"How can you have an air intake under the water?" asked Max.

"Ah. I think I may have misled you. This sub is designed

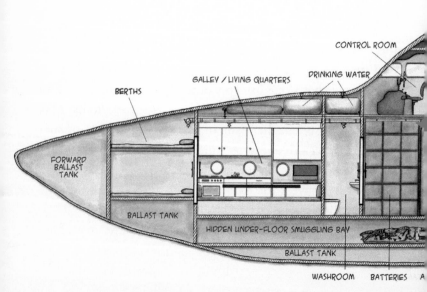

PERISCO

CONTROL ROOM

DRINKING WATER

GALLEY / LIVING QUARTERS

BERTHS

FORWARD BALLAST TANK

BALLAST TANK

HIDDEN UNDER-FLOOR SMUGGLING BAY

BALLAST TANK

WASHROOM   BATTERIES   A

to travel just below the surface. That way, we stay hidden, but we can pump in fresh air."

"Like snorkeling?" asked Lola.

"Exactly."

Max's face fell. "I thought we'd be deeper than that."

Lucky smiled. "Sorry, Max. The engine needs oxygen from the air intakes."

"What's the point of a sub if you can't dive? Uncle Ted was a smuggler. He must have needed quick getaways."

"Diving is for emergencies only. This sub can go down to about sixty feet," Lucky conceded, "but let's hope she doesn't need to. It uses up battery power and puts a lot of stress on the shell."

Max tried to reboot and focus on the positive. "It's cool that it looks like a shark."

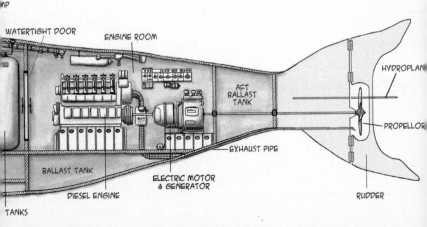

"*She* looks like a shark," Lucky corrected him. "Ships are feminine. But the shark thing is good camouflage, eh? Mr. Murphy designed her himself." He looked at Lola. "Did you notice the name?"

She shone her flashlight on the hull. "*Lily Theodora*. Dad named her after me!"

"He should've called it *Monkey Girl*," said Max.

"He should've called *her*," Lucky corrected again.

"I can't believe you said that." Lola took a swing at them with a bag of oranges.

"Hey! Stop using our rations as lethal weapons!" Hermanjilio scolded her. "Now, get those oranges stowed away. It's time to go."

"All aboard," said Lucky, ushering Hermanjilio through the hatch in the fin.

Max and Lola followed and found themselves in a minuscule cockpit. Lucky and Hermanjilio looked like giants squashed into the two little seats.

"Go below and make yourselves at home," said Lucky. "We're about to launch."

A metal ladder led down to a narrow corridor lined with storage lockers and tanks and banks of batteries. At one end of the corridor was the engine room. At the other end was a tiny bathroom, galley, and sitting area. Beyond that, Max and Lola found a bunkroom with four stainless steel bunks.

Max tried one out for size. He couldn't straighten his legs.

"It's like everything's child sized," said Lola.

"Or howler monkey sized," said Lord 6-Dog, hanging upside down in the bunkroom doorway. He still wore his pajamas.

Max bumped his head on the top bunk as he sat up in surprise. "Lord 6-Dog! Have you come to say good-bye?"

"I have come to assist thee on thy quest," said the monkey, jumping down.

"I thought you were afraid of the sea?"

Lord 6-Dog squared his shoulders in his little pajamas and stood as tall as he could. "A Maya king is afraid of nothing." Even as he spoke, his eyes betrayed his fear.

"It's good to see you, Lord 6-Dog," said Lola gently. "But you don't have to do this."

"I know that." He climbed regally up to the top bunk. "Is this my berth?"

"What changed your mind?" asked Max.

"I had a dream," replied Lord 6-Dog, lying down. "And now I plan to have another one. Wake me when we make land." With that, he turned his royal back on them and started snoring.

Max and Lola were still staring at him openmouthed when Hermanjilio came down the ladder. His frame filled the whole corridor. "Well, kids, looks like I won't be coming with you after all. The sub takes four, and Lord 6-Dog will be a lot more useful to you than I could be."

"But we need you! You're an expert on everything!" Lola cried.

"What you need in Cahokia is an expert on the Jaguar Stones, and no one knows more than Lord 6-Dog on that subject. I know he'll look after you. Just be careful, okay?"

"We'll be fine. It's not the jungle," said Lola. "We're going to a land of hotels, and hot showers, and round-the-clock pizza."

"Even so, be on your guard. Don't take any chances. If

this plan fails, we'll come up with another one. I just want you back safe and sound." He passed Lola his wallet. "You should have enough dollars in here for everything you need. Just don't let Max spend it all on food."

Lola gave him a hug. "We'll miss you."

"Take care of each other," he said, climbing back up the ladder. "Oh, and one of you better get up here and take my copilot seat."

Lola's reactions were faster than Max's, and she shinnied up the ladder to the cockpit. "Here we go!" yelled Lucky.

The craft vibrated like one big engine room.

Down below, in the cramped cabin, Max looked out of the porthole but saw only thick black water. Hermanjilio had left guidebooks and maps on the little table, but he couldn't think about reading. The smell, heat, and noise of the engine were dizzying. He'd expected the sub to glide silently through the water like a killer shark. This was more like riding inside a diesel lawn mower. He closed his eyes and tried not to think about puking.

He must have dozed off because the next minute, Lola was shaking him awake. "It's your turn, Hoop! Wait till you get up there. It's amazing!"

He climbed up and squeezed himself into the seat beside Lucky. The sub was close to the surface now, and the cockpit was filled with turquoise light. Bubbling streams rushed past the windscreens and sunlight danced on top of the waves. By squinting upward, Max could see a distorted version of the sky and the clouds. It was beautiful.

Then he turned his attention to the complicated array of controls, screens, and gauges on the console in front of him. "All this makes sense to you?" he asked Lucky.

"It's simpler than it looks," Lucky explained. "This screen shows our position, so you can see we're approaching Puerto Muerto. There are a lot of reefs along this bit of coast, so we're sticking to Morley's route. Here, do you want to take the wheel for a moment?"

Max leaned in to steer the sub. "So how do I dive?"

"I told you, that's for emergencies only." Evidently not trusting Max to steer a steady course, Lucky took back the wheel. He pointed at two video screens. "That's your job. Man the periscope. We've got cameras on the mast feeding in pictures from the surface."

Max tried out the camera controls. "I've got a video game like this. Do we have torpedoes?"

Lucky laughed. *"No."*

"So what am I looking for?"

"Planes or choppers that might spot us from above. Boats getting too close. Anything suspicious . . ."

Max zoomed in on a black fin cutting through the water. "Hah! That looks like a shark, but I bet it's another sub in disguise! We should dive before it sees us!"

Lucky checked the screen. "Look at the curve behind the dorsal. It's a dolphin."

As if performing for the camera, the dolphin made a graceful leap.

Max watched it, unconvinced. "It still looks suspicious to me."

"I promise you, it's a dolphin. But if you're worried, we have radar tracking as well."

"Can other boats track us?"

"We have a few tricks up our sleeves. Our shell is fiberglass, which is harder to detect than metal. And we cool our exhaust

115

before releasing it, so the heat isn't picked up. The only thing we can't disguise is the engine noise. The vibrations carry for miles underwater."

"Who'd hear us down here apart from the fish?" asked Max.

"Never underestimate the San Xavier coast guard," said Lucky ominously.

"That reminds me of one of Uncle Ted's stories," said Max. "He was dragging a crate of booty behind a banana boat one day, and the coast guard homed in on him. He had to cut the crate free and let it sink. But it had a radio-transmitter on it, so he went back another day and found it again."

"I was with him the day he found it," replied Lucky.

"In the secret cave? With the shipwrecked galleon?"

Lucky nodded. "I'll never forget that day as long as I live. It felt as if we were meant to be there. As if something wanted us to find the cave."

Max continued the story. "And besides Uncle Ted's crate, you found a hoard of Spanish treasure—including two Jaguar Stones." Max stared at him for a moment. "I've never thought about it this way before, but if the current hadn't carried you into the cave that day, my dad wouldn't have gotten his hands on the White Jaguar, and he and Mom wouldn't have vanished into Xibalba, and I'd still be at home in Boston, and none of this would have happened."

"Things have a way of happening anyway," said Lucky. "Mr. Murphy bought this sub with the proceeds of that dive." He tapped the nearest video screen. "How about less talking and more watching?"

As they passed the mouth of the Monkey River, Max spotted the Gran Hotel de las Americas. It was there he'd first encountered Count Antonio de Landa, the crazy, cape-twirling Spanish aristocrat who was buying a Jaguar Stone in a shady deal with Uncle Ted.

A sharp nudge from Lucky brought him back to the moment. "Radar! Behind us! Ship!"

Max rotated the camera and stared at the screen. At first it showed only a smudge on the horizon, but the smudge quickly grew into the shape of the one vessel they had hoped not to see.

"Coast guard!" Max exclaimed.

"Zoom in! Show me!" Lucky sounded frantic.

Max went to full magnification. His stomach flipped as he made out the silhouette of a gun mounted on the front deck.

"Have they seen us?" he asked Lucky.

"Only one way to find out." Lucky pushed the throttle forward to maximum and pointed to a narrow peninsula on the GPS screen. "If we can get past that headland, we'll be clear of the reefs and out in open sea. They'll never catch us then."

Max had thought it was loud before, but now the engine noise seemed to be coming from inside his brain.

"What's up?" yelled Lola, climbing through the hatch.

"Coast guard!" Max screamed back. He jabbed at the camera. "They're gaining on us."

Ahead of them, he could see big waves crashing onto the rocks of the headland.

It was going to be close.

Lola looked at the screen. She narrowed her eyes to see better. The coast guard vessel was so close, she could almost make out the faces of the individual sailors on deck.

Then, suddenly, she could see nothing but a flash of light.

The sub lurched in the water.

"They fired at us!" cried Lola in disbelief.

Lucky was flicking switches and pulling levers in a blur of movement. "Looks like you're getting your wish, Max. We need to dive—and fast!" The engine shut down, the screens went dead, the lights cut out, and the emergency lights came on.

Straightaway, they heard seawater rushing into the ballast tanks to weigh them down.

Just as they started to sink—BOOM!—another shell hit them and the fabric of the sub screeched like it was in pain.

Max and Lucky were hurled forward. Lola lost her grip and fell down the ladder.

Max sat up and rubbed his head. "Are you okay?" he called down to Lola.

"I think so," she said. "I'll have a few bruises, though." She climbed painfully back up. "How about you and Lucky?"

Max peered at Lucky through the gloom. He was slumped over the instrument panel. "Lucky! Are you okay?"

Lucky didn't answer.

"He's out cold!" cried Lola. She felt his wrist for a pulse.

All was dark outside the portholes. The depth gauge spun around. The only sound was the creaking of the hull as the water pressure increased.

"He's not dead, is he?" Max was panicking at the sight of Lola bending over a lifeless Lucky, both of them illuminated in the faint green glow of the emergency lights.

"He's concussed," replied Lola.

"Coast guard!" Max screamed. "They're gaining on us."

"He must have hit his head really hard. I think he'll come around in a moment."

"We need him NOW!" wailed Max.

"There must be a way to stop it," muttered Lola, inspecting all the switches on the console. "Why don't they label these things?"

Max watched in despair as the depth gauge spun lower and lower. "Maybe it will stop on its own. Lucky said it goes to a maximum of sixty feet."

At a depth of sixty-one feet, water started leaking in around the seal of the porthole.

"Lucky! Lucky! Wake up!" yelled Max.

By sixty-five feet, the ocean was streaming in. Max imagined that leaks were springing up all over the vessel. How long before the whole sub filled with water?

Seventy feet!

The walls of the sub made a terrible groaning sound, as if the sea was about to burst through.

At eighty feet, the depth gauge seemed to slow down.

All was dark around them. They were drifting at the mercy of the current.

Max was willing the coast guard to detect them. Far better to be caught red-handed than stuck in this aquatic coffin. How long would the air last? How long would it be before the sub imploded under the water pressure?

But, as it turned out, he had a much bigger problem, and it was right in front of his eyes.

"We're going to crash!" Lola was pointing, terrified, at the windscreen.

Through the darkness, Max discerned the outline of the sheer wall of rock that stretched from the cliffs above them down to the seafloor. They were heading straight for it.

"Lucky!" screamed Lola. "Wake up!" She tried again in Mayan: "Ahen! Ahen!" His eyelids fluttered, but his eyes stayed shut.

The rock wall loomed nearer and nearer.

"What do we do?" yelled Max.

"I don't know!" Lola yelled back at him.

"Cease this confounded racket!" boomed Lord 6-Dog, standing at the top of the ladder in his pajamas. His angry expression faded as he took in the situation:

Lucky slumped in the driver's seat . . .

Lola and Max in full-on panic mode . . .

Water sloshing around on the floor . . .

A collision about to happen . . .

. . . All bathed in the unearthly green emergency lighting that gave the scene a ghoulish quality.

"Ah Pukuh is behind this, I'll wager," muttered Lord 6-Dog, squeezing into the already overcrowded cockpit. He peered out of the nearest porthole, as if expecting to see the god of violent and unnatural death swimming past.

"Brace yourselves!" yelled Max as the great black wall of rock filled every windscreen. But the impact never came.

They simply floated into darkness.

"What just happened?" Max hugged himself to see if he still had a body. "Did we vaporize through the rock? Are we dead?"

A school of fluorescent blue fish swam toward them.

"I think we're in some kind of canyon," said Lola.

"One that leads to the underworld, I'll be bound," growled Lord 6-Dog. "I command thee to stop this vessel!"

"We would if we could," replied Lola. "But the current is carrying us forward. Only Lucky knows how to get us out of here."

They all looked hopefully at Lucky.

"I command thee to wake up!" Lord 6-Dog barked at him. Lucky was still out for the count.

"Maybe we should look for life jackets in case we have to swim for it," suggested Max.

"Swim?" Lord 6-Dog looked appalled. "Who knows what infernal monsters may await us in these deeps?"

A small squid floated by, glowing pink against the dark water.

Max shuddered, remembering the giant octopus in Venice that had tried to drag him down to Xibalba. "Please wake up," he begged Lucky. "We need you."

Lucky opened his eyes blearily. He looked at Lola.

"We were diving to escape the coast guard," she reminded him. "They fired at us. You got knocked out."

Max quickly picked up the story. "We don't know how to stop. . . . We're eighty feet deep. . . . The water's coming in."

Lucky tried to focus on the controls. As he snapped on the exterior lights, they saw that they were floating down a narrow tunnel of rock.

"I know this place," said Lucky.

"Where are we?" asked Max, but Lucky didn't answer. Every bit of his energy was focused on steering the sub through the narrow space.

As the canyon walls opened up to a sea of black, Lucky relaxed. "It's just as I remember it," he said, smiling to himself. Then he looked around at Max and Lola. "Prepare to surface!"

"Surface?" repeated Max in alarm.

"No, Lucky," protested Lola. "Not yet! What about the coast guard or whoever that was?"

"Not a problem," said Lucky with a mysterious smile.

Four things happened in quick succession.

The control panels lit up.

The cabin lights came on.

The ballast tanks starting pumping out water.

The sub began to rise.

"It's getting lighter," said Lola after a moment.

Surprisingly quickly, they broke through the surface of the water.

Max monitored the video screen and the GPS. "I don't get it." He tried to make sense of the picture. "It says we're inland."

Lucky leaned over to throw open the door. "It's an underground lake. But not just any lake."

Max, Lola, and Lord 6-Dog looked out in astonishment.

"What is this place?" asked Lola.

Back aboard the coast guard ship, the crew of zombies cheered. Their mission had been a success. For once in their lawless zombie lives, they'd followed their orders to the letter; they'd driven the little sub into the ocean depths, for the current to carry it the rest of the way. The two brats and the fleabag monkey would find what they were meant to find. Tzelek would be well pleased. There would be feasting in Xibalba tonight.

CHAPTER NINE
THE SECRET OF THE *ESPADA*

Max leaned out of the submarine hatch and gasped in awe. The cave looked like a pirate's treasure chest. Its limestone walls were as white as pearl, and rays of sunlight as bright as gold doubloons played on the emerald water. Flashes of topaz sky were visible through holes high up in the cave roof. Fish glinted like gemstones and were gone. At the far end, a pebble beach sparkled like diamonds.

Then he saw it.

In a corner of the cave, marooned high up on the treacherous rocks by a long-ago tide, was the wreck of a Spanish galleon.

A bell rang in Max's brain. He turned to Lucky. "Is that . . . is that . . . the . . . *Espada?*"

Lucky nodded.

"The *Espada?*" Lola was confused. "That was Antonio de Landa's yacht."

"This is the original *Espada,*" Max explained. "The one that sailed from Spain with the conquistadors. It sank off Puerto Muerto and was never seen again—until Uncle Ted and Lucky found it in a cave. *This* cave!"

"So, you've been here before?" Lola asked Lucky. "You know the way out?"

"I sure do."

"We're safe?" Lola breathed a huge sigh of relief.

"I wouldn't go that far," said Lucky. "We should hide down here for a while and give whoever was aboard that coast guard vessel time to lose interest."

"I still can't believe they fired on us," said Lola.

"Maybe they were trying to stop me leaving San Xavier," suggested Max.

"The real coast guard would never open fire without warning," said Lucky.

"So, who was it?" asked Lola.

"Who knows?" replied Lucky. "Maybe pirates. I'd report it, but with one passenger who's on the lam, one whose house has been destroyed by mythical Maya monsters, and one who's a talking howler monkey, I think I'd just as soon lie low. Will you help me tie up, Lord 6-Dog?" The monkey king looked horrified. "Me? Tie up? I have no nautical skills. I left those to my navy and trading fleets."

"It was your monkey skills I was interested in."

When Lucky had explained his plan, Lord 6-Dog took the rope and climbed onto the roof. Then he took a flying leap and landed on a flat shelf of limestone. For extra strength, he looped the rope around his tail before pulling in the sub.

"If Mother could see me now," he bragged. "I am king of the fiery pool."

While Lucky tied the rope securely around a jutting rock, Max and Lola went down to the galley for food. "I found some bananas for you after all your hard work," said Lola to Lord 6-Dog as they set out the picnic on the rock.

Lord 6-Dog didn't seem to hear. He was staring at the galleon. "That wreck is my doing," he whispered. "I cursed that ship." He stood with his head high in his striped pajamas, like a Maya king in his battle finery, reliving that fateful moment. "It was in the eleventh *bak'tun*. I had been called back by my people to the city you know as Puerto Muerto. They begged me to avenge the deeds of Diego de Landa, most hated of the Spanish invaders and"—he nodded to Lola—"ancestor of that fool, Antonio."

"The eleventh *bak'tun*? During the Spanish conquest?" asked Lola. "So you'd been dead for five hundred years by then?"

Lord 6-Dog waved his monkey hand to dismiss such boring details, then regained his heroic stance. "I stood on the dockside in Puerto Muerto and watched that very ship"—he pointed to the *Espada*—"being loaded with the riches of my people. Many of the chests were branded with the crest of Diego de Landa. I was consumed with rage. These invaders had already burned our books and destroyed our families. I vowed they would not have the little that was left. So I appeared to the Spanish sea captain and decreed that his accursed cargo would never leave Maya waters."

Lord 6-Dog hadn't really thought that one through, reflected Max. It hadn't been much help to his people to send all their stuff to the bottom of the ocean. But he saw the sadness on the monkey king's face and decided not to point this out.

126

Instead, he tried to look on the bright side. "And then it sat safely in this cave until my uncle came along and recovered all the treasure."

"He bought this sub with the proceeds," added Lucky.

Lord 6-Dog looked like he might explode. "The cargo was not his to sell."

"Fair's fair," Max blurted out. "If Uncle Ted and Lucky hadn't found this cave, the treasure would have stayed down here forever."

Lord 6-Dog curled his hairy fingers into fists. "Why must history always repeat itself? If only the cycle could be broken. Once, I cursed that ship to avenge my people. Now I find it broken on the rocks and the heritage of my people has been plundered again."

"It was my heritage, too," said Lola softly. "And my father who plundered it."

"Thou art descended from the Jaguar Kings. We are kin, thou and I. Thou art Maya."

Lola stuck up her chin. "*Half*-Maya. I'm also half-Murphy, which means a quarter Spanish and a quarter Irish."

Lord 6-Dog glared at her. "Then perchance it is time to take sides."

Lola glared back at him. "I *have* taken sides. I'm with the good guys."

There was a moment of tense silence, then Lucky jumped up. "I need to stretch my legs." He offered his arm to Lola. "Want to walk?"

Max watched them picking their way over the rocks. "Why did you get so angry at Lola?" he asked Lord 6-Dog.

"I fear she is ashamed of her birthright."

"Why would you say that?"

"I look at this galleon through her eyes and all I see is the story of our people, wrecked on the rocks of history."

"But that's not your fault."

"I wish I could believe that, young lord."

Max tried to think of a subject to distract Lord 6-Dog. "Will you tell me about your dream? The one that changed your mind about coming with us?"

Lord 6-Dog looked even sadder. "It was from my father, Punak Ha. He told me that my destiny lies across this ocean."

"Well, that sounds hopeful," said Max.

"He said that this will be my final journey."

"Oh. We're not going to sink, are we?"

"He said that Tzelek awaits me at journey's end."

"For your final battle? That's what you want, isn't it?"

"He said I will not beat Tzelek if I fight him."

"Oh."

They sat in miserable silence.

"Let's explore the *Espada*," suggested Max. "Maybe we'll find some Spanish gold."

"I doubt thine uncle has left us any pickings."

"You never know."

Max fetched some flashlights from the sub, then he and Lord 6-Dog climbed over the slippery rocks to where the galleon sat in stately decay. Bits of ship—splintered beams, broken spars, rotted canvas, and rusty nails—lay everywhere. An upended cannon, covered in barnacles and plugged with seaweed, pointed uselessly at the cave roof. But the vessel itself was still more or less intact, as if it had sailed straight out of a history book and into this cave. Only the nylon rope ladder that hung over the side gave any clue that they were not the first to discover it.

Max and Lord 6-Dog climbed up the ladder and onto the deck.

The ship had come to rest at a crazy angle and Max had to walk slowly, with his arms held out like a tightrope walker, to keep his balance.

"Hold on to my tail to steady thyself," Lord 6-Dog instructed him as they walked over the buckled and broken boards.

In the center of the deck was an open hatch. Max shone his flashlight into the darkness and saw a steep staircase that disappeared into oily black water. Disturbed by the beam of light, something slithered into the water with a splash, leaving ripples on the surface.

"That must be the hold where they found the treasure," said Max.

Lord 6-Dog peered down. "Naught down there now but rats."

"Aren't rats supposed to desert a sinking ship?"

"Rats can survive anywhere. Ask Tzelek."

Changing the subject quickly, Max said, "Let's find the captain's quarters. You go first."

Using Lord 6-Dog's tail as a rope, Max inched his way to the stern of the boat and pulled himself up to the quarterdeck, where the Spanish sea captain had once stood.

Max gripped the broken spokes of the ship's wheel and imagined setting sail for home, full of hope, and treasure, and tales of adventure. Then he imagined the terror of sinking right there in the bay, still within sight of the teeming jungle.

"Do you remember when we went to Spain?" he asked Lord 6-Dog, who was sniffing at the green mossy mold on the woodwork to see if it was edible.

"Of course I do, young lord. A dry and barren place where the cheese stinks like dung beetles. No wonder those barbarian conquistadors sailed far and wide."

"I don't think it was the cheese—" began Max, when a noise behind him made him jump. He spun around with the flashlight to see a skull tumble to the floor in the cabin behind them. A small crab climbed guiltily out of an eye socket and scuttled away.

"It is the Spanish sea captain," said Lord 6-Dog, sounding slightly shaken. "I last saw him on the dock at Puerto Muerto. I cursed him and he laughed at me."

The open doorway of the cabin was draped in cobwebs like lace curtains. Spiders of all sizes ran for their lives into cracks in the door frame as Max cleared the cobwebs away with the handle of his flashlight. There, inside the cabin, sat the headless skeleton of the long-dead captain.

"He's not laughing now," said Max.

The skeleton was posed in a carved wooden chair, elbows on the armrests, hands in his lap. The chair had been nailed to the cabin floor to prevent it rolling on the high seas. Dried seaweed draped the chair back like a cape, and sea snails left silver trails on the captain's yellowed bones.

"So," said Lord 6-Dog to the moldering rib cage, "we meet again, thou lily-livered coward."

"He went down with the ship," Max pointed out. "That was brave."

Lord 6-Dog looked with scorn at the skeleton. "Not brave," he said. "Greedy."

"Greedy?"

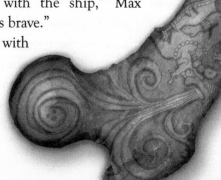

"It seems there was one piece of treasure he would not relinquish even in death."

Max looked around the cabin. It was completely empty, apart from bits of rotting debris. "I don't see anything."

"Look harder. Thine uncle missed the most precious thing of all."

"He did?" Max looked around again. He didn't see so much as a rusty spoon.

"There." Lord 6-Dog pointed at the hands of the skeleton, resting calmly in his lap.

"His bones?" Max was confused.

"Not *his* bones. The bone that he holds in his hands."

Now that Max looked more closely, he saw that in among the dusty, cobwebby tangle of yellow finger bones was a larger bone from a leg or an arm. It was browner than the rest and looked much older.

Lord 6-Dog fell to his knees and chanted in Mayan.

"Are you talking to that bone?" Max asked him incredulously.

"I am addressing its owner, Yax Tuun Ah Muuch. Jade Frog to thee. He was the founder of my dynasty."

"And he owned that bone?"

"It was in his leg."

"Gross. How do you know it's his?"

After reciting what sounded like a Maya prayer, Lord 6-Dog delicately picked up the leg-bone and blew off the dust.

He held it out reverently, and Max saw that it was covered in faint inscriptions. "It is unmistakable. It was carved after his death."

"But why would a Spanish sea captain be holding a Maya king's leg-bone? I mean, of all the things he could have grabbed when he was going down with the ship. Do leg-bones float?"

"This leg-bone is special. Perhaps he hoped it would give him immortality."

"What's so special about it?"

"It is the scepter of the Jaguar Kings. It was handed down from king to king through the generations. I had thought it was lost forever. With this, I can beat Tzelek."

"But what about your dream? I thought your father said—"

"Maybe sometimes, young lord, dreams are just dreams!"

"So what does it *do*, this scepter?"

Lord 6-Dog's eyes glittered with triumph. "It changes everything!"

CHAPTER TEN
THE GULF

Lola and Lucky were sitting on the rock slab waiting for them. Lord 6-Dog bounded over, holding high the leg-bone of his ancestor. Max made his way more slowly over the rocks and wasn't there to hear the king's announcement about his find. But from the lack of excited voices in response, he guessed that Lucky and Lola had also failed to greet Jade Frog's moldering leg-bone with enthusiasm.

"Dost thou not see?" Lord 6-Dog was saying when Max arrived at the makeshift dock. "It was the Jaguar Kings who guided us into this cave. It was they who put this scepter into my hands. They have given me what I need to vanquish Tzelek once and for all."

They all looked at the ancient brown bone.

Lola voiced their skepticism. "You're going to vanquish Tzelek with that old thing? How?"

"It is the scepter of the Jaguar Kings."

"But what does it do, exactly?"

"It channels the power of the Jaguar Stones."

Understanding dawned on Lola's face. "He doesn't know how to use it," she whispered to Max.

Lucky stood up. "The tide is turning."

Lord 6-Dog patted the leg-bone. "Indeed, it is."

"No," said Lucky. "The actual tide is turning. It's time to go." He went to open the hatch to the submarine. "All aboard. Again."

"Dibs on copilot," said Lola.

"Get ready to dive, everyone," said Lucky. "We're going back the way we came."

This time their descent was smooth and slow.

Lucky was studying the radar. "I don't see the coast guard vessel anywhere. They must have found bigger fish to fry."

A large grouper swimming by the windscreen puckered its lips as if blowing a kiss.

Max went and lay on a bunk to study the guidebooks, but once again the heat and vibrations and smell made his head spin.

Above him, Lord 6-Dog whispered in Mayan to Jade Frog's leg-bone.

Soon, both boy and monkey were in the land of dreams.

"What did I miss?" asked Max hours later, climbing up to the cockpit.

"Whale sharks, dolphins, and a giant barracuda," said Lola. "The fish in the gulf were amazing."

Max peered out of the porthole, but all was dark. "Did you see the coast guard again?"

"No. But we nearly collided with a trawler."

"So where are we now?"

"Coming into New Orleans. Is Lord 6-Dog still asleep?"

"I'll go wake him up."

Max ran back down and tapped Lord 6-Dog on the shoulder. "Rise and shine!"

Lord 6-Dog shot up, snarling. He clutched at the leg-bone, as if Max had been trying to steal it.

"Chill," said Max, backing away. "I just came to tell you that we're nearly there, so if you want to, um . . ." He was going to say *take off your pajamas*, but he wasn't sure about the etiquette of giving wardrobe advice to a Maya king, so he finished vaguely, ". . . if you want to get ready."

"I have the scepter of the Jaguar Kings, I am ready for anything."

"Um, okay, then. Let's go up."

Lola greeted them excitedly. "Look!" she said, pointing to the video screen. "New Orleans! Look at all the lights! *Please* surface, Lucky, so I can see it properly."

"It's too dangerous," replied Lucky. "We have to sneak around the back, find a quiet bayou to tie up in."

"A bayou?" Max pulled a face. "I don't like the sound of that. The guidebook said that bayous have alligators and leeches."

Lucky rolled his eyes. "I'll tie up close to the bank."

"Pleeeeeease," Lola was begging. "Can't we just surface for one little minute?"

"We're not tourists," Lucky reminded her. "We're here on business."

"But I've never been on vacation in my whole life."

Lucky relented. "Just a quick look, but then we need to stay under. None of us have documentation if we get stopped."

"Speak for thyself," said Lord 6-Dog. "I have the leg-bone of my ancestor."

"I'm fairly sure that's not a recognized form of identification around here," said Lucky. He brought the sub up until they were floating on the water. "Now take a quick peek, Lola, and let's get out of here."

As soon as she opened the hatch door, they were serenaded by the sounds of distant trumpets, trombones, and snare drums. The sub filled with aromas of spicy gumbo, boiled crawfish, and those impossibly light donuts called beignets.

"I'm so hungry," wailed Max. "Let's get off and eat. There's a dock over there."

"No," said Lucky. "We're going to do this my way. We'll tie up somewhere quiet and walk back into the city for dinner. I'll find you a hotel and tickets upriver for tomorrow. With luck, we'll find a boat going all the way to Cahokia."

"You're not coming with us?" Lola made a sad face.

"I have classes to teach, remember? But I'll be back to collect you. Just call me."

"What if the phones are still out?" asked Max.

"I'll find you somehow."

Max furrowed his brow dubiously.

"You'll be fine," Lucky assured him. "This place is a lot safer than the jungle. Besides, you have Lord 6-Dog to look after you."

Max and Lola regarded their so-called protector. He was in a world of his own, intent on polishing the leg-bone of his ancestor on his pajama top.

136

"You'll be fine," repeated Lucky, less convincingly this time. "Now let's get that hatch shut and find somewhere safe to tie up."

"HALT!" bellowed a voice.

Lucky clapped his hand to his forehead. "Too late! We've been spotted!"

Max looked around for the coast guard but saw no other boats on the water.

"STORM WARNING IN EFFECT. ALL TOUR BOATS INTO PORT. THIS IS AN ORDER."

"There's a guy with a megaphone on the dock," said Lucky.

"Police?" asked Max.

"It's hard to see. He's wearing a rain cape. He looks pretty official."

"Let's just go," Lola urged. "Let's dive and get out of here!"

Lucky assessed the situation. "No, it's okay. We'll play along. This could work for us. He thinks we're a tour boat, so I'll keep him talking while you three disembark and melt into the crowd." He turned the sub toward the dock. "Just keep your cool and act like tourists."

"Easier said than done," Max pointed out. "One of us is a howler monkey in pajamas."

Lola pulled out a blanket from a cubby. "Here," she said, draping it over Lord 6-Dog's head. "Wrap this around you and we'll say you're seasick. They'll think you're a little boy."

"What about his hairy feet?" said Max.

"It's getting dark," said Lola. "No one will notice."

Lucky put his hands on her shoulders. "I wish I could come with you. Are you sure you'll be okay?"

"You said it yourself," Lola pointed out. "It's a lot safer here than in the jungle."

"New Orleans looks like a beautiful city," agreed Lucky. "But it has its dark side. I've heard tales of ghosts and voodoo and haunted houses."

"Now you tell us," joked Max.

Lola laughed. "We've survived the Maya underworld. I think we can look after ourselves."

He nodded. "So when you get off the sub, promise me that you'll go straight to a hotel. Then you'll come back to the waterfront in the morning and look for a boat to St. Louis. They're supposed to leave every day. Do you have enough money?"

"*Yes!* Stop worrying. We'll be fine."

Lucky, who was not a natural hugger, hugged each of them awkwardly. "Let's get this over with, then."

Lucky disembarked first. "Good evening, Officer," he said to the guy in the rain cape. Then he stood at the hatch to help the others out onto the wooden dock. "Watch your step," he said to each of them as they emerged. "Sharky's Sub Tours welcomes you back to New Orleans."

"We didn't finish our tour," grumbled Lola. "We want our money back."

"Sorry, lady, read the small print. No refunds."

"And my little brother got seasick."

"Then it's a good thing we docked early." Lucky winked at the officer. "Tourists. There's no pleasing 'em."

"Very true," the officer agreed. "How's business? I never heard of Sharky's Sub Tours before."

"We're new in town." Lucky looked as guilty as only a man driving a smuggler's submarine in foreign waters on a mission from the Maya Death Lords could, but the officer didn't seem to notice.

"Next time, you should check the weather forecast first."

"I did but—" Lucky stopped himself arguing and nodded meekly. After casting one last worried glance at his former passengers, he got back in the sub and headed out across the water.

Max, Lola, and the blanket-swathed Maya king crossed the broad waterfront sidewalk and ducked around the first street corner.

"Did that cop follow us?" asked Max, flattening himself against the wall.

Lola peered around the corner. "All clear! We did it, Hoop! We're in New Orleans!"

Max exhaled with relief. "So let's find a hotel."

"Can't we explore a little first?"

"No. We're sticking to the plan. Besides, there's a storm coming, remember?"

"I smell no storm," said Lord 6-Dog suspiciously.

"Can you speak a bit higher?" Lola asked him. "You're supposed to be a little boy."

"I smell no storm," squeaked Lord 6-Dog.

Lola looked at the sky. "Not a single cloud," she agreed. "Maybe the weather changes quickly here."

"Whatever," said Max. "Let's get going. It looks like there's loads of places down this way. I'm pretty sure this is the French Quarter. It's full of hotels and restaurants. We should come back out for something to eat when we've found a place to stay."

They walked along, laughing and chatting and looking in store windows. But gradually their high spirits faded. One after another, the hotels they passed had NO VACANCY signs posted outside.

"This is hopeless," sighed Lola.

The streets were getting quieter now.

"This looks like the end of the French Quarter," said Max. "What should we do?"

"If we were in the jungle, we'd just sling our hammocks in some trees." Lola looked around doubtfully. "Maybe we could sleep in a doorway."

Max pulled a face. "I want fluffy towels and cable TV."

"I'd settle for shelter from the storm," said Lola.

Lord 6-Dog sniffed the air. "Battle stations!" he yelped.

"What? Why?" Max and Lola tuned to see what he was looking at, and a burst of raucous music made them jump out of their skin.

"It's started," said Lola. "Look!"

A band of skeletons was dancing down the road playing their instruments. They were led by a small skeleton with a baton.

Lord 6-Dog brandished the leg-bone at them. "Be gone, evil spirits!"

The skeletons waved back cheerily.

"Are we in New Orleans or Xibalba?" whispered Lola.

The small skeleton with the baton handed her a piece of paper.

"What's this?" she asked defiantly. "A ransom note for my parents?"

The little skeleton stared at her in alarm and high-tailed it back to the group.

"'Crescent City Middle School Marching Band,'" read Lola. "'Halloween Parade Route.'"

Max burst out laughing. "They're schoolkids. In costumes. They're rehearsing for Halloween. That poor little skeleton, you scared him to death."

Lola laughed, too. "I'm so on edge," she said. "I wish we could find a hotel."

"There's one," said Max.

All around them were smart, white-painted houses, some with imposing pillars and others with ornate iron balconies on their upper stories. But across the street sat a dark patch of gloom, a house entirely in darkness. A single flickering lightbulb illuminated the peeling sign that swung miserably outside:

BARON SATURDAY'S

Olde Tyme Inn

COME IN AND REVIVE YOURSELF

VACANCY

"At least it doesn't look expensive," said Lola.

A horse-drawn carriage rolled past. "And this is the most haunted hotel in New Orleans," said the driver to his passengers. "Guests who've lived to tell the tale speak of strange goings-on in the middle of the night. . . ." His voice faded away as the carriage clopped down the street.

"Are you sure about this place?" Max asked Lola.

"It's the only place we've seen with a vacancy sign," said Lola.

She crossed the street and opened the gate. It creaked like a cackling witch with a sore throat.

"Is this a good time to remind you that we're not good at choosing hotels?" asked Max. "Remember Casa Carmela in Spain? And the Grand Hotel Xibalba?"

"It's just for one night," said Lola firmly. "What's the worst that can happen?"

Max and Lord 6-Dog followed her down the path to the front door.

Like the other buildings on the street, the hotel was three stories high with ornamental balconies. But it was detached and set back from the sidewalk, with a dead-looking front garden surrounded by a rusty wrought-iron fence. A massive oak tree in the front yard was draped in a tattered veil of gray Spanish moss. Black shutters covered every window.

"This is the creepiest hotel I've ever seen," said Max.

"It will be fine," Lola said. She put her ear to the front door. "Sounds like there's a party going on inside."

Max breathed a sigh of relief. "That explains it. An early Halloween party. I bet someone in a creepy costume opens the door. I'm guessing Dracula. What's your guess, Lord 6-Dog?"

Lord 6-Dog murmured something noncommittal under his blanket, which Max took to mean that a Maya king in a monkey suit was in no position to make jokes about other people's Halloween costumes.

Lola rang the bell.

In fact, the man who opened the door was dressed very smartly in an ornate purple velvet coat, white ruffled shirt, black britches, and buckled shoes. He had black curly hair falling to his shoulders and a jaunty black mustache, like one of the Three Musketeers. The only alarming thing about him was his face. He looked startlingly like a slightly younger version of Uncle Ted's butler, Raul.

"*Bonsoir,*" he said.

"Er, *bonsoir,*" said Lola. "Do you have any rooms? There are three of us."

"But of course. We 'ave been expecting you."

CHAPTER ELEVEN
BARON SATURDAY

Max stared at the man who'd open the door. "You've been expecting us? But we didn't know we were coming here."

Their French host shrugged. "My name eez Louis. I am at your service." He gave an elaborate bow to welcome them into the house.

Behind him, a crystal chandelier blazed into life, illuminating a spectacular marble hallway. A wide, curving staircase with carved oak banisters led to the upper floors. It looked like a Hollywood mansion.

"Eet eez late," said Louis. He took in Lord 6-Dog's pajama-clad legs under the blanket. If he also saw hairy feet, he gave no sign of it. "Zee leetle boy must be tired. I will show you to your rooms."

As they followed Louis up the stairs, they glimpsed inside the parlors off the hallway, each more lavishly decorated than the last. It seemed that the interior of Baron Saturday's Inn was as sumptuous as the exterior was run-down. Music and laughter floated out from every room.

"Are you having a party?" asked Lola.

"Zees eez New Orleans. Zee good times zey always roll."

Louis led them up two flights of stairs and down a long corridor to a grand double door at the end. Pulling an old-fashioned brass key out of his pocket, he unlocked the door and motioned for them to enter. "Zees eez your suite," he announced. "Eet 'az two bedrooms."

They entered a floral-papered sitting room, plush with velvet sofas and swag curtains. In front of the French windows was a dining table set for three. It seemed that they really *had* been expected.

Louis opened a door on one side. "For Mamzelle, we 'ave zee Marie Laveau Room. They call 'er zee voodoo queen of New Orleans."

Lola peeped inside. An oil painting of a beautiful dark-skinned woman in an elaborate turban dominated the room. On a four-poster bed sat a collection of rag dolls with large pins sticking into them. There was a crystal ball on the dresser.

Louis crossed the sitting room and threw open another door. "And for zee gentlemen, we 'ave zee Lafitte Room, named for zee famous pirate, Jean Lafitte." This room had a nautical theme, with wood-paneled walls, pictures of sailing ships, a pair of crossed cutlasses above the fireplace, and a spyglass on the windowsill. A stuffed green parrot sat on a brass perch.

"You like eet?" asked Louis, looking around the room proudly. "If everything eez to your satisfaction, I weel leave you to settle in. But I weel return soon weez your dinner."

Finally, he left and they were alone.

"I'm so glad we found this place," said Lola, flopping down on a sofa.

"This is the life," agreed Max, flopping down on the other sofa.

"There is sorcery afoot," called Lord 6-Dog from the other room. "These chambers reek of the underworld."

Lola sniffed. "It's just air freshener. I'll open a window." But she couldn't get any of the windows, or the doors to the balcony, to open. "Looks like we need a key," she said. "I'll ask Louis when he comes back."

Soon there was a knock on the door. "Zee room service!" came Louis's voice.

"Quick! Lord 6-Dog! Hide in the bathroom!" called Lola.

Louis rolled a wooden cart loaded with dishes into the room. "I 'ave brought you zee specialties of zee 'ouse. I 'ope you enjoy." He looked around. "Where eez zee leetle boy?"

"In the bathroom," said Lola. "We'll start without him."

"Very well, mamzelle. For your first course, we 'ave one of our most popular deeshes." He lifted the silver dome off a serving tureen to reveal a heaped serving of bugs. They were about the size of crickets, bright red in color, pincers and antennas tangled together.

"Are those . . . scorpions?" asked Max, horrified.

"Zey are crawfeesh. Like shrimp. Zees eez a crawfeesh boil. Eet eez a local delicacy." Louis peeled one of the little crustaceans and offered it to Lola.

She tried it. "Delicious!"

Encouraged, Louis pointed to another dish on the cart. "'Ere we 'ave jambalaya."

"What's that?" asked Max.

146

"Eet eez rice weez sausage and chicken."

"It smells wonderful," said Lola.

"And 'ere we 'ave zee gumbo."

"What's that?" asked Max again.

"Eet eez sausage and chicken weez rice."

Neither Max nor Lola noticed that the stuffed parrot on the perch ruffled its feathers every time Louis said *chicken*.

"Thank you," said Lola. "This is a feast."

Louis bowed. "*Bon appétit!* When you 'ave finished, please come downstairs for zee dessert. Zee Baron likes to greet all eez guests personally."

"Baron Saturday?" asked Lola. "He's a real person?"

Louis gave a nod and left, closing the door behind him.

"Gah! I forgot to ask about the windows," said Lola, jumping up.

"Ask him later," said Max. "Can we eat? I'm starving."

"Okay," agreed Lola. "Will you tell Lord 6-Dog that the coast is clear?"

Max grabbed a roll to eat on the way, and then knocked on the bathroom door. "Dinner!"

After a pause, Lord 6-Dog's head appeared around the door. He sniffed the air and wrinkled up his face. "I care not for spicy food. Please bring me the flowers from the table."

"I know it's a nice bathroom, but don't you want to eat with us?"

"I am cleaning the scepter to better read the inscription. The glyphs are muddied with the dirt of the ages. And now, if thou wilt excuse me . . ."

Lord 6-Dog shut the bathroom door.

When Max returned with the flowers, he heard strange sounds like many voices chanting in Mayan.

He banged on the door. "Lord 6-Dog? Who's in there? Are you all right?"

Not getting an answer, he tried the door.

It opened.

Lord 6-Dog was alone. He was hanging by his tail from the shower rail and addressing the bathroom mirror.

"Are you talking to yourself?" asked Max.

He followed Lord 6-Dog's eyes and saw, with a shock, that the mirror reflected a crowded room. Sitting on the floor, leaning against the walls, even huddled in the bathtub were groups of Maya men. Old and young, tall and short, they were dressed like ancient nobles, in embroidered loincloths, jaguar pelts, and jade jewelry, their hair flamboyantly festooned with seashells and feathers.

As one, the reflections turned and stared curiously at Max. Some of them pointed at his hair.

Lord 6-Dog quickly dismounted and rushed to push him out the door. "I am sorry, young lord. This is a private council meeting."

"But who are they?" asked Max.

"They are my revered ancestors, the Jaguar Kings."

"How did they get here?"

"It seems that I summoned them with Jade Frog's legbone." The voices in the bathroom were getting louder. "I must go back in before they declare war on each other."

Max ran back to the dining table, where Lola was delicately dissecting a crawfish. "You won't believe what I just saw," he announced. "Lord 6-Dog has accidentally summoned the Jaguar Kings! They're in the bathroom mirror right now!"

"You're kidding me? The Jaguar Kings are here? In this

hotel room?" She ran off in the direction of the bathroom. Max heard her banging on the door.

He piled his plate high with food.

"How much weirder can this whole thing get?" he asked the stuffed parrot.

The parrot flapped its wings.

Max dropped his fork with a clatter. "You're alive? I had no idea! That's amazing! Can you talk? Can you say 'Pretty Polly'?"

The parrot gave him a dirty look and turned its back on him.

Lola came back in, walking slowly, as if in a trance.

"The parrot is alive!" announced Max.

She didn't seem to hear. "That. Was. Incredible. I. Just. Met. My. Ancestors."

"Did they talk to you?" Max asked.

"Yes! I'll never forget it. Lord 6-Dog was going to introduce me to his father, Punak Ha, but one of the other kings shouted: *It's a woman! Get her out of here!* And then they were all arguing in Mayan and Lord 6-Dog pushed me out of the bathroom."

"He pushed me out, too."

"It was so cool. And the whole mirror thing. Do you understand it?"

"It's a mirror," said Max. "You look in it."

"No. I mean, yes, but it's in the Maya creation story. The gods make it so that humans see the world as if they were looking through a fogged-up mirror, so they don't get too clever. It's so poetic."

"Cool," said Max unenthusiastically. "Did you hear what I said about the parrot?"

"Forget the parrot. I'm telling you about one of the

greatest moments of my life. I hope Lord 6-Dog isn't mad at me for barging in."

"Actually," said Max, "I think that secretly he'll be pleased. He told me in the cave that he thought you were ashamed of your Maya side."

"He did? That's awful." Embarrassed, Lola buried her face in a pillow.

"You *have* been acting strangely. I thought you didn't like me either."

Garbled sounds escaped from the pillow.

"What did you say?" Max asked her.

"I said: life is so confusing."

Max tried to look sympathetic. "We could go down for dessert," he suggested.

Lola looked at him over the top of the pillow. "Is dessert your solution to everything, Hoop?"

Max shrugged. "It's worth a try."

Lola laughed. "Okay. I'll go see if Lord 6-Dog wants some, too."

While she was gone, Max offered a crust of bread to the parrot. "Who's a Pretty Polly?" he asked it over and over. The parrot ignored him.

Lola came back with her hands up. It was obvious that Lord 6-Dog had yelled at her for interrupting him again. "He wouldn't let me in. He said he's not hungry. He sounded a bit panicky. I think he's having trouble getting rid of his guests."

Downstairs, the party was in full swing.

Guests in carnival costumes, all in shades of black, white,

and purple, thronged the hallway. Security guards—purple-uniformed musketeers—were posted at every door.

In one room, a jazz band played.

In another room, several raucous card games were in progress.

Lola spotted an open window. "I'm going to get some air."

"I'm going to get dessert," said Max.

Minutes later, Max came running back. "You won't believe it!" he said, his eyes as big and round as two chocolate tarts. "You have to come see! They have a whole room just for desserts. Pies, cakes, custards. Everything you can think of. And bowls of whipped cream. And jugs of chocolate sauce."

Lola smiled. "I love this place!"

Horse-drawn carriages clopped by in the street outside. Sightseers and souvenir shoppers were out in force, but they kept to the other side of the street, making a wide arc around the hotel.

"That cop was wrong," said Lola, looking up at the sky. "There's no storm coming tonight."

"So do you want dessert?" asked Max.

"Lead the way."

They were ambushed by Louis en route. "Good evening. I 'ope you enjoyed your dinner. And now zee baron eez waiting to speak weez you."

"Of course," said Lola politely.

"Can't we get dessert first?" asked Max.

But Louis was leading them in the opposite direction.

Casting a last longing glance at the dessert room, Max followed Lola and Louis into the card room. At the biggest table, with his back to them, a figure in a top hat and black tuxedo was dealing cards. Louis touched him on the shoulder. "Baron, may I present our new arrivals?"

The figure rose and turned around. Beneath his hat, his face was as thin and white as a skeleton. "Welcome to my humble abode. I am Baron Samedi, or, in English, Baron Saturday." His voice was hoarse and raspy.

Max stared at him in confusion. "You look familiar. Have we met before?"

"I can assure you that you'd remember if we had." The baron gave a wave of dismissal to his card-playing companions, one of whom looked suspiciously like the cop who'd ordered the sub to dock. The card players threw down their cards and, casting hostile looks at Max and Lola, vacated their seats.

"Please, sit," said the baron, indicating the newly empty chairs.

"I know why he looks familiar," Lola whispered as they sat down. "He looks like a Death Lord."

Baron Saturday overheard her. "You are observant, young lady. We are indeed related, the Death Lords and I." He grinned. "And, of course, we are in the same family business."

Lola stiffened. "The Death Lords aren't innkeepers."

"Except for the Grand Hotel Xibalba," said Max. "Is that what you mean? Because I think it's closed down now."

"No," replied the baron, sounding irritated. "That is not what I mean. I am talking in metaphors."

Max and Lola stared at him in confusion.

"Must I spell it out for you?" asked the baron. "What is an inn but a stop at the end of the journey? Do not the Death Lords welcome mortals at the end of their lives? I am talking about the business of death."

"Do you work with the Death Lords?" asked Lola nervously.

Baron Saturday shook his head. "Perish the thought."

"Welcome to my humble abode."

"Then what do you mean?" asked Max.

"The Death Lords," explained the baron, "specialize in wiping out humanity en masse. Mine is a more personal service. I dig your grave. I meet you when you die. I escort you to the underworld." He smiled at them. "I can give you a demonstration if you'd like. Tonight."

"We can't stay," said Lola quickly. "We'll pay for our room. But we're leaving right now."

The baron laughed. "That's what they all say. But it's too late for that. Where's my lagniappe?"

"*Lanny-app?*" repeated Max. "What's that?"

"You don't know the word? We use it a lot in this town. It means a little something extra, like a tip or a gift. If your lagniappe is generous enough, it might persuade me *not* to dig your graves tonight. So, what can you give me?"

"You can have all our money," said Lola.

"Look at this room," said the baron. "The crystal chandeliers, the solid gold picture frames. Do I look like someone who needs money? You will have to do better than that."

"We'll clear up after your party and wash all the dishes," offered Max.

"Do I look like someone who cannot afford servants?"

Max ran quickly ran through his possessions. "I have a bracelet made out of bat intestines. I bet you don't have one of those."

The baron raised an eyebrow. "Your lives are at stake. And that is what you offer me?"

Max and Lola looked at each other in a panic.

"Never mind. Let us get down to details. Pine or oak? Satin lining or velvet?" The baron clapped his hands and

Louis appeared behind him. "Measure them for their coffins. And polish up my best spade."

Louis produced a tape measure from his pocket.

"And now," said Baron Saturday, standing up and tipping his top hat, "I must mingle with my guests. We will meet again at midnight, one hour from now. I suggest you wear black."

As Louis took their measurements, he whispered: "You must pay the baron, weez a gift or weez your lives."

"But we have nothing," Lola whispered back.

"What about zat 'airy leetle boy?" suggested Louis.

"I can't give away my brother," said Lola, shocked.

"But your brother, 'e 'az something, does 'e not? What was 'e 'iding when 'e arrived?"

Max and Lola exchanged a nervous glance.

"Oh that," said Lola. "It's just an old bone, probably from a dinosaur, or something. You know what boys are like. It's disgusting. The baron doesn't want that."

"Zee baron likes old things." Louis finished measuring and stood up. "Zees bone might save you from zee graveyard."

"It's my brother's favorite toy," said Lola.

"Ask 'eem," urged Louis. "Before eet eez too late." He made a big show of jotting down their measurements in a notebook. "Or you weel not get out of 'ere alive."

Lola pulled Max out of Louis's earshot. "What should we do?"

"We'll have to get that stupid bone off Lord 6-Dog. It's our only chance."

Louis popped up behind them. "Why don't you take up some dessert for zee boy? We 'ave many specialties of New Orleans. I zeenk 'e would like zee bananas foster."

CHAPTER TWELVE
ESCAPE IN THE NIGHT

"**B**ananas foster! Did you hear that?" Lola said to Max as they ran upstairs. "He said to bring bananas to Lord 6-Dog. He knows he's a monkey! He knows who we are!"

"This is bad," agreed Max. "Very bad."

When they opened the door to their suite, it got worse. There were feathers everywhere.

Brown feathers.

Green feathers.

All over the floor.

"What happened?" cried Max.

"Where's Lord 6-Dog?" cried Lola.

"Here." A disheveled monkey head appeared from behind one of the sofas.

Lola ran over to him. "Are you all right?"

Lord 6-Dog got shakily to his feet. "Thank Itzamna thou hast returned. Thou didst miss quite a battle."

Lola picked up a brown feather and a green feather and studied them. "Was it a battle between an owl and a parrot by any chance?"

"Just so." Lord 6-Dog sounded disappointed that she'd guessed the scenario so easily. "The parrot was outflanked." They looked to the perch where the bedraggled parrot sat almost comatose.

"Where did the owl come from?" asked Max.

"It was Lord Kuy."

"Kuy was here?" Lola looked around fearfully. "What did he want?"

"He wanted the scepter of the Jaguar Kings."

"Not him, too," said Max.

Lord 6-Dog turned sharply. "Explain thyself."

"We just met Baron Saturday, the owner of this hotel. He's a New Orleans version of a Death Lord. It's his job to dig people's graves and escort them to the underworld."

"And he's going to dig our graves tonight," added Lola, "unless we give him your scepter."

"That cannot happen."

"Please, Lord 6-Dog," begged Lola.

"This guy means business," Max agreed.

Lord 6-Dog shook his head. "It is impossible."

"It's all right for you," Max exploded. "You've been dead already. Don't you care about us? Is a stupid old bone more important than our lives?"

"No," said Lord 6-Dog, "it is not. But I cannot give thee the scepter because Kuy has already taken it."

"No!" Max groaned and fell back on the sofa.

Lola sat down heavily next to him and buried her head in her hands.

"There is trouble in the air in Xibalba," said Lord 6-Dog. "The Jaguar Kings told me all about it. Apparently, there are mutinies brewing over who controls the Jaguar Stones. Tzelek was planning his own rebellion and had the idea to steal the scepter. It was his zombies who fired at us from the coast guard boat and sent us to the cave to find the scepter for him. But then the Death Lords got wind of his plan and called on their relative Baron Saturday to grab the scepter for *them*. But it seems that Kuy has beaten them all to it."

Lola looked up. "Who's Kuy working for?"

"Ah Pukuh, I assume," replied Lord 6-Dog. "But he was gone before I could ask him."

"So what happened?" asked Max.

Lord 6-Dog sighed. "I had finally bid farewell to my ancestors and was lying on the sofa to recover my strength. Stupidly, I had left the scepter in the bathroom. The first I knew of its theft was when the parrot alerted me. I flew into action, as did the parrot, but Kuy was too fast for us. Owls are rapacious hunters. He nearly killed that brave bird."

They all regarded the little green parrot asleep on its perch. It had lost more than half its plumage in the fray, and its pink dimpled skin, like raw chicken, shivered in the breeze from the ceiling fan.

"Does he look familiar to you?" asked Lola.

"Never mind the parrot. We have to get out of here," said Max.

"My thoughts exactly," said Lord 6-Dog.

"But how?" said Lola. "The doors and windows are locked. The baron has security everywhere. Could we get a message to Lucky?"

Max shook his head. "He'll be under the Gulf of Mexico,

halfway back to San Xavier. We have to get out of here right now!"

The parrot opened its eyes. "Cahokia!" it said.

"Did anyone else hear that?" asked Max.

Lola and Lord 6-Dog were staring at the parrot.

"That mangy coat," said Lola. "Those bald patches. It's Thunderclaw! I know it is!"

"Don't crack up on me," said Max. "I know how much you loved that chicken. But you saw Thunderclaw plummet into Xibalba with Chan Kan."

Lord 6-Dog backed away. "Thunderclaw? The Chee Ken of Death? The mighty Fowl of Fear? The bird that bestrides the halls of Xibalba with claws like obsidian razors?"

"We made that up," confessed Max. "It was the night you and Lady Coco became howler monkeys. You needed bodies, and you were giving us a hard time, so we said that stuff about Thunderclaw to frighten you. I'm sorry."

"Thou hast no need to apologize, young lord. It was no deception. This bird is a brave and noble warrior. He fought beak and claw tonight, and I am honored to have fought alongside him. He is truly the embodiment of the mighty Thunderclaw."

"I'd recognize him anywhere," agreed Lola.

Max looked like his head might explode with frustration. "Please don't waste our last minutes on earth by talking about a stupid bird who—" He was cut off by an unearthly shriek a sounded like a demented banshee. He had heard that racket before. And it came from the little yellow beak of the parrot. His mouth dropped open. "It *is* Thunderclaw."

Lord 6-Dog clapped his hands. "If I can reappear as a howler monkey, why should not the Chee Ken reappear as a parrot?"

Lola tickled the parrot under his chin, and he rippled what was left of his tattered feathers with pleasure. "Did Chan Kan send you?" she asked him.

"Cahokia," he repeated, nodding his head.

"I knew it!" Lola kissed the parrot's bald little head. "Chan Kan is trying to help us. I told you he was a good guy, Hoop!"

"I wish he'd sent us a helicopter instead of a parrot." Max looked at the bird. "Can you get us out of here?" When he nodded again, Max almost kissed him, too. "Show me."

The parrot flew to the top of a large armoire.

"Cahokia!" he said.

"That's not Cahokia, it's a cupboard," said Max.

"Give him a chance." Lola threw open the doors of the armoire. It had drawers down one side and shelves down the other, with a hanging space in between. "Maybe it leads to Cahokia like that wardrobe in those Narnia books my dad told me about."

"I hate to break this to you," said Max, "but they're fiction."

Still, he stood next to Lola and inspected the inside of the armoire. It was empty except for a few old coat hangers and a spider weaving a web in one corner.

Thunderclaw landed on Lola's shoulder. He seemed to be scrutinizing the inside of the armoire as well. With a squawk, he flew inside and began pecking at the base.

"Must be spilled birdseed," said Max in disappointment. "We haven't got time for this."

"Wait!" said Lola.

"I believe the fowl has found something." Lord 6-Dog peered into the armoire. "There's an indentation." He felt around with his monkey fingers, and a small square of wood sprang open, revealing a secret box built into the base. He pulled out an old-fashioned key. "Is this what you were looking for?" he asked Thunderclaw.

The parrot took the key in his beak and flew across to the balcony doors.

"Got it," said Lola. As quietly as she could, she unlocked the doors, opened the shutters, and edged outside. "All quiet out here," she whispered to Max and Lord 6-Dog. The three stood on the balcony contemplating the distance between them and the street beyond the inn.

They heard church bells strike twelve.

Someone banged from the hallway. "*Ouvrez la porte!* Open zee door!" came Louis's voice.

Thunderclaw flew into the big old oak tree and sat there looking at the group expectantly.

"He wants us to follow him," said Lola.

Max was sweating with fear. "We're too high, it's too far, I can't do it."

There was more pounding on the door. It would fly open any moment.

"I will catch thee." Lord 6-Dog took a flying leap off the balcony railing and landed on the nearest branch. He gripped it with his tail and held up his arms to Max. "Look into my eyes, and jump."

Funereal music floated up from the first floor of the inn.

Max climbed over and sat on the railing.

Then he stood.

Then he jumped.

He didn't travel as far as he'd hoped. He grabbed a piece of Spanish moss, but it broke under his weight. Quick as a flash, Lord 6-Dog grabbed him in mid plummet and pulled him to the safety of a thicker branch.

"Me next!" Lola did one practice knee bend on the railing, then launched herself at the oak tree. She caught a branch, hung there for a second, then swung herself up like a gymnast.

"Ta-da!" she said.

"Show-off," muttered Max, who was hugging his branch for dear life.

"Focus," commanded Lord 6-Dog. "Make thy way along the branch toward the trunk."

"Uh-oh," said Lola. "We have company."

Max looked down. The tree was surrounded by angry-looking musketeers. They threw down their hats and held their swords in their teeth as they began to scale the trunk.

"Higher! Climb higher!" Lord 6-Dog commanded Max and Lola.

"That's easy for you to say," complained Max. "You're a monkey."

"Do something, Thunderclaw!" begged Lola. "Tell Chan Kan we need help! Tell him we're trapped and we don't have much—"

Thunderclaw let out an almighty shriek.

New Orleans seemed to go quiet.

Then Max heard *clip, clop, clip, clop*, and something large and white loomed out of the dark toward them down the middle of the street. As he stared openmouthed, Max made out rickety wheels and tossing manes.

The parrot flapped his wings excitedly.

"We're saved!" cheered Lola.

"It's not real," said Max. "Look at it. You can see right through it. It's a mirage, or a trick of the light, or something."

Thunderclaw squawked, as if rebuking him.

As the carriage drew closer, the white-clad driver doffed his white top hat at them. The two white horses shook the white plumes in their bridles. The white paintwork of the carriage glistened in the moonlight and the plump white velvet cushions on the four rows of seats shimmered invitingly.

"Cahokia!" squawked the parrot, and flew onto the driver's shoulder, a patch of lime green in the mass of white. The carriage stopped right outside the inn under an overhanging branch.

"Okay," said Lola. "So we get to that branch and we drop."

"But it's a ghost carriage!" protested Max. "We'll fall right through it."

"The parrot found a solid perch," observed Lord 6-Dog.

"Of course he did." Max was losing his temper. "The parrot is a ghost, too! It's the ghost of Thunderclaw. Is there anything in New Orleans that isn't a ghost?"

"Thunderclaw wouldn't trick us!" Lola had reached the overhanging branch and, as Max watched, horrified, she let herself drop. She bounced slightly as she landed on the padded white velvet seat. "It's safe!" she called. "Your turn!"

Lord 6-Dog took Max's hand and, after some intense pulling, prying, and persuading—with the musketeers getting ever closer—together they let go.

Max braced himself for the impact of hard asphalt.

He landed, as Lola had done, in the carriage, although not quite as perfectly placed.

Just as Max and Lord 6-Dog scrambled onto the seat, a troop of musketeers burst out of the inn. They looked up and down the street but appeared not to see the carriage that was almost right in front of them. The musketeers still in the tree looked equally baffled.

"By the beard of Itzamna, we are invisible!" exclaimed Lord 6-Dog.

Lola waved at a guard.

No reaction. He looked straight through her.

The driver flicked his whip and the horse trotted on.

Max relaxed back into his seat. Chan Kan and Thunderclaw had saved them. But how many weeks, he asked himself, would it take to reach Cahokia at this pace?

It was a strange feeling, being invisible.

They rolled through the tourist quarter, still brightly lit and throbbing with music even at this late hour. No one turned to look at the ghostly carriage trotting down the street. If a group of revelers got in their way, they passed right through them unseen and unnoticed.

Soon they pulled up at a large iron gate in an old white-washed wall.

"Do we get out here?" Max wondered aloud, but the driver motioned with his gloved hand to tell them to stay seated.

"It's a cemetery," said Lola, sounding worried.

Thunderclaw turned and looked at her. "Cahokia!" he squawked. Then he made a little cooing noise.

"He says this is the way," she said.

"So now you can talk to parrots as well as howler monkeys?"

"This isn't any parrot. This is my old friend Thunderclaw."

"I don't like it," said Max. "If this was a movie, and the good guys got in a ghostly carriage of their own free will and allowed themselves to be taken to a spooky old cemetery in the middle of the night, you'd say they were asking for trouble."

"Shut your eyes if it helps," suggested Lola.

But Max kept them open, wide open, with fear.

On the other side of the wall, carved marble angels stared back at him. The tombs they guarded were above ground—some big, some medium, some small—all jammed in together, so that they looked like houses, palaces, and apartment blocks in a miniature city: a city of the dead.

With a creak that made Max jump out of his skin, the gate opened and out came a family in old-fashioned clothes: the mother and little daughter in crinoline dresses, the father in a frock coat.

"The spirits walk abroad tonight," observed Lord 6-Dog.

Max sneaked a peek at these new passengers as they climbed into a row of seats at the back. "You mean they're ghosts?" he whispered.

Lola turned and waved at the little girl. The little girl waved back.

"She sees you!" said Max. "That ghost girl sees you! Does that mean we're ghosts, too? Are we dead? Did Baron Saturday win?"

"No," said Lola. "I think Chan Kan sent these ghosts to help us. They seem very friendly. Be nice to them."

Max turned and smiled at the little girl.

She burst out crying.

"What did you do?" asked Lola.

"I'm not good with kids. I think I scared her."

"You frightened a ghost? Way to go, Hoop."

Max shrugged. "It's payback for all the times ghosts have scared humans."

"What should scare thee," said Lord 6-Dog, "is the fact of riding through a city of shadows in a phantom carriage with no clue where these specters are taking us—or why."

CHAPTER THIRTEEN
THE *PHANTOM QUEEN*

"**W**here are we going?" Max wailed as the ghostly carriage clopped on through the night.

"Our destination is our destiny," observed Lord 6-Dog unhelpfully. "And vice versa."

They stopped at two more cemeteries, each time taking on more passengers.

"I didn't know ghosts traveled so much," Max whispered to Lola. "I thought they just hung around in one place and haunted it."

"I think the rules are different in New Orleans," she replied. "It reminds me of my country. Everything is mysterious. Everything has a story."

"In Boston," muttered Max, "the only thing that's mysterious is why the Red Sox lose so much."

"The Red Sox? Like on your cap?"

"Yeah. They're the greatest team in the history of baseball."

"But you just said they lose a lot."

"It's complicated." Max searched for the words to explain his feelings. "With the Red Sox, it's not about winning. It's about believing."

"You don't want to win?"

"Of course we do. But there's more to it than that."

"More? Like what?"

Max shrugged. "You know. Traditions. Legends. Stories."

"Now you're sounding Maya. Tell me one of your stories."

"Well, every Boston kid knows about Babe Ruth and the Curse of the Bambino."

"A curse? That sounds exciting."

"It wasn't. They sold a player named Babe Ruth to the New York Yankees, their big rivals, and didn't win the World Series again for eighty-six years."

"Wow. And their fans stuck with them?"

"Of course. It was a tough time, but the Red Sox are heroes in Boston."

"Lola smiled. "So the Maya have the Hero Twins. And you have your Red Sox."

"I guess. You should come to a game with me. See them for yourself."

"I'll add it to my road trip list!"

They turned into another cemetery. Instead of little houses, this one had orderly rows of gravestones.

A soldier in a Civil War uniform was waiting for them. He took a seat and they headed through a gap in an old stone wall into the adjoining field.

Here, cannons lined their route.

They passed a visitor center all in darkness.

"It's a battlefield," whispered Max, reading the sign.

Lord 6-Dog looked around with interest. "I should like to know more about this place."

But the carriage rolled on toward a stately two-story brick house. It had tall white pillars at the front and back, with a balcony running the length of the second floor.

"Is this another inn?" asked Lola. "Can you see any signs?"

The other passengers were alighting and walking toward a grassy slope behind the house.

"Cahokia!" said Thunderclaw, flapping his wings again.

"You mean Cahokia is over that hill?" Lola asked the bird.

"There is but one way to find out. You two stay here." Lord 6-Dog leapt out of the carriage, bounded up the slope, and disappeared from sight.

"Sometimes," said Max, "his bravery surprises me."

"Maya kings led from the front," Lola explained.

Max thought about her statement. "They must have gotten killed a lot."

They both scanned the hilltop anxiously.

After what felt like forever, Lord 6-Dog appeared on top of the hill. He bounded back down the slope to them. His face looked grim.

"Bad news," he said.

"What did you see?" asked Lola warily.

"A great river."

"The Mississippi?"

"I know not its name. But there is no way forward except by water. The carriage passengers are boarding boats."

"Boats? That's what we need! Why is that bad news?" Lola asked.

"I am not a sailor. I am still sick to my stomach from thy submarine."

"You'll be fine," Lola reassured him. "It can't be far to St. Louis."

"How far?" persisted Lord 6-Dog.

"I don't know exactly," admitted Lola. "But you're a howler monkey. You're really good at sleeping. Just pretend the motion of the boat is a breeze blowing through your tree in the jungle. We'll wake you up when we get there."

"What motion?" Lord 6-Dog looked like he might vomit on the spot.

The night air was pierced by the mournful blast of a steam whistle.

"Let's go!" Lola began to run up the slope, then she stopped and looked back. "Are you coming, Thunderclaw?" she called.

The parrot landed on her shoulder, brushed his mangy feathers against her cheek, and took off again. "Cahokia!" he squawked as he wheeled in circles over her head. Then he flew back to the carriage and everything—the vehicle, the horses, the driver, the bird—evaporated like a morning mist.

"Good-bye!" Lola shouted after him. "Please thank Chan Kan for me!"

Behind them, the sun was beginning to rise.

In front of them, toward the river, the sky remained stubbornly dark.

They scrambled up the hill and stopped at the top. The hill, which was actually a man-made flood defense, sloped down sharply, ending in a mossy, slimy swamp. On the far side of the swamp was the mighty Mississippi. And stretching across the swamp, from the top of the hill to the water, was a modern metal dock where the ghostly passengers were now lined up to board a variety of ghostly river craft.

Max, Lola, and, reluctantly, Lord 6-Dog joined the line.

"St. Louis?" called Lola. "Are any of these boats going to St. Louis?"

The ghosts ignored her.

Down in the swamp, frogs croaked, cicadas buzzed, and swarms of mosquitoes zoomed in to attack. Max could see red eyes peering through the night.

"Crocodiles," said Lord 6-Dog.

"Alligators," said Max. "You don't get crocodiles this far north."

"As a mere Central American primate, I beg thy forgiveness for my ignorance. It looks like a crocodile to me."

"I read it in the guidebook on the sub," said Max. "Alligators have wider snouts."

"Remind me, when the beasts attack, to measure the girth of their snouts."

"Please stop squabbling and help me find a boat," said Lola.

"If I never see another boat, it will be too soon," muttered Lord 6-Dog.

A mist, green as the algae in the swamp, rose off the river.

Another blast of a steam whistle. This time it sounded much closer.

They were alone on the dock now.

Out of the mist, glowing pale green, emerged a Mississippi steamboat. No smoke came from its twin smokestacks, and the great paddlewheel turning in its stern made no waves in the water. As it pulled alongside the dock, they saw its name: *Phantom Queen*.

It looked old.

Historic, even.

Out of the mist, glowing pale green, emerged a Mississippi steamboat.

It had three decks. The lower one housed the engine room (great pistons were visible through the windows), while the upper two (which had picturesque verandas running all around) seemed to be for passengers.

But the vessel was deserted. There was no sign of a crew, no pilot in the wheelhouse, no captain barking orders through a megaphone.

As they watched, the boat docked and a front gangplank lowered itself silently down.

"Here we go," said Lola.

Max surveyed the shimmering ghost ship dubiously. "Are we sure about this?"

"Is there not another way?" agreed Lord 6-Dog.

"Come on, you two! What's the matter? Thunderclaw wouldn't trick us."

"But how do you know this is the right boat?"

Lola pointed at a small chalkboard on an easel. "It says so right there."

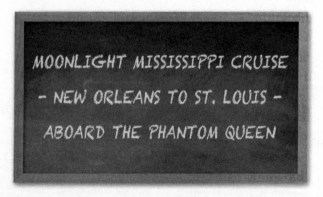

MOONLIGHT MISSISSIPPI CRUISE
– NEW ORLEANS TO ST. LOUIS –
ABOARD THE PHANTOM QUEEN

She marched across the gangplank and onto the boat. The other two followed her less confidently, but there was no time for second thoughts. The moment their feet touched the deck, the gangplank was raised and the *Phantom Queen* began to pick up speed.

Lord 6-Dog groaned. "I must find a bed."

"Let's explore," suggested Lola.

"I can't believe you're okay with this," said Max.

"We're headed to Cahokia, aren't we?" she called to him as she ran up the stairs to the upper decks. "We might as well enjoy ourselves. I've never been on a cruise before."

"Wait!" shouted Max. "We should stick together!"

"Why?"

"Haven't you ever seen a scary movie? They always split up and get picked off, one by one."

"Come on, then! I want to look around."

It was as if the boat had been abandoned in a hurry a hundred years before. There were old-fashioned clothes hanging in the cabins. Books moldered in the library. Sheet music lay open on a piano. The tables in the dining saloon were grandly laid with three settings of silverware for every place. Only the diners were missing.

"Do you think there's any food?" asked Max.

"There's no one to cook it," Lola pointed out.

Lord 6-Dog leaned against an open window. He didn't look good. "How canst thou even think about food?"

"You *can't* be seasick. This thing is like a hovercraft. We're just gliding over the surface." Max pointed to the river. "Look, no waves. It doesn't even feel like we're moving. It's the smoothest ride ever." But one look at Lord 6-Dog's face told Max that the mere idea of water transport was enough to make him feel ill.

"Let's find him somewhere to sleep," said Lola. "Those cabins are too musty."

At the bow of the ship, out on the veranda, they found some reclining wooden steamer chairs. They tucked Lord 6-Dog up and sat down next to him.

"We're moving fast," said Lola. "It's all a blur out there."

Max tried to make out the banks of the river, but they were engulfed in swirling mists and darkness. A strange orange glow, like the promise of sunrise, tinged the edges of the sky.

"It's been a long night," he said. "Shouldn't it be getting light?"

"I think it's a ghost ship thing," said Lola. "It's always midnight on this boat."

"Great," said Max sarcastically.

"Relax," she told him. "Try to get some sleep."

But neither of them shut their eyes.

Sometimes strange objects rushed past in the water: oak barrels, refrigerators, a department store mannequin, a dead pig.

Other times, music drifted over from the shore. "Memphis," guessed Max, when they caught a soulful snatch of blues.

"Memphis? As in Elvis Presley?" Lola jumped up and tried to see the shore. "His house, Graceland, was on my list!"

"Your road trip list?" Max squished a mosquito. "What else was on it?"

"The Statue of Liberty, Mount Rushmore, San Francisco, Hollywood, the Grand Canyon, Niagara Falls . . . I want to see everything!"

"That's going to be quite a road trip."

"If I ever get my parents back."

"We're on our way to Cahokia, aren't we? Your parents are as good as rescued."

"I don't know, Hoop. The more I think about it, the more I worry about what might be waiting for us at Cahokia."

"Then stop thinking about it. There's nothing we can do till we get there."

Lola sighed. "You're right. I think I'll go look in the library. Find a book to take my mind off things."

"Good idea. I'll see if there's any food on this boat."

And so, forgetting his own advice about the inadvisability of splitting up, Max went one way on the ghost ship and Lola went another.

When he first heard the scream, Max was poking around in the galley, looking for something edible. He dropped the rusty tin of cherries he'd just found and ran out to the deck. "Lola! Monkey Girl! Are you all right?"

Lola screamed his name again and he headed in the direction of her voice. "Where are you?" he yelled. "What's happened?"

As he turned a corner into the saloon, Lola barreled straight into him, giving them both the fright of their lives. (Well, maybe not quite the fright they'd gotten in the Grand Hotel Xibalba when they'd suddenly lost their superpowers in the middle of a turbocharged ball game against the Death Lords—but a really *big* fright nonetheless.)

Max was relieved and angry at the same time. "Why were you screaming like that?"

"Look at this!" Lola thrust an old photograph album at him. Her hands were shaking.

"Calm down." Max brushed a half-finished card game off a tabletop and pulled out two chairs. "Here, sit. Show me."

"It's them!" cried Lola, flicking through the pages of the album. "Look at the faces!"

She showed him a sepia photograph of a mountainside.

"That's Mount Rushmore," he explained. "They're presidents."

"Look closer."

Max did. And he saw that, carved into the rock were the heads of four Death Lords—the Demons of Pus, Jaundice, Filth, and Woe.

Lola turned the page and showed him a green-faced, diadem-wearing One Death grinning for the camera as he held aloft his torch on Liberty Island.

Next came various Death Lords larking around at the edge of the Grand Canyon, taking selfies in front of the Hollywood sign, looking tough at

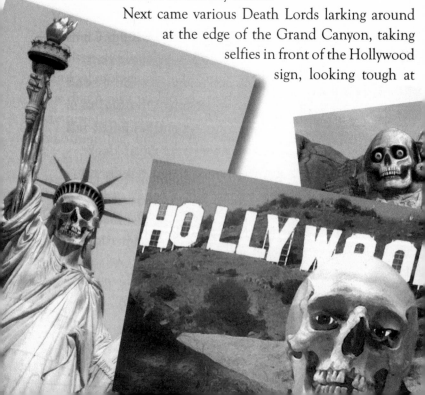

the Alamo, waving from a cable car in San Francisco, wearing rain ponchos on a boat at the foot of Niagara Falls.

The final photograph was of Ah Pukuh, bulging out of an Elvis Presley jumpsuit, as he posed with a guitar in front of a fur-clad sofa.

"My dad described that place to me," said Lola. "It's the Jungle Room at Graceland." Her voice cracked. "I told you, it was on our list."

Max tried to console her. "Don't cry. You'll get there soon, you'll see."

"I'm not crying," said Lola indignantly. "I'm angry. The Death Lords are taunting me, don't you see? *All* these places were on my list. I don't know how this album got on this boat, but it's proof that the Death Lords are playing with us. They're laughing at us, Hoop."

"Not necessarily," reasoned Max. "Maybe they're trying to encourage us, remind us of the good times ahead when all this is over." He looked more closely at Ah Pukuh's bloated, pockmarked face under its ludicrous black quiff. His pudgy lips were curled in a sneer. It didn't look encouraging. But was it directed

at them? Or was it just an Elvis impression?

"Do you think we're nearly there?" asked Lola wearily.

Max peered into the gloom. "Who knows? I can't see anything."

Lola sighed. "I'm so tired. I can't think straight."

"It's been a long day," agreed Max. "Or night. Or week. Or however long we've been on this boat. I've lost track of time. I just want to see the sun again."

"We should sleep," suggested Lola.

Max shook his head. "Sleep on a ghost ship? Are you crazy?"

But he did.

And so did Lola.

What woke them was the sound of the ship's whistle.

Lola groaned. "I think we've arrived."

Max opened his eyes. He turned to Lord 6-Dog and saw that he was gone.

Beyond his empty chair, looming out of gray mist on the opposite bank, was a huge stainless steel arch. "St. Louis! We're in St. Louis! This is it!"

Somewhere in the distance, a howler monkey roared.

"That's Lord 6-Dog!" Lola put her hands to her mouth and roared back into the darkness.

A reply came almost instantly.

"He's up there!" she cried. Max looked where she pointed and saw a little figure in striped pajamas, silhouetted against the glow of streetlights, sitting on top of an electricity pylon on the bank.

The riverboat had let its gangplank down against a rusty barge. Max and Lola walked across the barge to dry land, where Lord 6-Dog was running to meet them.

"I saw it! I saw Cahokia! It is a great city!"

"How far is it?" asked Max.

Lord 6-Dog stroked his hairy chin. "I would estimate leagues due east."

"How far is a league?"

"About three miles," volunteered Lola sleepily.

"So nine miles? That's a long walk," protested Max.

"It is a wonder to me," said Lord 6-Dog, "that thy legs d not atrophy from lack of use."

Behind them, the gangplank lifted and the *Phantom Queen* melted into the dark, rippling water.

"You know when Cortez burned his boats?" said Lola.

"No," said Max.

"He did it when he landed in Central America. So his crew couldn't mutiny and sail back home. He burned their boats on the beach, so they had no choice but to go forward, no matter what terrors awaited them. That's exactly how I feel right now."

"Good to know," said Max, his stomach lurching with fear.

CHAPTER FOURTEEN

BLUE AND THE BIRDMAN

They walked along the grassy, litter-strewn bank, crossed some train tracks, and found themselves on a potholed road.

"Which way now?" asked Max.

"Due east," said Lola. "Toward the sunrise."

"That's not helpful," Max pointed out. "The sun hasn't come up yet. East could be anywhere. We should ask someone."

"No need. We can read the signs."

"We're not in the jungle anymore," Max pointed out. "I know you're good at tracking in the wild, but this is the city. We need a map."

"Why?" asked Lola. "You can read the signs, too."

She pointed at a group of illuminated billboards at the junction with the main road.

THIS WAY TO OLD CAHOKIA
AND THE FESTIVAL OF THE SUN

YOU'LL HAVE MOUNDS OF FUN
AT OLD CAHOKIA!

OLD CAHOKIA
COME AND AD-MAYA IT!

Now that Max looked properly, he saw signs everywhere, all of them pointing to Cahokia—or Old Cahokia, as it seemed to be called now.

"'Come and *ad-Maya* it'?" Lola made a face. "Who writes this stuff?"

Lord 6-Dog growled. He was staring angrily at a billboard that showed five smug-looking kids each holding a Jaguar Stone. The headline proclaimed:

HOLD HISTORY IN YOUR HANDS
AT OLD CAHOKIA

"How dare they?" cried Lord 6-Dog. "The Jaguar Stones are the stones of kings, not the playthings of commoners. Those children are not even Maya."

Max looked at the endless line of billboards stretching to the horizon. "It's going to be a long walk," he said.

A car horn honked behind him.

He turned to see a camper van with a big peace symbol

painted on the side. "Need a lift?" asked the driver, a smiley-faced boy with dreadlocks.

"Are you going to Cahokia?" asked Max.

"Where else, man?"

Max and Lola nodded gratefully.

"No talking allowed," Lola cautioned Lord 6-Dog in a whisper.

"Cute pajamas, dude!" yelled a voice from the van.

"Is biting allowed?" muttered Lord 6-Dog.

The door of the camper slid open and Max, Lola, and Lord 6-Dog found seats inside.

"Thank you very much," said Lola to the driver. "Why are you going to Cahokia?"

"Same reason as everyone else: to catch the vibe." He held out his hand over the seat. "I'm Blue Sky, by the way. You can call me Blue. And these are my friends, Phoenix and Rainbow." Phoenix sat in the passenger seat, with a small drum on his lap, which he tapped from time to time. Rainbow

sat behind Blue, braiding yellow flowers into her hair.

"Nice to meet you all," said Lola politely. "My name is Lola Murphy and this is my cousin, Max."

"Hi," said Max, without enthusiasm.

Lord 6-Dog looked at Lola expectantly, waiting to be introduced.

"And this," she said, "is, um . . . er . . . Dog."

"Dog?" queried Rainbow.

"As in *The Dawg*," explained Max. "Because he's cool."

Rainbow slowly took in the hairy face, the pajamas, the tail. "The Dawg is, like, a monkey," she said at last.

"A howler monkey," agreed Lola.

"Is he, like, tame?" asked Phoenix.

Lord 6-Dog bared his teeth.

"He doesn't like the word *tame*. He prefers, um, *civilized*."

"He, like, understands what you say?" Rainbow was entranced.

"He's very intelligent."

"Wow! Did you, like, train him?" Rainbow asked. "Is he, like, your pet?"

"He's . . . um . . . more of a companion. He comes everywhere with us."

"I really, like, dig him." She giggled. "I dig The Dawg."

Lola patted Lord 6-Dog to remind him to keep calm. "So, tell us about Cahokia," she said to change the subject. "How many people are there right now?

"Last I heard there were, like, twenty thousand," said Phoenix.

"That's as many people as lived in Cahokia when it was built," added Blue.

"Blue's, like, our history buff," said Rainbow.

Max wondered what Blue the history buff would say if he knew he had a real-life Maya king in his van.

As Lola chatted to their hosts about Cahokia, Max leaned his face against the window.

It felt good to be traveling in something that wasn't powered by ghostly vapors.

He looked down the road, but all he saw were red taillights and the glitter of glass and metal from a line of cars stretching to the horizon. With every junction, more and more vehicles joined the predawn traffic jam. There were walkers, too, and cyclists and motorcyclists.

All of them had a festive air that Max had never before associated with visiting an archaeological site. (And his parents had dragged him to many.) People held hands or linked arms as they walked, car passengers waved, everyone smiled at everyone else. Sellers of jewelry, hats, and bottled water lined the route under battery-powered lights. Food trucks clattered up their shutters and opened for business. Max was tempted to ask if they could stop for a quick bite, but he knew Lola wouldn't approve.

He forgot all thoughts of food as he saw the flashing lights of police cars ahead. Had New Orleans put out a warrant for their arrest? He and Lola had, after all, skipped town without paying their hotel bill.

He felt for the door handle, ready to make a fast getaway.

An officer in a high-visibility jacket waved them to a stop.

"Parking lots for Cahokia are full," he barked at Blue. "Follow the signs for overflow parking."

Blue turned back to Max and Lola. "We'll let you out here, guys. See you at the sunrise ceremony!"

Max, Lola, and Lord 6-Dog clambered out of the van and looked around for the entrance.

"Which way?" asked Max.

"Follow the crowd," said Lola.

The throng carried them through a set of park gates where attendants were handing out maps. "Don't get lost in the lost city," they chanted robotically.

Once inside, Max found himself in a vast open campground teeming with people.

"Whoa!" exclaimed Lola. "When Phoenix said twenty thousand people, I thought he was exaggerating. But this . . . it's incredible."

Max tried to study his map without getting jostled by the endless stream of people. He looked around for higher ground. "Let's climb up that hill," he suggested, "so we can see the whole site."

"It's not a hill, it's a mound," Lola corrected him.

"Whatever," said Max.

The view from the top was spectacular.

"Is this a burial mound?" asked Lord 6-Dog.

"I'm not sure," said Lola. "Blue said they found bodies in some of them. Evidence of human sacrifice, too."

Lord 6-Dog lay down on his back and stared up at the fading stars.

"What are you doing?" asked Max.

"I'm communing with the mound."

"Why?"

"It gives me a sense of who lived here if I see the night sky through their eyes."

Lola threw out her arms and spun around. "It's awesome up here. I love this place!"

"You said you loved New Orleans until they tried to dig our graves," Max pointed out.

Lola ignored him. "To be standing here, on this ancient site, and the lights of St. Louis just across the river! Why didn't you tell me there were places like this in North America, Hoop?"

"I had no idea," said Max.

He looked down at Old Cahokia, trying to take it all in.

The huge park was split by a highway, which had been closed off for the festival. On one side, beyond some low mounds, a large area of flat, grassy parkland housed a makeshift city of RVs, buses, caravans, tents, yurts, teepees, geodesic domes, art installations, campfires, market stalls, food vendors, and people. There were people everywhere—dancing, sleeping, doing yoga, rocking babies, painting each other's faces by lantern light.

On the other side of the road rose an enormous earthen pyramid. It was too dark to make out the details, but there seemed to be steps up the front and a tall structure on the very top. The pyramid was blocked off from the rest of the site by barriers and security lights and NO ACCESS signs and guards mumbling into walkie-talkies.

Lola was reading the notes on the back of the map. "That's one of the biggest pyramids in the whole of North and South America! Why isn't it famous?"

Max tried to look interested, but he was actually more curious to know where the smell of fried onions was coming from.

"And look," said Lola, pointing beyond the pyramid to where a group of people danced inside a circle of tall wooden poles. "That's a prehistoric sundial. They call it Woodhenge."

Lord 6-Dog sat up and looked around. "Those pennants," he said to Lola, pointing at the yellow flags that marked the pathways throughout the site. "They have a figure on them. Who is it? Dost thou know?"

"It's the Birdman of Cahokia. Weren't you listening to Blue?" Lola chided him.

"I was fully occupied in trying not to bite him," said Lord 6-Dog.

"He told us the story. The guy on the flags was a king, like you. They found him buried in a mound like this one, with hundreds of seashells arranged around him in the shape of a bird."

Lord 6-Dog looked relieved. "I had thought it was Lord Kuy."

Max's attention had been caught by a different feature of the site. "The food stands are opening down there," he observed. "Let's get some breakfast before the show."

"Good idea," agreed Lola. She pointed to a little dread-locked figure at the bottom of the mound. "Look! There's Blue!"

They ran down to meet him.

"Hi, guys," he said. "We found a parking spot right away. Good karma for giving you a lift, I guess."

"Thanks again for that," said Lola.

"No problem. It's not every day you get to meet a real, live howler monkey." Blue reached out to Lord 6-Dog. "You said he's tame, right?"

"I wouldn't—" began Lola.

Too late, Blue tried to pat Lord 6-Dog on the head.

"Keep thy peasant hands to thyself!" spat Lord 6-Dog before leaping into the nearest tree.

Blue stepped back, his eyes wide in amazement. "Did you hear that?"

"What?" Lola and Max tried to look innocent.

"The Dawg! He spoke to me!"

"I don't think so," said Lola gently. "Monkeys can't talk."

Blue stared at her for a moment. Then a look of understanding spread across his face. "You're right," he said in hushed tones. "Monkeys *can't* talk. The Dawg must have communicated with me, mind to mind, on a different plane."

"I don't think—" began Lola, but Blue was on a roll.

"I heard his voice in my head. It's like he's a spiritual being and he chose *me* to convey his message." Blue's blue eyes shone with excitement. "Wait till I tell Phoenix and Rainbow! This is huge! I have to go—but I'll see you at the Sunrise Ceremony!"

"What is the Sunrise Ceremony exactly?"

"That's the big deal here. Sunrise and Sunset at the great pyramid. Let's hang out in between!"

"Wait, don't tell—" called Lola, but he was gone. They watched Blue's dreadlocks bobbing behind him as he ran across the grounds looking for his friends.

"Great," said Lola glumly. "Now he's going to tell everyone that Lord 6-Dog is some kind of monkey god."

"To be fair," said Max, "the monkey did talk to him."

"It's a disaster," said Lola. "The last thing we need is word getting out about a telepathic monkey."

"Maybe no one will believe him."

"Don't get your hopes up. They seem to be a gullible crowd."

"Well, nothing we can do about it now. Let's get breakfast."

"Too late, Hoop. Everyone's headed to the Sunrise Ceremony." She cupped her hands around her mouth and grunted loudly.

"Talk about not drawing attention to ourselves. What was that about?"

"I was telling Lord 6-Dog to stay hidden. I don't think he has the temperament for this place. He's better off staying in the trees."

"You said all that in a few grunts?"

"I'll teach you to speak howler one day, if you want."

"Will it count as my high school language requirement?"

"Definitely," said Lola.

They found a place far enough away from the great pyramid to be able to see to the top.

"I can't believe the size of that thing," said Max. "The base is huge. What do you think? Three football fields? Four?"

"If by *football* you mean American football, I haven't got a clue." Lola consulted the notes on the back of her map again. "It says here that it's as big as the Great Pyramid of Giza in Egypt. So how big is that?"

"Who knows?" Max shook his head in wonder. "I can't believe that we didn't study this place in school. I had no idea that Native Americans built cities."

"Maybe because it doesn't fit the story," said Lola.

"What story?"

"That before the Europeans arrived, the natives were uncivilized savages. It makes it easier to justify wiping them out. It was the same with the Maya and the Spanish conquest."

Max shuffled his feet. "I'm sorry."

"It's not your fault." Lola shrugged. "The conquerors get to rewrite history. That's how it's always been."

People all around them had fallen to their knees.

"We are ready," they chanted. "We are ready."

"What are you ready for?" Lola asked a friendly looking girl in a knitted poncho.

"We are ready to go home."

"Already? Have we missed the ceremony?"

"We are ready to go home to the stars."

"You have a home in the stars?"

"We all do. Great Sun has told us so."

"The sun speaks to you?"

"You must be new here," said the girl, smiling. "Great Sun is the king of Old Cahokia."

As the sky began to lighten, a sense of expectation built in the park. Some people knelt while others swayed and held their hands in the air. As the first rays of the sunrise bounced off the pyramid, the people whooped with joy.

Now Max saw the shape of the pyramid clearly. There were steps up the front and a terrace halfway up. On the top platform was a smaller pyramid made out of stretched canvas over metal scaffolding. It was open at the front like a stage at a rock concert and stacked with banks of speakers and video screens. Above it all soared a modern sculpture, a figure made out of wood and metal cable, with massive canvas wings. As the highest point for miles around, the sculpture seemed to attract and channel solar energy, reflecting it back onto the onlookers so that their faces glowed pink in the sunrise.

"That sculpture is amazing," Lola said to the girl in the poncho.

"It's the Birdman. He symbolizes our connection between the earth and the heavens. You know he was an old king of Cahokia, right?"

Lola nodded.

"And you know he was buried on a bed of seashells shaped like a bird?"

Lola nodded again.

"But do you know why?"

She shook her head.

"He was a space traveler! An extraterrestrial!"

Lola gaped at her.

"I know, right!" The girl hugged herself. "The shells are the ocean and the bird is the air and we are the earth. Great Sun says that one day soon the Birdman will come back for us. He says the Maya predicted it."

Lola looked confused. "The Maya? What have the Maya got to do with it?"

The girl took Lola's hand. "Pyramids. We're connected by them. You, me, everyone. We all came from another world and, wherever we landed, our masters built pyramids."

"You're saying that aliens built all the pyramids?"

The girl nodded, her eyes shining. "Cahokia, Central America, Egypt . . . They built pyramids all over the world."

"I'm sorry," said Lola, "but that's not right. I know for sure that the Maya built the Maya pyramids."

The girl snickered. "Yeah, right! Like a bunch of savages could build those amazing pyramids! They're astronomically correct, you know."

Lola looked like she might explode with anger.

Max stepped in to give her time to calm down. "That's interesting," he said to the girl. "We came here to find out about Great Sun. What else can you tell us?"

"You should look on the Internet," she said. "There are whole Web sites about this stuff."

"Wow." Max pretended to be impressed. "It must be true, then!"

"No, I'm sorry," Lola burst out. "I can't listen to this. My ancestors built those pyramids with brains and brute strength.

194

How dare you give the credit to some spacemen?"

"You're Maya?" The girl looked surprised. "I thought the Maya had all vanished in spaceships already."

"No," said Lola. "There are still quite a few of us actually."

"That's great," said the girl unenthusiastically. "You should do a workshop while you're here. You could learn a lot."

Lola made a noise like a teakettle coming to a boil.

Max pulled her away. "You're as bad as Lord 6-Dog. You have to hide your emotions or we'll never learn anything."

"But it's so insulting. How can she believe everything she reads on the Internet? Her logic defeats me."

"Nothing defeats you, Monkey Girl."

Lola groaned. "What's happened to me? We've swapped roles. You're supposed to be the hothead and I'm supposed to be the sensible one."

"You're always so touchy about Maya stuff. It's your Achilles' heel."

"Wrong mythology."

"Yeah, well." He looked toward the stage. "Now what's happening?"

As the audience shielded their eyes from the dazzling sunrise, there was a fanfare of conch shell trumpets and Great Sun made his entrance.

He was carried in on a litter held by four men in jaguar-patterned Lycra loincloths. Great Sun was dressed as a Maya king. His features were obscured by his black-and-white face paint and the shadow cast by his magnificent black-and-white-feathered headdress.

"It's Tzelek," gasped Max.

CHAPTER FIFTEEN
THE CHILDREN OF THE STARS

"What do you mean, Great Sun is Tzelek?" hissed Lola.

"That's exactly what he looked like the night the monsters came. We need to get out of here. I'm not fighting Tzelek, not for anyone. We don't stand a chance."

"I don't think it's him," said Lola.

"I'm telling you, it *is* him."

"Even if it is, he can't see us in this crowd. Let's hear what he has to say."

Max pulled his baseball cap lower over his face.

The crowd fell silent as Great Sun raised his arms.

Giant video screens flickered into life all over the site so that everyone could see.

Great Sun boomed a greeting in Mayan.

"What's he saying?" asked Max. "Do you understand him?"

"No, it doesn't even sound like Mayan to me. But there are nearly thirty Mayan languages. Maybe it's one I've never heard."

A woman in traditional Maya dress stepped forward to translate, and Great Sun's microphone was shut off. They could see his lips moving on the video screen but, sound-wise, the interpreter forged on alone.

"Hail to the sunrise," intoned the translator. "Hail to the Jaguar Sun as he starts his journey across the sky. May we take this new day to prepare for our own journey across the sky. In the first rays of the rising sun, let us signal to the Birdman with the sacred stones to tell him that we're ready to go home."

There was another blast of conch shell trumpets and a rough-hewn Maya stone altar rose slowly through a trapdoor behind Great Sun. Lola nudged Max. It wasn't the altar, but what was on it, that excited her. For there, shining in the early morning light, were five carved jaguar heads.

One white as alabaster.

One red as Mexican fire opal.

One green as jadeite.

One yellow as amber.

One black as obsidian.

The crowd went crazy.

Great Sun picked up the red stone and held it up to the morning sun until the carved jaguar blazed as red as fire, and Max saw the world through a filter of red. "Behold the Red Jaguar of Chahk, stone of the east, stone of the rising sun," said the interpreter.

The same process was repeated for each Jaguar Stone.

"Behold the White Jaguar of Ixchel, stone of the north, stone of the moon and the stars."

"Behold the Green Jaguar of Itzamna, stone of the center, stone of rebirth."

"Behold the Black Jaguar of Ah Pukuh, stone of the west, stone of the setting sun."

"Behold the Yellow Jaguar of K'awiil, stone of the south, stone of the past and the future."

Each time, the crowd was bathed in the appropriately colored light. Now, as Great Sun put the last stone back on the altar, stage lights like lasers beamed their colors across the adoring crowd, whipping them into a frenzy.

"Apart from the compass points, this is all wrong," complained Lola. "Tzelek wouldn't say those things. It's not him."

"May the stones set us free!" intoned the interpreter. "Hail to the Jaguar Stones!"

A troupe of twirling dancers took the stage, wearing various Lycra interpretations of Maya dress. At a signal from the woman, they joined hands and danced in a circle as the trapdoors opened and the altar bearing the Jaguar Stones sank back into the depths of the pyramid.

Great Sun mumbled an incantation.

"It is time to set your spirits free," continued the interpreter. "Let your spirits fly. Are you ready?"

"We are ready," chanted the crowd.

"Are you ready?" asked the interpreter again.

The crowd, once again, declared their readiness.

Great Sun looked skeptical.

"Some are still not ready," lamented the interpreter.

"Teach them!" called a voice.

"Those who seek enlightenment must first enlighten themselves. Those who would be children of the stars must free themselves from their earthly possessions."

Tears streamed down the face of the girl in the poncho as Great Sun bowed to the audience and made a blessing in his peculiar Mayan.

"From sunrise to sunset, may your joy be infinite," said the interpreter. "May wild honey drip into your mouths."

To tumultuous applause, Great Sun was carried offstage on his litter.

"I don't get it," said Max. "When I saw Tzelek a few days ago, he was his usual homicidal self. Why has he suddenly gone into show business?"

"It's not him," replied Lola. "It can't be."

"But he's wearing the identical clothes that he wore at the Villa Isabella."

"It *is* a great Maya king costume," conceded Lola. "It's exactly how I imagine the real thing."

"And those Jaguar Stones looked pretty real, too," Max pointed out.

Now a man's prerecorded voice boomed over the site. "If you wish to shed that which weighs you down . . . cash, jewelry, small electronics . . . baskets will now circulate for your convenience." Smiling dancers began passing through the crowd carrying large wicker baskets. "These baskets are handmade by Maya women in the rainforest. They are available for sale at the merchandise concessions, along with a wide selection of Birdman items, T-shirts, hammocks, and postcards."

"I wouldn't mind a T-shirt," said Max.

Lola glared at him. "Concentrate, Hoop. What do we know about Tzelek?"

Max thought about it. "He's tried to kill me twice. He's

Lord 6-Dog's adopted brother. He's based at the Black Pyramid. He formed the Undead Army to take on Lord 6-Dog's Jaguar Warriors. He killed Lord 6-Dog's father. He's the craziest, most evil, most ruthless maniac in Xibalba. And he's obsessed with battling Lord 6-Dog."

"Exactly. So why would he be selling T-shirts? It doesn't make sense."

"That doesn't mean it isn't true," said Max. "This whole place is nuts."

In front of them, a man with a ponytail removed his gold earring and placed it into a basket. "I am ready," he said.

The girl with the poncho removed her nose stud. "I am ready," she said.

All around them, people were enthusiastically taking off their jewelry, emptying their wallets, and switching off their phones to place in the baskets.

Now drums began to beat and the newly unencumbered danced wildly in concentric circles. "We are free!" they sang. "We are ready!"

"This stinks!" exclaimed Lola, her eyes blazing brighter than the morning sun. "It stinks worse than tapir pee. Whoever Great Sun is, he's inventing Maya rituals to get money from his followers. How can people be so stupid?"

Blue waved from across the crowd.

"Talking about stupid . . . ," said Max.

"Be nice," said Lola. "We need all the friends we can get."

"Hey, guys," said Blue, coming over. "What did you think? Wasn't it amazing? Have you ever seen anything like those Jaguar Stones?"

"Actually—" began Max.

"No," said Lola firmly. "We haven't. Where did they come from? Do you know, Blue?"

"Great Sun says he found them here at Cahokia. He says the Birdman showed him where they were buried."

"What do you know about Great Sun?" asked Lola. "Who is he?"

"I've only ever seen him onstage. But they say he's a great king from a faraway land come back to claim his inheritance. I assume he's a descendant of the kings of Cahokia."

"And what's the deal with the star children thing?"

"I thought *you'd* know that."

"I would? Why me?"

"Your people, the Maya, were big star watchers, right? Great Sun says they predicted all this. He says we all came from the stars, and one day, we'll go back there."

Lola sighed. "Seriously, Blue? Think about it. Why would my people, way down in Central America, care about anything except their own cities and their own children and their own lives? And if they couldn't predict the Spanish conquest, why would they make predictions about a bunch of hippies in the twenty-first century?"

"I'm not a hippie," said Blue. "I'm on a gap year."

"Sorry. But this"—she indicated the bustling tent city—"has nothing to do with the Maya."

"Then, why did you come here?"

"I wish I hadn't."

"Even if you don't believe any of it, the people here are good people."

Lola nodded. "I know. That makes it worse. Good people being sucked in by an evil confidence trickster."

"Shh," Blue warned her. "Don't talk like that. I've heard

Great Sun has spies to root out troublemakers—interplanetary agitators, he calls them."

"Why does that not surprise me?" said Lola.

"Please," said Max, breaking in. "Can you two stop talking? I'm dying of hunger here."

"Come to our camp," said Blue. "You can't miss it. It's the big blue tent with yellow stars. Oh, and bring The Dawg. Rainbow's got some organic mangoes for him."

"Do you have human food, too?" asked Max.

Blue laughed. "Of course. But humans can eat mangoes, you know."

"My cousin wouldn't know that," joked Lola. "He lives on pizza."

"You like pizza? No problem. See you at the camp!"

"Yesss!" Max punched the air.

Lola looked at him quizzically. "I don't get you, Hoop. One minute you're freaking out because the most evil being in Maya history is possibly right here, right now. And the next minute you're happy as a clam because someone mentions pizza."

"I can't think when I'm hungry," said Max defensively.

"Which is always," Lola teased him. "So let's go find Lord 6-Dog, have some food with Blue, and think things through."

The crowds were clearing now, and as they walked toward the trees, Max and Lola saw that the base of the pyramid was blocked off all the way around. A security team in black shirts guarded the barriers. On one side, a gaggle of media crews were conducting interviews in a dozen different languages with anyone who'd talk to them. At the back, through the autumnal trees, the silver roofs of trailers were visible.

"That must be where Tzelek lives," said Max.

"I can't imagine Tzelek living in a trailer," said Lola.

"But if it's not him, how did he get that costume?"

"That's the big question. Let's see what The Dawg thinks about it."

They found him in a hickory tree.

Lola called up to him in howler sounds. He ignored her and carried on munching leaves.

"Did you tell him it's about Tzelek?" asked Max.

At the sound of his enemy's name, Lord 6-Dog stopped eating and dropped down out of the tree.

Lola looked quickly around to make sure the coast was clear. "There's no one around, I think we can talk."

"About Tzelek?" asked Lord 6-Dog. "What of him?"

"We think he's here," said Max.

"Max thinks Tzelek's here," Lola corrected him.

"Here?" Lord 6-Dog sniffed the air. "I smell him not. Where didst thou see him?"

"At the Sunrise Ceremony," answered Max. "Did you watch it?"

"Alas, I did not. My attention was distracted by a persimmon tree."

"Max thinks that Great Sun is Tzelek," explained Lola.

"Curse those persimmons!" Lord 6-Dog grunted in frustration.

"I'm pretty sure it's not him," Lola soothed him. "He doesn't seem Maya enough."

"Where can I find this Great Sun? I would know if it were Tzelek in a heartbeat," said Lord 6-Dog.

"He'll be at the Sunset Ceremony this evening," said Lola. "Until then, we should keep a low profile. Let's just hang out in Blue's tent." She smiled at Lord 6-Dog. "Rainbow's got some mangoes for you. But no more talking until we're alone."

"Thou dost expect me to keep quiet when Tzelek is at large?"

"Yes," said Lola firmly. "And it's not Tzelek."

On the way to Blue's tent, they passed many unusual structures. There was a giant hand the size of a house with grown adults sliding down its fingers. There was an open-top London bus with the upper deck made into a dance floor. There was an archway made of old bicycles for no apparent reason. And there was every size and color of tent you could imagine.

But the biggest tent was the blue one with yellow stars.

It was round with a pointed roof, like a circus tent—an impression underlined by the stilt-walkers and fire-eaters who were practicing outside. Inside, it had a Moroccan air, with rugs, and pillows, and swathes of cloth draped from the tent poles.

"You're here!" cried Blue happily. "Look! I've made a special place for The Dawg. It's supposed to remind him of the jungle." He showed them a corner of the tent that was curtained off with green muslin and piled-up mountains of green pillows. A low table was loaded with bowls of fruit and trays of nuts. "And for you," Blue said to Max, "we have something extra special." He brandished a pizza box.

Max opened it eagerly. Then his face fell. "What *is* this?"

"Eggplant and lentil pizza. The crust is made from spinach and celery. It's the Cahokia Special. You won't find it anywhere else."

"Glad to hear it," said Max, appalled at this subversion

of his favorite food and very much hoping to never find it anywhere else ever again.

"What would you like, Lola?" asked Blue. "Tamales? Burritos? Nachos?"

"Pizza's great," she said. "If Max can spare some."

"Help yourself," said Max. "Have it all."

"Would you like dessert?" asked Blue.

Max looked up eagerly.

"Cabbage cake? Beet brownies? Prune pie?" offered Blue.

"Do you have any chocolate ice cream?" asked Max.

"That sounds good," said Blue. "I bet I can find some."

"Thank you, Blue," said Lola. "This is so kind of you."

"Thank my father. It's all on his credit card."

"Is he here?"

"No, he's a dentist in California." Blue pointed at a big bowl of toothbrushes on a side table. "Help yourselves, by the way. He keeps me supplied. When I told him I didn't want to be a dentist, he kind of lost interest in me. He gave me a credit card and told me to get out of his hair."

"I'm so sorry," said Lola.

"It's okay. Coming to Cahokia has been like finding a new family. Speaking of which"— he hesitated—"if you're cool with it, I do have some friends who'd like to meet The Dawg."

Reluctant, but not wanting to sound ungrateful, Lola said: "The thing is, Blue, he's shy. He's not good with people. He's a wild animal."

They both regarded the howler monkey, who was reclined on the pillows dangling grapes over his mouth like a Roman emperor.

"Just one or two," begged Blue. "They'll be quick."

Lola sighed. "I guess. But no photographs."

205

"You got it," said Blue. "I'll go tell them."

He ducked out of the tent and was met by excited voices.

"This pizza is disgusting," said Max.

"Forget the pizza," said Lola. "We need to talk before Blue comes back. How can we find out more about Great Sun? Do you have any ideas, Lord 6-Dog?"

He paused mid-grape. "At nightfall, I will infiltrate his quarters."

"I'll come with you," said Lola. "We'll go after the ceremony."

"No. Thou wilt stay safely here. Thou art a good climber, Lady Lola, but only a monkey could scale that wall. Besides, if it truly is Tzelek, I should prefer to face him alone."

Lola opened her mouth to protest, just as Blue stuck his head around the curtain. "Knock, knock. Is The Dawg ready for some visitors?"

"Just a moment," called Lola. She crouched next to Lord 6-Dog. "I'm sorry to say this, your majesty, but please remember you're an animal."

"What should I do? Swing from the tent pole?"

Lola shook her head in horror. "Why don't you just sit there and look mystical?"

"I am a monkey. I have limited dramatic options."

"Let's practice. Show me your mystical face."

Lord 6-Dog opened his eyes wide and pursed his lips.

"That looks like your seasick face."

Lord 6-Dog tried again.

"That's worse. You look like someone punched you."

"Imagine you can smell a freshly built termite nest," suggested Max.

Lord 6-Dog lifted his nose quizzically.

"Perfect!" said Lola. "I'll tell Blue."

Soon, a nervous-looking Rainbow entered the tent. Besides mangoes, she brought a garland of yellow flowers, which she gave to Lola to place reverently around Lord 6-Dog's neck over his striped pajamas. He looked more mystical already.

Rainbow knelt in front of him.

"What should I do with my life?" she asked him.

"He can't talk," said Lola quickly. "He can't answer you."

"He spoke to Blue," said Rainbow. "Maybe he will speak to me."

"He's just a howler monkey," Lola insisted, but Rainbow ignored her and carried on kneeling there, eyes closed, swaying slightly.

"I hear you," she said. "Thank you." She appeared to be talking to the monkey.

When she stood up her face was flushed with excitement. "This is the best day of my life."

Max and Lola looked at each other, baffled.

"Did he answer you?" Lola asked her.

"He spoke to my heart. He told me to follow my dreams and become a librarian. How cool is that?"

Before Lola could protest, Rainbow had whipped out her phone and taken a photo of herself with Lord 6-Dog.

"No photos!" said Lola, but Rainbow was gone.

Max was muttering to Lord 6-Dog. "How did you do that? Did you really communicate with her?"

"Of course not, young lord," the monkey muttered back. "I was thinking about termite nests."

"Then what just happened?"

"In my opinion, she listened to her heart."

Outside, it had taken approximately five seconds between

Rainbow posting her photo online to word spreading around Cahokia about The Dawg's message for her. A line of people clutching bunches of bananas soon wound from Blue's tent all around the park.

"I'm sorry," said Blue. "Word got out. I'll try to get rid of them." There was a scuffle at the door and they heard his voice saying, "Hey! Stop! Where are you going? You can't just barge in like that."

"Out of my way, you idiot," came a female voice.

In marched a young woman wearing a business suit and a headset microphone. "Come with me," she said to Max and Lola. "Great Sun wishes to speak with you. Now."

Behind her tramped in four burly bodyguards with SECURITY written on their sweatshirts. They pulled down curtains and kicked over bowls of fruit and toothbrushes as they searched the tent.

"What are you looking for?" asked Lola. "What do you want?"

"We're shutting you down," said the woman. "You've been fortune-telling without a license. There is only one guru at Cahokia."

She went to take Lord 6-Dog's garland and he bared his teeth at her.

"Do you have a muzzle for that thing?"

"No but—" Before Lola could even finish her sentence, a guard had pulled out a gun and shot the monkey. With a deep echoing groan, like a tree falling in the jungle, Lord 6-Dog fell lifeless to the ground.

CHAPTER SIXTEEN
GREAT SUN

"**W**hat have you done?" screamed Lola. "You've killed him!"

"It was just a sleeping dart," said the woman with the headset witheringly. "Get it out of here, boys."

One security guard took the howler's hands, another took his feet, and between them, they carried Lord 6-Dog out of the tent. Lola and Max tried to follow, but the remaining two guards blocked their way.

"You two are coming with me," said the woman.

Lola was still trying to push past the guards and go after Lord 6-Dog. "Where are they taking him?" she demanded.

"Just do as you're told and the beast will be fine. Now follow me, both of you."

Outside the tent, a golf cart was driving away, presumably with Lord 6-Dog inside it, while another one waited for Max and Lola. The carts had the Birdman logo painted on the side.

As they emerged from the tent, Max and Lola were greeted by the shocked faces of the line waiting outside.

"What's up with The Dawg?" called a voice.

"Is he dead?" called another.

With two security guards trying to push her into the golf cart, Lola called back: "You're all witnesses. If we don't come back, call the police."

As the line began to murmur in protest, the woman stood on the footplate of the cart, her mic now somehow linked into the public address system. "Do not be alarmed. These criminals have been detained for your safety. Rest assured that Great Sun is unharmed and will appear as usual at tonight's Sunset Ceremony. Until then, please concentrate on freeing yourselves from material possessions. Collection centers can be found throughout the park."

With that, she ducked behind the wheel and they took off at speed, squashing bananas and scattering flowers in their wake. When they reached the paved road, they turned left, and left again, until they were behind the great pyramid. They drove through a security checkpoint into the media village, where the world's press were busily interviewing each other, on through several more checkpoints, and up to a pair of tall gates made out of wooden logs like a stockade.

"Incoming," barked the woman into her headset microphone. The rough-hewn gates were slowly opened to reveal the slick, shimmering nerve center of Great Sun's operations: a settlement of double-wide silver trailers with smoked black windows like the ones movie stars use on location.

After more shouting into her headset, the woman pulled up outside the biggest trailer.

"Out!" snarled the woman to her passengers.

She punched a security code into the trailer door.

"Follow me," she said when it clicked open. The security guards followed behind as she led them down a black spiral staircase into a warren of corridors.

"Those trailers are just a smokescreen," whispered Max. "There's a whole underground city down here."

Lola nodded grimly. "I just hope it doesn't lead to the Maya underworld like the Grand Hotel Xibalba."

Max groaned. He hadn't even considered that possibility.

The woman ushered them into a large meeting room. The walls were lined with video screens, control panels, and important-looking technology. In the center of the room was a long, polished wood table surrounded by leather office chairs. The red lights of security cameras glowed silently in the corners.

"Wait here," she commanded. "Don't touch anything."

As soon as she'd gone, Max started panicking. "We've got to get out of here! Help me find a way out! In a few minutes' time, Tzelek is going to walk through that door! We're toast!"

Lola stayed calm. "We don't know for sure that it's Tzelek. And why would anyone go to all the trouble of setting up this place, just to start killing off the tourists?"

"Because we're not tourists, are we?" Max pointed out. "Tzelek has a history with us. A history of trying to kill us."

"One thing's for sure," said Lola, stroking the polished wood of the table. "This is exactly the kind of table Tzelek would choose. It's mahogany. That's an endangered species in the rainforest. I'll bet these trees were cut down illegally."

"Who cares about the furniture? *We're* about to be cut down illegally."

"I'm just saying." Lola looked around at all the high-tech equipment. "I wish Blue and his friends could see how Great Sun spends their offerings."

"Shame we won't live to tell them."

"Stop it, Hoop. We're the good guys. We'll find a way out. We always do."

"I wish I could be sure about that."

"So what *are* you sure about?" asked Lord Kuy, his owl face suddenly filling every video screen. "What have you found out? Anything to report? How's the mission going?"

"Very badly," said Max. "Did you come to watch us die?"

Lord Kuy blinked at him. "What are you prattling about?"

"Where's Lord 6-Dog's scepter?" Lola yelled at the screen. "He needs it to fight Tzelek."

"Tzelek?" Lord Kuy's head spun around in surprise. "What does Tzelek have to do with anything? Have you two lost your minds?"

"He's Great Sun," said Max. "As if you didn't know."

Lord Kuy looked confused. "Where's 6-Dog? Perhaps I can get some sense out of *him*."

"He was shot," said Lola accusingly.

"This is most unexpected," said Lord Kuy, his feathers ruffling uneasily. "I must consult with Ah Pukuh."

"But Tzelek is on his way here right now!" Max yelled. "What are we supposed to do?"

"My advice," said Lord Kuy, "would be to try not to make him angry."

They heard numbers being punched into the security pad outside the door.

Lord Kuy vanished as the door flew open and the two security guards marched back in. They stood behind the two

212

empty seats at the head of the table, arms folded, looking ready for a fight. They were followed by the woman with the headphone mic, this time carrying an important-looking executive case.

"Sit!" she barked at Max and Lola, in a voice so loud it slammed them into their seats. She placed the case on her chair, went back to the door, and held it open for the two people who entered last.

The first was a small, thin man in a black tracksuit with a towel rolled around his neck, like a rap star who'd just come offstage. He wore his hood up, and big black sunglasses covered half his face. His companion was a glamorous Maya woman with long black hair, wearing a ton of makeup, high heels, and a glittering green evening dress.

They took their seats at the head of the table.

"You are now in the presence of Great Sun," said the headset woman. "You may speak only when spoken to."

Max and Lola stared at the man in the tracksuit. Could he be Tzelek? They watched carefully as he put down his hood and took off his sunglasses.

He had traces of face paint on his skin.

Lola gasped loudly.

"*Buenos días*, Señorita Lola," lisped Count Antonio de Landa, the cape-twirling, trigger-happy Spanish aristocrat who'd been paid by Lola's grandfather, Chan Kan, to kidnap her from her parents when she was a baby.

"It's you? You're Great Sun?" Lola looked like she'd seen a ghost.

"*Y buenos días* to you, Señor Murphy," added Landa to Max.

Max was too stunned to respond.

"You know these people, Toto?" the Maya woman in green

213

asked suspiciously. "Who are they? Are you going to introduce me?"

"But of course, *mi amor*. They are cousins. Their names are Lola Murphy and Max Murphy. I did some business with their family in San Xavier." He smiled at Max and Lola, showing his little rodent teeth. "It is my honor to present to you my wife and queen, Lady Koo."

Now Max was staring at Landa's wife. "Your name is Koo?"

"Lady Koo," she corrected him.

"Didn't you used to work in the beauty salon at the Grand Hotel Xibalba?"

Lady Koo gave a little shudder. "You are mistaken."

Max tried to jog her memory. "I was waiting for Lola one day. . . . You were bored. . . . You tried to give me a tattoo . . . ?"

Lady Koo pursed her lips. "A tattoo? How vulgar."

"No, it was amazing. You were going to use a stingray spine. You had charts showing ancient Maya tattoos and all the ways they used to decorate their teeth. Don't you remember?"

Lady Koo smiled wistfully. "Cosmetic dentistry was my specialty."

"So you *did* work at the hotel?"

She nodded. "But I have tried to put those dark days behind me. The only good thing to come out of that place was meeting my husband." She put her hand over Landa's and squeezed it. He winced in pain.

"You *must* remember me," Max insisted. "You helped me after the ball game against the Death Lords. You threw me a stingray spine to cut myself free."

"That was you?" Lady Koo looked delighted. "And you were the girl?" she asked Lola. "You two were the Hero Twins?"

They nodded.

"This is amazing!" she said. "What a stroke of good luck! The Hero Twins right here at Cahokia!"

"We're not actually the Hero Twins," Lola pointed out.

Lady Koo was excited. "You're the modern-day Hero Twins. Not many people can say they've fought the Death Lords face-to-face! This could go viral!" She saw Lola's stony face. "I'm so sorry if my guards were a little rough with you, my dear. All I knew was that someone was operating an unlicensed fortune-telling concession. Oh, Toto, why didn't you tell me it was them?"

"I wasn't sure myself," said Landa. "I wondered when I heard about the howler monkey. But we attract so many strange people, I could not be sure."

"There's a monkey?" Lady Koo clapped her hands. "This gets better and better!"

"There *was* a monkey," said Lola. "Until your thugs shot him."

"Is this true?" Lady Koo looked angrily at the headset woman.

"The brute tried to bite me. It was just a sleeping dart, your majesty. No harm done."

"No harm done? I will be the judge of that! What about the harm to our image? You didn't think about that, did you, before you went around jabbing needles into cuddly animals?"

"But, your majesty—"

"I'll deal with you later," snapped Lady Koo. "Why do I have to do everything myself?" She rubbed her temples as if she had a headache. "Is there anything else you haven't told me, Toto?"

Max wondered if Toto had mentioned how he'd kidnapped

Lola as a baby. Or how he'd once chased Max and Lola down an underground river in San Xavier, taking potshots at them, in pursuit of a Jaguar Stone. Or how he'd once dreamed of marrying Lola for her royal Maya blood. Or how his brain had once been invaded by Tzelek, and his palatial home in Spain had been invaded by his pig-herding ancestors. Or how he'd once ended up swinging upside down from the cathedral ceiling on his wedding day.

As if he could read the boy's mind, Landa gave Max a warning look. Then he smiled his rat smile at his wife. "I have told you everything, *mi amor*. You are the queen of my heart."

"I am the queen of Cahokia," she said haughtily. "I run this place and don't you forget it!"

"*Si, mi amor,*" lisped Landa meekly.

"I would be Great Sun if I could," said Lady Koo to Lola, "but tradition demands a man for the role. Apparently, people are unaware of the great warrior queens in Maya history."

"But who is Great Sun supposed to be?" asked Lola. "A Maya king, a Cahokian, a spaceman—or what?"

Landa opened his mouth to answer, but Lady Koo cut in. "That kind of detail is unimportant to our followers. They seek merely to be led. And we seek merely to divest them of their riches."

Lola tried to hide her disgust. "But why? Your husband is already one of the richest men in Spain."

"There is no such thing as too much money. Besides, we make a good team, Toto and I. He had his money and the altar from the Yellow Pyramid. I had my Maya blood and my creative talent. I suggested that we pool our resources, and here we are."

"Why Cahokia?" asked Lola. "Why not a Maya pyramid?"

Lady Koo sniffed. "With all those archaeologists poking around? Impossible. But this place is perfect. Cahokia is a lost city. It's as if it was sitting here waiting for us to find it. With Toto's money, we soon made the necessary renovations."

"And your Jaguar Stones?" asked Max.

"We excavated them here at Cahokia," said Lady Koo.

"No, you didn't," said Lola.

"Yes, we did. The Birdman told us where to dig."

"No, he didn't," said Lola.

Lady Koo smiled. "No one else has questioned that story."

"Well, no one else knows as much about the Jaguar Stones. I'm pretty sure there are only five in existence. Your husband used to own one. He bought it from my father. But now they're all in Xibalba."

"Or are they?" countered Lady Koo.

There was a dramatic pause as she and Lola stared at each other.

Lady Koo giggled. "I'll tell you if you sign the confidentiality agreement."

The headset woman opened her case and fished out a sheaf of papers. "Sign on the dotted line," she said, pointing with her pen to a place on the last page.

Lola flicked through the pages. "It would take me days to read this. The type is tiny." She peered more closely. "Wait, this gives you the right to all my possessions and my firstborn child. I'm not signing this."

Lady Koo shrugged. "You'd be surprised how many people sign it without reading. It was worth a try. So, where were we?"

"You were telling us if your stones are fakes," Max reminded her.

"*You* tell me." Lady Koo clicked her fingers and the

headset woman extracted a long, thin, wooden box from her briefcase. Lady Koo's eyes shone excitedly as she flicked open the catches and lifted the lid.

Max and Lola watched, unimpressed. There was no way a Jaguar Stone would fit in such a slim box. Then Lady Koo turned the box around so they could see its contents, and suddenly they sat up straight.

Inside the box was a necklet of yellow stones.

To Max, it looked exactly like the necklet worn by Inez, the ghostly princess he'd met in Spain—the necklet that was made out of the Yellow Jaguar to disguise it.

Landa got up and came and stood behind Lola. "You wore it," he whispered, "at our betrothal. And then you stole it from me."

"What are you saying, Toto?" asked Lady Koo.

"*Nada, mi amor.*"

"Then come back here and sit down immediately!"

He flinched at her voice, like a dog that has been mistreated, and slunk back to his chair.

Lola's face was bathed in yellow light. She stared at the necklet, mesmerized. "This can't be the same one," she murmured.

"It is the same," said Lady Koo. "I dare you to find a difference."

"But Princess Inez took it down to Xibalba. How could it end up here?"

"Perhaps Toto stole it back from Xibalba?" suggested Lady Koo.

"He's not brave enough," said Lola flatly.

Lady Koo snorted with laughter. "It seems she knows you well, Toto."

"But here's the thing," said Max. "I'd always assumed that the necklet turned back into a Jaguar Stone when it went to Xibalba. And you held up a yellow stone onstage this morning."

"Did you also assume that anyone cares what you think?" snarled Landa.

"He's joking," said Lady Koo. "He knows very well that we made both, just in case."

You could almost hear all the necks in the room swivel toward her.

She put her hands up. "Yes, I admit it, we made them. We used technology, like the Maya kings used technology."

"But they look so real," said Lola admiringly.

"It's called 3-D printing," said Lady Koo. "It was practically invented by archaeologists. But we don't use plastic, like they do. We melt down real stone: black obsidian, red fire opal, white alabaster, yellow amber, green jadeite." She couldn't hide the pride in her voice as she counted off the minerals on her fingers. "All the colors of the Jaguar Stones."

"But the shape . . . ?"

"Toto had always thought he might try his hand at—" She groped for the word.

"Forgery?" suggested Max.

"Sculpture," said Lady Koo. "So, by chance, he had a mold made of the Black Jaguar when it was in his possession."

"And how do you make them glow like that?" asked Lola. "I assume they don't need blood like the real ones."

Lady Koo put on a mystical voice. "We connect them to a source of pure energy—otherwise known as batteries. Sometimes we use a little theatrical blood for effect. It's so much easier to wash out than the real thing."

"Your stones are amazing. You certainly had me fooled," said Lola.

Lady Koo slammed the table. "Fooled? No! Do not use that word. I do not fool people. I share my dreams with them. People believe what they want to believe. It is not my fault if others lack the ambition to make their dreams a reality! I have suffered enough. Now it is my time to shine!"

They all sat slightly stunned as Lady Koo tossed her hair and pouted.

It was Lola who broke the silence. "So, where's Tzelek?"

"Tzelek?" Landa looked around terrified. He motioned to his guards to come closer. Having once had Tzelek occupy his brain, it was obviously not an experience he cared to repeat. "Why do you ask about Tzelek?"

"You were wearing his costume this morning," said Max. "That black-and-white headdress. It's his."

"It *is*?" Landa turned to his wife in horror.

She laughed. "Of course, it's not Tzelek's. Don't be ridiculous. It came from our wardrobe department like all our costumes." She leaned forward to Max and Lola conspiratorially. "But if you want to talk about show business, let me just say that was quite a performance you put on at the Grand Hotel Xibalba. The Hero Twins were the talk of the hotel. Or what was left of it, anyway. So how would you feel about reprising your roles?"

"What do you mean?" asked Lola.

"Perform tonight as our guest stars. Be our Hero Twins. It will be easy money for you, and the publicity for us will be huge. Name your fee."

Max shook his head. "I don't think—"

"We'll do it," said Lola. "But our fee is your Jaguar Stones."

"That is out of the question," said Lady Koo.

"You can always make more," said Lola.

"Absolutely not."

"We'll put on a fantastic show. Plus we won't sue you for animal cruelty."

"Do you understand how long it took to make these stones?"

"Do you understand how quickly I can spread the word that you shot our monkey?"

Lady Koo thought about it. "Why do you want our stones? Are you setting up a rival attraction?"

"I'll tell you the truth," said Lola. "We were sent here by Ah Pukuh, the Maya god of violent and unnatural death. He's jealous of all your followers and he's holding our parents ransom until we get your stones."

"How did Ah Pukuh hear about this place?" Lady Koo sounded flattered.

"I think he saw you on cable news. Old Cahokia is very famous—even in Xibalba."

Lady Koo slapped Landa on the back, possibly harder than she'd meant to. "What did I tell you? It's a new age of social media. If you want to stay on top, you've got to stay online." She checked her phone. "One thousand new followers in the last hour. Yay, me!"

"You'll lose all your followers if they hear about the monkey," Lola pointed out.

"Can the monkey dance?" asked Lady Koo.

"No!" said Lola indignantly.

"*Por favor, mi amor*, don't do this," begged Landa.

"Oh, loosen up, Toto. I think this could work for us. We'll announce that our stones have been stolen and then they will be miraculously returned. It's a win-win! Think of the publicity! Perhaps we could even get Ah Pukuh to put in an appearance. It's genius."

"So, do we have a deal?" asked Lola.

"We have a deal," confirmed Lady Koo.

"Por favor, mi amor," Landa begged her. "We should not tangle with the Maya gods."

Lady Koo turned on him. "Don't tell me what to do. I am the brains behind this operation—and don't you forget it!"

Lola almost felt sorry for Landa, the way he cowered in the shadow of his wife.

"You are a little out of sorts today, *mi amor*. Perhaps you should take a siesta before the Sunset Ceremony?"

"There is no time for a siesta!" snarled Lady Koo. "I have a show to put on!"

CHAPTER SEVENTEEN

HERE COME THE HERO TWINS

When everyone else had left the room, Lola did a little victory dance. "Can you believe how well that went? We just need to do this stupid show, collect our Jaguar Stones, and get out of here. It's in the bag, Hoop."

Max looked at her like she was crazy. "You're kidding, right? You don't seriously think that Landa will hand over his stones? And that Ah Pukuh won't care if they're fake? And that everybody will live happily ever after?"

Lola jutted her chin stubbornly. "The deal was to go to Cahokia and bring back the Jaguar Stones. End of story."

Max noticed that she couldn't look him in the eye. She was desperate to believe that their quest was over. He realized how terrifying it must have been for her to face Landa again, the person who had done so much to ruin her life. His tone softened. "Yeah. Why not? Maybe you're right. Hey, you were right about Tzelek."

Lola smiled weakly.

"Are you okay?" he asked her.

"It was so creepy seeing him, Hoop."

"Landa?"

Lola nodded. "But he's not quite as scary as he used to be. I think he's met his match."

Max laughed. "Yeah, Lady Koo's the scariest one. Did you see her eyes when she got mad at him?"

"They deserve each other."

There was knock at the door and a smiling young woman entered. She was dressed in denim overalls and had a bandanna tied around her magnificently wild hair. "Hi, I'm Fay from wardrobe. I've come to get you ready for your big performance. Please follow me."

As Max and Lola trotted behind her through the network of underground corridors, they passed offices filled with people piling up coins, counting banknotes, and jabbing numbers into calculators. There was a room piled up with leather goods—purses, wallets, and shoulder bags—arranged by size and color. Another room had tubs of small electronics—cell phones, tablets, laptops—all neatly labeled by brand. In yet another room, the workers were processing jewelry, sorting gold from silver, rings from nose studs, precious gems from fakes.

"What do they do with all this stuff?" asked Max.

"Lady Koo sells it online," said Fay. "Or she has it melted down. It's so sad. People get carried away and donate their wedding rings and family heirlooms, and they will never be able to get them back."

"How can you bear to work here?" asked Lola.

"It's a job. I'm an archaeology major in St. Louis and I thought it would be good for my résumé. But no one here is interested in the real facts about Cahokia. They even shut down the visitor center. Now, it's all about costumes and special effects. No one cares about the truth."

They went up in an elevator to a trailer and out into the stockade area behind the pyramid.

It was late afternoon. All around Cahokia, the trees were turning the color of the setting sun. Fay wove expertly around stagehands carrying pieces of scenery on their heads, actors saying their lines, and dancing girls in macaw feather headdresses practicing their high kicks.

The great pyramid loomed over them.

"Nearly there," said Fay. "The dressing rooms are at the top."

Max groaned. "How many steps?"

"None," replied Fay. "We'll take the escalator."

And there it was.

A steep hundred-foot escalator rumbling up the back of the pyramid. And another one, next to it, rumbling down.

Fay saw the disbelief on his face. "Lady Koo calls it her Taj Mahal," she said.

"Isn't the Taj Mahal a palace in India?" asked Lola.

"Exactly. It was built by an emperor out of love for his wife. Lady Koo tells everyone that Great Sun built these moving stairways as a tribute to the wife who every day brings him closer to the stars." Fay dropped her voice. "The truth is she couldn't walk up the stairs in her high heels."

As they neared the top of the pyramid, they looked down on Old Cahokia. The flags around the campsite fluttered in the evening breeze. Campfires sputtered. A faint smell of boiling lentils wafted up to them.

They stepped off the top of the escalator and Fay guided them into the wardrobe tent. "You'll have to help me," she said. "I'm not exactly sure what the Hero Twins wore."

"Their Maya names are Xbalanque, which means Jaguar Sun, and Hunahpu, which means One Hunter, if that's any help," said Lola, looking through the racks of clothes. "So where do you get all this stuff?"

"The costumes? All sorts of places. Online, thrift stores, auctions. I'm always on the lookout for unusual pieces. A lot of them I make myself. Great Sun wants an ancient Maya feel, but there isn't much to go on. No textiles have survived from that period. I study wall paintings and pots and do the best I can."

"That black-and-white feather costume that Great Sun wore this morning was amazing. Did you make that?"

Fay didn't think twice. "I wish! I love it! It looks so authentic."

"So where did you get it?"

"It was the strangest thing. I just turned up to work one morning and there it was. Like someone had just taken it off and dropped it there."

"When was this?"

"A couple of days ago."

"And you have no idea where it came from?"

"I assumed that the local thrift store dropped it off. They're always looking out for things for me. It probably came from a movie or a play or something." She took a notebook out of her pocket. "Would you excuse me for a moment while I sketch a few ideas?"

Max and Lola went into a huddle at the other end of the tent.

"Tzelek is here somewhere," said Max. "But the question is where? Who's he picked to occupy this time?"

"Maybe Lord 6-Dog can sniff him out," said Lola. She clapped her hand over her mouth. "Lord 6-Dog! If Tzelek's here, Lord 6-Dog's in danger. We have to find him!"

Lady Koo entered the room, a white coat over her evening dress, followed by a retinue of assistants carrying makeup cases, mirrors, and hairstyling tools. "I haven't lost my old touch," she said. "I was top of my class at beauty school."

"I'll be back in a moment," said Lola, heading for the door.

Lady Koo caught her by the arm. "Where do you think you're going?"

Lola tried to wriggle free. "I need to check on the monkey."

"No," said Lady Koo, dragging Lola back to a chair. "You need to sit here while I do your makeup. I've got a million things to take care of before the show starts. But I'll have the monkey brought up for you. In fact, I'm writing a little part for him into the show. Everyone loves a dancing monkey."

"He doesn't dance," said Lola.

"The sooner we get you ready, the sooner you can teach him," said Lady Koo.

So Lola sat back and watched in the mirror as she and Max were transformed into Xbalanque and Hunahpu, the kids who saved the world from the Lords of Death.

CHAPTER EIGHTEEN
SUNDOWN

Lola and Max stood side by side, staring at themselves in the mirror.

"You look good," said Lola.

"So do you," said Max. "Apart from the beard."

Lola stroked the wispy hairs glued to her chin. "You don't like it?"

The rest of her hair was tied back, and all her visible skin was painted in jaguar spots. She wore a brown cotton tunic.

Max's skin had been painted in a leafy camouflage pattern. He wore a black bandanna tied around his hair and a pair of green baggy shorts.

Fay stood between them, watching their reactions anxiously. "If you're happy with your costumes, I'll take you to the greenroom. They're bringing your monkey up. I can't wait to meet him. He's called The Dawg, right? Everyone's talking about him." She looked alarmed. "Will he need a costume? I didn't think of it. We don't have much to fit a monkey. . . ."

"He has pajamas," Lola reassured her. "I just want to see him. Come on, Hoop!"

Max took a deep breath. "I think I've got stage fright. I keep getting flashbacks to my Thanksgiving play in first grade."

He paused for Lola to make a snarky comment about Thanksgiving not being Thanksgiving for Native Americans, but she said nothing, so he pressed on. "I was a corncob. I had to hold hands with the fish that fertilized me. I didn't get very good reviews."

"It doesn't matter, Hoop. We go on. We get off. We go home. It will all be over before you know it."

"This way," said Fay. "I'm sure you'll both be amazing."

She took them to another tent, nearer to the stage, where lots of extras in vaguely Maya costumes milled around.

"Do I smell food?" asked Max.

"Help yourself to the buffet," said Fay. "The grilled scallions are delicious."

Max didn't need telling twice.

"Bring me something back!" Lola called after him as he made a beeline for the table. "I'm waiting for The Dawg."

The guards brought him in on a stretcher—"Where do you want it?"—and tipped him and his blanket onto the couch. "He should wake up soon," they said. "Lady Koo says he has to practice his dancing."

"Like that's going to happen," muttered Lola. She wanted to hug Lord 6-Dog and tell him how glad she was to see him and how scared she'd been when he was shot, but she knew that a mighty Maya king wouldn't approve of such an emotional display, so she just sat there, gently rubbing his fur as he slept and willing him to wake up.

"Here comes a runner with your script," said Fay, taking a thick stack of pages from a backstage helper. "Still warm from the printer! Lady Koo's been writing like a demon. She's very excited about tonight's production."

Max returned with two loaded plates and watched as Lola weighed the script in her hand. "It's like a book!" he said. "She can't seriously expect us to learn all that?"

Lola flicked through the pages. "I hope they have plenty of fake blood. The stage directions are pretty gory. Listen to this, Hoop: *Xbalanque chops Hunahpu into little pieces, then puts him back together again.*"

Max put down his plate. He was feeling nervous. "How am I going to act that? This is going to be a disaster. It's the Thanksgiving corncob all over again."

"So what happened?" asked Lola, trying not to smile.

"I jumped up and down to welcome the fish and all my niblets fell off."

Lola and Fay burst out laughing. The noise woke Lord 6-Dog, who opened one eye and commanded sleepily, "Stop torturing that toucan," before going back to sleep.

"So, that's the famous Dawg," said Fay. "Did you know they're selling little Dawg Dolls of him in his pajamas?"

"They are? That was quick!" Lola made a face. "I hate to contribute to the profits of this place, but will you get me one for his mother?"

"Sure. But isn't his mother a monkey? Will she even know it's him?"

"Howler monkeys are very intelligent," said Lola.

"You should wake him," said Fay. "It's nearly sundown and—" The rest of her words were drowned out by a fanfare of conch shell horns and wooden trumpets. "Quick! The show is starting!"

Max and Lola woke Lord 6-Dog enough to be able to half carry, half drag him along between them.

"I have to check the dancers' costumes," said Fay. They were in the wings at the side of the stage, hidden from view of the audience. "Be sure to listen for your cue."

This is what they heard:

—Above everything, the noise of the crowd, clapping and chanting for Great Sun to appear.

—Some taped background music with drums and wailing.

—A painful whistle of feedback from the PA system every time a stagehand walked in front of a speaker.

"There you are!" barked Lady Koo, coming up behind them and making them jump out of their skins. "Do you know your lines?"

Lola shook her head. "We only just got our script."

"Then get to it!" Lady Koo's forehead was wrinkled with worry under its thick layer of makeup. "Tonight is a very special night. The TV cameras have arrived. This could be huge for us! I don't want any mistakes!"

"We're going to be on TV?" Max looked terrified.

"Isn't it amazing? I sent out a press release after our meeting, but I never expected such interest. All I said was that the Hero Twins would be performing, and the media have descended like locusts. For some reason they've got

231

it into their heads that the Birdman will land tonight."

"Will he?"

Lady Koo looked at Max like he was mad. "Of course not. But it means that you two need to be spectacular. We have to give them a show to remember."

"There's not enough time to learn all our lines," Lola pointed out. "Can we take our scripts onstage with us?"

"And make me look like an amateur in front of the entire world? Give me those!" She grabbed the scripts out of Max's and Lola's hands and, with the immense effort of someone trying to rip up a phonebook, tore them into little pieces. "If you want those stones, you better not let me down," she hissed, before hobbling away on her towering heels. "Someone put that monkey in roller skates for the big finale!"

Lord 6-Dog, who was slumped under his blanket in a director's chair, paid no attention. Max and Lola stood there, shocked.

"I think her shoes are hurting her," said Lola.

"That's no excuse to rip up our scripts."

"She's just nervous. This is like a dream come true for her, to be on TV."

"It's my nightmare."

"But it's great for us, Hoop. If we can put on a good show, she'll be so grateful, we'll have our hands on those Jaguar Stones tonight!"

"How does she expect us to put on a good show with no scripts?"

"Improvise. She knows we know the story. My guess is that she'd rather we made something up than stumbled around reading off our scripts. Just remember the big finale where I chop you into pieces."

"How do I act getting chopped into pieces?"

"It doesn't matter. Just scream a lot. Whatever. As soon as this is over, we're out of here."

More trumpets, more drums, then a roar from the crowd as Great Sun was carried out on his litter from the opposite side of the stage. He wore the same black-and-white feathers and black face paint as he had that morning.

Lady Koo was carried out next on an ornate chair with carrying poles. When her bearers had set her down, they detached the poles and left her seated in throne-like splendor. She looked around for the cameras and smiled a fake smile for the viewers at home.

As Great Sun stood up and began his incomprehensible chanting ("At least now you know why you can't understand him; he's making it all up," Max whispered to Lola), Lady Koo spoke her "translation" into a microphone.

"Ladies and gentlemen, boys and girls, welcome to the world-famous Sunset Ceremony at Old Cahokia," she began. "We would especially like to welcome our television viewers from around the world and inform you that a wide range of souvenirs from this evening's festivities is available on our Web site with free shipping."

"I'm fairly sure that's not what Great Sun said," muttered Max.

Now Lady Koo stood up and tossed back her hair dramatically. "As the great fire jaguar of day prepares to dive into the sea of night, we gather here, as children of the stars, to celebrate our special place in the cosmos."

From out of nowhere a man's voice that somehow managed to sound smooth and gravelly at the same time boomed out across the park. "Here we are at the lost city of Old Cahokia in America's heartland, home of the fabled Jaguar Stones and earthly base of the mysterious Birdman of Cahokia. Join me and millions of viewers around the world as we watch Great Sun, self-proclaimed king of Cahokia, attempt to summon back the Birdman from somewhere out there in the stars."

"Who's saying that?" asked Lola, straining to see where the sound was coming from.

"I know that voice," said Max. "He's a TV announcer. We must be going out live."

A stagehand tapped Max on the shoulder and pointed to a monitor showing the TV audience's view of the stage.

"We don't know exactly what Great Sun has planned for us tonight," continued the announcer, "but we've been promised a spectacular show. Social media is buzzing about nothing less than the return of the Birdman himself. That's right, folks, tonight we are hoping to see the world's first televised UFO landing!"

Great Sun and Lady Koo exchanged baffled glances.

There was a burst of music, the twirling dancers invaded the stage, and the altar bearing the Jaguar Stones began to rise.

The announcer dropped his voice to a loud whisper: "And it begins, as always, with the lighting of the Jaguar Stones. These legendary stones are the landing lights that will guide the Birdman home to Cahokia."

When the altar was in position, Great Sun made some bogus magician-type moves, somebody somewhere flicked a switch, and the Jaguar Stones glowed into life. Now five dancers came forward, hoods pulled up so that, from the side, they looked like monks. To a sound track of monastic chanting, and with great solemnity, they processed forward with the stones, placing them at even intervals along the edge of the stage.

After some banter with a female colleague about the value of the stones and the designer of Lady Koo's dress, the TV announcer leapt into the fray again: "So what surprise does Great Sun have planned for us tonight? Will the children of the stars be returning to their celestial home? Join us, after these messages, as we watch the skies in southern Illinois and wait for the messenger of destiny to arrive."

"This is all so stupid," said Lola. "I can't believe anyone would watch this trash."

"I bet Raul's watching it," said Max. "And Hermanjilio and Lucky and Lady Coco."

He wished he was safely curled up on a sofa with them at the Villa Isabella. (Assuming, of course, that new sofas had been delivered by now.)

"Okay, so remember to smile into the cameras, Hoop. Let them know that we're okay."

Max imagined their friends at the villa clapping and cheering when he and Lola walked onstage. It made him feel a lot braver. "What about Lord 6-Dog?" he asked her. "Do you think we should warn him about Lady Koo's plans for a roller skate solo?"

Lola shook her head. "She has zero chance of making him do it. Let him sleep. Whatever they shot him with was strong stuff."

"Silence in the wings!" snapped a stagehand. "You're on in *Five . . . Four . . .*"

"As our ancestors believed that blood kept the wheels of the universe turning," Lady Koo was saying, "so tonight we will reenact the ancient ritual of sending our blood to the stars.

And here to help us—for one night only!—are two very special guests from the world of ancient myth, the Hero Twins!"

"... *Three* ..."

"What did she just say about blood?" asked Max, suddenly remembering some dicey experiences on other pyramids when villains had tried to sacrifice him.

"... *Two* ..."

Lola read his mind. "Relax! This time it's all fake blood, remember? They have gallons of it backstage."

"... *One!*"

The stagehand gave them the thumbs-up.

"Okay, Hoop, this is it! Hold on to your niblets! We're on!"

The conch shells and wooden trumpets went crazy and, over the noise, Lady Koo could be heard assuring the crowd that it was not too late to make donations.

As Max and Lola walked onstage, Lady Koo opened her arms in welcome. "Hail to the heroes of the Maya creation story," she yelled over the mic. "Welcome Xbalanque and Hunahpu, the Hero Twins."

She thrust her mic under Max's nose. "Thank you for having us," he said politely.

Lady Koo rolled her eyes and gave the mic to Lola. "Act!" she whispered.

Lola thought for a moment, then said with authority: "The Hero Twins salute Great Sun and praise his solar greatness." She passed the mic back to Max and he repeated her words.

Lady Koo nodded approvingly, but Max knew that if there were any critics in the audience, his performance would score worse reviews than his grade-school interpretation of the corncob.

On the other side of the stage, Great Sun bowed to them. Max and Lola bowed back.

"Go to him!" whispered Lady Koo. "There's an X on the stage where you stand."

As they walked across the stage, Max decided to go further off script with a cheery wave to the camera for the guys at the villa. He could feel death rays from Lady Koo's eyes piercing his back.

Great Sun was waiting for them in between a wood-burning brazier and a small table. The table had been neatly laid with two footed bowls containing strips of bark paper, sachets of fake blood, and, next to them, a small dagger. His lips were mouthing Great Sun gobbledygook at them, but Lady Koo provided the translation.

"Advance, Hero Twins," she said, "and give your blood for the universe."

Great Sun picked up the dagger. Its steel blade glinted in the light of the flames from the brazier.

"I should speak to Fay about the props," muttered Lola. "The Maya had flint and obsidian knives, and Native Americans had wood and stone tomahawks. Either way, these guys could try to be authentic. Children are watching."

"How about a rubber knife?" said Max. He eyed Great Sun's dagger. "Something that doesn't look very sharp and extremely lethal."

As the dancers twirled in reverence, a strangled howl from behind the altar followed by a yelp of pain made Max and Lola turn. In the shadows, Max could see a scuffle involving a leg in blue striped pajamas, a hairy foot, and an empty roller skate.

"I think he bit the guy who's trying to put skates on him,"

whispered Lola, trying to keep up her stage smile. "Should I go and help him?"

"He can defend himself," Max whispered back, secretly looking forward to seeing a monkey on roller skates. "You don't want to make Lady Koo even angrier."

"I guess." Lola was so intent on watching what was going on behind her that Great Sun had to cough to get her attention. His arm was shaking from holding up the dagger. They could see the sachets of fake blood hidden in his hand.

"Now Great Sun will nick the earlobes of the Hero Twins and let their blood drip onto paper strips. We will then burn the paper and send their blood to the heavens," announced Lady Koo.

The dancers knelt in reverence.

Lola nudged Max to show him that Lord 6-Dog had escaped the stagehand and was now snuggled up to his blanket and attempting to sleep on the altar. "Looks like he won the fight," she whispered, turning back to the ceremony. Max didn't mention that he could see the stagehand gathering rope, presumably to tie the monkey down and attach skates to his sleeping feet. He guessed that Lady Koo's commands were not easily disobeyed.

"The excitement builds," enthused the TV announcer.

As Max and Lola held up their bowls to catch the fake blood, Max whispered: "What excitement? It's not exactly the Super Bowl, is it?"

The next moment, his bowl was knocked out of his hand.

"If you want entertainment," said Lady Koo, "I'll give you entertainment!"

She grabbed the dagger out of her husband's hand and headed for the altar. By the time Max and Lola had registered the fact that she'd kicked off her high heels and was limping severely, one leg dragging behind her, she was holding the dagger over Lord 6-Dog's chest.

"Tzelek! She's Tzelek!" yelled Lola.

"Prepare to die, brother!" shouted Lady Koo, in Tzelek's devilish voice.

"Quick!" Lola yelled to Max. "We have to save Lord 6-Dog!"

Max met Lady Koo's eyes and Tzelek's red orbs glared back at him. "You're next, boy," he said.

Max heard himself scream.

Then an even louder noise than his screams filled the air.

The stage was bathed in a ghostly blue-green light.

Tzelek stared up fearfully through Lady Koo's eyes at the massive spaceship that was descending from the sky.

Max thought he might save Tzelek the trouble, and just die of terror.

"He's here! He's here!" the TV announcer was shouting. "The Birdman of Cahokia has returned!" The muffled thud and radio silence that followed his words suggested he'd fainted.

The dancers and extras scattered. The cameramen and the stagehands cowered in the wings. Great Sun looked from his wife to the spaceship and back again, before tearing off his headdress and running offstage in the direction of the escalators.

Only Max, Lola, and Tzelek stood rooted to the spot.

"What's happening?" whispered Max. "Is this another special effect?"

"I hope so," said Lola. "I really, really hope so."

CHAPTER NINETEEN

ALIEN INVASION

Picked out in a beam of light from the spaceship, Tzelek was transfixed. The sequins on his dress shimmered and sparkled. He held the dagger above his head, as motionless as a statue. From the stream of curses flowing from his lips, Max and Lola, who were the only ones close enough to hear, understood that his immobility was involuntary. Also caught in the alien's headlamps, Lord 6-Dog lay flat on his back on the altar. Max noted that the stagehand had been successful in strapping the skates to his feet.

Down below in the plaza, the audience had completely lost track of the plot, but, assuming that the woman in the green dress was striking a dramatic pose, they applauded enthusiastically.

"Look at the altar," Max whispered to Lola. "It really *is* the one from Spain. You can see the scorch marks from the fire at Landa's palace."

"Yes," replied Lola sarcastically. "And if you look even more carefully, you can see that Tzelek is trying to kill Lord 6-Dog on it. We need to help him!" She strained to move but got nowhere. "I'm stuck! What's going on? It's like my feet are glued to the floorboards."

Max found that he couldn't move either. Only his mouth.

"I think it's the spaceship," he said.

As they looked angrily around, they saw that anyone who hadn't fled the stage was immobilized. Below them, the audience was going wild. It must have looked amazing from down there, Max thought. A human tableau frozen in the beam of an alien spaceship.

He narrowed his eyes and tried to look up. "Cigar-shaped," he observed. "That's a classic UFO description."

"It's not a cigar. It's a canoe," said Lola.

"A canoe?"

"Look at it. The ancient Maya had huge, oceangoing canoes with roofs. That's exactly what it looks like."

"A space canoe?"

"Why not? Modern space rockets look like jets, so why wouldn't an ancient Maya spaceship look like a canoe?"

"Okay. But why would a Maya spaceship land at Cahokia?"

"It's not real, Hoop! It's another trick!"

"I'm not so sure about that, Monkey Girl. They're letting down a ramp."

"You'll see. It will be another pathetic attempt to sell merchandise."

When the ramp was in place, the lights dimmed and the door of the ship slid open. A figure stood in the doorway, backlit from the cabin, and visible only in silhouette.

Twenty thousand people gasped at once.

"It's him!" yelled Max. "It's the Birdman!"

"No way!" said Lola scornfully. "It's just some guy in a costume."

The audience fell silent—the entire watching world fell silent—as the Birdman figure walked down the ramp. When he reached center stage, he spread his huge feathered wings. The moonlight danced on their silvery plumage, making them glitter and sparkle.

A distorted voice boomed out from the spaceship: "HAIL TO YOU, CHILDREN OF THE STARS."

Constellations of camera flashes lit up the night.

The voice continued:

"YOUR PLEAS HAVE BEEN HEARD. THE BIRDMAN HAS RETURNED."

"Hey you there, Birdman!" called Tzelek. "Would you mind turning off the spotlight? You're blinding me and I'm in the middle of a very important sacrifice here!"

The Birdman turned to see who had spoken.

He pointed a wing at Tzelek and extended a claw. A ray of red light, like a laser beam, shot out and exploded the dagger into pieces.

"Okay," said Lola. "this is looking real."

"Birdman, I beg of thee!" gasped Lord 6-Dog. "Use thy magic light to cut these ropes."

"*I'll* cut them," said Tzelek, "and use them to strange you."

The Birdman extended a claw and pointed it at Tzelek.

"No!" screamed the evil priest. "No!"

Another beam of red light shot out and Tzelek-in-Lady-Koo's-body slumped to the ground, holding his/her head.

The Birdman's shoulders shook as if he was laughing.

242

"Looks like Tzelek's been sent back to Xibalba," whispered Max. "Maybe this Birdman is on our side."

"Maybe," agreed Lola. "But I don't like the way he's looking at our Jaguar Stones."

"THE BIRDMAN BRINGS GREETINGS FROM YOUR NEW MASTERS," announced the voice from the spaceship. "OUT WITH THE OLD AND IN WITH THE NEW."

He pointed a claw at each Jaguar Stone in turn, and, one by one, they exploded in a fizzing tangle of wires and batteries.

Max and Lola looked at each other in despair. Despite the fact that a spaceship was hovering over their heads and something had gone very wrong with Lady Koo's show, they'd still hoped to grab the stones and head back to San Xavier. But now their plan was hopeless.

"We're doomed," whispered Max.

"Don't say that."

The spotlight moved to shine on them.

"Uh-oh," said Max. "What's this?"

"THE NEW AGE HAS BEGUN," the voice was saying. "STAY TUNED FOR DETAILS OF THE OPENING CEREMONY. AND TO SYMBOLIZE THE JOINING OF OUR WORLDS, THE HERO TWINS ARE NOW INVITED TO BOARD THE SPACE CANOE."

The Birdman gestured toward the ramp.

"Excuse me?" Lola called to him. "You know we're not the actual Hero Twins, right?"

"Take *me*! Take *me*!" volunteered voices in the audience.

"At least we can move again," said Lola, running over to the altar. Carefully, she picked up a piece of the dagger's shattered blade and began to saw at the ropes.

"HERO TWINS FOR IMMEDIATE BOARDING!" commanded the voice.

"We're not coming with you!" Lola shouted at the Birdman.

Lord 6-Dog had worked himself free of the rest of the ropes and was climbing down. "Who dares to—?" he began, and immediately lost his balance on his roller skates. Before he could pull himself up again, a red light focused on his heart.

The Birdman looked questioningly at Lola.

"Hoop?" she said in a little voice. "I think we have to go with them."

The Birdman nodded in agreement.

"What, and live on another planet for the rest of our lives? Are you crazy?"

The red light on Lord 6-Dog's heart grew brighter, and he clutched at his chest in pain. "As long as we're alive, we can escape," said Lola. "I'm sure we'll be back. They said something about opening ceremonies."

"No." Max was adamant. "It's too dangerous."

The red light flashed. There was a smell of singed monkey fur.

"Stop!" Lola shouted at the Birdman. "We get the message." She crouched down to Lord 6-Dog. "Are you okay?"

He nodded weakly.

Lola looked at Max. "With or without you, I'm getting on this spaceship. Lord 6-Dog can't take any more." She helped the howler to his feet. "Well, this is exciting," she said, trying to sound brave. "You're going to be the first Maya king in space."

"I care not for flying," grumbled Lord 6-Dog

"Where's your sense of adventure?" asked Lola, pulling him on his skates toward the ramp.

Max watched them go.

Fay pushed her way through the petrified stagehands. "Here," she said, putting something into Max's hands. It was a Dawg Doll in striped pajamas. "Lola wanted it."

Max looked at the little toy monkey. It had an almost mystical expression on its face. And whether it spoke to him or whether he listened to his heart, he suddenly knew what he had to do.

"Wait for me," he called. "I'm coming with you."

To Blue, somewhere in the audience, it was the most remarkable thing he'd ever seen.

A howler monkey wearing blue-striped pajamas and roller skates, his red blanket flying out behind him, was being towed by a jaguar-painted girl with a beard and a red-haired boy dressed in camouflage as they followed the mythical Birdman of Cahokia up the ramp of a shimmering space canoe.

"I have to find Wi-Fi," he said to Rainbow. "My Facebook friends will never believe this."

CHAPTER TWENTY
BLASTOFF!

The door of the spaceship shut behind them and the Birdman took his seat at the controls. "Seat belts should be securely fastened," commanded the recorded voice. "Tray tables stowed in the upright position. A crew member will not be pointing out emergency exits, as there aren't any. Prepare for takeoff."

Lola and Max looked at each other.

They had no words.

They'd set out to rescue their parents and now they were leaving planet Earth on a spaceship, and they didn't know if they'd ever be back.

There was nothing to say anymore.

In any case, words would have been lost in the screaming of the engines as the ship blasted off through the night sky.

Eventually, the ship seemed to steady itself and the noise was reduced to a hum.

Max gathered his thoughts. "Right up until the last minute," he said, "I was hoping it was another little trick of Lady Koo's, a special effect. But I guess we really are in space."

"I can see the moon," said Lola.

Lord 6-Dog looked out of the porthole. "Canst thou see the moon goddess, Ixchel?"

Max smiled. "I seem to remember that she had quite a crush on you at the White Pyramid, Lord 6-Dog. Maybe she'll help us."

"No one can help us," said Lola.

"I feel unwell," said Lord 6-Dog.

"Go to sleep," Lola told him. "We'll wake you if it looks like we're landing."

"He's been sleeping all day," Max pointed out.

"He's a howler monkey. That's what they do. Plus, he's had a hard day. He's been shot by a tranquilizer gun and singed by a laser. He deserves to rest."

"I wish I could sleep," said Max. "I don't want to know what happens next."

In fact, what happened next was that the Birdman stood up, walked over, and made strange garbled sounds at them.

"We don't speak your language," said Lola. "We don't understand you."

The Birdman held his head with his clawed hands. Then slowly he peeled off his face. At first, Max was repulsed, but then he realized it was a latex mask.

"Is that better?" asked Lord Kuy. "Sorry about the bumpy takeoff. I've never flown one of these before." He threw the mask on a chair. "I think that went well, don't you?"

Max and Lola were staring at him in disbelief.

"You're welcome," said Lord Kuy.

"What for?" asked Lola coldly.

"For building this thing and rescuing you. Tzelek was about to ruin everything."

Lola gaped at him. "You built a spaceship just to rescue us?"

"We Maya can build anything. You know that, Ix Sak Lol."

Max felt a furious anger bubbling inside him. "Why did you send us to get the Jaguar Stones if you were just going to zoom in and destroy them?"

"It was a surprise to us, too," explained Lord Kuy. "When you told us that Tzelek was at Cahokia, we had to think quickly. And we came up with an even better plan."

"So how are we supposed to get our parents back?" asked Lola.

"I am just the pilot," said Lord Kuy. "That would be a question for the captain."

"Did somebody call?" The voice came from a high-backed chair they had assumed was empty. It spun around to reveal Ah Pukuh, his bulging body squeezed into the silver Elvis jumpsuit he'd worn at Graceland, his black hair gelled into a quiff with a captain's hat balanced jauntily on top. His face and his many chins were painted with silver makeup.

"What do you think of my outfit, Maxie? Is it too much? I was going for a nautical space-age vibe."

"Yes, it's too much," said Max. "It's all too much."

Ah Pukuh's face clouded over.

"No, it's just right," Lola assured him. "You look amazing."

"I thought so." Ah Pukuh relaxed. "Back to the bridge, Kuy," he commanded. "The cosmic crocodile is frisky tonight." He smiled at Max. "So, Maxie, have I been a good friend?"

248

"What do you mean?" asked Max sulkily.

"You said friends give each other space. Look out of the porthole. Have I given you enough space?"

"Oh, very funny. Is this another setup? Did you send Tzelek to Cahokia like you sent the monsters to Uncle Ted's?"

"Tzelek is a loose cannon. Even I cannot control him. He runs on hatred for his brother, like the universe runs on blood. You know that."

"Then why did you come for us? What do you want?"

"I have a new proposition. A better one."

"No. We've done what you asked us to do," said Max. "Pretty much."

"Don't you get it? We never cared about Great Sun's Jaguar Stones. We sent you to Cahokia to ignite world interest in the Hero Twins. And I think that alerting the media to this evening's little alien abduction has done the trick, don't you?"

"What's the point of all this?" asked Max wearily. "Where are you taking us?"

"It's a good question. I am still deciding. I need somewhere with excellent satellite communications, a good tourist infrastructure, and established media links. I'm thinking Chichen Itza."

Again Max asked, "Why?"

"To play the game."

"What game?"

"The game of life and death."

"I'm guessing," said Lola, "that the deaths would be ours."

"Absolutely."

"Why does it have to be us?" asked Max. "We're not actually the Hero Twins."

"Try telling that to the crowds at Cahokia. As of tonight,

the whole world knows you two as the Hero Twins. And, let's not kid ourselves, it's personal. Much as I hate every mortal on this planet, I hate you two the most."

"So you and I, we're not BFFs anymore?" asked Max sarcastically.

"You never know. I might reconsider if you just do this one little thing for me, Maxie."

"Which is?"

"I just told you. A ball game to the death. Hero Twins versus Death Lords."

"But didn't we already do that at the Grand Hotel Xibalba?" said Lola. "And we won?"

"Exactly!" exclaimed Ah Pukuh. "I'm proposing a rematch. But this time, we'll get the ending right. And thanks to your visit to Cahokia, we'll have millions of viewers all over the world. There won't be a single mortal who hasn't heard about Ah Pukuh, the new king of Middleworld, after this game is over. And once we have their undivided attention, the new age of suffering can begin."

"What happened to the peace train?" asked Max.

"It crashed," said Ah Pukuh. "No survivors."

Max shrugged. "Well, your master plan won't work."

"Why not?"

"No one in Middleworld cares about the Maya ball game. You might get a few nerds and archaeologists tuning in, but apart from that, forget it."

"Forget it?" Ah Pukuh's plague sores were bursting through his silver face paint and throbbing red with anger. "Forget the ball game? It is what the Maya have done since the beginning of time. When we want to settle a dispute, or celebrate a new king, or mark an important occasion, we play ball. That's what we do." He reached out and grabbed Max by the neck. "You better make this work or I'll throw you overboard right now."

"You could . . . you could play *our* ball game," croaked Max.

Ah Pukuh released him. He smiled. "Where is the finest ball court in all of Middleworld?"

Max didn't have to think. "Fenway Park. In Boston, Massachusetts."

"How many mortals watch these games?"

"Millions. All around the world."

"In that case," announced Ah Pukuh, "it is decided. The Hero Twins will play for the future of the cosmos at Fenway Park."

"What if we refuse to play?" asked Lola.

"Then, I win by default. And the losing team is sacrificed. Including their parents and supporters."

"You do understand," said Max, "that our ball game is different from yours? It's called baseball. It has different rules."

"Whatever. " Ah Pukuh waved a fat hand dismissively. "We'll cheat anyway." He stood up and smoothed out his jumpsuit. "I take it there are costumes?"

Max nodded.

"Good. I will be in touch about the details. By the way, on your travels, did you happen to meet Baron Saturday?"

"You know we did," said Lola.

"Did he talk to you about your funeral arrangements?"

"Just stop," said Max. "You're not funny."

"I am trying to be helpful. Now is a good time to start planning your tombstones. I suggest something fun and catchy like: *Death Lords Rule, Hero Twins Drool*. Anyway, it's your choice. I have to get to work on my media platform. This is going to be mega. Finally, I'll get the recognition I deserve."

"Can we get off now?" asked Max.

"You can get off when we land." Ah Pukuh swiveled in his chair. "Kuy, set the controls for Boston, Massachusetts!"

And so, that night, unseen by any radar, a space canoe sailed over the sleeping cities of the Eastern Seaboard. Its pilot was half man, half owl. Its captain was a Maya death god on a mission to extinguish the twinkling lights of planet Earth forever.

CHAPTER TWENTY-ONE
STEALING HOME

They landed, in the dead of night, on a deserted wharf beside the Charles River.

"Welcome to Boston," Max said to Lola. "You said you wanted to see it."

"I'm guessing this isn't the tourist district," she replied, taking in the piles of garbage and snuffling rats.

Lord 6-Dog was wide awake and full of energy after his epic sleep. "How happy I am to be back on terra firma," he said, executing a twirl on his roller skates.

"You're getting good on those," said Lola, sounding impressed.

"I cannot believe that my people put wheels on children's toys and never thought to put them on their own feet. The stone roads we laid between cities would have been excellent for skates."

"An ancient Maya king on roller skates?" said Max. "I can't get my head around this."

"It makes perfect sense," Lord 6-Dog explained. "My monkey side is loving the breeze in my fur. It's like swinging through the trees. I feel like I'm back in the jungle." He threw back his head and emitted a throaty howl, a sound that carried for miles in all directions.

"Hush," said Lola. "We're not in the jungle, we're in the city now."

A faint roar of response floated back over the wharves.

"That sounded like a jaguar," said Lola, surprised.

"Must be the zoo," said Max.

"Let us go there at once," suggested Lord 6-Dog.

"No." Max sounded tired. "We're going to my house. We can walk from here. But no howling, okay? And if anyone stops us, you're a kid in a monkey mask on roller skates."

Sneaking like thieves in the night through the sleeping streets, staying in the shadows and avoiding the street lamps, they made it safely to Max's home.

Home.

Even in the dark, Max could see that the house was still covered with vines and the front yard looked suspiciously jungle-y. The vegetation, now dying in the chill of fall, was a relic from a prank the Death Lords had played on the Murphy household while Max and Lola were in Spain. Their house had acquired its own jungle biosphere, with the climate, plants, and wildlife of a tropical rainforest.

As he unlocked the front door, Max hoped that the last of the exotic creatures—the toucans, gibnuts, iguanas, snakes, and spiders that had made themselves at home—had all long since departed.

"Here we are," he said, throwing open the door. "Home, sweet home."

It still smelled of damp and fungus.

"Mmmm." Lord 6-Dog breathed in great lungfuls of the moldy air. "It reminds me of my palace in the rainy season."

"Mom and Dad were hoping it would dry out while they were away," said Max. He surveyed the peeling wallpaper and crumbling paint. "Sorry it's such a mess."

"It's amazing to be here," said Lola. "Just think. This is where my mom was living all those years when I thought I was an orphan."

"You can sleep in her room if you like," said Max.

"I need no bed," announced Lord 6-Dog. "I have slept enough. Now I have work to do."

"Suit yourself," said Max. "But feel free to use the couch."

The howler began to peruse the Murphys' bookshelves.

"I give him ten minutes before he needs a nap," Max whispered to Lola.

Lola yawned. "I give me five minutes before I'm asleep."

"Okay, so make yourself at home. Help yourself to anything you need. It's great to have working phones and Wi-Fi again. I'll e-mail Lucky before I go to bed and tell him we're safe." He reconsidered. "Or, at least, I'll tell him we're in Boston."

There was someone else in Boston that Max e-mailed that night, too.

And texted. Quite a few times.

But there was no reply.

Early the next morning, he was awakened by the sound of pounding on the front door. Certain it was Ah Pukuh,

255

Antonio de Landa, or the police, Max hid under the covers.

He heard the front door being opened.

He heard shouting.

He heard footsteps running upstairs.

He closed his eyes tightly, curled into a ball, and braced himself.

The bedcovers were pulled off him suddenly.

"Rise and shine!" said the perpetrator cheerily.

Max opened his eyes. "Lucky? What are *you* doing here?"

"We got your e-mail and took the first flight."

"*We?*"

"Lady Coco and I. She still had her travel documents from Spain, so we sailed through customs. Hermanjilio's coming as soon as he can. We're here to help."

"What about your class? Shouldn't you be teaching?"

"This is more important. I'll stay as long as you need me." Lucky held out his arms for a hug. "I'm here for you."

Max sat up in alarm. If tough, inscrutable Lucky Jim had started hugging, a crack must have appeared in the fabric of the universe. "What's happened now?" he asked warily.

"I'm sorry, Max." Lucky pulled a balled-up piece of paper out of his pocket. "This was stuck to your front door."

Max smoothed it out. It was a poster for a ball game. Quite possibly, he realized as he read it, the last ball game he would ever attend.

Hero Twins versus Death Lords, the paper said.

Fenway Park. Gates Open at Sunset, Day of the Dead. Sacrifice of losing team to follow game!

Max decided to ignore that last bit.

"When's the Day of the Dead?" he asked.

THE MIGHTY AH PUKUH PRESENTS

A GAME OF LIFE & DEATH

DEATH LORDS VS HERO TWINS

FENWAY PARK

GATES OPEN AT SUNSET, DAY OF THE DEAD

* FOOD * MUSIC * FUN FOR ALL THE FAMILY *
SACRIFICE OF LOSING TEAM TO FOLLOW GAME!

For broadcasting rights, advertising sales, merchandising opportunities
and social media links, contact Head of Marketing at Xibalba Corp

"This was stuck to your front door."

"It's actually two days," replied Lucky. "And it starts on November first, otherwise known as tomorrow."

"Tomorrow?" Max leapt out of bed. "But we haven't got a team yet!"

"We'll talk about it downstairs. Lord 6-Dog has been up all night learning the rules of baseball and Lady Coco's making breakfast." (Now that Lucky mentioned it, Max noticed a delicious smell of baking.)

"Where's Lola?"

"She was reading all the Cahokia reports in the newspapers. Now she's looking through your family albums. We all laughed at that baby snap of you in the bathtub! Speaking of which, you might want to take a quick shower before you come down."

Max looked at himself. He was still wearing his green shorts and camouflage paint from Cahokia. His mom wasn't going to be happy when she saw all the paint on his sheets, he thought. Then he remembered where she was, and realized she had bigger problems.

After his shower, he quickly checked his messages. Still nothing from Nasty Smith-Jones, the Boston music blogger he'd met in Spain and who was possibly, or more possibly not, his first girlfriend in an on-off sort of way. (He leaned more toward on; she leaned more toward off.)

He reread the last text he'd sent her:

Hey Nasty! Haven't seen you since octopus attack in Venice, lol. I'm back in Boston now. Lola's here, too! Did I tell you she's my cousin? Long story! Wanna meet up? IOU pizza and movie, remember?

He sighed. His exhaustion had made him sound like a crazy person. Maybe he'd do better this morning. He began typing again:

```
Hey Nasty, me again! Remember guy with
exploding stomach at Spanish wedding?
We're playing ball against him at Fenway
tomorrow. We need a team! Know anyone who
plays? You??????????
```

It was only after he pressed SEND that Max realized this text made him sound even crazier than the first one. He severely doubted that Nasty would want to be on his team.

With a heavy heart, he set about composing a more persuasive recruitment e-mail to his friends at school:

Hey guys. Hope you're having a good semester. Did you miss me? Well, I'm back in town and trying to get a team together to play at FENWAY tomorrow night. That's right, I said FENWAY. So if you've ever wanted to play at FENWAY, this is your chance! Call me!

Max paused, pleased with his efforts. Who wouldn't want to play at Fenway? Did he need to add any more details? Like, maybe:

P.S.: We're playing the ancient Maya Lords of Death. Losers to be sacrificed.

Nah, no sense in scaring them off. He deleted the P.S.,

copied in everyone he knew, and ran downstairs to eat breakfast.

Lola, Lord 6-Dog, and Lucky were sitting in glum silence at the kitchen table. Aside from a half-eaten banana in front of Lord 6-Dog, it looked like they hadn't touched their food.

Max's eyes took in the platter of bacon and eggs.

He was surprised to find that he wasn't hungry either.

"Seen the headlines?" asked Lola, passing him a pile of newspapers. She was wearing a big robe that he'd seen Zia wear a million times. Lola still had a few bits of beard stuck to her chin. "Looks like Landa got away."

"They'll catch him soon. It's on every news channel," said Lucky.

Max tossed the papers aside. "That's exactly what Ah Pukuh wants. Maximum publicity. So people will know who he is before he crushes them. It looks like his little plan is working."

"We're not beaten yet," said Lady Coco, carrying over hot buttered toast and a jar of honey. She was wearing one of Max's mom's flowery aprons cut down to fit. She surveyed the untouched food with displeasure. "You need to eat, all of you. You're our team. You need to be strong for the challenge ahead."

"Four is not a team," said Max.

"How many *is* a team?" asked Lola.

"Nine on the field, and a lot more in reserve."

They all sighed.

"How is your batting, Lady Coco?" asked Max.

260

"I have good eyes and strong arms, young lord."

"So five of us, then," said Max.

"At least we are the home team at Fenway," said Lord 6-Dog. "I learned last night that visiting players are at a disadvantage, due to the quirks of the field."

"Only if the home team knows the field," Max pointed out.

"So tell me," said Lola. "What quirks?"

"Fenway isn't like any other ballpark," Max began.

Lola sighed. "Is this a good moment to remind you that I've never seen a ballpark? And I've never seen a baseball game?"

"Seriously?" Max looked at her in horror and began jabbing into his phone. "The season's pretty much over, but I think they still do tours of the ballpark." He studied his screen. "Yes, here it is. And they have tickets for today! Let's go!"

"Wait," laughed Lola, "I can't go in a bathrobe! I need to borrow some clothes."

When he'd found her a hoodie, jeans, and sneakers, Max turned his attention to Lord 6-Dog. "You need a disguise," he said. "Someone will call the zoo if they see a howler monkey loose in Boston."

"What's a zoo?" asked Lady Coco.

"They keep animals in cages," explained Lola.

"A jaguar called to me last night," Lord 6-Dog told his mother. "He sounded melancholy."

"I'm not surprised," said Lady Coco, shuddering. "If you don't mind, young lord, I will stay home today."

"Will you be all right on your own?" Max asked her.

"I have little 6-Dog to keep me company," she said, pulling the Dawg Doll from Cahokia out of her apron pocket.

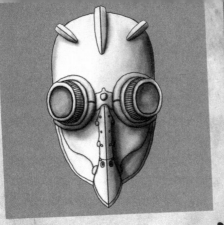

Spaceman or Conman?
The "Birdman" Returns

Who's That Simia

Mystical howler monkey
enter of Cahokia mystery

. LOUIS, Missouri
estigators are baffled by
orts of a talking howler
key at the center of

ModernTimes
freaky phenom

ALIEN ABDUCTION –
OULD IT HAPPEN TO YOU?
ERE'S HOW TO AVOID IT –
ND WHAT TO WEAR IF YOU CAN'T

"But don't you want to see Boston?"

"My heart is in the rainforest. I care not for cities, unless they are Maya cities. I would rather stay here and cook a dinner. What does your mother make for you?"

Max grimaced. "My mother is the worst cook in the world. But she likes buying cookbooks." Max showed Lady Coco the crammed kitchen bookshelf. "Look"—he selected a book—"this one's from a restaurant here in Boston."

Lady Coco's eyes lit up as she looked through the photographs. "Clam chowder, Boston cream pie . . . this all sounds delicious."

"Tonight we feast like kings!" declared Lord 6-Dog. "For tomorrow we fight like kings!"

Lola gulped. "So let's go inspect the battlefield. Did you find a disguise for Lord 6-Dog?"

"I have an idea!" said Max, turning to run upstairs. "Follow me!"

They found him in his room, rooting through a closet. "I know it's in here!" he called, throwing out footballs, and plastic toys, and stuffed animals, and assorted action figures.

"Aren't you a bit old for all this?" asked Lola, trying on a pirate hat.

"I know. I keep meaning to clear it all out, but it's easier to just never open the closet."

"I think you should keep them." Lola took off the pirate hat and picked up an old teddy bear. "It must be amazing to have your whole childhood around you like this."

Max was in the depths of the closet and didn't hear her, so she continued wandering around the room, inspecting his stuff.

"*Adventure Stories for Boys,*" she read, taking a book off

the shelf. "Anything in here about meeting a Maya girl and some talking howler monkeys, Hoop?" She opened the book. "'Happy birthday, *bambino*,'" she read. "'Wishing you many adventures.'" Lola smiled to herself. "Well, that came true all right." She took the book over to the closet. "I like how your mom always calls you *bambino*," she called.

"She's Italian," Max called back. "It means 'little boy.'"

"I know that. It's cute. I bet she's called you *bambino* every day since you were a baby."

"Yeah. I kinda wish she'd stop now."

Lola went quiet, and when Max looked up to see why, she had a weird expression on her face.

"Sorry," he said. "It smells a bit funky in here. I need to clean up."

"It's not that. I was just thinking that my mom doesn't have a pet name for me yet. We haven't had time." She looked away for a moment. "Did you find what you were looking for?" she asked, a little too brightly.

"Here it is!" said Max, pulling out a white helmet from under a pile of board games. The rest of the costume was stuffed inside the helmet. "It looks perfect."

And it was.

"Who am I?" asked Lord 6-Dog, his voice muffled by the helmet.

"It's from a movie called *Star Wars*," Max explained to Lord 6-Dog. "You're a Stormtrooper."

"A Stormtrooper, thou sayest? What might that be?"

"An elite fighter of the Galactic Empire."

Lord 6-Dog nodded his approval and went to study himself in the mirror.

Lola was checking out all of Max's video games—"You have

a lot of stuff, Hoop"—when she noticed his drum set, half hidden under a pile of laundry. She cleared off the clothes and sat down to play.

"You'll need these," said Max, handing her the headphones. "It's electronic. You can hear yourself but no one else can."

"Seriously?" Lola looked horrified. "You sit in your room drumming silently? That's the saddest thing I've ever heard."

"The neighbors like it."

"They don't dance in the streets when they hear drums?"

"No," said Max. "Maybe in Vermont, but not in Boston."

"What are you doing up there?" called Lucky. "Daylight's burning."

"I think I'd like Vermont," said Lola as they went downstairs.

"Add it to your road trip," said Max.

"First I need to get my parents back."

CHAPTER TWENTY-TWO
HALLOWEEN

Out on the gray streets, the fallen leaves were crispy under their feet and they kicked them as they walked along. Lord 6-Dog skated ahead. They were barely halfway to the T station when Lord 6-Dog let out a howl that set all the dogs of Boston barking.

"Death Lords approaching! Take cover," he shouted, diving over a low garden wall in his roller skates. The other three followed him without thinking and found themselves crouched behind some scraggly bushes in someone's front yard.

A trio of skeletons walked past them, chattering excitedly.

Max noticed how small they were.

And how they carried orange plastic pumpkins.

"It's Halloween!" he said. "The kids are wearing their costumes to school!"

A witch and a dead bride skipped happily by on the other side of the street.

Max, Lola, and Lucky waited until the coast was clear, then stood up, gave Lord 6-Dog a hand up on his skates, and brushed themselves off.

"Now I understand why Ah Pukuh chose tomorrow for the game," said Max. "Halloween is the only time that ghouls and ghosts can come in to town unnoticed, since all the kids are in costumes."

"And tomorrow, on the Day of the Dead," added Lucky, "the doors on the graves are opened and the dear departed return to visit their loved ones. It's a spooky time of year."

Max's phone pinged. "It's Nasty," he said, reading the message. "She says: Hey Mac! Hey Lola! I'll put word out. Everyone talking about game. Posters everywhere. Line about sacrifice putting off players. See you there."

"Why does she call you Mac?" asked Lucky.

"It's a private joke," said Max. To be honest, Nasty Smith-Jones had gotten his name wrong so many times that he wasn't sure if it was a joke or not.

"So, is she on our team?" asked Lola.

"I guess we'll find out tomorrow." Max put his phone away. "But if everyone's freaking out about the sacrifice, that explains why none of my friends have called back."

"Thy friends are cowards," opined Lord 6-Dog as he skated around a confused squirrel on the sidewalk.

"You can hardly blame them," said Max. "No one wants to get sacrificed after a game. Anyway, it's a school night."

Nasty was right. Ah Pukuh's posters were up everywhere. On lampposts, in shop windows, on bus sides, on subway walls.

When they emerged from the green line to Kenmore Square, they felt sure that no one in Boston could be unaware of the event.

"Looks like Ah Pukuh has publicity covered," said Lucky.

"He's been studying PR," said Max. "He's convinced it's the way forward for the villains of the world."

On Yawkey Way, outside the stadium, a large group of people milled around.

"Who is that?" asked Lord 6-Dog, eyeing a bronze statue. "Is it one of your kings?"

"Yes," said Max. "It's Ted Williams. They call him *the greatest hitter who ever lived.*"

"I wish he was on our team," said Lola.

"He's dead," said Max.

"Like us," wailed Lola.

"Next tour departs in two minutes!" called a guide. They bought tickets and mingled with the rest of the tourists.

"Did you see that poster for tomorrow's game?" one woman asked another. "Hero Twins versus Death Lords. I haven't heard of those teams. Have you?"

"They let all sorts of riffraff play here in the off-season," said her friend.

"I heard that tickets are free," said the first woman.

"In that case, we'll definitely be there. The whole of Boston will probably be there!"

Max and Lola exchanged a look of terror.

For the next hour they tried to forget their fears as they listened to their tour guide telling stories from the history of the Red Sox. They posed for photographs in the stands. They sat on the Green Monster, the high scoreboard wall at left field that routinely turned home runs into doubles. They inspected the red-painted seat that marks the landing spot of the longest ball ever hit at Fenway, shot by Ted Williams of statue fame.

But whatever part of the ground they were being shown or whatever piece of local pride was being pointed out, their eyes kept straying back to the home plate.

Max's stomach did a double-flip every time he imagined standing there in the footsteps of all the great Red Sox players, waiting for a pitch from a cheating Death Lord. Even the mighty Ted Williams would have trouble hitting under those circumstances. Max felt a lump in his throat. Once news of his brave self-sacrifice got out, maybe the Red Sox would erect a statue to him next to Ted Williams on Yawkey Way.

"Hoop!" Lola interrupted his thoughts. "Come on! The tour's over."

"So what did you think?" asked Max.

"It's smaller than I expected," said Lola, "not quite as intimidating."

"Those stories were really neat," said Lucky.

"I sensed the history in every brick and every blade of grass," said Lord 6-Dog.

Max asked, "Any ideas for getting a team together?"

"Leave it to me, young lord," said Lord 6-Dog. "This ball court has inspired me. I would be honored to form a team to play on this hallowed ground."

"You?" Max stared at the little Stormtrooper. "But you don't know anyone in Boston."

"Dost thou not trust me, young lord? When have I ever let thee down?"

Max remembered all the tight spots they'd been in, all the

narrow escapes they'd survived, all the times that the monkey king's wisdom had saved his life.

"Of course I trust you," he said. "But—"

"But nothing. I will be your manager. Lucky will be your coach. My mother will be your nutritionist. By sunset tomorrow, I will have found seven players, plus reserves, to join you and Lady Lola on the Hero Twins' team. I have a most excellent plan. Do not give it another thought."

Max knew he would think about nothing else.

Lola pointed to the team shop. "We should get some stuff to practice with—bats and balls."

"And Red Sox gear," said Max, "so people will know we're the home team."

Loaded up with their shopping, they walked to the nearest park and tried out their skills with their new bats and balls. It didn't go well. Then they sat down and ate the lunch that Lady Coco had packed for them, and watched little monsters trot by on the candy trail.

"Feels like it's getting dark already," said Lola. "The days are short here."

"This time tomorrow," said Max, "we'll be warming up for the game." He shivered. "Let's go home and practice some more."

"What's the point?" said Lola. "It's not going to make any difference. I'd rather forget about baseball and be a tourist for my last night on Earth. I've never been a tourist before."

"I guess it will be too dark to practice by the time we get home. But you have to promise to watch baseball with me on TV tonight." Everyone nodded. "So what do you want to see?"

"What is there?" asked Lola.

Max shrugged. "There's the aquarium. Or a duck boat down the river. Or the swan boats."

"No fish, no boats, and no water," demanded Lord 6-Dog, skating backward past them. He'd tied his red blanket over his costume for warmth. "And somewhere indoors, it's getting cold."

"I have a suggestion," said Lucky. "How about the Peabody Museum? Their Maya collection is famous."

"That would be of great interest to me," agreed Lord 6-Dog.

"I'm down with that," said Lola. "Isn't that where your parents work, Hoop?"

"Yeah, it's just across the river. At Harvard."

"Harvard?" Lola's eyes were shining.

Lucky smiled at her. "Thinking about applying?"

She rolled her eyes at him. "Yeah right, like Harvard would admit someone who grew up barefoot in a hut with no electricity."

"You're as smart as any Harvard student," Lucky said. "We need to believe in ourselves if we're going to stand a chance tomorrow."

"Hear, hear!" cheered Lord 6-Dog, executing a perfect double axel, his red blanket streaming out behind him like a cape.

He looks like a monkey superhero, thought Max.

Which, in many ways, he was.

It was twilight by the time they reached Harvard Square. Students dressed as vampires and werewolves flitted through the shadows.

"This place is beautiful," said Lola.

"Then you'd fit right in here," said Lucky.

Max thought he saw her blush.

They crossed the road to a big redbrick building and ran up the steps.

"Welcome to the Peabody Museum of Archaeology and Ethnology," said the lady at the desk. "You're my only guests this afternoon. But I must warn you that we close in one hour. No roller skates inside the building."

"We'll be quick," Max promised her.

He led them up the stairs to the third floor, home of the Americas exhibits. After so many rainy weekends being dragged around this museum by his parents, he knew it like the back of his hand.

Lucky pointed out a display of Maya fabrics and backstrap looms to Lola. "Look at the craftsmanship. See how the strength of our people comes out in every stitch."

She nodded. "They look like the patterns the women weave in my village. I wish I could tell them that their shawls and tablecloths are on display in a fancy museum in Boston, Massachusetts."

"You can tell them when you go back. After we win."

"Like that's going to happen," she said.

"I had hoped that coming to the Peabody would inspire you," Lucky said. "At this moment, you are surrounded by the achievements of your people. Try to draw strength from it. With our pyramids, our writing system, and our calendar, we Maya have always defied people's expectations. I would add to that list the fact that we have endured so much and lived to tell the tale. The impossible is what we do. And tomorrow we will continue that tradition."

"I just wish," said Lola, "that we had a tradition of playing baseball. All this old stuff is not going to help us."

She caught up to Max at the Day of the Dead exhibit, where an altar decorated with skulls and paper flowers dominated a room full of tributes to the dead. Skeletons in hats and party dresses hung from the ceiling, dancing in the breeze from a ceiling vent. On a table, sugar skulls and coloring pages awaited the next day's school visits.

Lord 6-Dog swooped into the room. "I sense danger!" he whispered. "Be on thy guard."

Before they could ask him to explain, he ran to the far end of the Americas floor and disappeared behind a large screen bearing the notice:

RESTRICTED
— AREA —
NO ENTRY
NEW EXHIBIT
IN PROGRESS

"Better follow him," said Max. "He's not supposed to be back there."

On the other side of the screen, workmen assembled stands and display cases. A museum director bustled around giving instructions.

She glared at Max over her spectacles. "Can't you read,

boy? This section is closed to visitors. Off you go now. Shoo. We're very busy."

Playing for time while he looked around for Lord 6-Dog, Max said: "I'm . . . I'm Max Murphy, Frank and Carla Murphy's son."

The museum director examined him more closely. "Ah, red hair like your father, I see the family resemblance. But that still gives you no right to come back here. I suppose they told you to come and check up on the new Maya pottery exhibition?"

Trying to keep her talking, Max decided to wing it: "Yes. That's right. How's it going?"

"Nothing broken so far, thank goodness. There were so many pieces in storage that have never been shown before. And of course, your parents' shipment arrived in the nick of time. Do thank them for us—what we've glimpsed so far is spectacular!"

"Thank them for . . . um . . . what exactly"—Max peered at her badge—"Dr. Delgado?"

She looked at him like he was stupid. "For sending the shipment."

"Mom and Dad sent a shipment?"

Dr. Delgado's laughter trilled like fingernails on a chalkboard. "Of course. It's from the Black Pyramid in San Xavier. It just arrived. Who else would send it?"

Max didn't know the answer to that question. But he did know that it was not from his parents. They'd been way too busy getting locked up in jail to be shipping any artifacts back to Boston.

"What was in it?" he asked.

"It's magnificent. A round lidded pot with a lizard handle.

Yale would kill for it! Of course, it's still in its crate and we haven't had time to translate the glyphs yet, but it's going to be a real showstopper."

Lord 6-Dog appeared from behind a screen. He carried his helmet under his arm.

"It's a monkey!" screamed Dr. Delgado. "A monkey in a space suit! I hate monkeys! Get it out of here!"

Max froze in panic.

"Excuse me, have you seen my little brother?" asked Lola, running in. "I think he came this way." She saw Lord 6-Dog and grabbed his hand. "There you are, you naughty boy. Don't you ever run way like that again. Come on, it's time to go home."

"Your brother is a monkey?" asked Dr. Delgado in shock.

Lola giggled. "It's his Halloween costume. He's a space monkey."

Dr. Delgado relaxed. "Silly me. It's Halloween. I quite forgot."

"The Peabody Museum is now

closing. All visitors are asked to make their way to the exit," came a voice over the public address system.

"Time to go home, children," said Dr. Delgado. "But do come back tomorrow for our Day of the Dead party." She was still looking at Lord 6-Dog suspiciously.

As they left, Max distinctly heard her comment to a workman that the boy in the space suit was the ugliest kid she'd ever seen.

"That was close," he said to Lord 6-Dog. "Why did you take off your helmet?"

"I thought I detected the smell of evil."

Max nodded knowledgeably. "That's probably from the Natural History Department. They have a lot of stuffed animals. Some of them are getting a bit old."

Lord 6-Dog shuddered. "Let us leave this place."

"Happy Halloween!" the woman at the desk called after them.

"Seeing all the pumpkins on people's doorsteps makes me think of Chan Kan," said Lola as they walked to the subway station. "I know you didn't like him, Hoop, but he did what he thought was right, and he taught me a lot. He was always saying that one little seed of good can change the world. So every time we ate pumpkin, I'd make him a necklace from the seeds."

"Nice," said Max. "But he was your grandfather and he paid Landa to kidnap you from your own parents. I don't see the seed of good in that."

"I don't either. But I know he regretted it. And he gave his own life to save you and me at the White Pyramid. We should buy some pumpkins. It's Halloween."

"Okay," said Max. "We can carve them while we watch old baseball games on TV."

It was rush hour and the train was crowded.

They squashed in by the door.

Lord 6-Dog pulled at Lola's jacket to get her attention. He pointed to one of Ah Pukuh's posters pasted on the car's window. Someone had scrawled Maya glyphs on it in red marker, like ancient Maya graffiti.

"What does it say?" asked Max.

"Too advanced for me," said Lola.

Lord 6-Dog pulled at her again and she crouched down. Unseen by the crush of commuters, he lifted his helmet slightly and whispered the translation into her ear.

"Did he tell you what it says?" Max asked when she stood up.

"The Death Lords reign supreme and the Hero Twins salivate!"

"I don't get it," said Max.

"Death Lords rule, Hero Twins drool! It's what Ah Pukuh said we should write on our tombstones. He's trying to psych us out."

Had Ah Pukuh been on this train? Max surveyed the faces of their fellow passengers. A few minutes before they'd looked tired, preoccupied, dazed, uncomfortable. Now they all looked sinister to him.

"You know, Hoop," whispered Lola. "I bet we're the only people on this train whose family members are being held prisoner by the Maya Lords of Death."

"And who are going home to a dinner cooked by a howler monkey," added Max.

Even with a stop at the store to pick up pumpkins and candy, it didn't take long to get back. As soon as they piled through the front door of the Murphys' vine-covered house, Lady Coco ran out to greet them.

"I'm so happy to see you!" she said. "You have no idea! This neighborhood's got more spirits than Xibalba! The doorbell's been ringing all afternoon, and every time I peeped out of the window, I saw ghosts and skeletons at the door."

"It's just kids dressing up for Halloween," said Max.

"How do you know it's not the Death Lords' supporters come early for the ball game?" demanded Lady Coco.

Max realized that he didn't know that at all. Which is why, after a quick discussion, he and his teammates decided that they should eat all their Halloween candy themselves and not open the door again until morning.

Back at the Peabody Museum, the workmen had gone home. Down in the basement, a crate sat waiting to be unpacked. Inside was the showstopping lidded pot with the lizard handle that had recently arrived from San Xavier. And inside it, something stirred. It was waiting for the Day of the Dead to dawn and the doors between worlds to open.

It wasn't a person or an animal, more like a seething gas that was the essence of evil.

"Trick or treat," cackled Tzelek to himself.

CHAPTER TWENTY-THREE
THE LAST PIZZA

The next day was Wak Ok in the Maya calendar, the day of 6-Dog the monkey king's birthday. Lady Coco made him a cashew and banana cake, and stuck a beeswax candle in it.

"How old are you, your majesty?" asked Lola.

"In thy solar years? About twelve hundred."

"We should have gotten you something," said Max.

"No, I shall give *thee* something. I shall give thee the greatest team in the history of baseball." He wiped his hairy chin with his napkin, jumped down from the table, and bounded to the front door to strap on his skates.

Max and Lola followed him.

"Lord 6-Dog, I'm worried. Please tell me who's on the team," begged Max.

"Why all the mystery?" asked Lola. "If this team exists, where did you find them?"

"Trust me. I will see thee at Fenway." And with that, Lord

6-Dog jammed on his Stormtrooper helmet and skated off into the Boston backstreets.

"If anyone can pick a team to take on the Death Lords, he can," said Max when he went back to the others. He sounded like he was trying to convince himself. Lola and Lucky gave him weak smiles.

"I was busy yesterday," said Lady Coco brightly. "Come and see my secret weapon." She lifted the lid off a pot that was boiling furiously on the stove.

Max peered in. It was dark and unctuous. "What is it?"

"Do you remember, young lord, when I used flatulence as a weapon at the Black Pyramid to fell several soldiers in Landa's army?"

Max nodded. "No one can beat you in that department, Lady Coco."

She pointed to an open page in the Boston cookbook. "I found a local dish that will serve my purpose well."

Max looked at the recipe and laughed.

"Boston Baked Beans," said Lady Coco. "Guaranteed to fell an army of Death Lords. Now you two go practice your ball game. And I will cook up more ammunition."

"I'll coach," volunteered Lucky. "I picked up a few tips watching those old games last night."

So Lucky coached, and Lola pitched, and Max batted.

Then Lola batted, and Max pitched, and they both argued with Lucky's coaching.

As the afternoon wore on, they gathered for one last meal in the Murphy kitchen and everyone chose one course. Max went for thin-crust pepperoni pizza with extra cheese. Lola chose tropical fruit salad. And they added a banana-pecan pie for Lord 6-Dog, who hadn't come home yet. Lucky suggested they finish up all the ice cream in the freezer as they didn't know when they'd be back.

"What about you, Lady Coco?" asked Lola. "Where's your favorite food?"

"Right here," said Lady Coco, tucking into another plate of baked beans. Or, as she called it, loading up on ammo.

CHAPTER TWENTY-FOUR
WARMING UP

"**R**eady?" asked Lola.

"No," said Max.

"Come on, Hoop, there's nothing else we can do. We've watched games, we've practiced all day, we've gone over the rules, we're wearing our Red Sox uniforms—it's time to get down to Fenway."

"Where's the rest of the team?"

"You know where. Lord 6-Dog said they'd meet us there."

"This has disaster written all over it. I should never have trusted him."

"Have faith, young lord," said Lady Coco, taking off her apron. "My 6-Dog always keeps his word. If he says he will find you a team, he will find you a team."

"But how can he? He's a howler monkey! It's not like he can just walk up to people on the street. Can you imagine?" Max put on a Boston accent and pretended to talk into a phone. "Yeah, a talking monkey came up to me today and asked me to play ball against the Maya Lords of Death. Did I say *yes?* 'Course I didn't say *yes.* I ran screaming down the street, is what I did."

"It's too late to worry now," said Lola. "Let's just get there."

"A lot of people are rooting for you guys," said Lucky, reading the messages on his phone as he came downstairs. "The word is out. I'm hearing from people all over the world."

A car horn honked outside.

"There's the cab," said Max.

Lady Coco pulled on her child-size Red Sox shirt.

"Time to go," she said.

It took a little while to persuade the driver to accept a howler monkey in his taxi, but in the end he agreed because of Lady Coco's shirt. "What's the game tonight?" he asked.

"It's a . . . a charity game," said Max.

"Looks like there's a good crowd."

Traffic around Fenway, always bad on game days, was even worse than usual. They were still several blocks away and not moving an inch.

All around them, people surged toward the ballpark.

"It's not the usual Red Sox fans," said Max. "Most of these people look Maya."

It was true. As soon as word had gotten out about this grudge match—in e-mails, texts, tweets, status updates, letters, phone calls, notices in hallways, and whispered messages— Maya people from all over the American continent had dropped everything to head for Boston.

A surgeon from San Francisco had laid down his scalpel and jumped on a plane. A bellboy from Atlanta had abandoned his luggage cart in the hotel lobby. A weaver from Maine had left her loom to catch a bus. A chef from Chicago put her sous chef in charge. Students from Seattle left their lectures, refugees from Florida hit the road, a university professor from Texas brought his entire class with him.

From farther afield were costumed performers from a theme park in Cancun; a gang of workmen from Chichen Itza; a party of archaeologists from Honduras; a whole village from the Lacandon rainforest—men, women, and children all with long black hair and wearing their distinctive white tunics; market traders from Guatemala, carrying their wares in straw baskets on their backs; a punk band from the Highlands in leather and jeans with their hair carefully gelled and spiked; village elders in straw hats with long flowing ribbons; old women in intricately woven shawls.

"Wow." Max stared at them all in amazement. "I can't believe it."

Lady Coco wiped a tear from her eye.

"What's the matter?" Lola asked her.

"I'm so proud. It's been a long time since I saw our people come together. All the costumes and the colors, it reminds me of markets in the old days."

"These folks need you to win today," said Lucky to Max and Lola. "If they see a couple of kids stand up to the Death Lords, they'll know that anything is possible."

"We are so doomed," said Lola.

"Look!" said Lady Coco, pointing through the taxi window. "Sacrifice victims!"

They looked where she pointed and saw three men painted blue from head to toe.

Max laughed. "That's the Blue Man Group. It's a show in town. They're actors."

"Well, I hope Ah Pukuh doesn't see them," fretted Lady Coco. "You know that my people painted sacrifice victims that exact same color. They're taking their lives in their hands, walking around in blue paint like that."

A Blue Man saw her looking and mimed falling in love by pretending to give her his heart. "That man has a death wish," said Lady Coco, shaking her head.

Max was panicking now. "This traffic isn't moving. It would be quicker to walk."

He started to open his door and quickly pulled it shut again as a motorbike almost clipped the paintwork. Next minute, the taxi was surrounded by bikes, their riders wearing black knitted ski masks.

Lucky rolled down his window and shouted something in Mayan to the leader of the gang, a woman with a bandanna across her face.

"What's he saying?" Max asked Lola.

"They're rebels from the mountains," she explained. "They fight for the rights of the poor. They're offering us a lift to the game."

Max, Lola, Lucky, and Lady Coco each took a seat on the back of a bike. Then, to the cheers of the crowd, the rebels took off, revving their engines, weaving through the traffic, and pumping their fists in the air.

When they finally arrived at Fenway, it looked very different from the day before—like some evil alien version of itself from a parallel universe. The usual red, white, and blue Red Sox pennants along Yawkey Way were gone, replaced by black Death Lord pennants with skulls on them. The

HOW CAN I HELP?

FRIED GRASSHOPP

GAME DAY S
HONEY ROA
SCORPIO

Fresh GRASSHOPPE
JUMBO SIZED BA

Fenway looked very different from the day before.

rotating baseball sign by the parking lot across the street had been swapped out for a rotating skull. Even the Red Sox merchandise in the team shop sat side by side with souvenirs of Xibalba.

Yawkey Way had been closed to traffic and now bustled with pregame excitement.

Max noticed that many of the food stalls had added fried grasshoppers to their usual offerings of peanuts and Cracker Jack. A program seller with a fearsomely painted face waved a brochure in Max's face. "Get yer programs and completed scorecards here."

"How can they be completed?" asked Max. "The game hasn't started yet."

"This game is a foregone conclusion, sonny," said the program seller. "The Death Lords win. End of story."

They headed for the players' entrance.

"Names?" said the one-eyed ogre on security.

"They're Max and Lola, the Hero Twins," said Lady Coco indignantly. "They're the home team in today's game."

The ogre checked his list and waved them through. Lucky and Lady Coco went to follow, but the ogre barred their way.

"I'm under strict instructions. No one but the twins gets through," he said. "You two, scram. You're not on the list."

"But we're with them," argued Lucky. "I'm the coach and—"

The ogre curled his massive fist.

"It's okay," said Max to Lucky, trying to sound brave. "Go get good seats. We'll be fine. It's too late for coaching, anyway."

Lola forced a smile. "We have to say good-bye sometime."

Lady Coco gave a little toot of melancholy. "Please come back safe to me," she sniffled.

They nodded unconvincingly.

"And remember," said the monkey queen. "I ate that whole pot of beans. So if you need artillery, just tell me where to point and shoot."

Lucky and Lady Coco watched as Max and Lola went inside, following signs to the home team locker room.

"Good-bye, Hero Twins!" they called. "Good luck!"

"I feel sick," Max said to Lola. "I'm so nervous I could throw up."

"It's just the smell of hot dogs," said Lola. She didn't look very well herself.

She looked even worse when they found their locker room and it was empty. "Great!" said Max, kicking a locker door. "Where's Lord 6-Dog? Where's the team?"

Lola bit her lip. "We still have time," she said. "Want to practice?"

"We should be practicing with our team," objected Max. But he grabbed a bat and ball and followed her anyway.

As they walked through the tunnel to the field, they heard a cacophony of drums and screeching guitars.

Lola put her hands over her ears.

Max winced. "This is the worst warm-up band I've ever heard."

When they reached the end of the tunnel and saw where the noise was coming from, they stood and gaped. Fenway's interior had also been transformed.

For a start, the Green Monster—that towering green wall—had been daubed blood-red. On top, instead of the usual seating, was a rock stage with a massive PA system and light show. Performing on this precariously high platform was Max's favorite band, the Plague Rats.

Or at least, it looked like them. But Max wasn't taken in. After all, the real Plague Rats took pride in bad musicianship, but this was something else. This was painful.

He instantly realized that the four skinny dudes in black leather prancing about on the stage were the same four demons of hell who'd impersonated the Rats in Spain. Apparently, Ah Pukuh was a Plague Rats fan, too.

Meanwhile on the floodlit field, pandemonium ruled.

Flaming trapeze artists flew high above the stands. Zombies with nothing left to lose were fire-eating, juggling chain saws, and sword-fighting on stilts. Heads and body parts flew everywhere, all in a swirling mist of dry ice.

It was chaos.

It was terrifying.

It was fantastic.

"I guess this is what Ah Pukuh meant when he said he wanted a spectacle."

They peered at it all from the safety of the tunnel.

"We can't let them intimidate us," said Lola. "We need to go out there. Get started with batting practice."

Max took a deep breath. "Let's do it!"

As soon as they ran onto the field, a cheer went up from the crowd, followed by a weak chorus of boos. Max looked around the stands. He estimated that the crowd was 20 percent ghouls and 80 percent good guys; about the same ratio as Yankees to Red Sox fans when the two arch-rivals played at Fenway.

He picked out Lucky and Lady Coco in a block of empty seats.

He tried to ask them in gestures if they'd seen Lord 6-Dog, but they just waved back encouragingly.

"And here are the famous Hero Twins," said a TV reporter, thrusting a microphone under their noses. "First of all, guys, on behalf of all of us, let me say how glad we are to see you. Last time you were on our screens, you were being abducted on an alien spaceship. We now know that it was just a publicity stunt by your opposing team. Tell me, were you in on the joke?"

"No," said Max.

"So, you actually thought you were being abducted?"

"Yes," said Max, starting to feel foolish.

"Well, let's hope the Death Lords don't dupe you so easily today." He turned to Lola. "And what about your pet monkey? It attracted a lot of attention at Cahokia. Will it be rooting for you today?"

"I hope so. It's our manager."

"Glad to see you've kept your sense of humor, Lila."

"My name is Lola."

"Of course it is. So tell me, Layla, the stakes are very high today. Do you have any pregame superstitions?"

"No," she said. "I've never played this game before."

"What a comedian! And how about you, Max? Any pregame rituals? What did you eat before the game?"

"Pizza," said Max. "Why do you want to know—"

"You heard it here, folks! The Hero Twins like to eat pizza before a game. I spoke to those crazy Death Lords earlier and, believe me, you do *not* want to hear about their rituals." The presenter laughed, then suddenly became serious. "And now the question on everyone's lips. Tell me, Lula, where's the rest of your team?"

291

Lola disliked this reporter intensely. "They're still changing," she snapped.

"Let's hope they're changing into the most amazing ballplayers the world has ever seen! They'll need to be to win this one today!" The reporter chuckled. His cameraman swung away from Max and Lola over to the Death Lords.

"What an idiot," said Lola. "He got my name wrong every time."

"Let's just practice," said Max, feeling sicker than ever.

"I'll pitch," said Lola.

Max couldn't focus on the ball. The bat shook in his hands. All he could think about was the fact that Lord 6-Dog had let him down. Was it even allowed to have a team of two, he wondered, or had they lost before they'd even started?

"It's no good," he said. "I can't do this. Let's go back to the clubhouse."

"Wait," said Lola. "I want to watch the Death Lords practice, see what we're up against."

There was a fanfare of wooden trumpets and conch shells.

Max and Lola sat down in their dugout as their opponents ran onto the field.

"I can't believe it!" said Max in disgust. "Of all the dirty, lowdown, rotten tricks . . ."

"What's the matter?" asked Lola. "They look pretty smart for once. No rotting flesh, no distended bellies, no spilled intestines. You can't tell who's who anymore without the trailing organs."

"Don't you see what they're *wearing*?"

"Those striped shirts? What's wrong with them?"

"They're *Yankees* shirts. The Yankees are the Red Sox's biggest rivals. They've done this deliberately to get under my skin."

Lola laughed. "That's pretty funny."

"No," said Max. "It isn't."

"Who cares what they're wearing? They're not the Yankees and we're not the Red Sox. The only thing that matters is how well they—"

Lola gasped as the first Death Lord to bat sent the ball soaring into the stands.

The second Death Lord to bat sent the ball hurtling into the sky, where it was last seen bouncing off the Citgo sign.

The third Death Lord to bat sent the ball flying over the band on the newly red Green Monster and out into the street.

"Cheaters," said Lola.

"I've seen enough," said Max grimly. "Let's go look for Lord 6-Dog."

In fact, they bumped into him in the tunnel.

"Where have you been!" yelled Max.

"I was submitting the team list. Everything is in order."

Max looked down the tunnel. "So where's the team?"

"They are on their way."

"They're not here yet? But it's nearly time—"

"Calm thyself, young lord. Thy reserves are in the locker room."

Max and Lola raced back to the locker room and barged straight in.

The wall of noise that hit them was incredible.

"It sounds like the monkey house at the zoo!" joked Max.

And that's exactly what it was.

A monkey house.

The locker room was full of spider monkeys.

Spider monkeys in caps and little Red Sox shirts.

CHAPTER TWENTY-FIVE
THE DREAM TEAM

"**Y**ou've got to be kidding me," said Max. "Our reserves are monkeys?"

A banana peel bounced off of his head.

"They are excellent pitchers," Lord 6-Dog pointed out.

"I trusted you," said Max coldly.

"They are but reserves. They were bored at the zoo, so I brought them along. They will not be called upon to play."

"How can you be so sure? Where is our team?"

"They will be here soon."

"We need them *now*."

Someone banged on the door. "HOME TEAM! TIME TO GO!"

"We'll have to go on without them," said Lola.

She put her fingers on her lips and made some little chirruping noises.

The spider monkeys chirruped back excitedly.

"I told them to spread out on the field," said Lola.

Neither Max nor Lola looked at Lord 6-Dog as they walked sullenly out to face certain mockery—and equally certain death.

Ever since he could remember, Max had daydreamed about how it would feel to walk out on the field at Fenway wearing a Red Sox uniform. But he had never imagined the humiliation of walking out with a team of spider monkeys behind him.

When he and Lola emerged from the tunnel, they were rewarded with another roar from the crowd. But when the monkeys came out after them, it went very quiet.

Then began the nervous giggles and the heckling.

Lord 6-Dog directed the monkeys to sit in the dugout.

"Everyone's laughing at us," said Lola.

"Hold thy head high," said Lord 6-Dog.

"Don't tell her that!" snapped Max. "You've made fools of us!"

Max and Lola angrily turned their backs on Lord 6-Dog and stood, arms folded, surveying the field.

"Maybe we should surrender," said Max. "There's no way we can win."

Behind them, a commotion began in the stands. It started quietly and built to a crescendo, with people yelling, chanting, and clapping:

"LET'S-GO-GOOD-GUYS!" *Clap, clap, clap-clap-clap.*

Max and Lola turned toward it. What they saw was mind-blowing.

It was everyone.

Everyone.

All the empty seats around Lucky and Lady Coco had

been filled with friends and family, all madly waving. There was Hermanjilio and Raul. There was a whole section of Max's friends from school and Lola's student friends from Itzamna. Lucky's entire family was there—his mother, brothers, and sisters. There was Eusebio, Och, his brother Little Och (looking fully recovered from his accident), and assorted villagers from Utsal; Oscar Poot from the Maya Foundation and Victor, the head waiter from the Hotel de las Americas, both of whom Max had met on his first day in San Xavier; Santino Garcia, the law student from Spain, and his distant relative Doña Carmela, who ran the hotel in Polvoredo where Max and Lola had stayed; Fabio the gondolier from Venice, and the posse of fishermen who'd killed the octopus that had tried to drag Max down to the underworld; Blue, Rainbow, Phoenix, and a big crowd of campers from Cahokia; of course, a huge archaeologist contingent in a swathe of khaki; and even the poncho family from the Grand Hotel Xibalba—innocent tourists who'd gotten caught up in Max and Lola's first ball game against the Death Lords and had now turned up to support them in this second bid. They still wore their bright yellow rain ponchos.

Everyone was there. And they were all waving and chanting and whistling furiously, even the normally dour Doña Carmela.

"I guess we're not on our own anymore," said Lola.

Nasty Smith-Jones had done a very good job of getting the word out. But where was *she*? Max was scanning the faces in the crowd for her. And then he saw some people he had certainly not expected.

"Look!" He gripped Lola's arm as some late arrivals took their seats behind home plate. Surrounded by a brigade of Maya guards were Frank, Carla, Uncle Ted, and Zia.

"That stinks!" said Lola, with tears in her eyes.

"Aren't you happy to see them?" asked Max.

"That pig Ah Pukuh has brought them here to watch us die."

"*Good evening, ladies and gentlemen, boys and girls,*" came the announcer's voice. "*Welcome to America's most beloved ballpark.*"

A blast of organ music was drowned out by the earsplitting *ker-rang* of electric guitars. In place of the national anthem, the bogus Plague Rats banged out a truly horrible cover of "Highway to Hell." The fog machines belched out dry ice, and laser lights sent colored beams spinning around the stands.

As the distorted guitars howled to a screeching crescendo, the ballpark reverberated with a massive bang as simultaneous explosions of fireworks shot balls of fire around the field. This was the cue for the Death Lords to burst onto the field doing wheelies on their motorbikes, like the Death Riders of the Apocalypse.

It was all too much for the monkey reserves. The noise, lights, and sheer chaos of the moment sent them fleeing from the dugout in terror. Max lost sight of them as they scampered up the supporting poles and disappeared onto the roof deck.

"Great," he yelled over the noise. "Now we've lost the reserves. Could this get any worse?"

The answer was yes, it could.

It could get a lot worse.

And it did.

The Death Lords circled Max and Lola on their motorbikes, spinning their tires and spraying them with earth, grass, and sand.

"So much for charm school," said Max.

Laughing maniacally, the Death Lords zoomed back to their dugout to get ready to bat.

"I think I'm done here," said Max. "Face it, Monkey Girl, we've lost. This is hopeless. Let's just get out of here."

"No!" Lola pulled him back. "What about our parents?"

"We can't save them. We can't save anyone. We can't even save ourselves. The Death Lords have won."

Lola sighed. "We can't give in, Hoop. Everyone's depending on us. We have to think of something."

"Like what?"

"I don't know. I . . . I . . ." Lola was looking around the grounds for inspiration, and suddenly she paused. "Hoop! Look at Lord 6-Dog! Why is he smiling to himself like that?" Her voice was getting more and more excited. "I think he has a trick up his sleeve!"

Lord 6-Dog was standing serenely, gazing at the Green Monster. He'd replaced his Stormtrooper helmet with a Red Sox cap. When he sensed their eyes on him, he grinned and gave them a thumbs-up.

"Maybe he switched sides. Maybe he's working for Ah Pukuh," suggested Max.

"You don't seriously think . . ."

"Tonight's game is between the Death Lords and the Hero Twins."

There was a blast of organ music.

"Tonight's umpires are the Paddler Gods."

A hush settled over the crowd as the two umpires were carried out on bamboo litters. They were dressed in the typical polo shirts and chinos of the American League—but they didn't look like any umpires Max had seen before. These were two wizened, wrinkly old men with no teeth and pointed chins. One of them had black jaguar markings on his skin and wore a jaguar-patterned baseball cap. The other one sported a stingray spine through his large hooked nose and wore a baseball cap with a shark's head on it, like something you'd get at a joke shop.

"I know them," said Lola. "They'll be great umpires."

Max looked dubious. "Why do you say that?"

"They're known for bringing cosmic order—so they have to be fair and balanced. They're like night and day, yin and yang. Their main job is to ferry the corn god down to Xibalba every night. They must have dropped him off and come straight here."

Max shook his head slowly as if he thought she was crazy. "Do they even know the rules of baseball?"

"Um . . . I doubt it."

The Paddler Gods stood at home plate and called for each team's manager.

Lord 6-Dog adjusted his Red Sox cap. "Remember this?" he said to Max. "It is the same cap thou didst give to me that morning we first met in the strangler fig tree."

"I didn't give it to you. You stole it from me," Max corrected him.

Lord 6-Dog winked at him. "Wish me luck."

He strode out with as much dignity as he could in the body of a howler monkey and bowed low to the umpires.

After another wooden trumpet and conch shell fanfare, Ah Pukuh rode out on a three-wheel motorcycle, his corpulent mass undulating like jelly under its Yankees suit as he skidded to a stop in front of the umpires.

"How d'ya like the show so far?" he said to them.

"It is time to set the ground rules," they said in unison.

299

"I'll tell you the rules," said Ah Pukuh. "No team, no play. The Hero Twins forfeit the game."

"Lord Ah Pukuh makes a valid point," said the Paddler Gods.

"But the game has not started yet," said Lord 6-Dog. "Please carry on. I assure thee that the team will be here."

Ah Pukuh snorted scornfully. "He's bluffing."

At a nod from the Paddler Gods, the announcer began again.

"Leading off for the Death Lords tonight will be the designated hitter, Lord One Death."

The huge video screen flashed up a picture of a grinning corpse in a wig made of rat tails.

"Batting second will be the left fielder, Lord Seven Death.

"Batting third will be third baseman, Lord Scab Stripper.

"Batting fourth will be the shortstop, Lord Packstrap. . . ."

And so on, through the roster of ugly, moldering so-called ballplayers.

The more the crowd booed them, the more Ah Pukuh laughed. "I hope the TV cameras are getting all this," he said. "Middleworld once dared to forget about us—they won't forget again!" He was enjoying himself tremendously. "Now it's your turn to introduce your team," he said to Lord 6-Dog. "Good luck in telling those monkeys apart!"

Lord 6-Dog ignored him. He was looking over at the Green Monster, seemingly riveted by some lingering fog patches from the dry ice.

"Leading off for the Hero Twins tonight . . . ," began the announcer. His voice faltered and he began again. *"Leading off for the Hero Twins tonight will be center fielder Dom DiMaggio."*

The crowd gasped.

Lola clapped a hand over her mouth. The fog was forming into human shapes.

The announcer fought to keep his voice level.

"Batting second will be the right fielder, Babe Ruth.

"Batting third will be hall-of-fame shortstop Joe Cronin.

"Batting fourth will be designated hitter Ted Williams.

"Batting fifth will be third baseman Johnny Pesky, Mr. Red Sox.

"Batting sixth will be catcher Hick Cady.

"Batting seventh will be first baseman Jimmie Foxx.

"Batting eighth will be second baseman Max Murphy.

"Batting ninth will be left fielder Lola Murphy.

"Pitching will be Cy 'Cyclone' Young."

As every name was called, the figures solidified further until standing next to Max, Lola, and Lord 6-Dog were eight ballplayers in their original Red Sox uniforms. The video screen flashed up old photographs of their greatest triumphs.

The crowd erupted into a roar that shook the ground and was heard all across Boston. Some said it could be heard as far as Yankee stadium.

"How did you get them?" Max asked Lord 6-Dog.

"The Red Sox have always played with their hearts. Once I explained the situation to them, they were more than willing to fight for the good guys."

Lola was cheering the apparitions wildly. "Who are they?" she whispered to Max.

"Only eight of the greatest players in Red Sox history. It's unbelievable."

"It's a scandal!" shouted Ah Pukuh, getting off his motorbike. "Umpires! Throw them out! They're cheating!"

The umpires stepped forward.

"All is in order," they said. "These players' names were on

301

the roster filed by Lord 6-Dog. The paperwork is correct. The rules say that we should start the game. Please leave the field, Lord Ah Pukuh."

"Whose side are you on?" fumed the god of violent and unnatural death.

"We ferry passengers between both worlds. We must be impartial."

"Just you wait till you need a new boat license," shouted Ah Pukuh, knocking both their caps off. He plopped himself back on his motorbike, revved the engine, and roared back to the dugout, leaving a gash in the turf.

"Let's play ball," said Ted Williams, the greatest hitter who ever lived.

CHAPTER TWENTY-SIX

THE GREATEST GAME

None of the baseball fans gathered in Fenway Park that night—whether living or dead—would ever forget the game that followed. Here were two teams of unmatched ability and both were determined to win.

Once he realized that there was nothing he could do to stop the game from proceeding, Ah Pukuh decided to focus on searing this night, as if with a branding iron, into the collective memory of Middleworld so that mortals would never, ever, again forget who was in charge.

To make things more interesting, in much the same way that he'd loaned Max and Lola superhero abilities at the Grand Hotel Xibalba, he'd given each of the Death Lords phenomenal skills in baseball.

But there were two things he hadn't counted on.

The first was that Max and Lola would show up with, excluding themselves, the greatest team in the history of baseball.

The second was that baseball is not just about the physical skills of pitching, hitting, fielding, and running. It also requires mental qualities like courage, patience, endurance, and the capacity for teamwork—none of which the Death Lords possessed.

Even though the Death Lords directed most plays toward the Hero Twins as the weakest links in their team, the seasoned Red Sox players anticipated this and covered for them. They also used their knowledge of the quirky layout of Fenway to their best advantage.

By the end of the third inning, the Hero Twins had crept into the lead and the crowd was beginning to sense that victory was possible. This strengthened the home team's mental resolve and further spurred them on.

Ah Pukuh was livid.

Realizing that the Death Lords could not win by out-playing their opponents, he called on a skill his team had been honing for thousands of years in Xibalba—the art of blatant cheating.

At his signal, the Death Lords began to use every trick they could think of to gross out, distract, disgust, and confuse their opposition.

Skull Scepter was the master of this tactic.

For example, when he'd just rounded third base and was heading for home. Jimmie Foxx sent the ball to catcher Hick Cady on home base, but Skull Scepter kept on running. Ten feet from home, he purposely disintegrated his body into a mass of bones, sinews, and intestines that slithered on independently, in order to get past Cady.

Undaunted, Cady calmly tagged several squishy parts of Skull Scepter before any of them hit home plate and called for a new, clean ball. The Hero Twins cheered the out. The Death Lords argued that Skull Scepter couldn't be out because his foot was still on second.

And there it was—his disembodied foot on second base, wiggling its toes in victory.

The Hero Twins appealed to the umpires.

After some deliberation, the Paddler Gods decided that in the nature of Maya duality, Skull Scepter was both in and out, and had both scored and not scored.

Max was tearing his hair out, but the bottom line was that the Death Lords were up by one and Skull Scepter was still on second.

Such wayward tactics, coupled with increasingly more baffling pronouncements from the umpires, helped the Death Lords edge forward. By the time they reached the bottom of the ninth inning, they were ahead by seven runs to five.

The game was winding to a close.

Jimmie Foxx was on third and Max was up to bat.

"We have two outs, kid," muttered Babe Ruth. "We need two runs to stay in the game. Think you can handle it?"

Max nodded, because how could he tell the legendary Babe Ruth that he didn't have any hope of hitting the ball? Max had had a really bad night. Not only had he failed to get on base, he hadn't even been able to get a good hit.

He stepped up to the plate.

The Death Lords smirked at each other. If it had been one of the Red Sox players, they might have been a little nervous. As it was, they knew the game was securely in their bony hands.

Max could feel the crowd willing him on.

Just hit it, he told himself. *Just hit it.*

The Demon of Pus was on the mound. His first pitch was

a curveball that seemed so far out of the zone, Max didn't even think of swinging at it.

At the last minute, whether by fair means or foul, the ball swung in over the plate.

"Strike one!" shouted the umpires.

The second pitch was a blistering fastball that blurred past Max and hit the catcher's mitt before he'd even started to swing.

"Strike two!"

This was it.

Max was two strikes down and one pitch away from defeat.

The future of the world hung on this next pitch.

Max stepped back and looked at the crowd. He saw Och's little face, so tense and worried. He saw his parents' faces, full of encouragement. He saw Lucky, nodding at him sagely, and Lady Coco, pumping her hairy little fists.

If he missed this ball, he was condemning everyone in this park and their children and their great-great-great-grandchildren to four hundred years of misrule by an unstoppable Ah Pukuh. If he got a hit, the Hero Twins would be on track to win for Middleworld.

He stepped back up to the plate and focused on the Demon of Pus.

He never even saw the ball.

All he knew was that he swung the bat with all the anger and frustration that had been building up inside of him since the day that his parents had announced they were canceling the family vacation and taking off for a dig in San Xavier.

Crack!

Against all expectation, logic, and common sense, the bat made solid contact with the ball.

There was stunned silence in the stands, in the field, and in the dugout.

But no one was more stunned than Max himself. He just stood there with his mouth hanging open in disbelief.

The bat dropped from his hands.

The ball floated out past the infield, past center field, and hit deep into the stands, where it was caught by Och. The crowd went wild.

A home run.

The only home run Max had ever hit.

Eventually, he came to his senses and, to wild cheering from the crowd, did the obligatory run around the bases.

The score was now tied and Dom DiMaggio was up to bat.

Rattled by Max's home run, the Demon of Pus struggled to get the ball over the plate and Dom walked to first base.

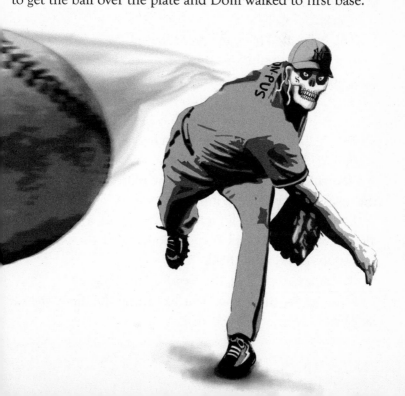

Babe Ruth was up next and the crowd went wild, sensing that a victory for the good guys was at hand.

Ah Pukuh pulled Skull Scepter out of center field and put in Lord Kuy.

Ruth came up to the plate, waved to the crowd, and then pointed with his bat to the single red seat in the stands that marked the longest home run ever hit at Fenway.

"That's what *you* think," snarled the Demon of Pus. He wound up and threw a fastball straight at the Babe, who only just jumped out of the way.

"Ball one!" shouted the umpires in chorus.

The next pitch bounced off the plate.

"Ball two!"

The next pitch was another lethal fastball, but Babe Ruth was waiting.

Crack!

The ball lofted high and arced toward the stands.

It was a home run for sure.

Until . . .

   . . . Lord Kuy spread his owl wings . . .

      . . . flew after the ball . . .

         . . . and caught it in his talons.

NO! NO! NO! The home team's fans protested, but the umpires ruled it a fair catch. Now the score was tied and the game was going into extra innings.

Lord Kuy's dastardly aerial defense had a devastating effect on the Red Sox players. Nobody could get a ball past the swooping owl in outfield.

In the twelfth inning, the Death Lords scored.

Once again, the home team had to tie the score or lose the game.

Joe Cronin, up first, was caught out by Lord Kuy's flying fielding.

The great Ted Williams stepped up to bat.

He hit low, fast and straight down the first base line. Kuy flew to catch it and crashed into Pesky's Pole. As the owl-man was carried away on a stretcher, Ted Williams smiled a "mission accomplished" kind of smile.

In his anger, Ah Pukuh's bloated body released a cloud of gas so toxic that a nearby popcorn seller passed out from the smell.

Johnny Pesky was up next and hit a single. Hick Cady and Jimmie Foxx both got hits. With the bases loaded and two outs, it was Max's turn to bat again.

He relished the moment.

This time, when he stepped up, the crowd didn't groan. They knew what he was capable of. They waited for him to repeat his home run.

"Go, *bambino!*" cried his mother's voice.

The first two pitches flew by as strikes.

Max let slip a curse word.

The crowd went quiet.

Someone said: "Did he just curse?"

Someone else said: "Did she call him *bambino?*"

Babe Ruth put his head in his hands.

With the fate of the world resting on his next ball, Max focused.

Time slowed.

He saw the ball coming at him and swung his bat hard.

He missed.

"Strike three!" called the umpires. "You're out."

The Curse of the Bambino had struck again.

CHAPTER TWENTY-SEVEN
PAYBACK TIME

So that was it. In the great rematch between the Hero Twins and the Death Lords, the Death Lords won. No bones about it.

"Thanks for coming," said Max to Ted Williams. He couldn't meet the great man's eyes.

"Our pleasure. We'll be off now, if you don't need us anymore."

Max nodded. "No sense in us all getting sacrificed."

Ted Williams rubbed his neck. "We can stick around if you want us to. We're dead anyway, so it makes no difference."

"You've done more than enough," said Max.

"Wish we could've got a win for you."

"Me too," said Lola.

Ted Williams smiled at her ruefully. "You know what they say about the Red Sox?"

Lola rolled her eyes. "It's not about winning, it's about believing."

"Yes," said Ted Williams. He looked embarrassed. "Good-bye, then."

"Good-bye," said Max.

Lola said nothing.

"Keep believing," called Ted Williams as he and the rest of the greatest players in Red Sox history vanished back into the mist.

Ah Pukuh's voice came over the loudspeaker.

"Ladies and gentlemen, zombies and ghouls, we hope you enjoyed tonight's game. The winners were, of course, the Death Lords, and the losers were all the rest of you. There will be a brief interlude while we set up for the human sacrifice portion of the program. Please do not attempt to leave the ballpark as all gates have been locked."

Max wanted to go and say good-bye to his family, but the field was ringed by Ah Pukuh's heavies, and they weren't letting anyone go anywhere. He could see his mother crying hysterically and his father arguing with a security guard. Uncle Ted and Zia were calling out to Lola. All over the stands, people were screaming and crying, and fighting to get out.

The noise was like hell on earth.

Max sat in silence with Lola and Lord 6-Dog in the dugout.

He was almost glad when the bogus Plague Rats launched into another set.

All was hustle and bustle on the field as Ah Pukuh's lackeys assembled a stage under the Green Monster. On it they placed a huge throne swathed in jaguar fabrics and a long, low table.

Next, a massive stone altar was rolled in and set in the middle of the field.

A procession of grim-looking priests, draped in black with

matted hair and painted faces, circled the field, each swinging a large incense burner.

When the priests' acrid smoke had dispersed, five monkey-faced monstrous little men paraded in, each carrying a Jaguar Stone on a cushion. They arranged the five Jaguar Stones on the table below the throne and sat in front of them to guard them.

Another squad of priests entered, this time carrying blue paint, knives, and special bowls to catch the blood.

Max felt sick to his stomach.

"We could run," he said.

"Where to?" said Lola.

"Do you think it will hurt?"

"Maybe not," she said. "Those obsidian knives are very sharp." They watched for a moment as the priests set out their equipment. She took his hand. "Hey, Hoop, do you remember the first time we met? Landa was chasing you, and I told you to follow me to the Blue Pool and we escaped down the underground river?"

Max nodded.

"I wanted to tell you that I've always regretted that. I should have taken you back to your uncle's house. Then maybe you'd never have gotten involved in any of this."

"And I wouldn't have gotten to know you. And you wouldn't have found your parents. And we wouldn't be cousins. It all happened for a reason. You can't go back."

Lola did a double take. "You're sounding a bit like Lord 6-Dog."

Max laughed. "And what an honor to meet an ancient Maya king. Shame I'll never get to tell my children about it."

"This wasn't your world. You're not Maya. You shouldn't

be here. You don't deserve any of this. I'm so sorry."

"You can't say that," Max pointed out. "The Death Lords chose me because I look like my ancestor, the Spanish conquistador Rodrigo Pizarro. They chose you because you look like your ancestor Princess Inez. They needed both of us to get their hands on the Yellow Jaguar. There was nothing we could have done to stop this from happening."

Lola was staring at him.

"What? What's the matter?"

"Really, Hoop? You're not going to say that it's not fair?"

"That used to be my catchphrase, didn't it? But I've learned a lot from you, Monkey Girl. And I get that life isn't ever fair. It's a challenge. A different challenge for everyone. And it's how we react to that challenge that says who we are."

"I think I've fainted," said Lola. "I'm hallucinating. I can't believe what I'm hearing. Are you sure you're Hoop? You're not some actor he paid to stand in for him?"

"I wish I *was* an actor. Because this is how it ends. We get sacrificed and Ah Pukuh gets to boast that he beat the Hero Twins *and* the Red Sox."

"In a Yankees uniform," added Lola.

"Stop it," said Max.

Lola groaned. "I kind of wish they'd get on with it. This waiting is torture, too."

"So what do you think Ah Pukuh will do next?" asked Max. "He's not going to settle for trophies on the mantelpiece. He's got the attention of the world and he's got the Jaguar Stones."

"You don't need Jaguar Stones to be unthinkably evil," said Lola, looking at the ground. A moment later, her head popped up excitedly. "That's it!" she said. "You don't need Jaguar Stones!"

Max shook his head. "Say what? We've been risking our lives to track down Jaguar Stones and—not very successfully—keep them out of the hands of the bad guys. Now you tell me it's not about them?"

"Yes! You know how the Maya don't look at things as black-and-white? Nothing is all good or all bad. Well, it's the same with the Jaguar Stones. They're not innately good or bad. They simply channel the powers of the king. It's all about how you look at it."

"I haven't got a clue what you're talking about." Max was too freaked out to follow her philosophical musings. He couldn't take his eyes off the obsidian blade that awaited him on the altar.

Time was moving far too quickly now.

The band stopped, the trumpeters played their conch shell fanfare, and Ah Pukuh swaggered onto the stage in a black sequined tuxedo jacket. This time, his headdress was made of three live quetzal birds, the most endangered creatures of the cloud forest, bound cruelly together chest to chest, so that their beautiful, long, iridescent tail feathers sprayed out like a waterfall over Ah Pukuh's fat head. His blotchy, pox-marked face was plastered in thick white makeup, his eyes were daubed in black, and his mouth was a red slash.

He looked repulsive, ridiculous, insane. But Max felt only fear at what this maniac was about to do.

Ah Pukuh picked up the microphone.

His ugly face was broadcast on the big screen.

"As Venus, the morning star, rises in the sky and heralds the start of a war that will never end, I want to thank the Hero Twins for ushering in my rule. You saw how I crushed them, outwitted them, broke them . . . and I will do the same

His headdress was made of three live quetzal birds.

to every living soul in Middleworld. So look your last at your loved ones, kiss your children good-bye. It's time to get real, Middleworld. You are entering the pain zone. And you have only yourselves to blame.

"When I first came here, I wooed you with hurricanes, floods, and epidemics. Instead of paying me tribute, you clubbed together and helped each other. That disgusting behavior will not go unpunished. It's payback time. We're playing by my rules now. And I am about to introduce you to the five Jaguar Stones that will make you wish you had never been born. Individually, they control time, weather, death, blood, and fertility. Together they form a Five-Headed Jaguar that will control every aspect of your miserable lives until the day I end them.

"As soon as we have dispatched the Hero Twins, symbols of all that is good, we can get on with my new age of all that is bad!" Ah Pukuh's minions applauded, he posed for some press photographs with a baseball bat, and then he kicked the photographers off the stage. "Sacrifice time!" he bellowed.

Lord 6-Dog, Max, and Lola were pulled to their feet.

A minion with a clipboard dashed over to babble in Ah Pukuh's ear. His voice carried over the war god's microphone.

"We need to spare the monkey, your lordship. Research has shown that many humans prefer animals to other humans."

"Why do I care about research anymore? I'm about to kill my entire demographic."

"Quite so, Lord Ah Pukuh. But it was my understanding that you intend to do it as slowly and as painfully as possible. If we are to sustain the fear factor without jeopardizing our broadcasting coverage, we need to spare the monkey."

Lord 6-Dog was thrown back, while Max and Lola were dragged forward to the stage.

"Here they are," boomed Ah Pukuh, "the famous Hero Twins, the last hope of Middleworld. Now watch, all of you here tonight, and"—he smiled into the TV camera—"all you viewers at home, and see how easily their little bones are broken, and how quickly their little hearts stop beating."

As if to dramatize his words, a marching band of drummers began to tap out a slow roll like a fragile heartbeat.

Chan Kan walked onto the field. He looked very different from the tired, broken, almost blind old man who had thrown himself into Xibalba to save Max and Lola. This Chan Kan walked tall in his flowing white robes, his long white hair streaming behind him, his sharp brown eyes taking in every detail of the stadium and the audience and the sacrifice setup. Few people looked back at him, as most were more interested in the creature he led in on a leather leash, a cross between a giant chicken and a Tyrannosaurus rex.

Fenway shook at the creature's footfalls.

"Behold the Chee Ken of Death," said Ah Pukuh, "the Fowl of Fear, the scourge of Xibalba. With its curved beak of doom, it will now peck out the hearts of these criminals."

The crowd gasped to see the twenty-foot chicken.

"What's happened to Thunderclaw?" asked Max. "I thought he was on our side. How did he get so big?"

Lola was staring at the chicken's handler.

Chan Kan rolled his eyes at her to indicate that a guard was right behind him with a blade in his back. Then he stared at her meaningfully. He seemed to be pushing out his chest.

Eventually, she saw what he wanted her to see: he was wearing a pumpkin seed necklace. They exchanged a little nod.

A smile twitched on Lola's lips.

"I saw that," whispered Max. "Please don't tell me you've had an idea."

"I've had an idea," Lola whispered back.

"Whatever it is, forget it," Max begged her. "Please don't make this harder than it has to be. Let's just give up and be sacrificed. I want to get it over with. We've lost, Monkey Girl. Accept it. If they don't kill us soon, I will literally die of terror."

"Pull yourself together, Hoop. We will die as we lived, as Hero Twins."

Max looked at her strangely. She was talking very loudly, as if she wanted the whole crowd to hear.

"Not me," he said. "I'm done."

Lola gave him a little wink. "It's not the winning, it's the believing, remember?"

She began to fight back against the guards who held her. "If I am to die," she called up to Ah Pukuh, "I demand the right to make a speech."

Ah Pukuh looked at the nearest producer for advice. The producer nodded furiously and encouraged the cameramen to get close-ups of this cute Maya girl. A makeup artist rushed over to dab her with powder and fix her hair. Someone put a mic in her hand.

She took a moment to look around the stadium, meeting the eyes of everyone who had believed in her. Then she began to speak: "Look at this creature," she said, pointing at Thunderclaw, "and what do you see? A monster?" The crowd shouted their agreement. "Well, I'll tell you what I see. I see my old friend, Thunderclaw. I knew him when he was just a little chicken. I saved him from the cooking pot more than once. I don't know what they have done to him in Xibalba to change his appearance so much. But I do know that he is not the Fowl of Fear. He is the Fowl of Friendship."

Thunderclaw regarded her lovingly. He seemed to be shrinking.

"So now, I want to ask the rest of you who've come here from Xibalba: Are you really on Ah Pukuh's team? Or are you just misunderstood like Thunderclaw? Which team are you really on? Think carefully before you answer. Because it's an absolute fact that good always wins. That's just the law of the universe.

"No matter how hard you try to destroy Middleworld, there will always be a little seed of good that you can't wipe out. And every day it will grow bigger and bigger, until one day it will find you and choke you like your own personal strangler fig."

The TV camera zoomed in on a zombie shedding a tear of self-pity.

Ah Pukuh reached down to grab the mic, but Lola ducked out of his reach.

"And while we're thinking about good and evil, let's talk about the Jaguar Stones." She pointed to the five stone jaguar heads that snarled in freeze-frame on the table. Every Maya head in the audience turned to look at them. "No matter what you've been told, they have no power over you. They're not good or bad—they don't control anything—they're just symbols of kingship. And, apologies to you, Lord 6-Dog, but we all know what happened to the Maya kings. They got lazy, they got greedy, they got fat." She pointed to Ah Pukuh, lolling in his throne. "Remind you of anyone?"

There were snickers in the crowd.

"When the Maya kings stopped pulling their weight, the Maya people walked away. And you can walk away right now. Yesterday, I saw the treasures of the Maya in the Peabody Museum, and I can tell you that they were not made by kings. They were made by people like you and me, people who honed their skills through training, and practice, and talent. Who do you think made the Jaguar Stones? It was a human sculptor, not a god. All Ah Pukuh knows how to do is steal, and cheat, and lie. He can't build a pyramid, or weave a shawl, or paint a pot. He even needed human scribes and artists to set down his own story. Every single one of us is more powerful than he will ever be.

"So let's tell Ah Pukuh that he has no power over us. That we don't care how many Jaguar Stones he has, we will never pay tribute to him." Lola was yelling now. "He can do nothing if we choose to ignore him. That's why he tried to steal Great Sun's media presence. Why he built a spaceship. Why he organized this game. He's a spoiled child who wants to be the center of attention. So let's show him and his bullying friends that we're not interested anymore. They belong to our past, not to our future. It is time for the good guys to stand up together and turn their backs on the oppressors. It is time for us to say NO MORE!"

And they did.

First it was the Maya people in the crowd, led by Chan Kan, who got to their feet. Then Lady Coco stood up and aimed her posterior at the Death Lords. Then the Hero Twins fans and all the other spectators, the poncho family, eventually even the visiting team's supporters from Xibalba. One by one, every single person in Fenway Park, living and dead, rose up and turned their backs and yelled "no more." At home, they turned their backs to their televisions and computer screens and tablets. The message was relayed around the world and picked up by everyone, Maya and non-Maya, who'd ever felt bullied, and cheated, and oppressed.

And that, it turned out, was pretty much all the people, everywhere.

Ah Pukuh didn't have a leg to stand on. Literally. He stood up to protest but his shaking legs gave way beneath him and he sank down, weeping with self-pity.

Max ran to join Lola.

"You were amazing," he said.

She grinned. "I was, wasn't I? Look at the mighty Ah Pukuh now."

The god of violent and unnatural death looked like a shriveled balloon. His makeup was running, his jacket was shedding sequins, his power was draining out of him. "What's happening to me?" he asked the Head of Marketing, who had lost her platter in the melee and was now being carried on an old pizza box.

"It's called losing brand loyalty," she said. "Our target audience is moving on without us."

"What will we do?"

"I vote we go back to Xibalba and play cards for the rest of eternity."

"But what about my glorious rule? Middleworld is mine! I won the ball game!"

"No," said the Head. "It isn't, and you didn't. PR is tricky. Mortals have a sense of right and wrong that's not about keeping score. As I tried to explain to you when we started this campaign, it's not enough to win the game. You have to win their stupid hearts as well."

"Mortals are complicated. I hate them. Let's grab the Jaguar Stones and get out of here."

"Not so fast," said Lucky, rapping Ah Pukuh's greedy fingers. "Those Jaguar Stones belong to the Maya people, not to you."

Oscar Poot carried over a cooler and a wad of bubble wrap.

"What do you think you're doing?" snapped Ah Pukuh.

"I claim the Jaguar Stones for the living Maya," said Oscar.

"Don't you dare touch them!" Ah Pukuh went to pick up the Black Jaguar. "Come to daddy," he said. The Jaguar Stone snarled and bit his hand.

Oscar Poot took the stone from him and stroked its head. It purred. "We will bring you home to San Xavier," he said to it, "and put you on display where everyone can see you. You will inspire our people to new heights, you will embody their past, and you will remind them never to let anyone oppress them again."

Gently, he picked up each stone in turn, wrapped it, and placed it in the cooler. If one of Ah Pukuh's minions tried to stop him, the stones would snarl and bite. But, otherwise, they sat still and quiet, glowing slightly in the moonlight.

When all five stones were safely wrapped, Oscar locked the padlock on the cooler.

"This was not supposed to happen," said Ah Pukuh as Fenway security slapped handcuffs on him. "I built my media platform. I tweeted. I blogged. I logged on. Middleworld was mine for the taking. Where did I go wrong?"

"You're a bully," said Lucky. "Bullies never have happy endings."

"How dare you speak to me like that!" said Ah Pukuh,

but no one was listening to him. Everyone was looking at his headdress, which was shivering pitifully.

"We must get those poor quetzals back to the cloud forest," said Lord 6-Dog. "It is too cold for them here."

"Shh, you said that out loud!" Lola warned him.

Lord 6-Dog smiled. "It has been such an extraordinary night that no one will blink at a talking howler monkey."

He whistled, and his spider monkey helpers carried over a cage hastily made from a large wooden crate covered with batting fence. With a little help from the security guards, Lord 6-Dog and his spider monkeys were able to lift the shameful headdress into the crate and cut the shivering birds free from each other.

"Sorry, little brothers," said the monkey king, "but this indignity will not last long." He fastened the mesh tightly across the crate. "Now find somewhere warm and feed them insects and fruit," he ordered the spider monkeys. "Animal rescue will come soon."

"Why all the fuss?" snapped Ah Pukuh, who was still hanging around unsure of where to go, as he didn't have any friends to tag along with. "Just strangle them and have done with it!"

The little birds squawked in fear.

Lord 6-Dog laid a protective hand on their crate. "They have been hunted almost to extinction; let us hope these gallant survivors find mates."

The quetzals made little cooing noises that suggested they liked that idea.

For Ah Pukuh, it was the last straw. "You are all so smug, and I am sick to death of you! Prepare to die right now!" he screamed. "Death Lords, bring it on!"

323

The Death Lords lined up and concentrated very hard.

"Earthquakes!" commanded Ah Pukuh.

A small crack appeared in home plate.

"Floods!" commanded Ah Pukuh.

A small puddle formed at the base of the Green Monster.

"Diseases!" commanded Ah Pukuh.

A small spot appeared on Oscar Poot's nose.

"That's it?" screamed Ah Pukuh. "That's all you've got?"

It was all they had.

As the moon shone down on Fenway Park, Ah Pukuh and his followers vanished back to Xibalba forever.

The audience turned to the front and cheered.

But one voice cheered louder than the rest.

"MAC! WOOHOO! MAC!" yelled a voice from the top of the Green Monster.

He looked up.

"Nasty!"

She waved. "I brought the band!"

The real Plague Rats took their places on top of the Green Monster and started a real concert.

"You're late," said Max when Nasty came down to talk to him.

"Yeah, my parents wouldn't let me leave the house."

"Why not?"

"They knew you were in town."

"Oh." Max had an unfortunate history with Nasty's parents, right from when they'd first met in Spain. They were always walking in just as he was leaping out of a coffin or somebody's stomach was exploding. Their dry cleaning bills had increased enormously since they'd met him.

"No," said Nasty, "it's great! They love you! You've won

them over! They saw tonight's game on TV and they've changed their minds about you completely! Look, they're over there."

Max looked. Nasty's parents were chatting to his parents and waving to him enthusiastically. Lola and her parents stood nearby.

He nodded approvingly. "This is a good party," he said in amazement.

"It's the best party ever!" said Nasty.

It was dawn before Max and Lola finally escaped all the people who wanted to hug them, and congratulate them, and date them, and shake their hands, and nominate them for high office. Eventually, they snuck out, found a spot in the deserted concessions concourse, and choreographed a victory dance on the spot.

"Can you believe it?" said Max. "We're alive!"

"It feels amazing," said Lola.

Then she screamed as a massive bat jumped out in front of her. Wait, not a bat, a man in a cape. Antonio de Landa.

"Ugh! Go away! What do you want?"

"Señorita Lola, I want to talk to you.

"I don't want to talk to *you*."

"I want to say I am sorry, *lo siento*. For everything. Everything I have done is wrong."

"I know. The police are looking for you. Why aren't you in prison?"

"I will surrender when I have talked to you."

"Save time. Do it now."

"*Por favor*, Señorita Lola, have pity. I am a broken man. Even before Tzelek, my wife was a monster. I want you to know that we are parting. She will have no claim on my estate."

"Why would I care?"

"Because I need to give this to you." He handed her an envelope.

"What is it?"

"It is the deeds to my property in Spain and everything I own."

Lola recoiled in disgust.

"There is nothing from Cahokia. That money has been returned."

"I don't want anything from you."

"Then think of it as a legacy for your people. My ancestors stole the treasures of the Maya and I wish to make reparation."

"You should take it," Max urged her. "His place in Spain is worth a fortune. You could do a lot of good with that money. Maybe even start that Maya school you've always talked about."

Lola thought for a moment. "Okay, then. On behalf of the Maya people, I accept your gift. But only on the condition that you and your descendants never ever come near me, or talk to me, or try to contact me ever again."

"As you wish, *señorita*. And now I will say *adiós*."

"Where are you going?"

"To prison, I expect. I am handing myself in. Do you know where is the nearest police station?"

As Max considered the question, a police car cruised slowly by.

"Wait!" yelled Landa. "Wait for me!"

With a final flick of his cape, he took off after the

police car to flag it down and begin his punishment for a lifetime of villainy.

And that should have been the end of the story of the city boy and the jungle girl who joined forces to save the world from the Maya Lords of Death. But life is never that simple, is it? Everybody's stories are as tangled as vines in the rainforest. And, as Max and Lola were about to find out, the end of one story is often the beginning of another.

CHAPTER TWENTY-EIGHT

THE WORLD TURNED INSIDE OUT

At first, they were too tired to even notice the outside world. When they got back to Max's house, they went to their rooms and slept for twelve hours straight.

They missed an epic breakfast and lunch cooked by Raul, and would probably have slept through dinner, too, if Max's mother hadn't rapped on his bedroom door. "*Bambino!* Phone!"

He was going to ignore her, but suddenly thought it might be Nasty.

"Who is it?" he called.

"Dr. Delgado!"

"From the museum? What does she want?"

"She wants to interview you and Lola!"

"Why?"

"About the Jaguar Stones, silly!"

"When?"

She passed him the phone. "Here, you talk to her. I will go and wake Lola."

"Dr. Delgado? This is Max Murphy."

"Hello, Max. Everyone is so excited about what you and Lola accomplished last night. I'm calling because I've been asked to interview you both for a spot on national TV. It will make a wonderful start to the fund-raising campaign for the new Jaguar Stones Museum—so I do hope you'll say yes!"

"Um . . . I guess—"

"Excellent! So shall we, say . . . meet in an hour?"

"What, now? Today?"

"Strike while the iron is hot, as they say."

"Where are you?"

"The TV station is scouting locations, but don't worry. They'll send a car for you. Oh, and Max . . . ?"

"Yes?"

"Bring those adorable monkeys with you!"

"I thought you hated monkeys?"

"No! Did I say that?"

"Yes, you did. On Halloween. At the museum."

"It must have been my little joke! Anyway, the producer says the viewers *love* monkeys! So, be sure to bring them. Remember, it's all in the name of charity!"

"Okay," said Max, still half asleep.

He pulled on a Red Sox hoodie and glanced in the mirror. He looked tired, disheveled, hollow-eyed. He assumed the TV people would be able to transform him into someone more heroic looking. As a gesture, he rubbed gel into his bed-head and tried to coax his hair into spikes.

His mother was waiting at the bottom of the stairs. "Let me see you, *bambino*." She regarded his hoodie with horror. "You can't wear that old thing on TV! Shall I iron a shirt for you?" She attempted to flatten the spikes in his hair.

Max ducked around her. "Where's Lola?"

"Here I am," she said, coming down the stairs. She looked well-rested, beautiful, shiny-haired, perfect. "I can't believe we're going to be on TV!"

"Quite right, too," said Ted Murphy, coming into the hallway. "You're big news! Well done, both of you. I'm so proud. The whole of Boston is proud of you!"

"So where is the interview?" asked Max's mother. "Shall I drive you?"

"No need, Mom. They're sending a car."

"You're getting the star treatment, *bambino*! Well, come and say hello to everyone, you two, before you go."

"Everyone" was people who'd come for the game and needed somewhere to stay. The house was full of guests, mostly Maya. They all clapped and cheered when Max and Lola walked in the room.

Lady Coco bounded over. She was wearing a fresh flowery apron. As ever, the head of her beloved Dawg Doll peeped out from the pocket. "This is so exciting!"

"Where's Lord 6-Dog?" asked Lola.

"Who knows? He's like a bear with a sore head today. I just hope he's on his best behavior for the TV cameras. I'll go and look for him."

"No need, I am here," said Lord 6-Dog, coming in with Zia. They both looked somber.

"The omens for this day could not be worse," he announced. "Calamity and tribulation await us."

"Let me guess," said Lola. "You two have been reading the days with Mom's crystals."

Zia smiled at her. "I know you don't believe in these things, but they kept me sane in that waiting room."

"Waiting room?"

"Where the Death Lords kept us when they grabbed us from the kitchen that day. I lost all track of time. And then, suddenly, we were at Fenway. It still feels like a dream."

Lola hugged her mother. "It was real, all right."

"Please be careful out there," Zia said to her. "I never want to lose you again."

"Those tribulations you saw in the crystals," said Max's mother, "I think I know what they are. Frank and I are still up to our necks in red tape in San Xavier. I'm hoping that if this interview goes well, Dr. Delgado may be able to smooth things over for us. Please do your best to impress her, *bambino*."

"I will, Mom." Max looked around the room. "Where's Och?"

"Lucky Jim and Hermanjilio took him to the Science Museum. You'll see him later. Call me after your interview and we'll all go out to dinner."

"Your chariot awaits!" called Max's father. He opened the front door. A black stretch limo was parked at the gate.

It was huge inside. Black leather seats as long as sofas, a pullout table, and a little fridge filled with sodas. There was even a basket of snacks with plenty of nuts for the monkeys. They could see the silhouette of the driver in his peaked cap through the dark window that separated him from the passengers, but even without the window, he was too far away for conversation. So Max, Lola, and the monkeys relaxed in the back as their limo glided through the streets of Boston.

"I could get used to this," said Max, opening a packet of gourmet potato chips. "You know, I've heard that film sets have really good food—huge buffets set out all day long and you can eat as much as you want. Do you think it's the same for TV?"

"Really, Hoop?" said Lola. "You're a world-famous celebrity about to star in his own television special, and all you can think about is food?"

"It's a survival mechanism. I like to know where my next meal is coming from."

Lola threw him a bag of dry roasted peanuts. "Here, put this in your pocket."

He did. Then he stuffed his pockets with candy bars and gum.

"What I want to know," said Lady Coco, "is whether 6-Dog and I should talk or not?"

"You'll be a sensation if you do!" said Lola.

"In that case," said Lord 6-Dog, "let us keep our silence. I have no desire to be a circus act."

"I suppose you're right," said Lady Coco, a little regretfully. "I expect I'd get tired of the fuss. My own cooking show would have been fun, though."

As they fantasized about how fame might change their lives for better or for worse, they forgot to wonder about where they might be going or who might be waiting for them at the end of this journey.

And that was a big mistake. Because if Max had kept his wits about him, he might have recognized that peaked-cap driver from a rainy summer night in Spain. And he might have remembered another limo ride that began at Landa's palace and ended at his own funeral.

But, so excited were they at the prospect of appearing on TV, not one of them suspected a thing.

The car came to a halt outside a small domed building on Massachusetts Avenue.

"What is this place?" asked Lola as they walked across to the massive portico.

Max stared at it. "It looks familiar. I think we came here once on a school trip."

The door swung open. "Good afternoon," said the tall, thin woman they'd seen at the museum. "Dolores Delgado. How nice to see you again." She shook hands with each of them. "You must be Lola? And Max? And, of course, your darling monkeys! What are their names?

"This is Lady Coco . . ."

"How cute!" simpered Dr. Delgado.

". . . and this is Lord 6-Dog."

"Who's a handsome boy?" She patted Lord 6-Dog's head, and Max could see that it took all the king's self-control not to bite her.

Dr. Delgado pulled a small bottle of sanitizer out of her purse and wiped her hands. "Super!" she said. "And we've found such a fun location for your interview. Follow me."

They followed her through marble halls until they came to some small double doors. Max was looking around for lights, cables, buffet tables, and other showbiz accoutrements. He was disappointed to see nothing at all.

"So," said Dr. Delgado, pressing a button and opening the doors, "welcome to the world turned inside out."

They walked through a set of double doors onto a clear glass bridge and suddenly they were inside a glass globe, three stories high, with a world map all around them lit up in brightly colored stained glass.

"I remember this place now," said Max. "They call it the Mapparium. It has weird acoustics." Even as he said that, his voice echoed loudly, bouncing off the glass.

"That's so cool," said Lola.

"*We* thought so," said Dr. Delgado.

"Who's *we*?" asked Max. "Where's your film crew?"

He distinctly heard the doors lock.

"It's just me tonight," said Dr. Delgado. "No one has the money for big shoots anymore. But don't worry, I'm quite a whiz with the old handheld." She pulled a small camcorder out of her purse.

"Which channel did you say this was for?" asked Max.

"It's an independent production company," she replied. "Shall we get started?" For no reason that he could identify, Max was getting a bad feeling. "If you'd like to just stand there, on the bridge, and maybe you could each hold a monkey . . ."

Lord 6-Dog bared his teeth at Max.

"They don't like to be held," he said.

"Never work with children and animals," muttered Dr. Delgado under her breath. She smiled, but it looked forced. "Okay," she said brightly, "we'll get to the monkeys later." She tapped a switch and a green standby light appeared on the camera. "Are we ready?"

Max and Lola nodded.

The green light changed to red. They were recording.

"So, Max Murphy, can you give me one word to describe what happened yesterday at Fenway Park?"

Max thought quickly. "Awesome."

He kicked himself. His mother hated that word.

"Lola—one word?"

She jutted out her chin. "Revolutionary."

"And Lady Coco—one word?"

Lady Coco whimpered.

"She's a monkey," Lola pointed out. "She can't talk."

"No?" said Dr. Delgado. She turned off the camera. "I have been misinformed. So, the other ape won't speak to me either?"

"He's a monkey," said Lola. "Apes don't have tails."

"But will he speak?"

"No," said Lola firmly.

"Even if he knew that I killed his father?"

Max and Lola stared at her in surprise.

Lord 6-Dog lunged at her, snarling savagely.

Dr. Delgado hurled the video camera at the attacking monkey. It hit him hard on his forehead and he fell backward. Blood trickled down his face and matted his hair.

Lady Coco rushed to his aid.

"What's happening?" cried Lola.

"What kind of interview is this?" asked Max angrily.

"The deadly kind," said Dr. Delgado in a very strange voice.

CHAPTER TWENTY-NINE
THE FINAL BATTLE

Dr. Delgado stood back, legs apart, hands in the air, and closed her eyes, as if she was concentrating hard.

Max ran back to the door and tried to open it. It was locked, as he knew it would be. He banged on it crazily with his fists, yelling: "Help! Help!"

"No one can help you now," said Dr. Delgado. Her hair was standing on end and her frumpy suit was blowing as if she was in a wind machine.

Max jabbed at his phone—no service.

Dr. Delgado screamed and, as she did, a figure stepped out of her body. It was a man, Maya by the looks of him, with an enormous nose, straggly black hair, and a receding hairline. He looked angry. Very angry.

He pushed the empty shell of Dr. Delgado to one side with his foot.

Lord 6-Dog let out an agonizing moan. "Tzelek!"

"Tzelek?" said Lady Coco.

"How did *he* get here?" asked Max.

"He's supposed to be in Xibalba. Lord Kuy sent him back there. We saw it with our own eyes," said Lola indignantly.

"You know what they say," said Tzelek. "You can't keep a good man down."

"You are not a good man," said Lady Coco.

Tzelek laughed. "Very true. That made it even easier. As soon as I landed back in Xibalba, I raced over to the portal at the Black Pyramid. There is so much evil in the air—mostly thanks to me and my efforts while I was alive—that the portal is always hazy. At this time of year, it's positively sheer. With the help of a rogue site worker, I infused myself into a prized pot, jammed on the lid, and had myself shipped to the Peabody Museum. As soon as this Delgado woman opened the pot, I leapt into her brain! And here I am, fighting fit and ready to crush you, Brother. You're going down."

"That is against the rules," complained Lady Coco. "You cannot jump between worlds. You must go back to Xibalba."

"It is still the Day of the Dead, Mother," said Tzelek. "And my brother is *so* dead."

Lord 6-Dog staggered to his feet and pushed in front of the other three to protect them. "Swear not to harm my companions. This is not their battle."

"I will do what I like," said Tzelek.

Lola took a deep breath. "You are beaten already. Ah Pukuh and all your little friends have gone running home with their tails between their legs. Xibalba is finished. No one is interested."

Tzelek focused on her with blazing eyes. "I don't care about Ah Pukuh and his Death Lords. I am greater than all of them. Under my leadership, Xibalba could be invincible again. Ask Lord Kuy. He has the wisdom of an owl and the instincts of a vulture. And he has chosen to side with me. But first, I must settle an old score with my brother."

Lady Coco glanced at Lord 6-Dog. The bleeding seemed to have stopped and he was looking stronger. "Why so much hatred, Tzelek?" she asked, playing for time.

"Why? Because it's all I've got. 6-Dog had the life, the riches, the power that should have been mine. All I *have* is the hatred. And now I have this moment." Tzelek looked scornfully at Lord 6-Dog. "Are you ready to die, mommy's boy?"

Lady Coco put out an arm to stop Lord 6-Dog. "Ignore him, Son. The Day of the Dead will soon be over. He will have to return to Xibalba."

"Then I must make haste," said Lord 6-Dog, shaking her off. He assumed a fighting stance. "This battle has been a long time coming."

"You think I would fight a monkey?" snorted Tzelek. "Reveal your true self, 6-Dog."

"No!" screeched Lady Coco. "If you leave your host body, you cannot rejoin it."

"So be it," said Lord 6-Dog.

He stood as Dr. Delgado had, legs apart, arms raised, eyes closed in concentration. There was a terrible roar, a howler monkey roar, and out stepped Lord 6-Dog, most fierce, most handsome, most mighty king of the ancient Maya. The gash from the video camera still glistened on his forehead.

His howler monkey body slumped to the ground.

As the two (im)mortal enemies faced off on the bridge, Max, Lola, and Lady Coco dragged the lifeless forms of the monkey and the museum director off the walkway and back to the relative safety of the doorway. Then they stood at the end of the bridge to watch and hope.

The battle was on.

Lord 6-Dog flexed his arms like a body builder, reacquainting himself with the muscles and nerves and reflexes of his former self. He pulled an obsidian-bladed battle-ax from his belt and spun it in his hand, weighing the heft and balance.

Tzelek stood watching him, a sneer on his face, one hand behind his back.

"Where is thy weapon?" Lord 6-Dog asked him.

Tzelek produced from behind his back the scepter of the Jaguar Kings.

"Where didst thou get that?"

"It was a gift from my friend Kuy."

"It belongs to the Jaguar Kings. It is their sacred scepter. Thou knowest thou canst not use it against me."

"Watch me."

Tzelek raised the scepter over his head, muttering incantations. Energy crackled in the air, gathering and swirling around the end of the leg-bone, meshing like cotton candy into a spinning ball of pure energy. With a flick of his wrist, Tzelek sent the ball hurtling toward Lord 6-Dog. "You have no idea how my powers have grown since last we battled, Brother."

"And thou hast no idea how much I have learned from Ted Williams."

Lord 6-Dog planted his legs and swung his battle-ax like a baseball bat. He hit the ball square on and sent it shooting straight back at Tzelek.

Tzelek ducked just in time and the ball went smashing

Tzelek produced from behind his back the scepter of the Jaguar Kings.

through the wall of the globe with a force that sent shards of glass flying and shook the room so hard, it knocked Max and Lola off their feet.

Now it was Lord 6-Dog's turn to sneer. "Surely, thou knowest that I cannot be harmed with the sacred scepter of my ancestors? Unlike thee, I am a Jaguar King. That bone comes from my flesh and blood." He paused a moment to look Tzelek up and down. "Which is more than can be said of thee, thou cuckoo in my family's nest."

"How dare you?" thundered Tzelek. "My mother died on the day I was born. Your parents were the only parents I ever knew."

"What a pity, then, thou didst repay their kindnesses by murdering my father."

"I did it because he favored you. He always favored you."

"Perhaps, because I never tried to murder him."

"You smug piece of dirt!"

"I speak only the truth. I was the legal heir. The blood of the Jaguar Kings flows through my veins."

"Why is your blood any better than mine?"

"My father was a king. My mother was a queen."

"And didn't you just love to remind me of that every day of our childhood? It was you who turned me to evil, 6-Dog. You and your constant jibes. I took my burning rage and I poured it on your family's happiness, like a vat of boiling oil. And when I had killed your father, I set out to acquire the power and wealth that had been denied me. I have worked my way through the echelons of evil to become the baddest bad guy standing. There is none more powerful than me. I am the inheritor of the universe. So tremble before me, 6-Dog, for today I begin my reign."

"Thou didst always talk too much. Put down the scepter and I will put down my ax. Let us fight, man to man." Lord 6-Dog put up his fists.

"Don't tell me what to do." Tzelek was shaking with rage. "If I can't use this butcher's bone, neither can you." He grabbed an end of the scepter with each hand and brought it down hard onto his knee to break it in two. But instead of breaking, the leg-bone bounced off his knee and out of his hands, and slid spinning across the glass bridge until it came to a stop at Lord 6-Dog's feet.

Lord 6-Dog picked it up and, after a moment's consideration, handed it to his mother. Then he kicked his own ax over the bridge.

"Are you mad?" asked Lady Coco.

"Tzelek is unarmed. There is no victory in winning without honor."

"You will regret that," muttered Lady Coco, shaking her head in despair. "You have been battling Tzelek for three *bak'tuns*, twelve hundred solar years. Have you learned nothing, Son?"

Tzelek listened jealously to this exchange. "You never called me 'son,'" he said in a quiet voice. "I am glad you are here today to see me rip out the heart of your favorite, and eat it for my victory dinner."

"Enough talk!" complained Lord 6-Dog. "Let us fight!"

"Very good," agreed Tzelek. "Since you chose the weapons—or the lack of them—I choose the arena."

"Are we not fighting here?"

"Here? In the confines of a room? This is hardly the site for the battle at the end of the world."

"I am weary of thy games. Let us fight, man to man, here and now."

"Look around you," said Tzelek. "I did not choose this room at random. We are literally in the middle of the world. We are in the middle of Middleworld. And we are outside time and space." Tzelek closed his eyes and stretched out his arms. Slowly at first, but faster and faster, the globe around them began to spin, and as it spun, it grew bigger and bigger until the walls melted away altogether. Max, Lola, and Lady Coco were still crouched, terrified, at the end of the glass bridge, but the bridge was no longer inside a building in Boston. It was now a raised platform standing on a large scrubby field, between two ancient Maya pyramids.

Tzelek and Lord 6-Dog stood facing each other in front of the bridge.

Behind Tzelek stood the Black Pyramid of Ah Pukuh. Behind Lord 6-Dog stood the Green Pyramid of Itzamna. Neither structure was as Max had last seen them; they both looked brand-new, freshly painted, clear of all vegetation. But the rest of the location looked like the setting for a nightmarish music video: the colors were too saturated, the contrast too intense and, around the edges where there should have been green jungle, there was nothing but a burnt purple haze.

"What is this place?" said Lady Coco.

"It is the scene of thy little 6-Dog's death," Tzelek replied. "You may say good-bye and wipe his nose one last time, if you like."

Lady Coco growled. "I will say good-bye to you first, Tzelek."

"I think not."

"In a fair fight, my 6-Dog could beat you with one arm behind his back," Lady Coco insisted.

"Who said anything about a fair fight?"

On the steps of the black pyramid, thick smoke billowed from hundreds of burning incense pots.

Tzelek clicked his fingers.

Out of the smoke, weapons clanking as they descended the steps, marched the most fearsome army that Max had ever seen, a sea of black-painted warriors in white-feather headdresses, a host of mythical Maya beasts (including Eek' Chapaat, the monstrous centipede, and Kamasootz', queen of the bats), assorted ogres and giants, and battalions of zombie warriors in their various stages of death and decay. Each and every one of them was armed to the teeth—including, for many of them, a set of fiercely sharpened teeth and flesh-ripping fangs. They raised their weapons as one and, with a thunderous noise, shouted, "Hail Tzelek, King of Xibalba, Lord of the Middleworld."

Lord 6-Dog shook his head in disgust. "Thou wert ever a sniveling coward. Canst thou not keep thy word and fight like a man?"

"You have your supporters," replied Tzelek, indicating the trio on the bridge. "It is only fair that I should invite my nearest and dearest. Since your family has disowned me, I have been forced to make a new family for myself." He smiled and indicated the crowd behind him. "Meet the guys."

"I'll show you family!" roared Lady Coco, whirling the scepter above her head and chanting in Mayan.

"No, Mother!" called Lord 6-Dog, but it was too late.

Down the central steps of the pyramid of Itzamna came a parade of Jaguar Kings. Max recognized many of them from the bathroom mirror at the inn. But this time, they all wore full battle gear and were accompanied by their bodyguards, warriors, and household retinues. At the very end, carried on a litter by his guards, came Jade Frog, the founder of the dynasty and owner of the leg-bone that had summoned them all here.

Lord 6-Dog's father, Punak Ha, peeled off from the rest to come and stand on the bridge with Lady Coco. They looked at each other tenderly, the old king and the howler monkey that used to be his wife.

"It is good to see thee, my dear," whispered Punak Ha, not commenting on her new appearance. "I have missed thee."

"I have so much to tell you!" Lady Coco's eyes were shining but she tried to assume a somber expression. "But, of course, I have missed you, too."

"If the worst parents in the world are ready," said Tzelek, "perhaps we can get this massacre started."

Both armies stood at attention, facing each other at opposite ends of the field. There was an echoing rattle as they lifted their weapons, ready to charge.

From his vantage point on the bridge, Max felt like a spectator at a medieval joust.

He switched his attention to the main players. They were working themselves up to battle, trading insults like the two little brothers they had once been. Suddenly, this whole scene looked ridiculous.

Childish.

How many times had this scene played out?

How many more times would it be played?

And all the while, the lives of ordinary people were torn apart because these ancient forces of good and evil went on fighting for all eternity.

There was a split second of silence before the conch shells blew to start the battle.

"I can't watch." Max buried his head in his hands.

"Here we go again," said Lola.

Lord 6-Dog put up his hand to stay the advancing armies. He turned to Lola, eyes blazing. "What didst thou say?"

"I'm sorry," said Lola, sounding terrified. "I didn't mean it."

"What didst thou say?" he asked again in a gentler voice.

"I . . . I just said here we go again because, you know, this is not the first time that you and Tzelek have battled to the, um, death."

She bit her lip.

Lord 6-Dog was still staring at her.

"What now?" asked Tzelek, irritated.

"Brother," said Lord 6-Dog, turning to him, "we need to talk."

"Talk? Is this a joke? We need to throttle and maim each other, is what we need to do."

"We have already done that and it got us nowhere."

"What has happened before will happen again," said Tzelek. "That's the whole point of history."

"Perhaps we need to move on."

"The only thing I need is to see you dead."

"I am already dead, and so art thou. We died twelve hundred solar years ago in the battle that destroyed us both."

"It may have destroyed you, but it drove me on. My hatred for you is even stronger than death."

"Who are we fighting today? We are all just ghosts. How can either of us win?"

"Not to give away my tactics, but I intend to win by ripping out your heart."

"I understand thy hatred. For twelve hundred years, since the day thou didst kill my father, I have lived and breathed my desire for revenge."

"That's more like it," urged Tzelek. "Bring it on."

"No, I will not fight thee. Thou art not my enemy."

"*What?* Yes, I am. What are you saying?"

"I am saying that my battle is within myself."

"You're scared," jeered Tzelek.

"No, fighting is easy. What I am about to do is much harder."

"If it's sorcery you're thinking about, don't bother. I am a master of the black arts."

Lord 6-Dog smiled. "Thou wert always good at magic, even as a child. Remember the day thou didst teach me to produce a cocoa bean from my ear? I wish I could still do that. Wilt thou teach me again?"

"What trickery is this?"

"No trickery. I just want to say that I am sorry, Tzelek. It must have been hard to lose thy mother and feel like an outcast in my family. I am sorry for the part I played in thine unhappiness. Wilt thou forgive me?"

Tzelek gave Lord 6-Dog a look of incredulity mixed with disgust. "What sick joke is this?"

"It is no joke, brother. I am serious."

Tzelek put up his fists. "Just fight, you coward!"

"My father—our father—told me that I would not win if I fought thee. Now, I see what he meant. I have been a terrible brother. Instead of welcoming thee into my family, I resented thy presence. I fought with thee when I should have shared with thee. It is my fault thou art cast as a villain."

"It's really not. Can we just get back to fighting? Remember

I killed your father. I destroyed your kingdom. I like being a villain!"

Lord 6-Dog stuck his hand on Tzelek's shoulder.

Tzelek winced.

"I forgive thee," said Lord 6-Dog softly. "What's past is past. Let us go forward as friends and brothers."

"No! You can't do this to me!" Tzelek turned very pale; so pale, in fact, that he was becoming transparent. "You hate me and I hate you. That is what nourishes me! I demand that you hate me again! I need your hatred. I feed on it! It is who I am."

"It is gone," said Lord 6-Dog. "I am free of it."

With agonizing cries, Tzelek and his armies shriveled up and dissipated like smoke in the wind. And when the smoke was gone, there was a silence, full of peace.

"Well played, Son," said Punak Ha.

"Thank thee, Father. In all honesty, it feels good to be rid of the hatred."

"And rid of Tzelek," added Lady Coco.

"Just one thing, Son."

"Yes, Father?"

"Now that thou hast vanquished all the foes of Middleworld, I assume thou hast no further need of the scepter?"

"Dost thou want it, Father? Take it. It is thine."

"Return it to Jade Frog. He has difficulty walking without it."

Lord 6-Dog borrowed a shield of brined cotton from a nearby warrior to use as a ceremonial platter. Then he laid the leg-bone on it and made his way through the ranks of kings to Jade Frog, looking rather like a chef serving up a Sunday roast.

"Venerable ancestor, I present the sacred scepter of the Jaguar Kings," he said, kneeling before the old man.

"I am proud of thee, 6-Dog," said Jade Frog. "Thou hast broken the cycle and restored the balance. I am glad to get my leg back after all this time. But now we must take our leave." Lord 6-Dog nodded. "I am ready to accompany thee."

"No," said Jade Frog, smiling. "Rejoin thy friends. It is not thy time."

As Lord 6-Dog made his way slowly back over the glass bridge, Jade Frog waved the leg-bone above his head in farewell and the Jaguar Kings vanished like smoke on the wind.

"Where did everyone go?" asked Max.

"Hold tight," said Lola. "Something's happening."

The towering pyramids crumbled in front of their eyes and, in seconds, the battlefield was entirely camouflaged by jungle. The glass bridge was now floating in the night sky, with planet Earth revolving below it.

Looking down, Max saw a bobbing, multicolored mass weaving across the land surface of the Earth, swaying and turning in rhythmic circles. "Are we trapped now?" he asked. "Will we ever get down?"

"They're dancing us down," said Lola. "All the Maya around the world. They're dancing the story of creation and the birth of the stars. They're dancing us back to Earth."

As they came nearer to the ground, the clouds engulfed them, gradually solidifying like frosted glass, until they stood once again inside the great globe of the world that sat hidden beneath the dome of a stately white building on Massachusetts Avenue in central Boston.

"Will Tzelek come back?" asked Max, trying to process what had just happened.

Lord 6-Dog shook his head. "No, he is gone for good." He smiled weakly at Max. "But there will be other enemies to subdue. Be always on thy guard, young lord."

"Where will you be?" asked Max.

"My strength is failing. My time here is done." Lord 6-Dog put a hand to his injured head.

"Let us take off that headdress," said Lady Coco. "The weight of it would give anyone a headache."

With the help of his friends, Lord 6-Dog unloaded some of his battle gear and sat down on the walkway of the bridge, leaning back against the glass sidewall.

"You were amazing out there," Lola said to him. "You broke the cycle of revenge."

"I was inspired by thee," he said, squeezing Lola's hand. "Thou wert magnificent at Fenway. What a great king thou wouldst have made."

"Thank you." She bowed her head, so he wouldn't see that her eyes were full of tears.

"Son, you're wounded," sobbed Lady Coco. "If you can just get back in your monkey body, we could get help."

"It is too late, Mother, you know that. When the Day of the Dead is over, I must leave this mortal world."

"Don't say that!"

"Good-bye, Mother," said Lord 6-Dog weakly. He lay back and closed his eyes.

"Noooo!" Lady Coco pulled at him. "You can't leave me!"

But he was already dead.

Lady Coco howled in pain. "He is gone. He was without a body when he passed. This time he cannot return."

A white light filled the globe room.

"Greetings," said Ixchel, the young moon goddess.

Lady Coco stared at her mournfully, her eyes red from crying, the fur on her face tearstained. "My son is dead, Ixchel. If only you had come sooner."

"He died a hero," said the goddess, her face shimmering like moonbeams. "I have come to honor him as a champion of our people." She knelt beside the fallen king and cradled his head. His body, bathed in her light, began to glow. He opened his eyes and looked straight at Ixchel.

"It is thee," he said.

They looked at each other dreamily for a few moments, then Ixchel cleared her throat and assumed a businesslike attitude. "Lord 6-Dog, I come to you from the ancestors. You have done us great service in silencing Tzelek. Now you must choose your reward."

"Seeing thee is my reward," whispered Lord 6-Dog.

Ixchel tried not to smile. "You have a choice," she said. "You may stay in Middleworld and live out your life in mortal comfort or . . ."

She hesitated.

"Or . . . ?" Lord 6-Dog was staring at her intently.

"Or you may rise to the heavens with me tonight."

"And if I choose to go with thee . . . ?"

"You will be a star in the night sky, the closest star to the moon." She lowered her glance. "We will be together for eternity."

"I would like that," he said.

"Please, no," Lady Coco begged him. "Don't leave me, Son."

"Come now, Mother. All my life thou hast nagged me about meeting the right woman. And now, finally, I am in

351

love. Surely even thou must think a goddess good enough for thy son?"

Lady Coco nodded through her tears. "Look after him for me, Ixchel."

"I am the goddess of motherhood, Lady Coco. I know how much you love him."

"He has been wounded."

"I am also the goddess of healing."

Lady Coco sighed. "Good-bye, my little 6-Dog. I will look for you in the sky."

"And I will shine down on thee, Mother, every night."

"Don't be sad, Lady Coco. It is a time of change for you, too," said Ixchel. "You have fulfilled your mission in Middleworld."

Lady Coco gasped. "But it's so sudden. I've been so happy here. . . ."

"You, too, shall have a choice. You may return to your husband, Punak Ha, in the underworld, or you may live out your days as a howler monkey."

"A talking howler monkey?"

"No, you would lose the power of human speech."

"You could express yourself through art!" burst out Lola excitedly. "The ancient Maya always depicted scribes and artists as monkeys! I could teach you to paint!"

Lady Coco's little forehead was furrowed with the effort of curbing in her monkey spirit. "It sounds nice, Lady Lola, but I must go to Punak Ha. In my day, a wife's duty was to her husband."

"You were a good wife," said Ixchel. "You pricked your tongue with thorns for royal rituals. You rose at dawn to knead the tortilla dough. You waited for your husband to return from battle. But times have changed. Now Punak Ha will wait for you. There is time enough to return to him when your adventures are over."

Lady Coco's eyes lit up. "Then I choose to be a howler monkey, wild and free, swinging with my troop through the beautiful forest."

"I hope you'll come and visit us at the Villa Isabella," said Lola.

"Every day," said Lady Coco. "I'll bring the troop to sample Raul's cashew crumble."

"So be it," said Ixchel. "I wish you a lifetime of happiness, Lady Coco."

"Thank you, my dear. Call me mother-in-law."

They all hugged each other, and Ixchel left a sparkle of moondust on everyone's cheek when she kissed them.

"Ready?" Ixchel took Lord 6-Dog's hand.

"Ready," he replied.

"Then let us go."

Lady Coco clutched her Dawg Doll close as the moon goddess and the handsome Maya king melted into the shaft of moonlight and disappeared.

The doors of the globe room unlocked themselves.

Dr. Delgado sat up and groaned. "Where am I?"

Lola helped her to her feet.

"How did I get here?" asked Dr. Delgado, looking around at all the broken glass.

"It's okay, he's gone now," said Lola.

"Who's gone?"

"Tzelek."

"Tzelek? That was the name painted on the pot with the lizard handle. I was unpacking it at the museum. . . ." She held her head. "I opened the lid and something jumped out at me. I . . . I . . . I don't remember anything else."

"He took over your body to get him here, so he could fight one last battle with his arch-enemy, Lord 6-Dog," explained Lola.

"Lord 6-Dog? The great king of Itzamna?"

"He was in the body of that monkey who came to the museum with us on Halloween."

Dr. Delgado stared at her like she was crazy. "Are you asking me to believe that the ancient Maya have the ability to come back to life?"

Lola laughed and shook her head. "It was the Day of the Dead, remember?"

"I don't remember anything."

"Then you're going to want to hear about the Red Sox game last night."

Lola picked up the body of Chulo, the howler monkey who had hosted Lord 6-Dog all this time. She kissed his sleeping head. "You won't believe what's been happening," she whispered to him. "But it's over now. Everything's going to be all right. Just sleep and dream about the forest. In the morning I'll bring you all the mangoes and bananas you can eat."

As they left the globe room, the shattered world reassembled itself.

So if the world didn't end, what happened next?

Well, Max Murphy and Nasty Smith-Jones finally went out for a pizza and a movie. They went quite a few times, actually.

Lola never made her road trip. She was too busy making plans with Lucky Jim for the Maya school they were going to build with Landa's money, after she graduated from Harvard.

Hermanjilio spent all his free time guiding tourists around the new Jaguar Stones Museum.

And somewhere deep in the rainforest, another tree was felled.

And another . . .

Down in the deepest depths of Xibalba, the Death Lords looked up from their card game and smiled. "There are many ways to end the world," they said. "We just need to be a little more patient. . . ."

GLOSSARY OF THE MAYA WORLD

AH PUKUH (*awe-poo-coo*): God of violent and unnatural death, depicted in Maya art as a bloated, decomposing corpse or a cigar-smoking skeleton. Ah Pukuh rules over Mitnal, the ninth and most terrible layer of XIBALBA, the Maya underworld.

BONE SCEPTER: Carved human femurs (thigh bones) have been found in royal Maya tombs and depicted in the hands of kings. Archaeologists believe that these carved relics were powerful symbols of office, showing the king's noble descent from a revered ancestor. The femur is the longest and strongest bone in the human body.

HERO TWINS: Brothers Xbalanke (*sh-ball-on-kay*) and Hunahpu (*who-gnaw-poo*), are the main characters in the Maya creation story. Challenged to a ball game by the LORDS OF DEATH, they outwit their opponents and make the world a safer place.

IXCHEL (*eesh-shell*): Traditionally, "Lady Rainbow" has been viewed as one deity with multiple personalities. As the malevolent Goddess of the Old Moon she is shown with a snake headband and a skirt embroidered with crossbones; as the Goddess of the New Moon, she is a beautiful young woman who reclines inside the crescent moon, holding her pet rabbit. Recently, scholars have made the case that she is two separate deities: Chak Chel "Great Rainbow" and Ix Uh "Lady Moon."

JAGUAR STONES: These five fictional stones embody the five pillars of ancient Maya society: agriculture, astronomy, creativity, military prowess, and kingship.

LORDS OF DEATH: In Maya mythology, there are twelve Lords of Death: One Death, Seven Death, Scab Stripper, Blood Gatherer, Wing, Demon of Pus, Demon of Jaundice, Bone Scepter, Skull Scepter, Demon of Filth, Demon of Woe, and Packstrap. It is their job to inflict sickness, pain, starvation, fear, and death on the citizens of MIDDLEWORLD. Luckily, they're usually too busy gambling and playing tricks on each other to get much work done.

MIDDLEWORLD: Like many ancient cultures, the Maya believed that humankind inhabited a middle world between heaven and hell. The Maya Middleworld was sandwiched between nine dark and watery layers of XIBALBA and thirteen leafy layers of the heavens.

MORLEY, SYLVANUS GRISWOLD (1883–1948): Thought by some to have inspired the character of Indiana Jones, Morley was a dashing, Harvard-trained archaeologist most famous for his work at Chichen Itza. Secretly, he was also an American spy, hunting for German sub bases on the coasts of Central America.

PADDLER GODS: So called because they are usually pictured ferrying gods around in a dugout canoe. They are both old men. The Jaguar Paddler has jaguar spots, while the Stingray Paddler has a stingray spine through his nose. It has been suggested that they represent night and day.

PITZ: The Mesoamerican ball game was the first team sport in recorded history. The game was played along the lines of tennis, but without rackets or a net—and using only hips, knees, or elbows. The game had great religious significance, and it is believed that the losing team, or a team of captive "stunt doubles," was sometimes sacrificed.

SAN XAVIER: A fictional country in Central America based on modern-day Belize.

XIBALBA (she-ball-buh): Maya name for the underworld, meaning "well of fear." Like its Norse equivalent, the Maya underworld was a bone-chilling place of mists, damp, and cold.

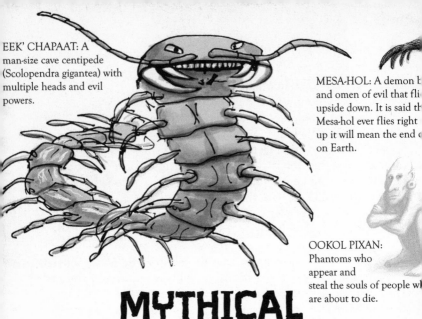

EEK' CHAPAAT: A man-size cave centipede (Scolopendra gigantea) with multiple heads and evil powers.

MESA-HOL: A demon b[...] and omen of evil that fli[...] upside down. It is said th[...] Mesa-hol ever flies right[...] up it will mean the end [...] on Earth.

OOKOL PIXAN: Phantoms who appear and steal the souls of people w[...] are about to die.

MYTHICAL
MAYA MONSTERS

IX HUMPETZ' K'IN: A lizard with a knotted tail he uses to to whack his victims. He can kill you by biting your shadow.

WAAY POP: Giant bird with wings made of flint daggers. He spikes his victims and then disappears without a trace.

ALUX: a sprite protects the fore[...] and plays tricks [...] humans. The A[...] loves sweets.

K'AAK'ASBAL: Malignant creature [...] up of body parts from different anim[...] that hate each other. His eyes flash lightning and he breathes a toxic vap[...]

WINIK: A
...ular giant
...o bones and
...ard feet. If you
...him laugh (a
...ance with a
...h works best)
...s to the ground
...n't get up.

WAWA' PACH: Giant
with three tongues like
knives and a necklace
of human kidneys. Kills
people by squeezing
them between his legs.

EEK' UNEHIL: Snake with
a forked tail. It tries to stick
the venomous tips of its tail
up people's nostrils.

...K TUUN HU': This man of stone is
...ent of death. Vultures sit on his head,
...eadlocks are the nests of scorpions, and
...s crawl around his toes.

...BAY: A
...iful fallen
...ss who calls to
...g men in the
... Her victims
...und snared
...rn bushes
... look of horror
...ir faces.

KAMASOOTZ': Huge bat and
queen of the deadly bat house
in Xibalba. Her giant claw can
decapitate a person in one swoop.

CAHOKIA MOUNDS

Just across the Mississippi River from present-day St. Louis stood one of the greatest cities of the ancient world. No one knows the name of the settlement that rose on what is now called Cahokia Mounds State Historic Site in Collinsville, Illinois. All we know is that a sophisticated civilization flourished here, long before Europeans came to North America. At its peak in 1250 CE, Cahokia was bigger than London.

Like the Maya, the architects of Cahokia built huge flat-topped temples. Where the Maya pyramids are made of stone, the mounds at Cahokia are made of earth. They include Monk's Mound (named for Trappist monks who farmed its terraces in the nineteenth century), one of the largest pyramids in the world. It's been estimated that Monks Mound comprises 15 million baskets of earth, carried by human labor.

In front of Monk's Mound was the grand plaza—a fifty-acre communal space for markets, ceremonies, and a game called chunkey, which involved throwing spears at rolling stone discs. To the east of Monk's Mound was a huge solar calendar, now called Woodhenge. It used a circle of cedar posts, each twenty feet tall and painted red, to track solstices, equinoxes, and other important dates in the agricultural cycle.

Cahokia gained its power partly from its location on the fertile floodplain of the Mississippi near the confluence of the Missouri and Illinois rivers. It grew maize on an industrial scale and its trade links reached as far as the Gulf of Mexico. To protect their wealth, its rulers surrounded their city center with a twenty-foot-high stockade wall.

Who were these rulers? We still don't know. But in one of the smaller mounds, the remains of an important man were discovered. The archaeologists called him "The Birdman" because his skeleton lay on 20,000 shell beads arranged in the shape of a bird. Also in the mound were 250 human sacrificial victims. Although Cahokia had fallen by the time Europeans arrived (and they mistook its grass-covered mounds for hill formations), it can be surmised from their accounts of other Mississippian settlements that the ruler of Cahokia was called Great Sun.

J & P Voelkel at Cahokia Mounds, June 201

JOURNEY OF THE *PHANTOM QUEEN*

The place known today as CAHO[KIA]
MOUNDS is the site of the lar[gest]
ancient Native American city. It was [built]
by the MISSISSIPPIANS, a sophistica[ted]
culture that emerged in the Mississ[ippi]
river basin and flourished from 80[0 to]
1300 [CE.]

ST. LOUIS, MISSOURI, is home to the 630-feet-
high Gateway Arch, also known as Gateway to the
West, the tallest man-made monument in the US.

ST. LOUIS

**CAHOKIA MOUN[DS]
STATE HISTORIC S[ITE]**

THE MISSISSIPPI RIVER is the longest river in North
America. From its headwaters in northern Minnesota it
travels 2,340 miles before draining into the Gulf of Mexico.

THE *PHANTOM QUEEN* is a fictional riverboat, based on
the many legends of phantom riverboats on the Mississippi
River. Witnesses claim to hear a steamship whistle at
midnight as the boat glides out of the mist, moving silently
over the water and giving off an eerie glow.

MEMPHIS

MEMPHIS, TENNESSEE, [also]
known as the Home of the Blues [and]
the Birthplace of Rock 'N' Roll, is [the]
largest city on the Mississippi R[iver.]

NEW ORLEANS, LOUISIANA, is a "liminal" city,
meaning that it's in between two states of being: in
this case, half land, half water. Much of it is below
sea level and protected by levees, like the
one Max and Lola climb to board the *Phantom
Queen*. The ancient Maya were fascinated by
liminality. (For example, they venerated the jaguar
because it could hunt by night and by day, on land
and in water.) Nowhere would have pleased the
Death Lords more than the spooky bayous
around the city where cypress trees rise out of
swampy water, draped in Spanish moss,
providing cover for lurking alligators and
snakes. The high water table also gave rise to
the many above-ground cemeteries known as
"cities of the dead."

One of New Orleans's most fam[ous]
citizens is BARON SAMEDI (or Ba[ron]
Saturday as his name translates f[rom]
French to English). He's the party-lo[ving]
boss of the dead in the city's voodoo [lore.]
He's usually pictured as a skeleton dre[ssed]
in a dark suit, top hat, and sungla[sses.]

NEW ORLEANS

THE *LILY THEODORA*, Uncle Ted's subma[rine,]
was based on a real sub that was captured f[rom]
smugglers in Ecuador in 2[010.]

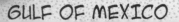

GULF OF MEXICO

MAX MURPHY'S GUIDE TO BOSTON

FENWAY PARK:

"This is my favorite place in Boston.
It's the oldest ballpark in Major League
Baseball and it's been the home of the
Red Sox since it opened in 1912.
Things to notice are the wall called
the Green Monster, and the single
red seat in the bleachers that marks
a 502-foot hit by Ted Williams—
the longest home run hit at
Fenway. And the Curse of the
Bambino? That began when
we traded Babe Ruth, nick-
named The Bambino, to the New
York Yankees in 1919. After that,
the Red Sox didn't win another
World Series for eighty-six years.

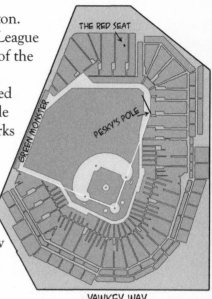

The curse was officially lifted in 2004 when we finally won the
World Series again."

MASSACHUSETTS AVE

MAPPARIUM: "This is where
Lord 6-Dog and Tzelek had
their showdown. It's a massive
stained-glass globe, and it's in the Mary Baker Eddy Library on
Massachusetts Avenue."

PEABODY MUSEUM OF ARCHAEOLOGY AND ETHNOLOGY:

"I wouldn't have come here if Lola and the
others hadn't made me, because I've been here
fifty million times. It's part of Harvard, where my
parents work, and it has one of the biggest Maya
collections outside of Mexico, if you like that
stuff. Oh, and it's not actually in Boston, but
across the river in Cambridge."

EEK' (Roasted Wasp Larvae)

With thanks to Sofi Pat Balam and Denis Larsen

INGREDIENTS:

- One volleyball-size
  paper-wasp nest
- 6–12 small green chilies
- Juice of six sour oranges
- Corn tortillas

(This recipe requires adult
supervision!)

PREPARATION:

1. Try to avoid getting stung as you harvest the nest. (Do not attempt at all if allergic to wasp or bee stings.) You may need to smoke the hive to evict the wasps.
2. Peel apart layers of nest until you reach the honeycomb-like structures at center.
3. Roast the green chilies and, using pestle and mortar, grind into a paste. Add water if necessary. Transfer chili paste to a serving bowl.
4. In a large frying pan, toast pieces of honeycomb, open side down, until you see a color change. Use a gentle heat and take care not to burn the comb.
5. Gently tap pieces of toasted honeycomb on cutting board to loosen and remove the cooked larvae. (If they don't readily pop out or are still moving, you haven't toasted the comb enough yet.) Discard empty combs.
6. Coarsely grind larvae with mortar and pestle, mixing in some ground chilies and the orange juice to make a coarse paste.
7. Spread on warm tortillas, adding chili paste to taste.

Enjoy!

ACKNOWLEDGMENTS

As this is the last book in the Jaguar Stones series and our last chance to thank everyone who's helped us, we'd like to start by thanking you.

Yes, YOU.

Whether you've read one Jaguar Stones book or all of them, thank you for coming with us on this wild ride. We've loved traveling with you and we hope you'll stay in touch. (You can always find us through our Web site.)

Huge thanks too to our agent, Daniel Lazar; to our editor, Alison Weiss, and everyone at Egmont USA, especially Bonnie Cutler, Margaret Coffee, Georgia Morrissey, and Michelle Bayuk; also to Elizabeth Baer, Sam Hadley, and Arlene Goldberg; and to Elizabeth Law, who made it all happen.

In the world of Maya archaeology, we're indebted to the mighty Marc Zender for his mind-boggling expertise; to marine archaeologist Heather McKillop for introducing us to the possibilities of 3-D printing; to the memory of George Stuart, Maya scholar, storyteller, gentleman, and real-life Indiana Jones; and to all the archaeologists, guides, and Maya people who've so generously shared their knowledge and experiences with us.

Thank you to all the wonderful booksellers, librarians, and teachers we've worked with along the way, especially Jill Moore of Square Books Junior, and Liza Barnard and Penny McConnel from the Norwich Bookstore.

Thank you so much to Judith Lafitte and Tom Lowenburg of Octavia Books and Elizabeth Kahn of Patrick Taylor Academy for masterminding our research in New Orleans (which included taking us on a creepy after-midnight tour of levees and old cemeteries, and scouring the streets of the French Quarter to find the perfect house for Baron Saturday). Thank you to Kenny Brechner of DDG Booksellers in Maine for inspiring the submarine storyline; thank you to Mary Magavern Sachsse, Christy Coverdale Voelkel, and Kate Messner for helping us compile our lesson plans and reading guides; and thank you to Donald Kreis for teaching us about baseball.

A big shout-out to our Jaguar Stones club members and our crack team of middle-school reviewers: Kayla Begin, Ben Gwilt, Bill and Sally Hodgkinson, Brandon Rosa, Sammy Spector, and Bailey Steele—plus Beth Reynolds and all her rapacious readers at the Norwich Public Library; to Loulou Voelkel for her stubborn and very wise advice on the naming of this book; to Eddie Case, Stephanie Kilgore, Brandi Stewart, Faith Hochhalter, and the Club Read kids at Changing Hands bookstore in Tempe, Arizona, for helping us choose the final title.

Lastly, to our three amazing children, thank you for all the adventures. (And sorry about all the bug bites.)

THE JAGUAR STONES SERIES
CLASSIC ADVENTURES—WITH A MODERN TWIST!

Jaguar Stones, Book One:
MIDDLEWORLD

When his parents go missing at an ancient Maya pyramid, a video-gaming, pizza-eating city boy must learn to survive in the perilous rainforest—with a little help from a local Maya girl.

Jaguar Stones, Book Two:
THE END OF THE WORLD CLUB

When Max and Lola follow a trail of secrets to the end of the ancient world in northwest Spain, they stumble across an enchanted castle and the craziest rock concert ever!

Jaguar Stones, Book Three:
THE RIVER OF NO RETURN

It's a wild ride to disaster when Max and Lola head upriver to flee the Maya Death Lords—and find themselves in a luxury hotel that is spookily similar to the Maya underworld.

Jaguar Stones, Book Four:
THE LOST CITY

When Max and Lola make one last desperate attempt to save the world from the evil Maya Death Lords, their secret weapons include a roller-skating monkey and the Boston Red Sox.

You'll find more fun for fans at www.jaguarstones.com, including free signed bookplates and a free Jaguar Stones Club for readers, plus free reading guides and lesson plans for teachers.

The Lacandon Maya
say that every time
a tree is cut down
in the rainforest
a star falls from the
sky.

J&P Voelkel
would like to thank
their publishers,
Egmont USA,
for only using paper
from legal and
sustainable sources.